The Home Recording Handbook

The Home Recording Handbook

Amsco Publications
New York/London/Sydney

First published in Great Britain in 1985 by
Virgin Books
328 Kensal Rd, London W10 5XJ.
This edition published 1986 by
Amsco Publications.

Order No. VV 20481
ISBN 0-8256-1105-9

Printed and bound in the United States of America
by Vicks Lithograph and Printing Corporation

Cover photo by Andy Knight

Cover design by Sue Walliker

Illustrations by Ursula Shaw

Designed and typeset by Type Generation, London

Exclusive distributors for the USA and Canada:
Music Sales Corporation
24 East 22nd Street, New York, NY 10010, USA

CONTENTS

Introduction

What is a bright-eyed and bushy-tailed lad like me, who works at the professional end of the recording and production business, doing writing a book on *home recording?* The question did not in fact occur to me until after I'd written the book, and the answer is not that simple.

Since 1978/9 and the release of the Fairlight CMI, professional recording studio concepts have completely changed. In the contemporary field, the control room has become *the* place where 99 per cent of the musical action takes place; a separate chamber is only required (sometimes) for vocals. Technology has brought the process of recording a single in a $200-per-hour studio closer to the way a demo is recorded on a Portastudio in a bedroom.

The old adage that professional recording techniques and those used at home are like chalk and cheese no longer holds good. Only classical recordings and specialist voice-overs require professional methods that are fundamentally different from those used by the home recordist.

Furthermore, with so much biased advice on hand, orientated round and originating from the manufacturers, it was time an *independent* set the general public at ease.

So, whether you are a Portastudio virtuoso, or have just picked this book up out of general curiosity, I suggest you buy it. It costs under a tenner, and even if you have no intention of becoming a home recordist, you'll no doubt find it useful as a doorstop or a last-minute Christmas present for a rarely-seen favourite nephew. Honestly, this book is ideal for anyone who is thinking about thinking about laying out a modest amount of greenies on a two track and a small mixer; it is also ideal for someone who has an advanced home recording set-up, maybe a sixteen track or larger, who wants to keep an eye on the latest equipment and learn a little more about how things actually *work*.

The *Home Recording Handbook* shows you how to set up your own home studio and explains a lot about recording equipment and techniques. However, you will *not* need a physics degree or a well stocked Swiss bullion account. It covers basic areas, such as picking your room and soundproofing it and offers practical advice, hints and tips on getting the best from your equipment. Record industry pundits – well-known faces from the charts, and the odd accomplished 'back room boy' – let you in on how they go about recording at home and (in certain cases) in professional studios. By the time you reach the back cover, you should have all the knowledge necessary to start a home studio from scratch and take it to an advanced stage, have an inside understanding of 90 per cent of all the relevant equipment available this year, be able to record and produce professional sounding demos (and masters), *and* have the confidence to take on small multitrack recording sessions as a recording engineer.

As this is a yearbook and as such a reference work, I have included sub-chapters entitled 'Basics' in some sections. These are really for the benefit of those who are utterly unfamiliar with the subject being discussed. People who are reasonably competent in recording on eight track can leave out most of the 'Basics' sections (though of course it's all up to you). The most effective way of using this edition is probably to read the whole book through once and then keep it in your studio for easy reference. Taking it with you when buying equipment (new or second-hand) will undoubtedly (he says modestly) save you from getting caught or being 'done' – and for this simple reason alone it's worth buying!

So now you know what this book is about and you've been standing in the shop reading this page for a minute or so, you'd better dig into your pocket for the money to buy it or you're going to look like a right Norman Bates, aren't you!

You won't regret it – brain damage has never come cheaper than this!

Chris Everard London 1985

SECTION ONE

Do You Need a Studio?

Choosing Equipment

Soundproofing

Putting Your Studio Together

Do You Need a Studio?

This section is for the benefit of those who are about to establish their first home recording system. If you have already decided on the amount, shape and type of recording equipment you want to own and where to put it, you can in theory skip this section – however, you may still find that parts of it are relevant to your circumstances.

First of all, you have to decide how much you *need* to do home recording. Do your musical ideas get jumbled, lost or, even worse, completely forgotten if you can't get them down on tape in a fairly structured and, in certain cases, quite detailed form? How fundamental a part will a 'studio' play in your musical creativity? Do you mostly play acoustic or reasonably portable instruments, such as electric guitar? If so, does sitting in the same room all the time with a microphone in front of you stunt your creativity? And, perhaps most importantly, are you going to do a large amount of home recording: does your present lifestyle allow you much time to devote to recording music; or will you just use your home recording set-up as a shorthand notepad, sketching ideas that will only come to fruition once in a blue moon?

Some of the above questions may seem a little irrelevant. However, while 80 per cent of home recordists may be happy in one room that is designated your 'studio' and home base, others (especially those whose music can be made without electricity – acoustic guitarists, for example) will find that recording music in the same environment *all* the time stagnates performances.

There is no real answer to this sort of problem. Musicians who tend to feel claustrophobic and whose creativity is frustrated by being in the same room all the time must combat it by trying to record in and around their humble abodes. This will almost certainly cause huge problems if you're trying to lay down anything half decent. Playing your guitar in the garden in the middle of summer, and going straight into a battery-driven Portastudio may be an ideal creative environment, but then you mustn't mind traffic noise and the unmusical sounds of your neighbours' barbecues leaking on to your potential masterpieces.

Recording in different places around the house may also put a strain on everyday family relationships – especially with kids in summer. Asking them to 'play quietly' in the garden in hot weather while you attempt some serious strumming on the patio is like giving an axe to an axe murderer and asking him not to kill anybody.

The best solution that I can come up with is to place oneself in the room with most windows, or the best available and enlarge the window area or even add another. Rooms with balconies and French windows are perhaps the least boring to spend a lot of time in. Increasing the amount of light and enlarging your view of the outside world can minimize the chances of feeling that you're caught between four walls with no way out. Failing all this, the next best step is to paint your chosen room white and fill it (moderately) with things that you like (and which don't take up a lot of space). Only spend time in your chosen room when you are playing, recording or doing both.

However, if your demos do not need to have a professional sheen, if background noises don't disturb your performance and if you play instruments which are on the whole portable and non-bulky, then storing your recording gear in a particular corner of a certain room seems the most workable situation. If we are talking eight track (above compact multi-tracker level, at least), the equipment is going to dominate a room of average proportions anyway.

In short, it's only worth going to the bother of arranging a whole room around one's recording exploits if the amount and *type* of recording warrants it. If you are lucky enough to have a spare room that you can use regardless, then designate it as a 'studio' and keep your equipment in there even if you can't handle being in it all the time. Space that you can call your own and use how you please is welcome at any time.

Basically though, I'd like this section to provoke thought before action. The best advice I can offer is *think* about what you need – do you *need* a studio or can you work better without one? If you are already established in a particular room and you feel tired or jaded after sitting at your mixer for even a short time, ask yourself whether you are happy and comfortable working in the room as it stands. Decorating it in bright (though not garish) colours will have an almost instantaneous effect on the way you perceive your music and how you go about recording.

Picking Your Room

Let's take a look at what makes a *good* home-recording room. Having sorted out your personal preferences you must now consider the practicality of your choice. Ground floor access to a ground floor studio is the ideal starting point, without forgetting the need for structural isolation from any neighbours. If your recording exploits are not going to involve live drums or any other loud acoustic instruments, then even a room that shares a wall with neighbours should fit the bill. But remember that late night vocal overdub sessions, loud piano runs at three in the morning and winding up combo amps when trying to lay down a guitar line with that 'certain' Clappo Layla feel will all do their bit in convincing inconsiderate neighbours (and unfortunately they nearly all are!) that a visit from the local environmental health inspector or the Old Bill is in order.

If you are lucky enough to live in a detached house, nine times out of ten *any* room can be chosen, as sound leakage from even mildly insulated studios will not travel far enough in consistent strength to be a major annoyance. Semi-detached properties are the next best, a room farthest from the partition wall shared with the neighbours being the most sensible choice. If you live in a flat, however, you are going to have to work out really seriously how to stop major sound leakage from music that is recorded or monitored at reasonably loud levels, something which I'll be covering in greater detail later.

In a less than ideal situation, you may be requested to find a room which is as isolated as possible from another place in the house. This is when we start running into all sorts of problems and where sensible soundproofing comes into its own. Never monitoring at more than 40 watts (which I feel is sufficient in *any* situation) and not recording live drums or brass should allow you to site your studio almost anywhere within a given building if you take basic and simple soundproofing precautions. Babies are invariably the biggest bone of contention in this sort of situation, but if you were recording under the above arrangements, there should be no reason at all why your studio couldn't be *next door* to the nursery!

It is when you are planning to record live drums and move heavy pieces of equipment in and out of your studio that 'picking the room' becomes a really difficult decision. Internal or external stairs are always the biggest pain in the neck when you're setting up new sessions, or finishing one in the small hours and the gear *has* to be loaded into the van for a gig tomorrow. If you don't live in a place with ground-floor access, then I'm afraid you're either going to have to start weightlifting sessions at night-school or find a roadie! If you live in a block of flats or whatever, at least always try to site your studio in the room which is most easily accessible once you get through the front door. If neighbours are within easy earshot of the communal stairways it may be an idea (weather and local vandals permitting) to stick a bit of carpet down so that when the odd Marshall stack has to be dragged up or down at midnight, the smallest possible amount of banging around is transmitted to ungrateful ears.

Of course, living above ground level does

have its advantages for home studio owners. Traffic and street noises are usually cut to insignificant levels, giving you one less criterion to take into account when making your choice. The room's structural arrangements must always be considered, especially if it is not at ground level. How much weight is there going to be when you and all your equipment are set up? Will the floor be able to take the weight? You can usually test this by scrutinizing the floorboards for any form of rot or general weakness. If the floor is stone or concrete, can the *general* structure support the extra weight?

Next, are there any major household controls concealed under the floor of your potential studio, such as water shut-offs for times of emergency, or gas taps or meters? If there are, and there is no alternative room, then it is very important that immediate access to these controls is possible by night and day, for instance via a hatch in the floorboards, in case of emergency. Remember, if you carpet a wooden floor (which I highly recommend), you will have to make access *through* the carpet possible too – this can create problems as moving equipment and simply walking about can ruck up the piece of carpet covering the trap-door.

Another *very* important thing to take into account is where the water tank(s) and pipes run. If there were a freeze-up one winter (or British summer!) would a burst pipe seriously threaten any of your major pieces of equipment? Without trying to use scare tactics, I would wholeheartedly suggest steering well clear of any room which has a water tank *above* it. In any circumstances a water catastrophe must *always* be guarded against when you have established your studio – water and electricity do not mix successfully!

Perhaps the most important question to ask yourself when making your choice of room is: does it have scope for the future developments that any home studio, however basic, always goes through? Is there enough room for you and your equipment, and for doing the necessary soundproofing safely and easily. When the room is empty, can you reasonably say that there would be enough space for you to work comfortably in if a one-and-a-half-foot border was put along each wall right round the room? One and a half feet is the optimum measurement in this case, as any soundproofing on any wall would almost certainly close the room in by about nine inches in either direction and it is always wise to match the depth of the soundproofing by an equal amount of space.

Some of you may be wondering why we are talking in terms of establishing a studio in only one room – isn't it better to have one room for recording and another for performing? There is no straightforward answer to this. Working equipment remotely from a 'studio' to a control or mixing room is not always a wise thing to attempt and will often cause level problems, as no matter how complicated your multitrack machine's remote or autolocater is you are still detached from observing the recording meters *during* recording. Over the last three or four years, at least since the introduction and widespread utilization of sampling keyboards, even professional recording artists and engineers have come to regard the control room as the place where almost everything happens, with only vocals and live drum overdubs needing a separate chamber.

As it is possible to inject directly almost everything into your mixer or compact multitracker, monitoring the sound to be recorded via the main monitors rather than from headphones in a separate area or room has become old hat. It has also brought about the realization that any sound, such as the one produced from placing a microphone in front of a valve combo, can be faithfully recreated using external effects devices without the hassle of actually setting the combo or amp up – or, indeed, without even owning them in the first place, let alone having a separate chamber to do it all in! So the line I shall take throughout this book is the professional one (or at least the most contemporary one): that is, that nine times out of ten a project will be recorded in the main room housing all the equipment and that only when vocals or particularly loud or expressively acoustic instruments whose sound depends upon perfect recording conditions (ie no background noise created by multitrack machines) need to be committed to tape should the artist or artists seek chambers away from the recording room or area. To cut a long story short, there is no need to make things more difficult than you have to: a single recording room is by far and away the most direct and simple way of establishing your home studio; it is also the optimum way of performing *and* engineering if you are working on your own.

Choosing Equipment

The inclusion of a chart in this chapter may seem at first glance an oversimplification of the choices on offer, but without it most of the book could have been burned up on this personal and practical subject alone. What you can afford and what you need are the two major factors to be considered when choosing equipment. However, several other things must be taken into account, not least of which is whether your multitrack will be required to link to a professional studio's machine so that you can complete your recording without re-recording your demo (always a headache if you've produced something on the demo that is hard to re-create in the studio).

Don't use the chart as a bible; indeed, look upon it merely as a list of examples, then pick the scenario closest to your own needs and use the equipment suggestions as a basis for your enquiries to retailers. It would have been impossible to include every piece of relevant equipment, but those which appear are usually typical examples of the sort of product I suspect would be best for the job described. If a certain piece of equipment isn't included in the chart, it doesn't necessarily mean that I think it couldn't do the job – check to see which other pieces would do the job by referring to the equipment review and fact-file section, but more importantly ask your local retailer whether there are similar pieces of equipment available, capable of the same work as the piece or pieces that I've included in the chart.

A home recording studio based around a compact multitracker whether it be the Fostex X-15 or the Akai 12-T at £6,000 or so, is always more compact and easier to set up. All the basic components are at your fingertips – the mixer and the multitrack in one package. This means that there is no need for lead harnesses running between the mixer and multitrack. Operating costs are much lower because the tape format is on cassette (either custom format or video or audio types). Indeed, everything about a compact multitracker system comes down to its being less of a financial burden. If you are looking to expand your system in the future you have no option other than to sell your compact multitracker and purchase a mixer and tape machine. With a basic reel system, components can be upgraded independently of one another, which is a major advantage.

The recording performance of a reel-based set-up can be improved by utilizing compatible (and, indeed, dedicated) noise reduction units. This is usually an ill-advised move with a portastudio as they nearly all have internal NR systems for which their heads have been lined up. One of the possible advantages of a reel multitrack is that you can stick a couple of dbx or Dolby units in front of it to improve the s/n ratio. Test to see if the multitrack is replaying at the right speed by recording a constant tone and replaying it.

There are, of course, other considerations which must be taken into account when choosing the other three major links in the chain; amplifiers, monitors and mixers.

Amps

Quality is the best guide when buying *any* home recording gear. However, there are different levels of quality even within groups of amplifiers that have the same specification. Visit a retailer or an obliging audiophile shop and audition several of the amplifiers that are recommended in this book. Whack them up

The JSG shop in Bingley, W Yorkshire

at three-quarter volume through a pair of appropriate monitors and decide where your monitoring threshold is going to be, bearing in mind the size of the room. Keep in mind the information to be found on monitoring levels in the soundproofing chapter. I cannot see any need to monitor higher than 30 watts per channel for home recording in the average home studio. Don't judge that statement by remembering what a friend's HiFi 50-watt system sounded like last week. A clean and powerful amp like a Quad or a NAD heard through some reasonably sensitive monitors (even small ones), such as the Tannoy Stratfords or Yamaha NS10ms, can produce face-pounding levels of bass and perfectly shrill trebles when listened to in close field – even at a mere 25 watts!

A good amp will not colour the signal in any way by expanding its bass content or by not transmitting its high frequencies in their full glory. Test any amp you audition for distortion at high volume levels by fitting it up to a pair of speakers whose minimum power threshold (the minimum number of watts required to drive the speaker components full enough to recreate the incoming signal faithfully) is below that of the amplifier's maximum output, but whose maximum power intake is at least 50 watts above that of the amplifier's maximum volume. If you hear distortion with the volume full up, you can bet your bottom dollar the amp is the one at fault.

For novice home recordists (those who have not developed that sixth sense which comes into play when trying to trace a fault in the recording chain), I would not recommend getting an amplifier that has no meters on it first time around. Several makes of amps such as Quad are renowned for having the absolute bare minimum of extraneous features – the theory being that concentrating on amplifying the incoming signal without putting it through any superfluous circuitry (like VU meters) will help the end signal be as pure and true an amplification of the original as possible.

My approach to these matters is very down-to-earth. A quality amp (you won't find a bad one reviewed in this book) will in no way effect or harm the incoming signal by converting (in branch circuits) the electrical energy into the sort that drives meters. The same applies to omitting the humble volume control(s). The amps in Yamaha's professional series, which I think are the best in the world at the moment, all have separate channel volumes. Again, only if you really understand your system should you get an amplifier with no master volume. It may seem that I'm underrating such well respected companies as Quad – well, before the letters start arriving, I have owned Quad amps in the past and will undoubtedly do so again. I've had two 303s, a 405 and a 50E – and all did me proud, executing their varied tasks superbly. However, I would not have purchased my first Quad amp if I'd had a recording system that was in any way organized.

Sackville Sound

Monitors

When it comes to searching for monitors, be ready for all sorts of advice to be thrown at you from all quarters. This area is looked at in much greater detail in the fact-file section for monitors. For the moment your first and foremost consideration should be deciding how much space you have in your studio. Close field monitoring (sitting within the field of stereo, the speakers close by on stands rather than mounted on a wall in front of the desk which is the option taken by most professional studios which have large budgets for acoustic installation) is the only kind you'll find me recommending for the average home studio recordist in this book. You'll notice in the aforementioned fact-file that the largest speakers I've included aren't very big at all. Monitors don't have to be huge to be good. The diameter of the woofer (bass driver to all you technical pundits out there!) is usually just a direct reflection on the amount of air that can be moved by the vibrating cone. Therefore, small woofers can only push around small amounts of air. However, sitting directly in front of a quality pair of bookshelf speakers will in some cases give you the same sensations as are experienced when listening to, say, a pair of custom Eastlake monitors eight feet away across the desk.

You may then be asking yourself why professional studios bother to have speakers mounted in the walls of a control room. The simple answer would be to say that every new professional studio has it done because every established studio has had it done! But there are some sound (geddit!) technical reasons for 'infinite baffle' designs. During a professional recording, there are usually at least three people who need to hear the same thing simultaneously from the speakers – the engineer, the record producer and at least one musician. Creating a wide and yet consistent stereo field from the speakers is difficult to do at the best of times. Getting a wide enough stereo picture from a small pair of speakers for three people to sit comfortably within it can be very difficult, some would say impossible; designers therefore incorporate the monitors as part of the room. However, due to the development of new cone materials such as carbon fibre, small speaker designs have progressed so far that, although the stereo field isn't any bigger in relation to the size of the cones, it is now more consistent – and that goes for outside it, too. Now with a pair of speakers such as the Celestion SL6s or the Monitor Audio R252s (or, indeed, with any of the other pairs of speakers I mention), you can happily seat people whose judgements are crucial to the recording project *outside* the stereo field, and know for sure that what they're listening to isn't so radically different from what you in the centre are hearing. This is the essence of close field monitoring.

More and more engineers in contemporary recording studios are recognizing the improved quality and, some would say (I certainly would), the greater detail of what one can hear when monitoring in close field.

Make sure the speakers you buy are well constructed. All manufacturers of any repute are only too pleased to deal with questions that your local retailer may not be able to answer. By the way, a speaker that isn't made of 'real wood' or that doesn't have 'real wood veneer' is no less capable than one made of Mexican monkey-tree splinters that have aged for a hundred years over a pot of simmering mineral water!

When auditioning speakers run them off an

Audio Services, Stockport

Sackville Sound, Brighton

amplifier that you have either already chosen or are considering. It's no good auditioning speakers off an amplifier that is not of the quality you will eventually be using. Take along on compact disc, ¼″ tape or metal cassette a recording that you know extremely well. Position the speakers in the room at the angle which you envisage recording, pointing the tweeters right at your ears. Listen for over-emphasized frequencies – but most importantly (and this is the ultimate judge of a good monitor) listen for things which you can honestly say you never heard before in the music when playing it at home. When seated well within the stereo field, with the amp at three-quarters volume, shut your eyes and concentrate on *listening*. Can you only hear the music? Or can you hear a nagging background tonal quality either in the mid range or the bass? If you can, then this is almost certainly due to the speaker cabinet resonating to the vibrations that the cones are transmitting.

Move about the room in front of and to either side of the stereo picture. Does the sound change *that* much? It should change a little, with things hitting your ears differently from the way they did when you were sitting in the stereo field. However, there should be no over-emphasis of any frequencies when outside the listening field. Only when you leave the room or go behind the speakers should there be major changes in the overall tonal quality.

The monitors that you audition and finally choose should be able to handle at least 15-25 (or more) watts more than your amp can push out at full blast. This extra 'headroom' is essential if transients, or peaks of musical power, are to be handled efficiently and safely by the monitors. Take for example the track 'King of Pain' by Police. Playing this through your monitoring system at full blast should be the ultimate test for discovering whether you have enough headroom. The track starts off reasonably quietly, moving on to a second stage which has quite a few loud transient peaks coming off Stuart Copeland's drums. When the chorus begins, there is a notable increase in the amount of music power, with snare and cymbal shots ricocheting all over the place. Your amp and speakers (although I don't usually endorse using amps at full volume) should both complement each other and let the music sail through: the speakers should become transparent when you shut your eyes and really *listen* and there should not even be a minor hint of distortion or woofer popping when the bass content gets a bit thick.

Mixers

Many digital drum machines and some keyboards (such as the Oberheim OB8) have multiple outputs which enable you to process and balance separately the individual components of the sound(s) that they produce. If you have such an instrument or plan to record backing tracks using a few sequencers simultaneously, then your choice of mixer *must* have enough input channels to deal with this stage of recording.

Personally, because of the sort of work I do in my own studios, I would never consider getting a mixer which had less than 16 input channels. However, many of you will be recording just single output instruments, one at a time, and will therefore need a twelve input desk at the very most.

Because the number of input channels on a desk is reduced at the mixdown stage by the number of tracks being used on the multi-track, you must always make sure when choosing your mixer that you will have enough input channels left when mixing for return signals from FX devices. Future expansion of your recording activities must always be considered when picking a desk. Are you, for instance, likely to increase the number of input channels required at certain stages of recording by investing in a drum machine with separate outputs?

The front of Gigsounds Catford shop. Mixer and outboard are mixed through a PA, while a high resolution VDU with separate audio control facilitates the viewing of demonstration videos.

Make sure the desk you buy is not going to degrade the performance of your multitrack machine by adding hiss to the finished recordings. Most mixers (even some costing thousands upon thousands of pounds), introduce systems hiss, commonly referred to as 'noise'. It's unlikely that you are going to find a perfectly quiet mixer on the average home studio budget. However, system noise is nine times out of ten generated by bad recording techniques. I'll deal with this in greater detail later. Suffice to say for now that the mark of a good mixer is this: when the mike gain knobs at the top of every input channel are turned up to increase the amount of signal coming into the desk no extraneous hiss should become audible. When you check out a mixer, check that you can send via the sub group outputs to the multitrack a signal which is coming through an input channel that has only minimal mike/line gain added. Desk faders are the quietest form of gain, so use them before you have to resort to turning the gain pots up.

Parametric EQ systems on desks are favourable, as they allow all sorts of bass and treble effects to be added into a straight input signal. Shelved or 'fixed' EQ sections on desks are usually less capable and flexible. A lot of desks have a mixture of the two. If you're trying to do any sort of accurate or serious recording on reel format, don't get a desk that has no mid range control.

Making sure a desk is well constructed is also important. Don't, however, immediately think that a mixer with a metal casing is better quality in audio than one with a plastic casing. Look for good quality input sockets and outputs. Carbon faders (commonly known as Alps faders) are shied away from by professionals as they tend to wear out. However, like so many institutionalized old wives' tales most commonly supported by senior engineers in the BBC and EMI, carbon faders are *not* (on the whole) *audibly* less capable than the more expensive plastic conductive types. If an Alps fader goes down or starts crackling when in motion, it usually costs less than $3.00 to replace!

Outboard

Outboard or auxiliary equipment is usually a phrase employed when referring to FX machinery, such as reverbs, analogue and digital delays, graphic EQs, harmonizers, flangers, etc. They are also known as 'toys'. For the home recordist, there are some toys that are more important than others when putting together your first system. A capable and stable reverb is the first important thing to acquire when building your library of FX. Make sure of all the units you buy – again, do

Another part of the Catford Gigsounds, showing their comprehensive array of keyboards and, to the back, their range of guitars and combos.

not degrade the performance of your multitrack machine by introducing noise into the recording chain.

Nineteen-inch rack-mounted units look very smart when housed in a dedicated unit. However, in certain instances there is no reason at all for buying them. Rack-mounted units are, on the whole, a third or maybe half as expensive again as their footpedal floor-standing counterparts. Notable advances have been made in the area of pedal FX, and Roland (or Boss) has managed to cram a *digital* delay into a standard-sized unit – quite amazing. So it may not look as chic or, indeed, be as versatile to have the auxiliaries on the desk sent to a batch of footpedals, but the arrangement does have considerable financial benefits.

You may have thought from time to time while reading this chapter that I was living in a fantasy land where recording equipment retailers are only too happy to help you choose equipment, set up speakers with the amp you're thinking of purchasing and let you spend half an hour auditioning FX pedals and checking input channels on various desks for input noise, etc. Well, to tell the perhaps surprising truth, that's exactly how they are! People like Turnkey and Don Larking and ITA make a point of giving you all the best possible advice and assistance they can. Even general retailers like Gigsounds and the London and Bristol Rockshops will go out of their way to give you the best possible choice in equipment and advice. If you happen to come across a retailer who is more interested in watching TV or listening to the radio than helping you set up a mixer, amplifier and a pair of speakers, then you know you're in the wrong place – they obviously don't deserve your money if they think you don't deserve their time!

If you do come across a dodgy retailer who gives out misleading advice about equipment then a quick phone call to the product and sales manager of the appropriate company should clear the air and the situation. However, you must be prepared to make the first move when choosing gear and be ready to weigh up several factors at once. Taking this book along will also help. First, you must decide (a) how many tracks you need (not want) and (b) how many tracks you can afford. After you've come to a practical compromise, you must then decide what sort of quality you require. Will your home set-up have to be good enough to allow you to bounce home recorded material on to a professional studio's multitrack? Rather than losing a generation would you prefer to sync your home multitrack to the studio's? There can be distinct advantages in doing this.

Now let's go through the choices available:

Application	Equipment
Notepad 2-T	Akai 4000 series Tascam A108 simul sync cas. dk. Tascam 22-2
Advanced 2-T	Revox B77 HS Fostex A2 Tascam 32 machines Soundcraft 2-T Tascam 42 and 52 Otari 5050B-II
Notepad 4-T	Fostex X-15 Tascam Porta One Tascam 144
Advanced 4-T	Cutec MR402 Tascam 244 Tascam 246 Fostex 250 Vesta Fire MR1 Clarion compact multitracker system Tascam 34/34B Tascam 44 Tascam A3440 Fostex A4 Otari ¼" 4-T BQII Otari ½" 4-T Mk.III/4
Compact (no fuss) 8-T	Cutec Octette Tascam 388
Advanced 8-T	Tascam 38 Tascam 80-8 Tascam 48 SMPTE Tascam 58 SMPTE Fostex A8 Brennell Mini 8
Compact (no fuss) 12-T	Akai MG1212
16-T	Tascam MS16 Tascam 85-16B Fostex B16 Soundcraft 760 series Otari 16-T Aces TR16
Basic 24-T	Soundcraft 760 series Aces TR24 Trident 24-T
Advanced 24-T	Otari MTR-90 Mk.II Studer A-80/A-800

Soundproofing

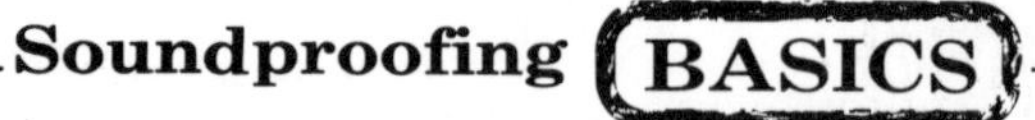

All sound is made up from waves of vibrating air particles, which are capable of making any objects with a pliable mass that are in their path vibrate in sympathy. Objects which have both mass and stiffness, or rigidity, will be forced to vibrate more freely at one particular frequency than at any other – this is termed resonance.

Some rooms have their own resonances, caused by sound waves being deflected from parallel walls and building up into what is sometimes referred to as a standing wave. At low frequencies, these standing waves can make the bass content of a piece sound loose and boomy. Non-parallel walls are the best solution, though completely out of the question for the vast majority of studios. Panelling fixed to the wall and ceiling is the next best thing.

Loudspeaker cabinets have their own resonating frequencies, which can be combated in a number of ways; these are dealt with in the loudspeaker section.

In space, where there is no air to vibrate, sound does not exist. If you isolate air pockets, effectively cutting down the amount of air which can be vibrated, you are in fact also reducing sound levels. This is the main principle behind double-glazing and some other forms of soundproofing.

Noise Control

As I've already pointed out, there are really two approaches you can take when soundproofing a room. If you play drums then you'll have to look at the room as a whole, whereas if you have no loud equipment (or do not intend to monitor at more than 30 watts per channel), the room can be looked at in sections. Isolate areas that leak sound badly, such as windows and doors, and deal with them one at a time until the amount of sound leakage from the room has been minimized.

Structural transmission of certain low frequencies via floor joists is the most common 'giveaway' to whether someone has a drum-kit or not. The neighbours hear the drums as deep, bellowing whoomphs and thuds through their walls, which can be very disturbing. The only really effective way of dealing with the problem is to isolate the studio or the drum area completely by building a room within a room. This is nearly always time-consuming and very expensive, and, even more importantly, very space-consuming.

Although it may seem defeatist, ask yourself how *important* your acoustic drum kit is to you or to your recording exploits at home. The chances are that if you're recording alone at home, some sort of drum machine is already at your disposal for laying guide tracks down. Electronic kits have huge advantages over the acoustic kind when it comes to volume control. An acoustic kit generally has to be played quite hard (loud) to sound good – even at gigs controlling drum volume in relation to the other instruments has always been a serious problem. Vocal signals are pushed beyond the limits of the PA, bass guitars are made far too boomy to cut through the relentless thrashing of the snare, and any delicate, high range keyboard work is made to sound crass and emotionless because of the sheer volume it has to be played at to cut across even the most conciliatory of beats. Onstage monitoring is also upset by drum volume, as the side-fills, which the drummer uses to hear what everyone else is doing, usually end up soaking across to the vocal mikes and causing unwanted feedback. So what with these hassles, plus all the ones it creates at home, is it really worth keeping your acoustic kit? Far better to get yourself an electronic kit, so that volume control is well and truly under your thumb once and for all.

Several electronic kits which have hit the market recently really do have affordable price tags, such as the Ultimate Percussion (formerly known as M&A) UP5, which has fully professional pads (they play like real drum heads) and a non-presetable brain, for around $800. The next best contender is the popular Simmons SDS8 which will set you back no more than about $1,500. There are also some others which are reasonably cheap, such as the Cactus kit (with solid plastic heads) and the kits and modules from MPC Electronics. Roland are also now taking a keen interest in the drum market, and buying a drum machine that can be fitted with pad controllers is fast becoming yet another popular alternative to the problem.

The acceptance and growing popularity of electronic kits has had a major effect on the way even professional studios are designed. Until a few years ago it was considered essential to have a dedicated drum area in the studio itself. Companies such as Eastlake Audio, which is responsible for some of the world's finest recording rooms and mixdown suites, used to install slate drum booths that reflected the sound of the kit and gave a very open, though isolated, sound. Once the first fully professional electronic kit, the Simmons SDS5, came into being, studio clients realized that *everything* could now be performed and recorded in the control room, which had the distinct advantage of allowing the drummer to hear the drum sound through the monitors while he was actually playing. Digital reverb and delay devices also had a major hand in changing the studio layout as they made it possible to give any electronic drum sound the ambience and reverberation that had been achieved by using an acoustic kit.

So, many professional control room studios are now being set up, with only small cubicles designed for vocal overdubs. Only doors and windows are properly soundproofed, now that there is no longer a need for an area that is completely isolated from the main structure.

Furthermore, when you are working out the financial pros and cons of acoustic versus electronic, remember that an acoustic kit needs microphones (reasonably good ones, too) before it can play any part in your recording projects, whereas many electronic kits have built-in stereo mixers and are easily direct injected into the average unbalanced mixer or compact multitracker. Those of you who plan to use sequencers to any great effect probably possess a drum machine already or have put it at the top of your shopping list – having the facility to link up pad controllers to your machine compensates for the lack of having a kit that can actually be 'played' when doing a gig. MIDI must also always be taken into account when considering electronic percussion of any sort.

However, in case you have the space, are willing to put in the graft and can afford the extra money on soundproofing, I shall now reveal some ways of minimizing altercations with the neighbours who have been upset by your love of acoustic percussion!

Floorboards and Risers

First, site your 'dead' area as far away from shared walls as possible. Secondly, try to position your gear in a corner. As you will have gleaned from the soundproofing 'Basics', sound is just vibrating air: therefore, in order to minimize sound leakage from an acoustic kit (or whatever) you must limit the amount of air transmissions which are created when each skin is struck, making the sound waves travel around the room bouncing from one hard area to another. It is also necessary to minimize the 'impact' area of the bass drum in relation to the floor itself. This can most effectively be done by constructing a raised platform (or riser) that has just a few small points of contact with the floor. The riser will decrease the amount of impact energy (mostly caused by the bass drum) directly transmitted to the building's structure. Natural shock waves will be forced to take 'the long way down' as they will have to travel to the floor via the riser's narrow points of contact, thus dispersing much of the energy before the joists are vibrated. Putting rubber on the riser's feet will also help.

For best results, always fit the riser into the corner of the room by cutting it in the shape of a very large 90-degree arrow head. Remember to make sure there is enough room for you as well as the kit! There should be at least enough space for you to stand beside the drum stool. If you're planning on any new acquisitions, such

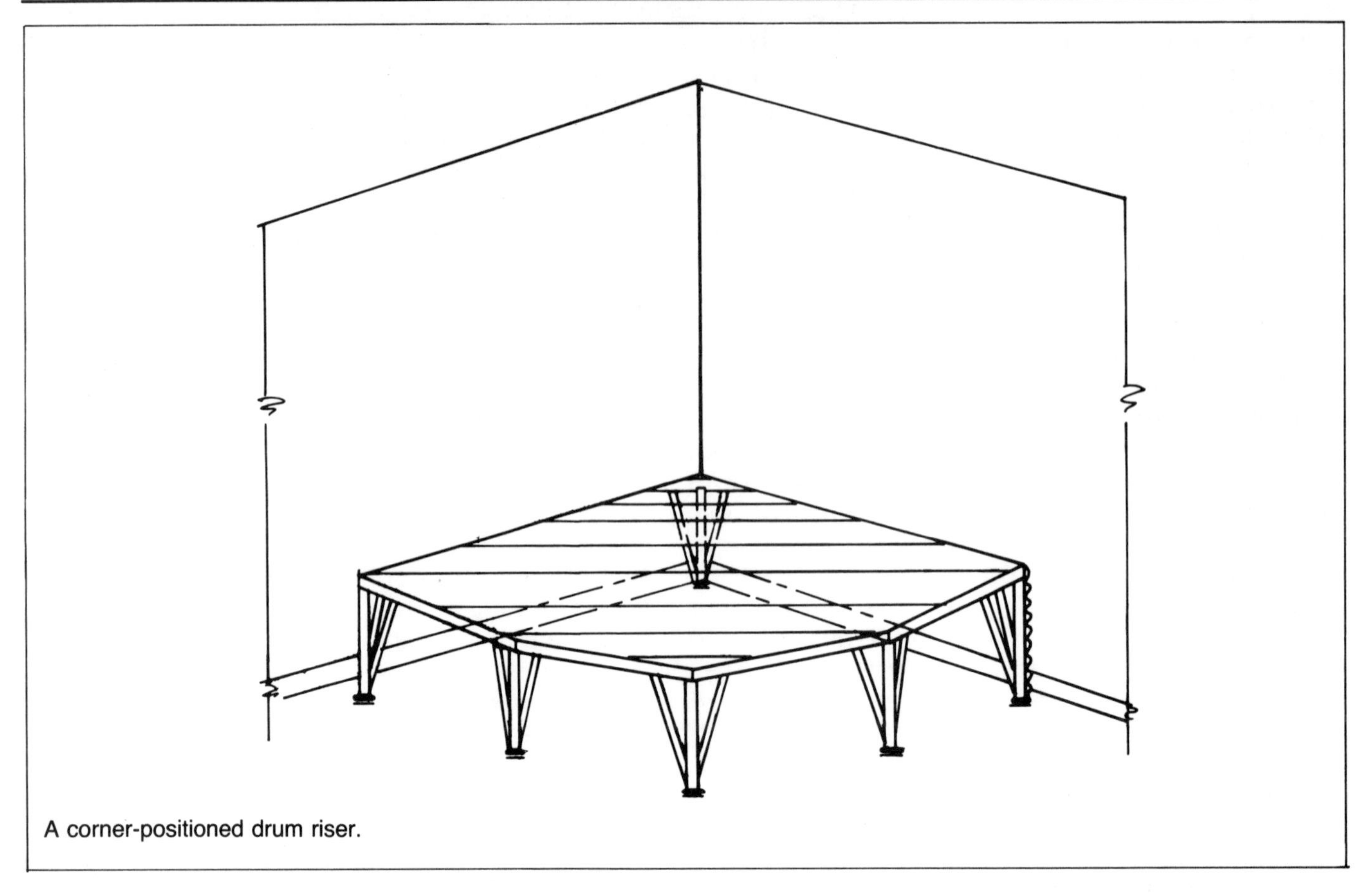

A corner-positioned drum riser.

as stands, make sure that there's room for them. The riser should stand about 1½-2 feet above the carpet.

Sound waves also vibrate the air in the cavities between floor joists. Breaking the air current or volume by placing dense, hard panels backed with absorbent foam rubber over the dead area's floorboards will limit the amount of vibrating air able to travel freely through the floor to the cavities, and will also reduce impact transmission to a minimum. However, the right sort of foam rubber must be used. The best sort is the resilient type sometimes found on the faces of table tennis bats. Normal bathroom tile sealer (rubber based) can be used to make a thorough job of sealing the gaps between the floorboards. This sort of attention to detail must be followed through if an acoustic kit is to be used happily in, say, a block of flats.

After sealing the floorboards and laying down the hardwood boards, try to cover the area with two layers of carpet underlay such as Tredaire or Duralay. In fact, the general rule is (assuming that you've covered the bottom of the riser's feet with foam rubber already) to put down as much underlay and carpet as possible without making the riser move or sink during performance playing. Underlay usually contains a lot of air which won't vibrate as it's held in foam rubber, and as such presents a formidable gap for sound waves to bridge.

Isolation Screens

The next step is to screen the area from floor to ceiling using a removable screen made up of several sections so that it stands (and can be folded) concertina-style. This will probably be the most expensive part of your soundproofing (and all because you want to use those acoustic drums!). Measure the length from wall to wall across the front of the riser. Make sure that you have allowed enough floor space around the perimeter of the riser for mike and cymbal boom stands whose ends jut out quite alarmingly.

Now divide the wall-to-wall measurement into three-feet sub-measurements – these represent the width of each isolation panel. For instance, if the measurement between two walls across the front of the drum riser (following its shape, of course) is 11 feet, you would make provision for four isolation screens. You can experiment to try to find exactly how many panels you should go for by measuring the perimeter of the dead area in straight three-foot lengths using a tape measure. Always remember that the potential overall width of the concertina screen is taken up by the natural zig-zagging arrangement that has to be employed with these screens to give them enough stability to stand (which I'll deal with a little later). In fact, looking back at the above example, I would probably go for five instead of four panels in my overall screen, so that the angles between each one (the point of stability) could be that much more acute, thus minimizing the risk of the whole thing keeling over should someone blunder into it or should the riser collapse (God forbid!).

The screen's design is governed by the length (or in this case height) of hardboard available. Usually, three-foot widths do not come in longer pieces than seven or eight feet at the most. Your average ceiling is usually higher than this (though not by much) and if you can get lengths which will span the distance from floor to ceiling, then all well and good – though a serious word of caution is necessary. Each hardboard panel in the screen must be strengthened with 2″ × 1″ pieces of timber. I would not advise making screens any higher than ten feet because of the rigidity and weight problems that arise when putting a lot of absorbent material on each side of such panels. Very high screens also become very awkward to move around – even manoeuvring the end panel in order to gain access to the dead area becomes quite problematic.

After careful measuring and having worked out how many pieces of hardboard you need, decide how many panels you want to have windows to aid visual contact with the rest of the people and equipment in the studio. For all but the largest screens I would recommend having a modest *vertical* window in *every* panel. These windows are made from pieces of clear (or coloured if you want to be psychedelic!) perspex which may have to be tracked down over a series of weekends if you don't want to pay through the nose for them. In any case, these perspex panels will almost certainly be the single most expensive items in the screen. I think the ideal size is about 2½-3 feet long by about nine inches wide; this won't give you a terrific view, but it will allow you to see all the major bits and pieces in the studio depending on how logical your equipment layout is.

Cut your window holes *before* you strengthen the hardboard panels with the timber strips – nothing destroys the old morale so much as successfully strengthening a panel only for it to crack and split when you cut the window hole! Most hardboard can be scored (or even cut right through with a bit of perseverance) with a common-or-garden Stanley knife. But first it is advisable to draw your window shape with a ball-point pen and a ruler (or other straight edge), pressing deep into the board. Then score heavily along the pen lines. Once scored, a clean break can usually be

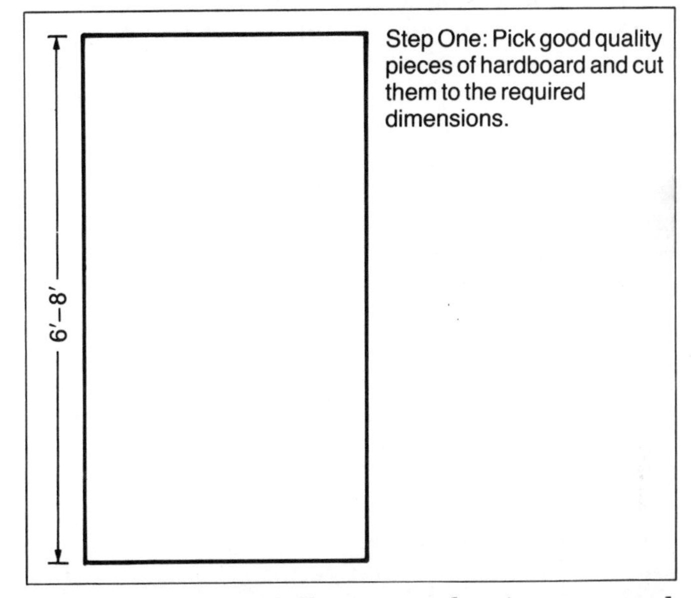

Step One: Pick good quality pieces of hardboard and cut them to the required dimensions.

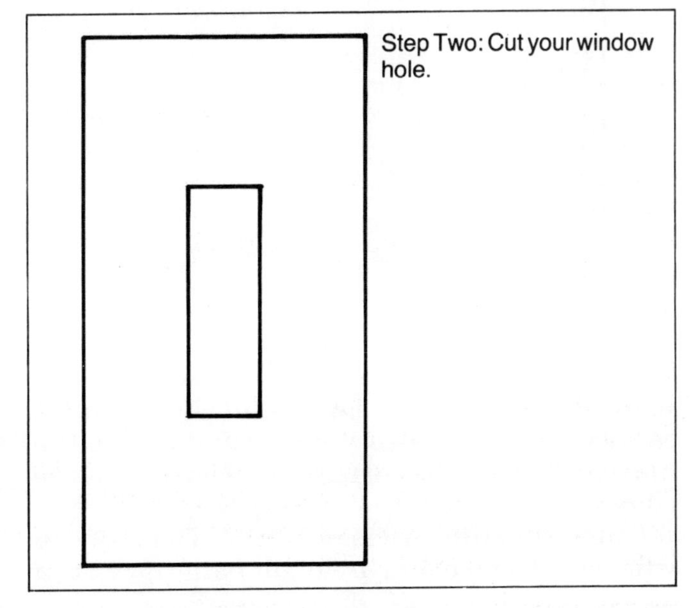
Step Two: Cut your window hole.

made by applying minimal pressure.

Of course you could always ask the timber merchants to do it for you, or enquire whether anyone produces something similar for specialist applications.

If you want double-glazed windows, edge each window hole with 2″ × 1″ timber strips on both sides of the panel and mount the perspex across them, so that the gap between the two sheets is the thickness of each piece of timber and the hardboard itself (negligible).

You will also need enough 2″ × 1″ timber to go round each panel, about nine inches from the perimeter, to make your frame. A good professional timber glue (of which you may need several bottles) should be enough to bond the strips to the hardboard, but you can add some pin-tacks as well to make doubly sure. There are some tricks to getting the hardboard skin-tight across its frame. One is to drench the hardboard with water (using a large paint brush), then glue the timber strips in place and wait for a sunny day! The hardboard must be left long enough to become bone-dry so that it shrinks round the battening as the water evaporates, resulting in a very professional look indeed. There are some problems with this method. You have to find a glue which will stick firmly to the wet board *and* withstand its contraction. You also have to make sure the hardboard isn't the sort that will curl up at the edges.

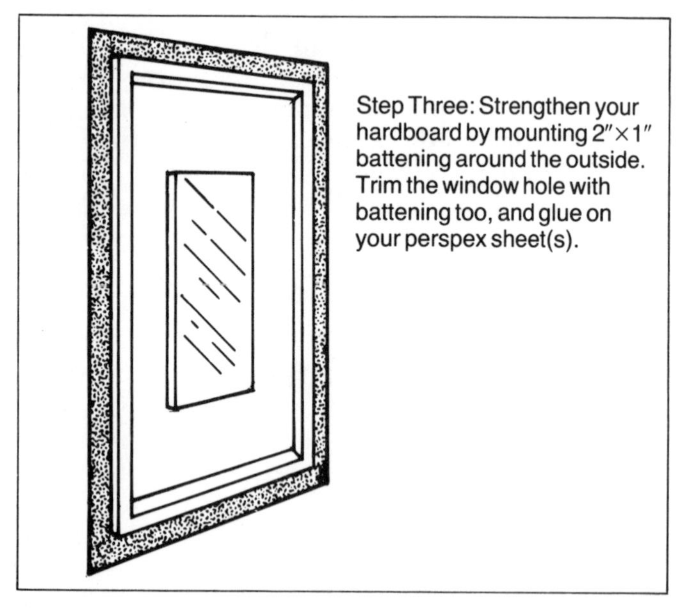
Step Three: Strengthen your hardboard by mounting 2″×1″ battening around the outside. Trim the window hole with battening too, and glue on your perspex sheet(s).

Step Four: Glue all your foam pieces to the hardboard within the battening.

Cutting hardboard is no picnic. Those of you who have to cut a four-by-eight panel down to a three-by-eight have my deepest sympathies – at least wear a mask, as the task creates a lot of dust. You have to be tough to survive the hardboard test, I can tell you!

Once you've cut and strengthened your panels, the next step is to find soundproofing material. This should have good absorbent properties, and suitable stuff can often be found at the back of industrial estates, supermarkets and department stores. Foam rubber is the best bet, but is generally quite expensive. Look in your local market for bargain prices.

Cut the foam rubber into blocks of different sizes. This is not as easy as it sounds – a hot wire cutter, such as is used to cut polystyrene, will work on some foam, but be careful as certain types of foam rubber give off toxic (and intoxicating!) fumes when heated.

When you have a mass of different sized blocks, stick them carefully on to the panel using a suitable adhesive, so that they form a solid but uneven surface. This method is far more effective than applying flat foam sections as the uneven surface breaks up the soundwaves as well as absorbing them. The same principle is behind using egg boxes to soundproof a room, although these will not neutralize sound (as we are attempting to do here) and, of course, they do nothing to stop structural transmission of impact energy or low frequencies.

To make the screen, you can either join your soundproofed panels together using two-way hinges, or make them into stand-alone panels by adding stabilizers on either side, protruding outwards to the floor. The biggest disadvantage of a hinged screen is the gaps between panels which can be a source of sound leakage if they are too big. So be careful to fit the hinges snugly. Hinged screens are also very bulky when folded. On the other hand, the stand-alone screens take up more floor space and the stabilizers (or feet) can be a hazard when moving your kit around.

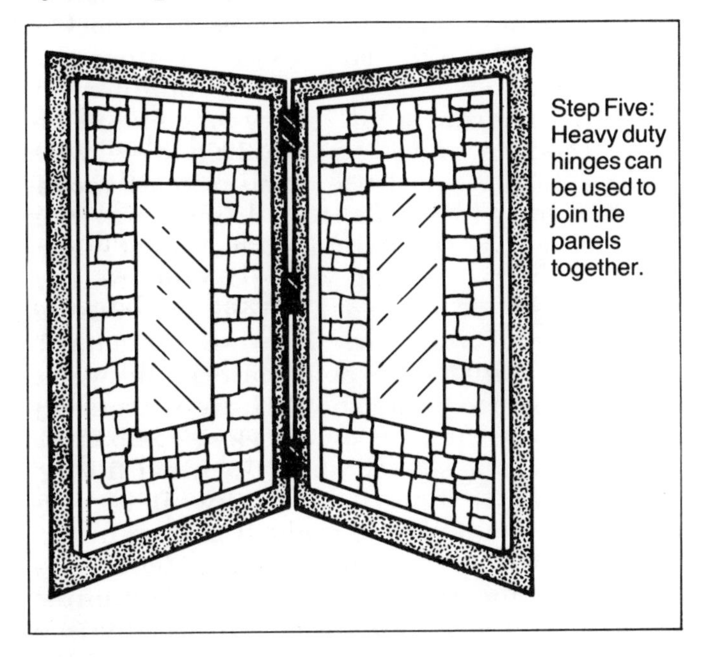
Step Five: Heavy duty hinges can be used to join the panels together.

The gap between the top of your screen and the ceiling is best taken care of by foam-covered baffles (preferably made from something light like hardboard). Flash Harrys will no doubt be able to fix them at an angle so that they form a nice little soundproofed cocoon between ceiling and screen. Less handy bods will just have to fix them so that they hang straight down.

It is very important to make sure your ceiling is structurally sound *before* you put the baffles up – plasterboard ceilings, for instance, will probably just be pulled down by the weight. Also check in the loft (if you've got one) that you won't be damaging any water or gas pipes. If you don't have access to the inside of your ceiling, ask a builder friend for advice on where any concealed pipes are likely to be.

Ceilings that cannot have things fixed to them (plasterboard or concrete, for instance) are best soundproofed by screwing brackets into the walls and fitting box or isolation screens into them. This method also overcomes the pipes problem and is really the only practical method in a flat.

Concertina screens, to be honest, at best look home-made (that is unless you're a master carpenter); at worst you'll be selling them after three weeks. Remember that their effectiveness stands or falls on the amount of shockwaves coming through unchanged from the drummer's side. A two or three inch gap between the panels and around the top will let a lot of transients through, although the floor treatments I have outlined will prevent major structural transmissions of soundwaves and impact energy.

A finished isolation booth, complete with foam-covered ceiling baffle.

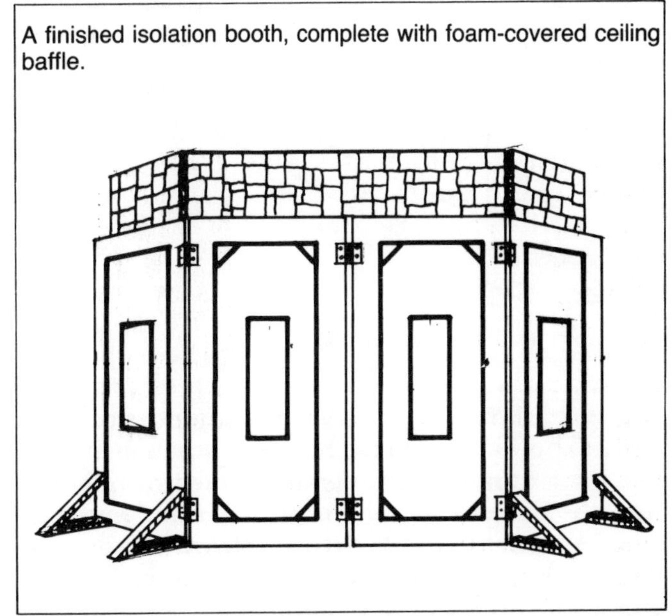

Box Screens

Which brings me happily to the box screen, an altogether more difficult thing to construct although it involves no specialist installation at all (such as ceiling baffles). These box screens are only really effective at drastically reducing sound transients if they reach from floor to ceiling without interruption. Box screens are good at stopping large linear shockwaves from seeping through the air in the studio. In other words (and you may have observed this yourself at one time or another), when someone is thrashing out a tribal rhythm on his bass drum you may find that the studio door (if not well insulated) is knocking backwards and forwards within its frame because of the amount of uninterrupted air

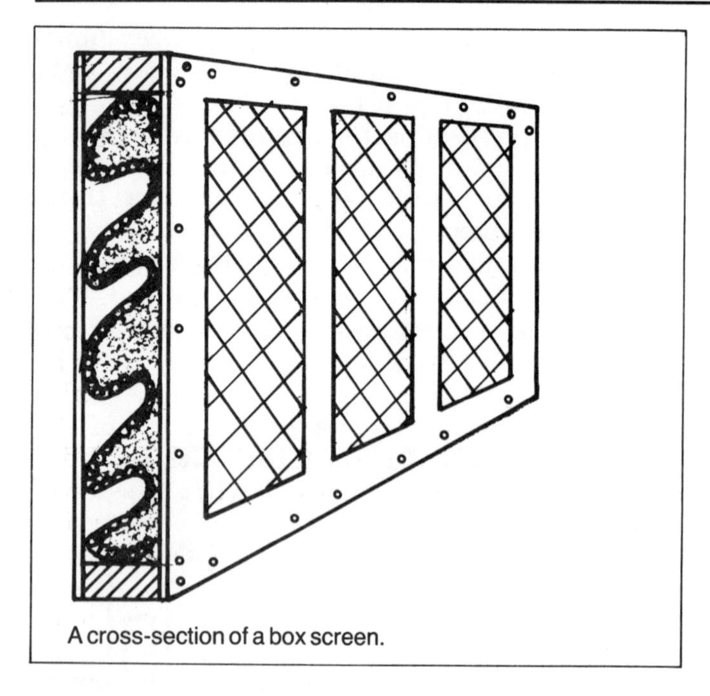
A cross-section of a box screen.

being violently pushed from inside the bass drum shell through to the large surface area of the door. Box screens (as the name implies) put an air barrier between the drums and the outside world which, while allowing free passage of air, will stop direct soundwaves leaving the room and causing havoc with the structure.

The interesting thing is that if you use, say, just two half-screens in front of the kit, linear soundwaves are cut down to nominal levels but the actual volume in the studio is unchanged. As a general rule of thumb, straightforward half and three-quarter box screens are fine for semi-detached residences. In a block of flats, however, if box screens are to afford real protection, they must be used in a similar way to isolation screens, with every conceivable air gap accounted for. Used in this way, with ceiling baffles and little or no free air movement allowed outside the drum area, box screens become the ultimate low-budget insurance against annoying your neighbours. Box screens can be looked at from the side as sandwiches – two layers of cloth-covered hardboard filled with absorbent material between. Each hardwood panel should have reasonably large holes in it to allow shockwaves hitting the screen to be soaked up by the inner filling.

A substance known as Rockwool is very popular amongst many professional manufacturers for this sort of job, but again it is hugely expensive for the home recordist's limited budget. A tried and tested substitute is a mixture of carpet underlay and foam rubber pieces. Some sort of inner barrier, such as chicken wire, will stop the innards spilling out through the holes in the hardboard. Use hessian or any other (preferably tasteful) loosely woven cloth as an overall covering.

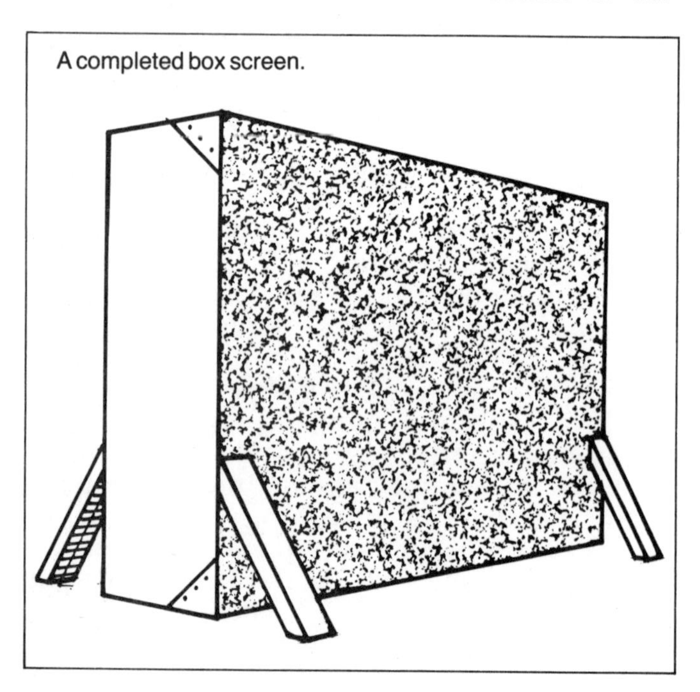
A completed box screen.

Walls, Doors and Windows

I must point out that insulating walls is only essential if you are going to monitor above 30 watts per channel or if you're using drums. Two sets of heavy curtain spaced away from each other and about six inches from the wall is an ideal way of starting to cut down direct transients. Professional foam rubber panels

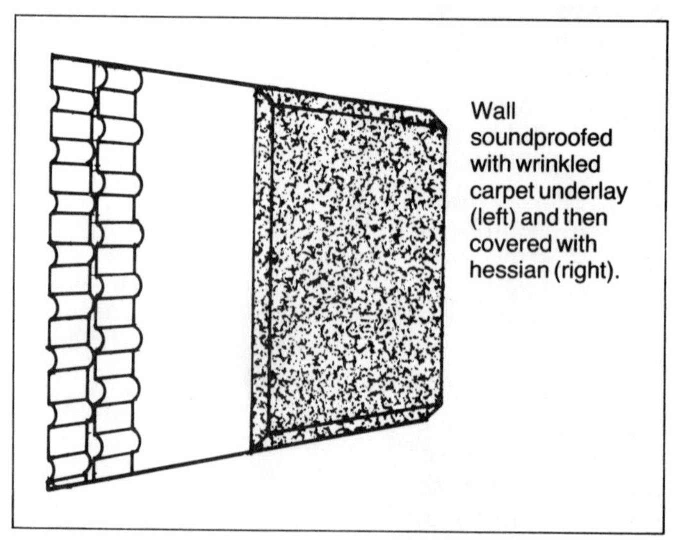
Wall soundproofed with wrinkled carpet underlay (left) and then covered with hessian (right).

can be got from various recording equipment retailers, such as Turnkey, ITA and Don Larking. I only recommend these for soundproofing walls (for which they are ideal) rather than your panels, but make sure you have a friendly bank manager as the popular Illsonic tiles, for instance, cost $15 each and only measure 16″ square.

A cheaper and very effective way is to glue carpet underlay to the wall but wrinkle it so that air pockets form between it and the wall, making it bulge out. These cavities can be left or filled with foam or more underlay. It's best to cut the underlay in strips no wider than about ten inches, and stagger the bulges in each strip so that they are an inch or two above or below the bulges on the adjacent strips. It is *not* a pretty sight – but it does cut down the amount of sound travelling through the walls. Do not be tempted to paint what you've done – for one thing it will look worse and secondly once the paint has dried it will leave a reflective and non-absorbent layer of hard underlay!

The most effective way to disguise wall insulation is to cover groups of strips with hessian from floor to ceiling. Make sure you don't crush the pockets which have been created. You may have to stretch the hessian over timber frames and then fix these to the wall with screws through the underlay.

More important than walls are the windows. What one should concentrate on is the window and door areas. Doors (if you stay within my guidelines) are a doddle to insulate. Common-or-garden draught excluder tape is the first thing to apply to the frame, not forgetting the door jamb. Then, if transients from your monitors are still coming through loud and clear, cover the inside of the door with a large sheet of uneven foam rubber, as with the isolation screen, but perhaps attempt to make the whole thing look a little more professional by covering it in a loosely woven cloth. If your door leaks sound badly, then it is advisable to put an industrial-sized draught excluder around the frame. Failing this, make your own draught excluder using adhesive and strips of foam rubber (preferably a mixture of the bath and resilient types) which should prevent direct sound waves escaping. To deaden the whole door you may have to build a box the same size as the door, and make it two to three inches thicker than an ordinary box screen. For maximum effectiveness, a porch can be added on one side of the studio door with insulated walls using wrinkled underlay (as previously described) and another door, this time with a box on each side. However, these 'air-lock' type porches are space-consuming and can restrict, and sometimes prevent, the movement of large pieces of furniture or equipment. Porches can also be an eyesore from the outside *and* be quite expensive to build. The most important thing to remember when constructing one is that the whole thing must be airtight when both doors are closed, and also that the adjoining timber on the edge of the porch walls is lined at the joints with resilient foam rubber so that structural transmission of shock waves and sound waves is not carried through. A double box-screened door that is well lined with thick draught excluder should offer all that any loud home recordist will need in the way of door soundproofing.

The most difficult areas to soundproof are, of course, windows. You will want to keep a reasonable amount of natural light coming through them, while at the same time reducing sound leakage. Home-made double-glazing is OK *if* you take the time to make at least one of the extra pieces of perspex (don't use glass unless you're forced to – mike stands break panes of glass, but just scratch perspex!) either completely removable or at least 'slidable'. This is particularly important if you have no other means of escape or calling for help in an emergency. Any DIY shop will be able to supply you with and give you advice on fitting plastic or aluminium runners that are designed to go on the inner walls of any window cavity. Sound transmission from outside and inside is reduced, but only on a domestic level. You will have to make sure that the runners you buy will be suitable for having thick draught excluder stuck on them wherever the butt of the panels ends. Usually, with a two-pane system, there is a gap between the two where the overlap occurs; this will have to be dealt with by sticking a foam strip on the first pane and making sure that it doesn't restrict the movement of the second.

If your windows do not sit in their own cavities and you are exceeding my advised monitoring levels or using a kit, then there is no alternative but to lose the window altogether. Bricks are cheap but bricklayers aren't. As it's a very small job, you could perhaps put your own price on it (say a tenner and a couple of pints down the local for doing an average-sized window). Make sure you are not going to weaken or damage the wall by knocking out the window frame. Bricking up a window may also contravene planning regulations in your area – especially if you live in a listed property. However, just bricking the cavity up is not the end of the matter; some sort of absorbent layer will have to be put over the new bricks to fill the remaining cavity. If there is enough depth to the wall and if it is structurally possible, two layers of bricks with an air gap in between them is probably the most effective form of sound insulation.

But most of us are unable to do such things to the buildings we live in. The most commonsensical and practical alternative I've found in dealing with window insulation is to create a foam-lined frame in or around the window cavity; you make a box screen of considerable thickness that fits tightly and snugly into the frame. When you are not using a kit and monitoring at sensible levels, the screen can be removed to allow natural light into the room and, more importantly, natural air! Good ventilation in a recording room is very important – some people go as far as installing ionisers which remove all the negatively charged ions which most electrical equipment gives off. The most notable benefit of having a framed screen over your window is that, when not in position, it can be used independently if you're clever enough to fit some stabilizers to it or make a stand-up frame for it to drop into.

As you complete each area of soundproofing, check how effective each section is by standing outside the studio (and perhaps going to your next-door neighbours) and listening to loud programme material (nothing exceeding your usual monitoring levels though).

Control Room Acoustics

If, at the end of the day, your studio resembles a dark and dingy padded cell with no natural ambience at all, you will have to take some steps to ensure that, when you are monitoring during recording and mixdown, the walls, floor and ceiling aren't sucking up frequencies straight out of the speaker drivers and so preventing your ears from making a balanced judgement about whether a recording has, say, enough treble in it or not. Having a very absorbent environment will make you add more high frequencies when recording and mixing. The tonal balance of the finished recording, when played in a different environment, will be too heavily weighted at the top end; guitar solos at the top of the fret board and cymbal crashes, for instance, which sounded perfect at home, will now come out as screechy and tinny.

If your monitors are pointed at a pair of

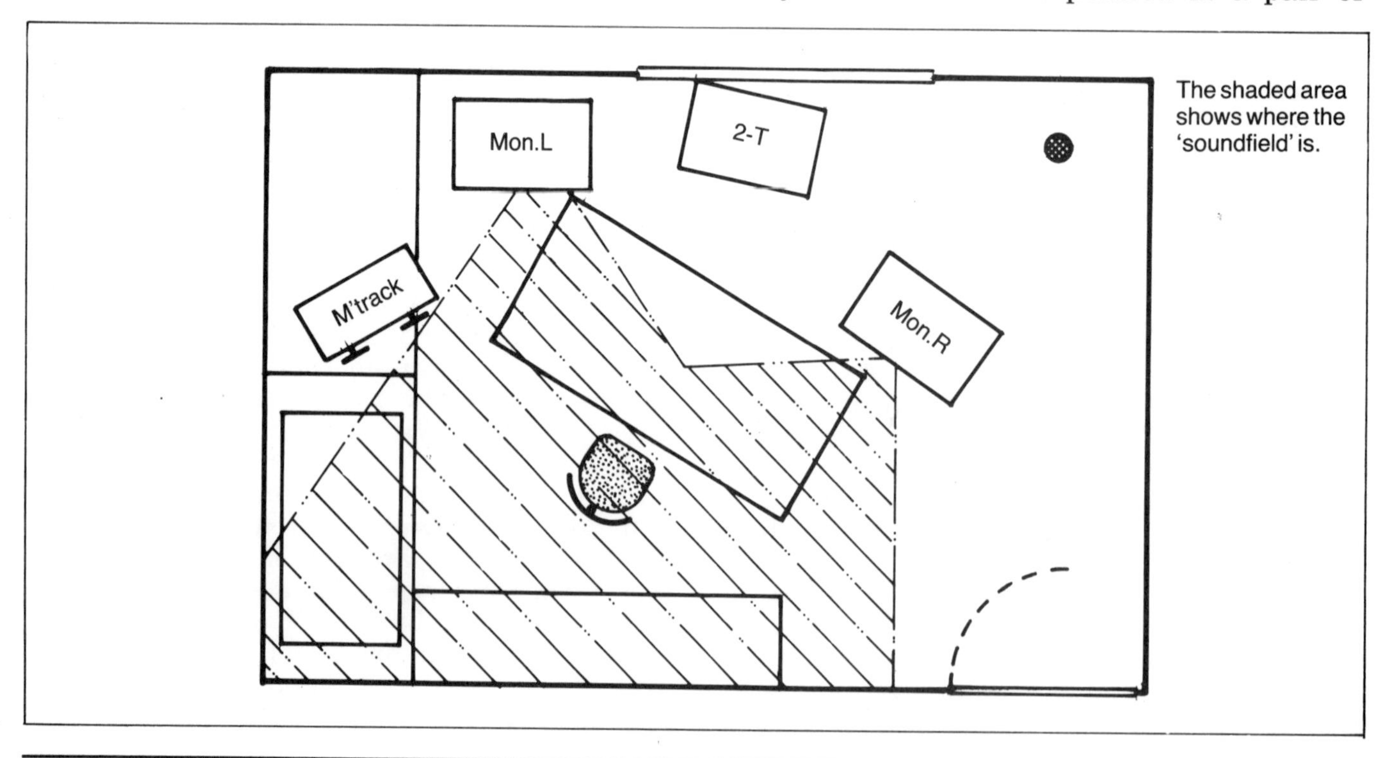

The shaded area shows where the 'soundfield' is.

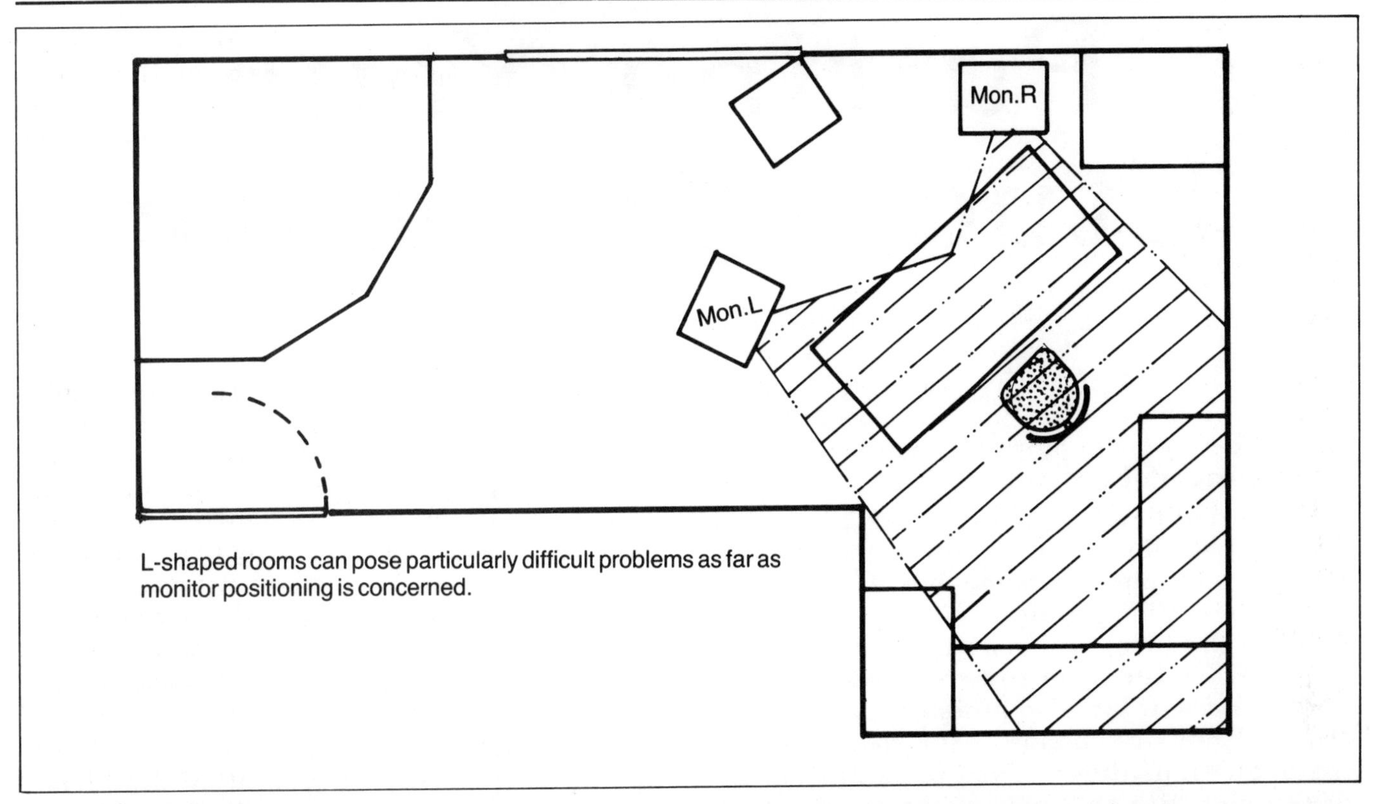

L-shaped rooms can pose particularly difficult problems as far as monitor positioning is concerned.

curtains and if there is no other absorbent material around, it can still have quite a strong effect on the overall treble and brightness that a speaker seems to be putting out. Make sure the monitoring field is over a wall area which is about 50 per cent reflective and 50 per cent absorbent. Hardboard panels can be fitted over wall-coverings which will have quite a marked effect on the brightness of the room. Quite nice decorative hardboard panels can be purchased which are reasonably cheap. Check what effect your additional reflective panels are having on the acoustics at regular intervals. Walking from side to side and end to end of the room while listening to material through your monitors will show up acoustic differences, such as 'dead spots' and the equally annoying 'live spots'. By erecting the reflector panels in foot-wide strips placed two feet apart you'll get the best possible mixture of reflective and absorbent wall-coverings. However, there are no hard and fast rules; you may find that you have a *very* dead spot which will perhaps require 80 per cent of the wall area to be boarded over.

Before you embark on any major soundproofing, it is always a good idea to contact your local recording equipment shop and ask if they know of any studios that are being refitted – you never know, you may be lucky enough to pick up some old unwanted isolation screens from Abbey Road or wherever! Independent local radio stations are another possible source for soundproofing hand-me-downs.

Don't be put off by this chapter – it does seem daunting at first reading. Your soundproofing needs will very much depend on your environment. There are many buildings, including council-owned blocks of flats, which have strong non-conductive structures and in which soundproofing will only have to be done as an afterthought to everything else – if at all!

Putting Your Studio Together

Equipment Layout

The type of music you record and perform in your studio will ultimately effect the way pieces of equipment are laid out in relation to each other. Visual contact with VU meters is usually the prime consideration when deciding where in the room you are going to record. Guitarists will have no problem, as leads can be run from side to side of the room if you're using an amp, allowing you to perform at the desk itself with the instrument on your lap.

Keyboardists using a reel system will have extra problems, created by the sheer amount of space their instruments need. Working behind the desk, with a clear view of the multitrack, is always the best solution – but what if your equipment won't fit into this space? The only logical alternative is to set up just the important instruments, usually your work-horse keyboard and drum machine, and do a bit of Pickfords removal work in between takes. If you're using a full MIDI system with, say, a couple of keyboards, a drum machine and digital sequencer there's really no practical alternative other than to invest in an A-frame stand. These stacking types of keyboard stands take up the minimum of space, while giving you the maximum amount of racking to mount instruments on.

Equipment layout will be dictated by the length of your lead harness between multitrack and mixer . . . wrong! You must always strive to achieve a layout that will use space most economically and have your leads prepared accordingly. I've walked into too many home studios to find that, for the sake of ten quid spent on wire, the multitrack stands askew to the mixer and that the outboard equipment is resting on empty suitcases because there isn't sufficient slack to place it neatly in a rack, away from the auxiliary outputs on the desk!

Your equipment layout must take all factors into consideration, not least of which is where the wires will run to and from. Rats' nests of multicoloured cable can soon appear when rigging up even a simple reel-based four track. Labelling important leads at both ends is always a sensible thing to do. Also, make sure in your room plan that you allow wall space here and there for hanging up leads neatly and tidily. Hunting for a lead is almost as irritating as 'finding the beginning' when in the middle of a heavy session. I've worked in major professional studios where leads – of all kinds – are kept in cardboard boxes in the maintenance room. This sort of petty disorganization is time-wasting and frustrating for anyone who's trying to put things down on tape seriously. Make sure you keep the equipment tidy, have a clean-up after every major session, and I guarantee things will go a lot easier.

Electricity, You and Your Studio

NEVER poke knitting needles into the holes in a mains socket! NEVER suck your fingers and then go and change a light bulb! Under NO circumstances pour liquids over equipment which is connected to the mains!

I may seem a little over-anxious in my warnings, but these sorts of things have happened in some studios I've worked in! Electricity is something which should *always* be taken seriously. No doubt you'll be using a couple of multi-way plug banks to subsidise the amount of mains points available in your studio. As long as you buy good quality banks and use cable which is more than capable of handling the mains current, then all should be well.

In winter, you may find it necessary to have

some sort of heating in the studio. If you use an electric fire which has a rating above 1000W (usually a one-bar job), then I'd seriously consider running it off a socket that is on a separate fuse. Most home recording studios never require a burn of more than 750-900W. However, if you are in a building which has not been rewired in the last ten years, I would thoroughly recommend spending thirty odd quid on an isolated transformer. This plugs into your mains and has a socket or two at the other end of the transformer chain. According to the type, about twenty or so things can be run off the other side with little or no chance of an overload. However, it won't give you *complete* protection, and if you're silly enough you'll get a shock anyway – even if you do the mixdown wearing a pair of Marigolds (rubber gloves)!

Lighting in the Room

I cannot overemphasize the importance of proper lighting in a studio. Bad lighting arrangements can be found even in the best studios and are, on the whole, responsible for the headaches and migraines that many people experience during sessions. The way light is used has a direct bearing on how tired your eyes get. The best policy is to acquire a couple (or more if you can afford it) of low-wattage spotlights (which you can buy for about £5 each). Position them far from the centre of the ceiling in such a way that pools of light fall on reflective surfaces and so *indirectly* light your equipment. However, it is a thin line that divides what is at first a soft and restful light from one which makes the task of reading legends that much more difficult. Lighting a mixer from one direction only must be avoided at all costs, as all the knobs (of which there are usually many) throw their own shadows across adjacent controls and labels. Sketching out some ideas before actually moving things about may save some time and energy.

Monitors in Relation to Your Ears

We'll cover the acoustic side (and the generally much more technical side of monitor placement and usage) a little later. When arranging the studio equipment, remember the *personal* needs of your monitors! If a manufacturer recommends that you place speakers with their backs to a wall, don't expect them to sound particularly good (or accurate) if you stick them on wall-mounts, two yards out into the centre of the room. But there are no real rules and you may find that positioning monitors in an unrecommended way has no adverse effect on their performance. The secret is to ask yourself – or, better still, the manufacturer(s) – *why* they recommend certain positionings for particular speakers.

When you plan your room, make sure that pieces of equipment are not going to protrude into the monitors' stereo field and unbalance the sound reaching your ears. If you intend to work behind the monitors (that is, facing the back of them) you may want to invest in some small additional monitors, to bring the sound nearer without going through the hassle of turning the speakers around in between takes.

This seems a good idea at first – and indeed solves the problem for a lot of home recordists. But it's important to make provision for turning the small speakers at the other end of the room off when mixing or doing any critical appraisal of your production, as the sound reaching your ears from them has reflected its way up through the entire length of the room and could make your work sound more live than it is. Secondly, crucial instruments such as synths – especially Yamaha's excellent DX keyboards which have particularly percussive overtones – may be inaccurately represented on a pair of small speakers. This could result in your committing to tape a sound which when listened to at close range on your main monitors sounds completely different! This is yet another reason for arranging enough space in front of the desk for keyboards, sequencers and drum machines.

The distance between your monitors will have an effect not so much on the sound itself, but on the amount of space you can freely move about in at the mixer before you start to hear 'too much' from one side or the other. If your monitors require floor-stands for them to sound accurate, you *must* take this into account when judging the height at which you want the mixer to stand off the floor.

You must also take into account in your plan the possible need to modify the wall-covering's properties directly in front of the monitors. A common complaint for many beginners is that the monitors go 'dead' when they start adding soundproofing to the room. All that's happening is that the high frequencies being pushed out of the tweeters are being absorbed by the wall surrounding the monitors. The simple solution is just to add reflective coverings over your absorbent layer, as I've already described. This sort of thing, however, can be made much more difficult if you've already mounted wall-hangers for leads and bits and pieces right on the spot where your monitors are now demanding a different covering!

In life in general, as well as in getting the best results from your studio, people don't plan to fail, they just fail to plan!

Back Access

Some would say that the most important thing to consider when putting your studio together is to make sure you have rear access to the major pieces of equipment. To a certain extent, I would go along with this. However, looking at the backs of pieces of metal spilling bits of spaghetti isn't very attractive, and that's something you have to consider if you're pondering the possibility of hiring your studio to outsiders. To my mind, you only need constant access to the FX units, due to repatching requirements. Second comes the mixer, with the tape machine third (you may need to access a tape channel output direct, ready to feed to a drum machine or sequencer for clocking purposes).

The Patchbay Necessity?

Lash-ups – studios running without a central point of connection such as a patchbay where separate pieces of equipment can be linked together by simply using short 'patch leads' as they are known – *do* work; there can't be any arguments where that's concerned! However, a patchbay is needed when you're using over and above the usual number of rack-mounting FX. I'm a great fan of partial patchbays which are semi-normalised.

Let me explain. Professional studios traditionally lean towards large, cumbersome and very expensive patchbays. They're usually referred to as GPOs, because the socket and plug types were common to the one the Post Office used to employ on their telephone switchboards before System X and fibre-optics came along. An average pro patchbay would have somewhere in the region of 2,500-3,000 holes (or connection points). I can honestly say that even on very complicated sessions – usually involving synching a Fairlight's Page R function to itself the second time around to aid programming flexibility *and* running video off the multitrack, I've never used more than 15 per cent of the patchbay. There are those who believe it's better to have the option than none at all, to which my answer is that at $5 per hole they could come up with something a little less expensive and expansive!

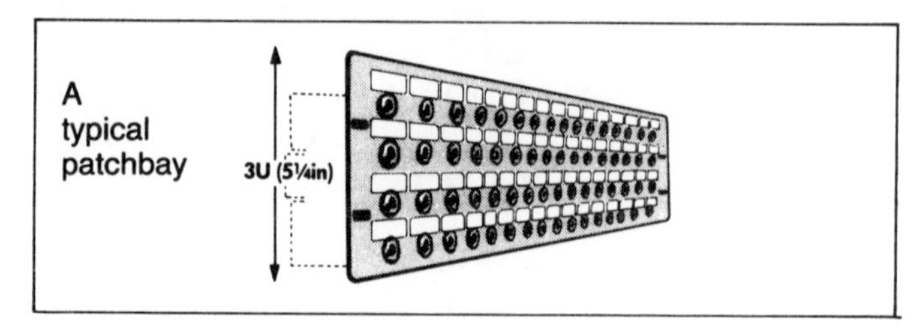

A typical patchbay

The most-used connection points on a patchbay in a home studio are the mastering machine's ins and outs; FX sends and returns from the insert points on the desk and master module(s); parallel or 'multi' strips of holes for quick linking of several previously unrelated signals and patching them all via one cord to another patch point; amplifier ins and outs; a limited number of line inputs; and finally the foldback output, ready for connection to a second amplifier – a need rarely encountered when recording solo at home.

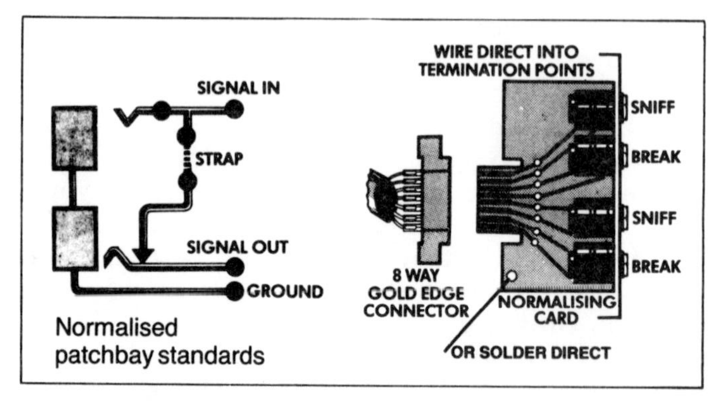

Normalised patchbay standards

A normalised patchbay is one that, although boasting line input sockets and tape return sockets, does *not* need these to be connected to each other via patch cords for the whole system to work. In other words, you may have the tape returns linked onto your patch bay so that you can take tape signals off the multitrack and process them (or whatever) *before* they reach the desk. However, if you need no pre-desk interference with the tape return signals, you can just leave that part of the patchbay empty, and the signal (because of some clever soldering work and lead running) will run to its required tape return channel on the desk without the need of patching it through.

There are many solutions to the patchbay puzzle – and I'll guide you through them at a later stage. Having a patchbay in your studio may or may not influence its overall layout – it all depends on whether you *want* it to or not . . . which could be applied to just about everything explained in this book!

SECTION TWO

The Art of Noise

The Art of Noise

The Recording Chain

PROBABLY second only to monitoring and speaker preferences amongst recording engineers comes the intensely personal subject of microphones and microphone techniques. Some engineers will doggedly stick to using just one type of microphone for *everything* except special effects. The Neumann U87 is a very popular microphone that has become valued for its clarity both in contemporary recording studios and in the claustrophobic, institutionalised world of classical recording where the *only* way to record an orchestra is to stick the mikes straight into the inputs on a Sony PCM F1. I myself have never been particularly keen on the U87, always preferring to use a selection of different mikes rather than stick to that one sort of sound. You may wonder whether mikes do actually have sounds of their own. Well, it is true that mikes accentuate certain frequencies they pick up – whether intentionally or not. 'Presence curves' are often quoted by manufacturers for mikes whose frequency pick-up characteristics accentuate frequencies in the mid range; these mikes are often very useful for vocal applications. Other mikes each have a 'sound' of their own because they have valves in the signal chain that are designed and constructed in such a way as to 'warm' or 'soften' the *tone* of the sound being relayed to the mixer. Nine times out of ten, microphones recommended by pro engineers accentuate frequencies in particular areas, which means they are especially useful for certain instruments. This is really the reason why the subject of microphone selection is so complicated and fraught with passionate extremes of opinion. A snare drum sounds excruciating at 1K, so a microphone that accentuates this frequency will be regarded as a bad snare mike. However, at 125Hz and 80Hz, with a crisp attack at 2K, the snare sounds full, deep, luscious and loud; a mike supporting one or all of these frequencies in preference to others will therefore be considered a good snare mike. On the other hand, the same 1K-loaded mike may be dug out of a cupboard by another engineer and used for an instrumental or vocal effect that sounds *good* with the 1K emphasis, so that that particular mike will thereafter be known as a terrible snare mike to one engineer and a terrific vocal mike to another.

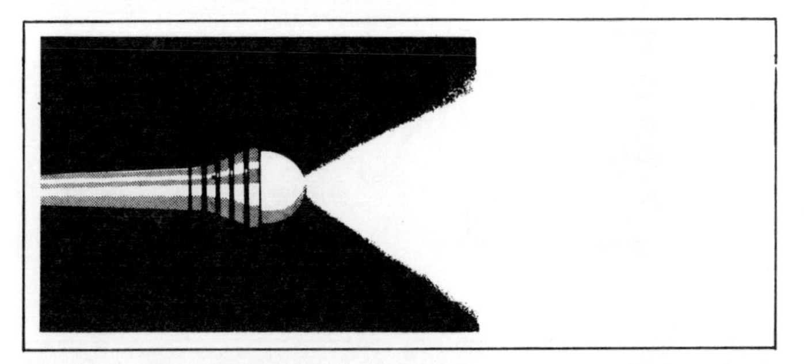

There are four types of microphone being used in the recording studio at present:

Pressure Zone Microphone (PZM). The newest and probably most controversial of all microphone designs. A PZM mike makes use of a diaphragm connected to a rather special electret capsule to produce the output signal or voltage. Sound waves are picked up on a plate via a small adjacent slit. A PZM mike possesses a pick-up pattern that is hemispherical and is continued down to a frequency determined by the surface area of the plate.

Dynamic (sometimes referred to as 'moving coil') microphone. In this type of mike the diaphragm is connected to a coil set in a magnetic cap that produces a voltage as it is moved. These mikes sometimes have a transformer added to increase signal output.

Condenser & Electret. In this sort of mike, the

diaphragm has been coated with an ultra-thin layer of metal which has a backing plate. A very high voltage is contained between the two; this is called the polarizing voltage. As the capacity fluctuates with the movement of the diaphragm, varying voltage is produced, and this has to be amplified in some way inside the microphone.

Ribbon. A ribbon mike contains a reasonably large magnet with a ribbon of metal set into it, which is cleverly capable of acting as both coil and diaphragm. As it moves, a low voltage is produced across the ribbon. A transformer is then needed to increase the output voltage.

Microphone placement in a string section.

Microphone placement in a brass section.

Microphone placements for other instruments.

Every microphone has a pick-up pattern, which corresponds to the area around the capsule of the mike within which sound is picked up. It is the shape of this area that determines microphone usage in professional studios. For example, an omni-directional mike will, as the name implies, pick up sound in a wide area from every direction. This is the mike most commonly used for general recording, and is the best for recording sound sources that move about a lot. However, when you are recording several instruments in the studio simultaneously, it is desirable to use microphones that have directional pick-up fields in order to minimize spillage or leakage. Such mikes are known as cardioids. A typical case in which spillage needs to be kept to a minimum is when you are trying to record a drum kit. Each drum has its own mike which in turn is fed into its own input channel on the desk, in order to facilitate fine EQing and processing. You don't want the bass drum mike to be picking up the snare if you're adding a lot of frequencies to the bass drum that make the

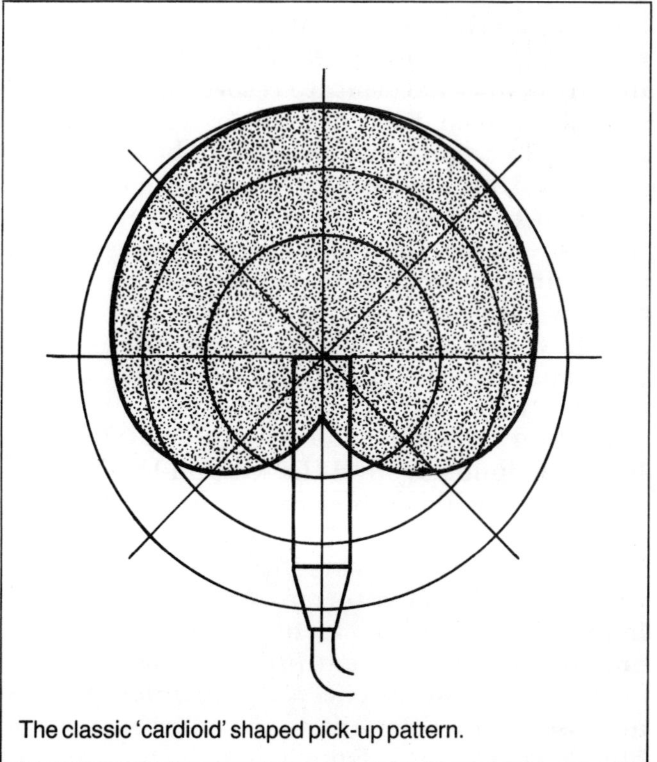

The classic 'cardioid' shaped pick-up pattern.

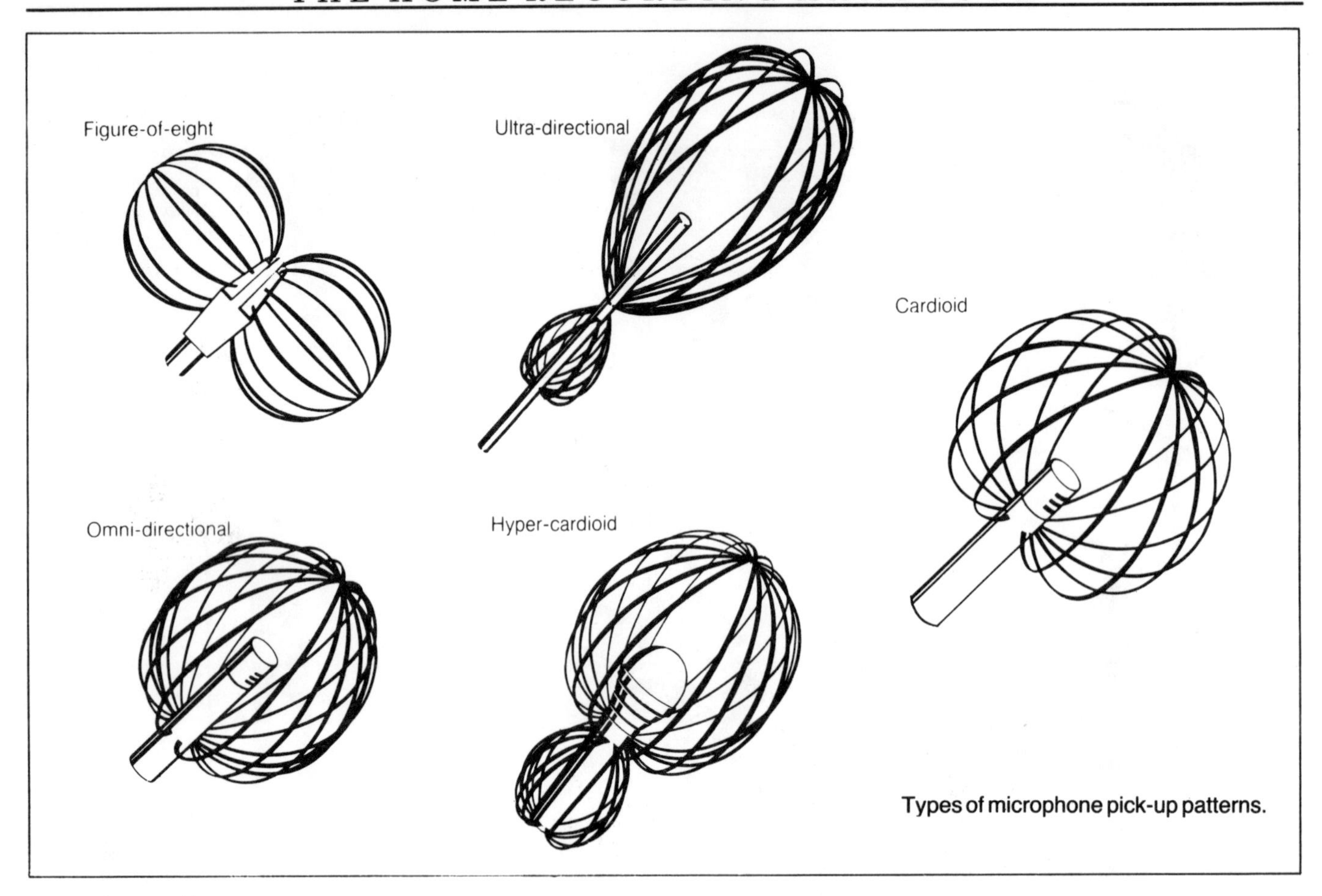

Types of microphone pick-up patterns.

snare sound hard and nasty. The same thing applies to other combinations of instruments; recording a Country & Western outfit, for instance, may necessitate recording violin and acoustic guitar together. If you're lacking in isolation screens and tracks, it becomes imperative that the mike recording one instrument in the studio doesn't pick up too much from the other instrument; otherwise sound-balancing between the two on the desk becomes very difficult.

However, an understanding of the pick-up patterns of your microphones is not enough to ensure the results you desire. When you are recording a drum kit, for example, setting up a lot of cardioids around the kit and leaving the capsules to isolate the sound source is just not good enough. If a cardioid is placed in front of a kit it will pick up everything regardless. For the best results (in terms of minimizing spillage) close miking techniques have to be employed. As the term implies, close miking entails positioning each of your microphones as close to the relevant sound source as possible. To get the most from a mike on a drum kit, it should be placed no more than an inch and a half from the top or bottom skin of the drum. This method does have its problems, the first of which is that instrument movement can cause mid-take collisions (*especially* with drum kits). When miking tom-toms in particular, whack each one as hard as it's likely to be hit during recording to determine how much the tom wobbles. You may have to tighten the centre drum holder in some instances, or even resort to taping the tom to the bass drum.

The second problem potentially arising from close miking is that many cardioids boost low frequencies when they're placed in close to the sound source. This effect can of course be used creatively; however, in many cases it just isn't acceptable to keep flattening out the signal coming from a mike on the desk's EQ section. It's easy to get caught up in vicious circles, and the end product doesn't sound 'right' after a lot of tweaking and cutting. So, to prevent this, mike manufacturers build into their mikes bass roll-off filters designed to pull the low frequencies down to a manageable level when close positioning is employed to

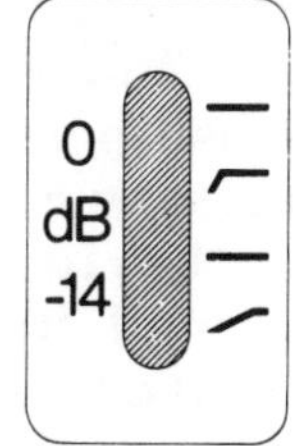

Many manufacturers include bass roll-off filters in their mikes. This diagram is typical of the selector switches found on many models.

minimize spillage.

As you can see from the mike-positioning suggestions in this chapter, there are many different ways of miking up instruments. Each different position will result in a different ambience and/or frequency content entering the desk. As is so often the case in the field of home recording, there are no rules and what's

Various microphone placements for drum kit and congas.

good for one person is terrible for another. Experimentation is the key to originality.

As a final word on the subject of mike positioning, there is one guiding principle: the closer you get to the source, the more direct the sound will be, while the further you go away, the more room noise (ambience) and side spillage will come into play. Therefore, a close-miked kit in a dead room can be a boring one. 'Overheads' is the term given to mikes that are placed *above* a sound source deliberately to introduce more room ambience (as far as the acoustic properties of the wall coverings allow) into the signal.

Ohms, Highs and Lows

Microphones with high impedances ('high-z' as they are known) have the awkward tendency to produce nasty microphonic effects and lose all your top end signal when you're using them with reasonably long cables. So why do manufacturers make them? Well, high-impedance mikes provide mixing-desk and compact multitracker manufacturers with a convenient means of getting a loud signal through from the mike gain amp (in the desk) and making the best of the equipment's usually rather poor signal-to-noise ratio. Microphones with a *low* impedance (say 200 ohms) usually produce signals between 2mV and 500mV (½ volt), so that the noise level created by the mike gain amp in the mixer needs to be 60 to 65dB below 2mV if systems hiss isn't to be audible on the lowest sound to be recorded. Units manufactured on a budget, such as affordable mixers and compact multitrackers, can't usually achieve the signal-to-noise ratio needed to enable one to record using low impedance mikes; the standard of craftsmanship and design and the quality of the necessary components would put the price of the finished product out of the reach of normal human beings (that is, people who still have to worry about how much things cost!).

So what *is* the point of having low-impedance mikes? Well, unlike high-z mikes they can be used without any audible side-effects in situations where cable lengths need to be anything up to a hundred feet. Even if you are never going to need a hundred-foot lead on any of your mikes, you may still encounter difficulties. The trouble with high-z mikes is that if you've bought one that is already attached to a cable measuring over 14ft. and with a capacitance above 100pF/metre, your delicate high vocals, flute solos and cymbals (in fact anything with a reasonable HF content) will inevitably suffer.

The way round the problem when you are using equipment that is designed with high-z inputs is to steer well clear of mike cables longer than 12ft. and always to make sure that the cable has a capacitance lower than 100pF/metre.

Building a Mike Library

I'm glad to say that the recent development of new manufacturing processes and materials has meant that home recordists can now afford very good mikes at extremely reasonable prices.

The key to building a good mike library (if

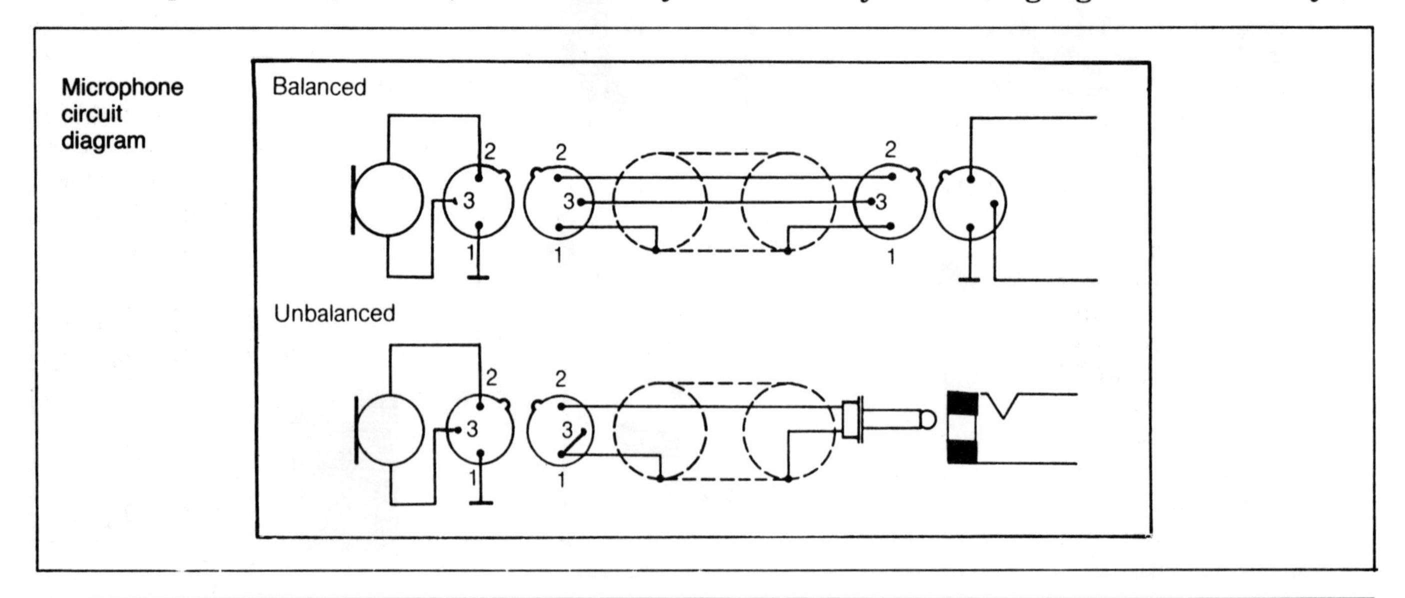

indeed you decide you need a microphone in the first place – you may prefer just to 'D.I.' your instruments, and vocals may not be part of your recording projects) is first sitting down and analysing the sorts of instruments and vocals you plan to record. Secondly, decide whether the mikes you're going to buy are to be used on stage as well as in the studio. Thirdly, work out which, of all the uses you intend the mikes for, is the one that crops up most often – it's no good going out and spending a fortune on a good bass drum mike when in fact you're recording vocals more often than drum kits! If it transpires that even after much deliberation you cannot pin-point the job you most frequently require of a microphone, then go initially for what is known in the business as a good 'all-rounder' – of which there are a good few on the market.

Unless you happen to be particularly wealthy, you'll be aiming to spend no more than about $75-$100 on your first couple of mikes – which I think is a realistic sum to start with. For this sum you're not going to get 'broadcast standard' high-quality mikes, but for around $50 you should be able to get hold of a mike that will both give you extremely respectable performance and withstand a fair amount of wear and tear. Because prices are so reasonable at the bottom end of the quality range, my advice is to buy your first mike new. Not much can go wrong with a microphone, I'll admit, but if it is to fulfil the important role of 'first and most used mike' in your library, then it's not worth allowing even a slight possibility of a breakdown or slight drop in signal quality (due to diaphragm damage inflicted in an earlier life) to jeopardize your recording projects for the sake of saving a few pounds. In short, make sure that your first mike is going to be reliable, and that if it *does* go wrong it's likely to be repaired promptly under guarantee; your first mike should be the one you can rely on should a second-hand mike subsequently purchased let you down.

I generally favour European-made mikes as opposed to American or Japanese efforts. People like Sennheiser, AKG and Beyer Dynamic have excellent servicing facilities in or just outside this country. Although Electrovoice and Cutec are two fine exceptions to the following generalization, mikes from the US and Japan are usually sonically at the bottom end of the market. Even some of the 'top-line' mikes from these two great countries struggle in terms of reliability and performance to measure up to some of the very modestly priced European mikes.

A good rule to stick to when auditioning mikes is 'European first'. If you find no joy at the price you can afford, *then* look towards the US and Japan.

Frequency Response

Frequency response is a simple term applied to many pieces of recording equipment. Sound is made up of many frequencies; what we generally refer to as a bass sound is in the 40Hz-800Hz range, after which mid range takes over until about 3kHz-3.5kHz when treble sounds begin. The human ear can receive frequencies up to about 17.5kHz. Music played through a pair of speakers whose components cannot handle more than 8kHz will sound a little dull and lifeless, with cymbals and vocals suffering. However, medium wave radio doesn't usually top more than about 4kHz-4.5kHz. The use of limiting, compressing and EQ-ing can make something which has a small 'bandwidth' (the two extremities of an individual's or piece of equipment's frequency range) sound acceptable. Home recording equipment should in all cases have the largest bandwidth available at the price. Speakers should be able to reproduce sounds from 40Hz-20kHz, in which case their sonic capabilities will be said to have a 'frequency response' of 40-20K.

You should under no circumstances buy a mike that has a 'top-end' (treble) capability of less than 12K. Even a beater hitting a bass drum contains frequencies as high as four, five or even 6kHz. Cheaper mikes usually have small bandwidths, unable to handle either bass below 60Hz or treble above ten or 11kHz. They should be used only as general-purpose, muck-around mikes, when they will not affect the overall tone of your recording. Always,

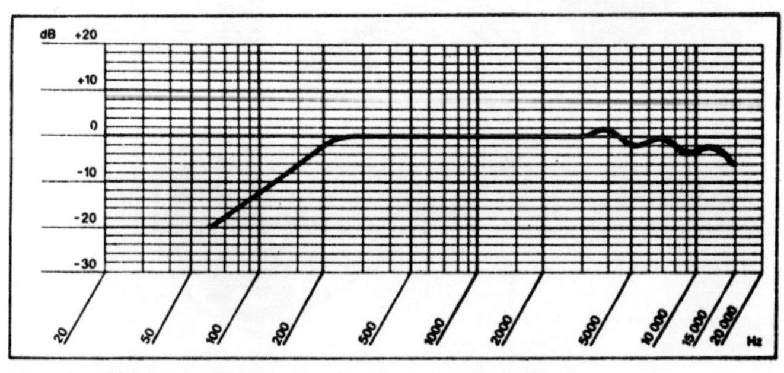

A typical 'flat' frequency tracing from a microphone.

always check the frequency response or bandwidth of any equipment you're thinking of buying.

It is difficult to give many hints on auditioning microphones, as so much is based on personal preferences. Try to record speech and/or music and play it back through headphones. Listen carefully for any unnatural colouring of the sound (bearing in mind what I've already said about bass responses when a mike is held close to your mouth or an instrument). Hold the mike in a variety of ways to see if you are comfortable with it – this is important if you're going to use it on stage. Be careful not to cover the 'sound ports' with your hand or the mike-stand clamp. These have not been put on the mike for decoration! The excellent D222E, D202 and D330 BT mikes from AKG, for instance, have sound ports in places on the body other than the front where the wind shield is! Blocking these will severely inhibit the mike's performance – so watch it!

Microphone Connections

You may notice that some of the more expensive mikes, which are constructed internally and externally to a higher standard, have what are known as XLR or cannon connections

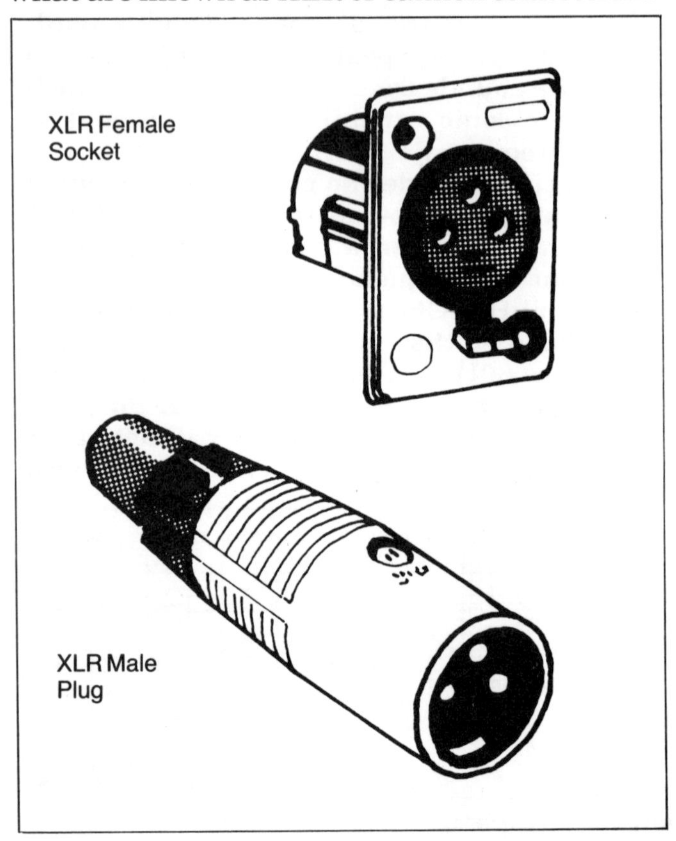

to their accompanying cables (where a cable is included in the price, that is). Three-pin XLR connections are the industry standard worldwide in professional studios. If a piece of equipment has XLR inputs or outputs (or both!), then you know it's aimed at the quality end of the market.

Many cheap mixing desks and compact multitrackers have no XLR connections, an omission that is designed to keep down costs (each XLR socket costs about $1). The next most popular connections in the professional field are the common-or-garden stereo or mono 1/4" jack plug and socket system, followed by the familiar and widely used (on home recording equipment and Hi-Fi especially) phono system. Less common on European speakers and amplifiers are Din and the scary bare-wire-and-pole system (not forgetting 'banana' types).

There is no audible difference between an XLR and a phono connection system, but they do have their own designated working levels. A jack input, for instance, is often referred to as 'line level' or a line input. This is designed to meet the output voltage (or signal level) from such things as electric guitars, direct amplifier outputs and synthesizers. The XLR inputs on a desk are designed for 'mike level', which is self-explanatory really.

Some home recording equipment is fitted only with phono connection systems whose working level is around -10dBm/15-20k on line input and -10dBm/10ohm on output. Professional studios also work to a standard, known as 'zero-level'; technically speaking, this is equal to one milliwatt or 0.775 volts into 600ohms. Don't let any of this confuse you – I don't! You'll be surprised how many professional engineers disregard the standard working levels, leaving all the 'setting-up' of the tape machines and mixer to the maintenance man! A lot of manufacturers make the inputs on their equipment capable of handling huge differences in working or systems level, so much so that it doesn't much matter what you stick in there – it'll all be well within the boost and cut torque of any attenuators or amplifiers built into the signal chain.

The input and output levels of home recording equipment are generally referred to as 'unbalanced'. A professional system is 'balanced'. If you have no such thing as a balanced XLR microphone input on your mixer or compact multitracker, then I'm afraid that your choice of mikes is confined to the best of the high-zs that I've already discussed. A professional microphone's output will be too low for the mike gain amp at the top of the input channel or module to relay the signal to the rest of the system without also conveying system hiss.

Tell your dealer which desk or compact multitracker you use or intend to use, and ask his advice on the most suitable microphone. Open reel/mixer set-ups usually have the advantage of having balanced XLR inputs, which can accept pro-quality mikes; these then attenuate the input signal internally to match the output of the system, if the mixer is indeed being run at home recording levels in an unbalanced set-up.

Direct Injection and D.I. Boxes

As mentioned earlier, direct injection is the term given to the method of plugging a direct signal output into the inputs on a desk or compact multitracker, without employing the use of a microphone. The vast majority of instruments, especially synthesizers (indeed, anything electrical) can be plugged into the line input (jack socket) of a mixer with no trouble whatsoever. Many synthesizers have an output attenuation control – High, Medium and Low – which enables you to get the best result. Similarly, many instrument amplifiers have direct outputs for the same purpose, even on low-budget units. However, you must never, *ever* connect an output into your line input which has a signal output rated in watts – e.g. a headphones output that has a built-in amplifier and volume control. Quite a lot of damage can be caused to the input circuits on your mixer or compact multitracker this way and it should be avoided at all costs.

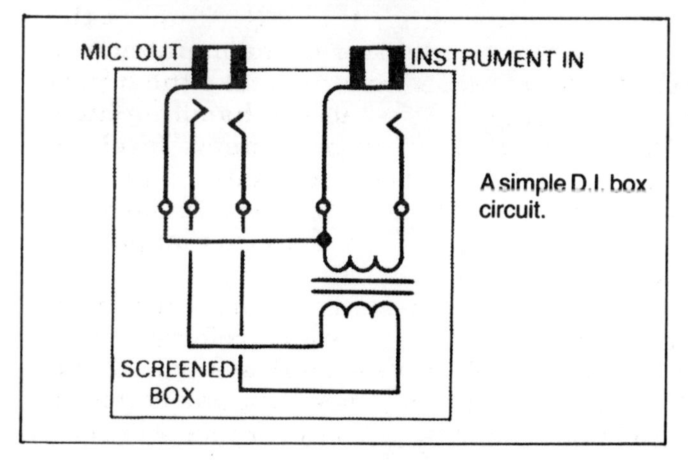

A simple D.I. box circuit.

D.I. boxes are a means of taking a feed from an instrument and connecting it directly (for whatever reason) to a low impedance mike input. If you connect the high impedance signal from an electrical source straight into a low impedance mike input, the signal level will suffer, and a definite loss in quality will also be audible.

D.I. boxes simply bring the high signal down to match the mike input. However, they can at times reflect nasty interference back to an instrument (not always a good thing if the 'instrument' is a microcomputer running MIDI software!). Cable capacitance and inductance (depending on the length used too – see what I said earlier for details) will also affect the tonal balance and quality.

It is doubtful whether using a D.I. box from a synthesizer into a mike input is any better than feeding straight into a line input (if one is available on your mixer). Usually – especially in PA applications – engineers take a D.I. signal from a guitar pick-up and mix this with the signal derived from placing a mike in front of the instrument amp. This way you get the best of both worlds, but it does tend to use up the number of free input channels you have left to play with on the desk.

D.I. boxes are great if you really need them. The best are the 'active' types, especially for applications involving low output levels from instruments or amplifiers and especially when there is no pre-amp being used. Active D.I. boxes don't usually suffer from the side effects mentioned above as they tend to transfer *all* the original quality.

The Monitor System

Impedance – Amp & Monitor Matching

For best results it is important that an amplifier's output is matched to the impedance of the speaker. A loudspeaker represents a load stretched across the amplifier output. Professional equipment traditionally has impedances between 12 and 15 ohms, although this figure is frequently less on some of the more technically advanced monitoring systems.

The average transistor based amplifier (as opposed to valve) has outputs of low impedance, 8 ohms being the most popular of impedances with manufacturers. The lower the impedance on the speaker, the more volume will be produced. An impedance too low for some amp circuits will result in bass distortion.

Amplifier BASICS

THE amplifier is one of the most crucial links in the recording and mixdown chains. The amplifier is responsible for receiving electrical impulses down wires (the signals) and boosting them to power a pair of speakers which reconvert the impulses via a paper cone and a magnet into air vibrations.

It is all too easy to get bogged down in complex statistics with amplifiers. Look for an amp which is clean and does not colour the sound or distort (due to transient peaks in the music) when at three quarters volume. When the input signal is exceeding the thresholds of the amplifier circuits, it lops the tops and bottoms off the outgoing transient frequencies; distortion of the music known as clipping will be heard.

Yamaha have a good reputation for making excellent quality HiFi amplifiers.

One of Soundcraft's new power amps. The SA2000 is probably the biggest type of amp ever needed in a domestic studio.

Quad recently introduced the 520 and 510 amps which look set to dominate the upper end of the domestic studio market.

Loudspeakers and Enclosures

There are three main types of loudspeaker design, all of them relating directly to the enclosure arrangement, designed to allow the listener to hear all the frequencies the tweeter, mid range and bass drivers are capable of producing.

The Bass Reflex Cabinet

The main principle in bass reflex design is to have the cabinet entirely enclosed apart from a small slit at the bottom of the front board. The soundwaves created by the backwards movement of the speaker cones are delayed slightly inside before emerging from the port into the room. The delay causes the waves to be in phase with those from the front of the cone(s); therefore an *addition* to the sound is produced rather than the cancelling out which occurs when waves created by rarefaction movements from the drivers escape unhin-

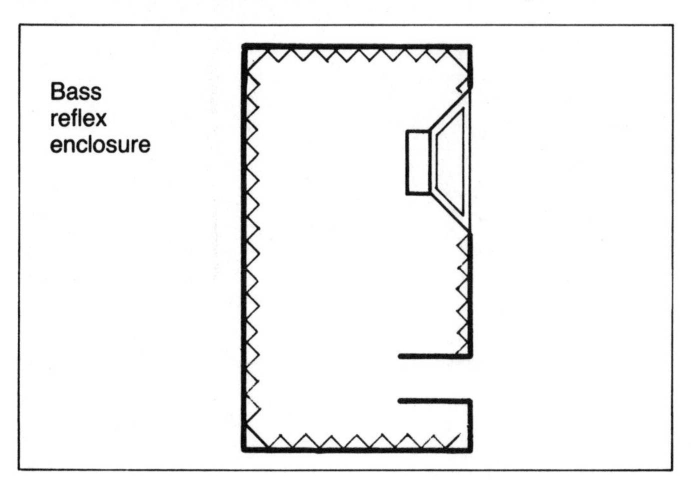

dered into the room. The enclosure and port dimensions are critical for this sort of design.

Cone loudspeakers, having mass and weight, have their own resonance frequencies, usually between 15-20Hz and 80Hz. To combat these, the inner walls of bass reflex cabinets are usually lined with a mineral wool or thick felt, though foam rubber is also used.

The Folded Horn

This method of getting the best from speakers involves the inside of the cabinet being partitioned off. This is designed to produce a long, winding (or folded) airpath between the waves produced by the backward movements of the cones (which are 180 degrees out of phase) and the waves being transmitted directly into the room by the front surface of any cone driver(s).

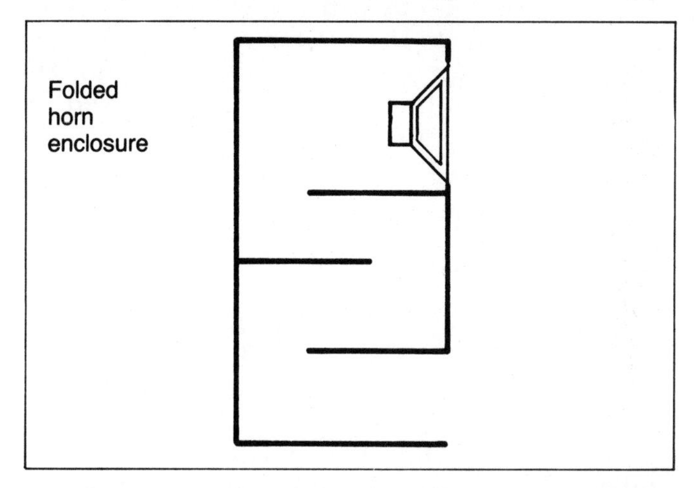

Care must be taken that the partitions are not made parallel to each other, otherwise the standing wave phenomenon may occur. However, the folded horn cabinet must be of fairly large proportions, as – in the case of speakers mounted on baffle boards in professional control rooms – the size of the speaker's enclosure (whatever shape, form or theory it takes) is directly related to efficient reproduction of bass frequencies. In this instance, the area/distance between the mouth of the horn and the rear of the cone determines the lowest bass frequency ultimately produced.

The Infinite Baffle Enclosure

This is the undisputed champion design which 90 per cent of the domestic speaker manufacturers go for, capable of producing a reasonably good low end response in fairly compact enclosures. Mineral wool, general acoustic damping material and foam rubber is compacted inside the enclosure, fitted snugly round the back of the drivers, with no openings

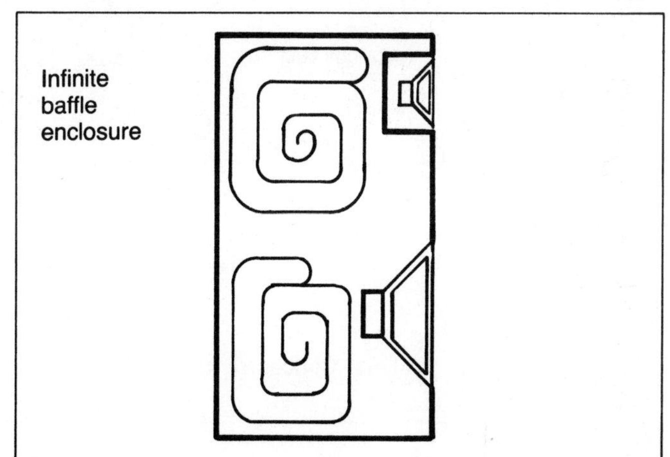

in the cabinet at all.

The size of enclosure can improve bass response – again the bigger you go, the lower you get. However, sensitivity, due to the amount of damping which is employed, is usually not so high (see comments on the Celestion SL6).

The Signs to Look For

Whatever its intended purpose, a speaker should be solidly built, with the enclosure being made of solid hardish wood or high density particle board, and not thinner than 2-3″.

It is a myth that, for a speaker to reproduce faithfully, it should have lots of different drivers. Many cheap domestic systems do have trouble portraying frequency integration with just a woofer and a tweeter, but you only have to look at Yamaha's excellent NS10Ms and the Ditton 100s to realise that successful integration is due to crossover frequency choices and quality components. Your average woofer can partake quite happily in transmitting reasonably high mid frequencies (if you let it). Having more than three drivers means you are going to run into integration problems sooner or later (especially in close field listening situations) and this will involve using extra attenuating components in the circuitry. The best advice is to stay simple.

If the frequency response of a speaker is good enough and it can handle the music you intend recording, then go ahead and buy a pair. There has to be a 'big plunge' sometime in your set-up and the monitors may as well be one of the biggest.

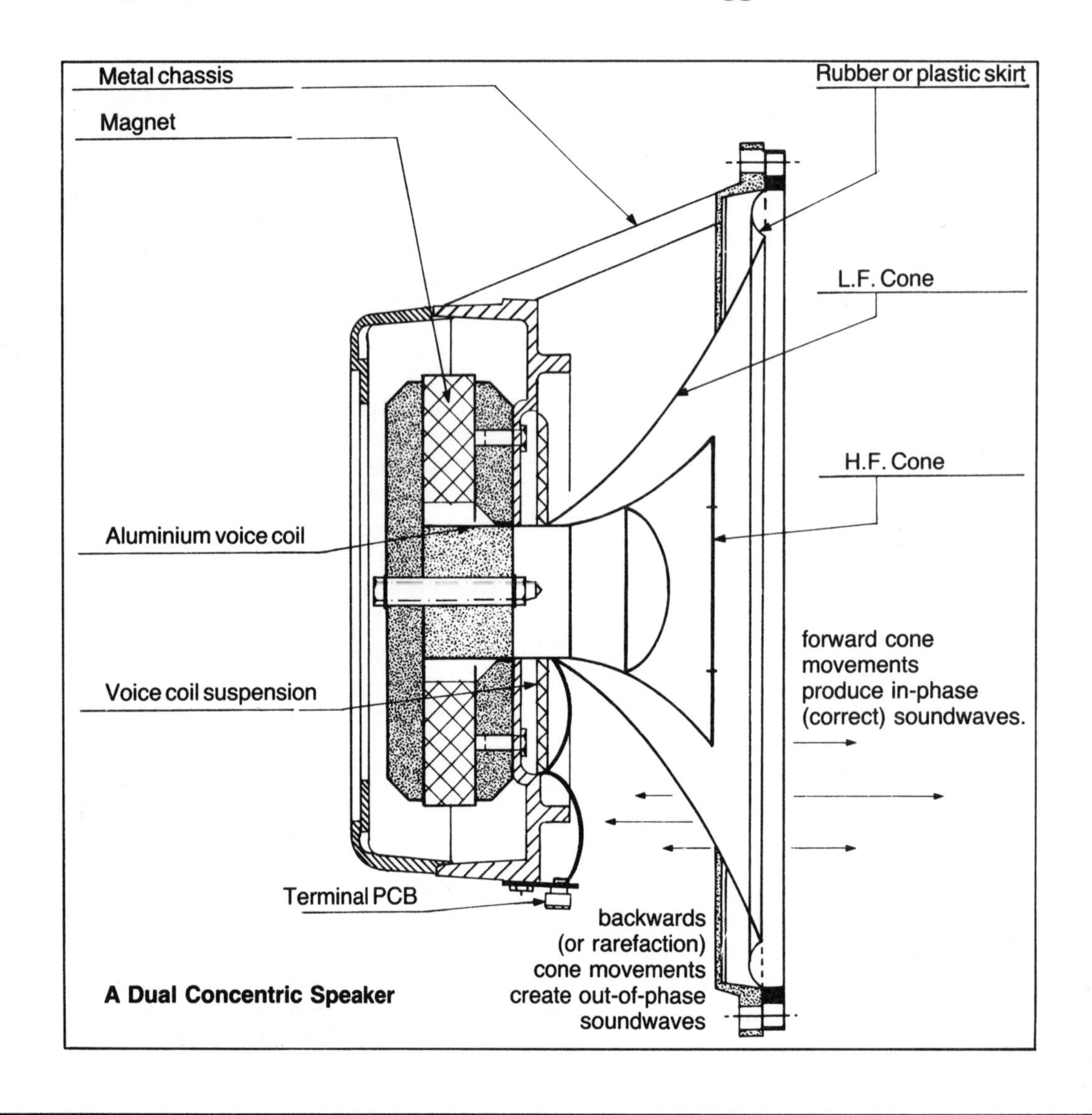

A Dual Concentric Speaker

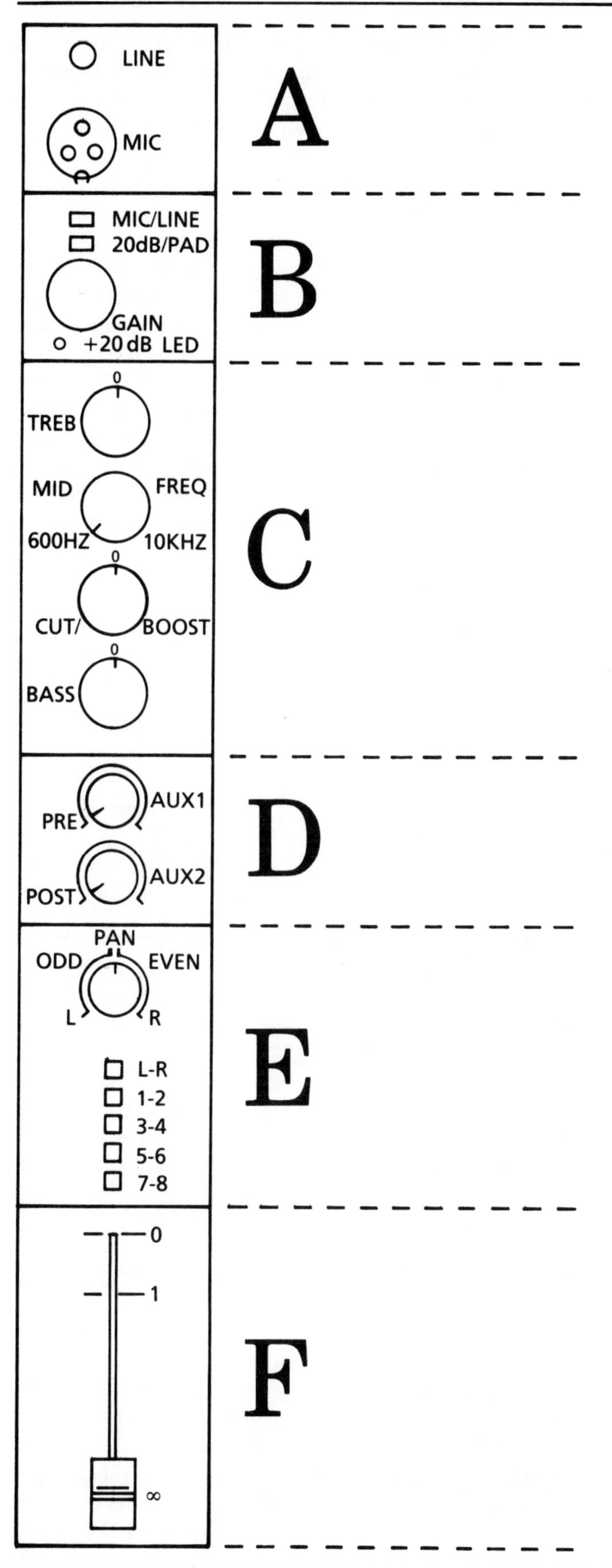

The Typical Mixer Input Channel

Section A: The Inputs

The input sockets that go to make up the input channel on a mixer are where the signal enters the chain of section, which can and do vary considerably in terms of content and layout between manufacturers. There are mainly three types of connections found on modern input channels; the most popular is the phono-type chassis-mounting socket which is commonly found on nearly all compact multitrack-

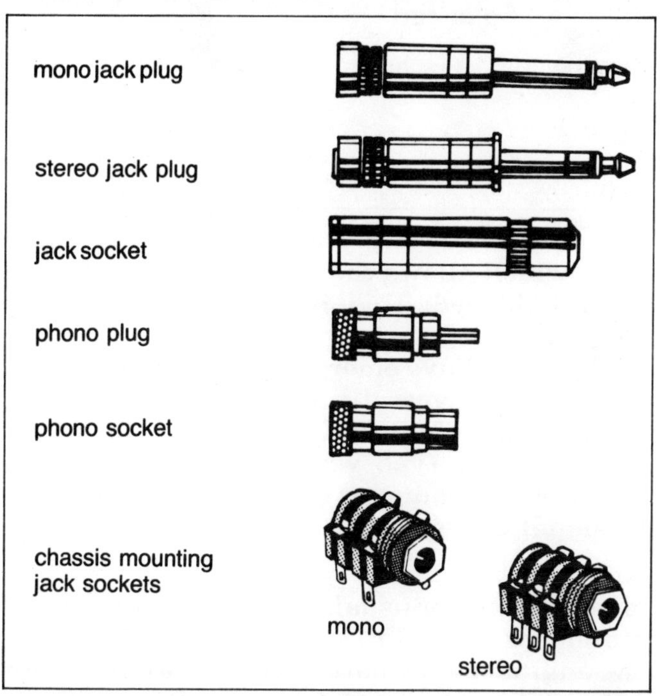

ers, practically to the exclusion of all other types of connectors. The other two socket ypes used (usually in conjunction with each other) are the aforementioned jack and XLR connectors. Quarter-inch jack sockets are always selected to receive line level signals and XLRs are always the candidates for microphone inputs. Mono jacks are two core terminal

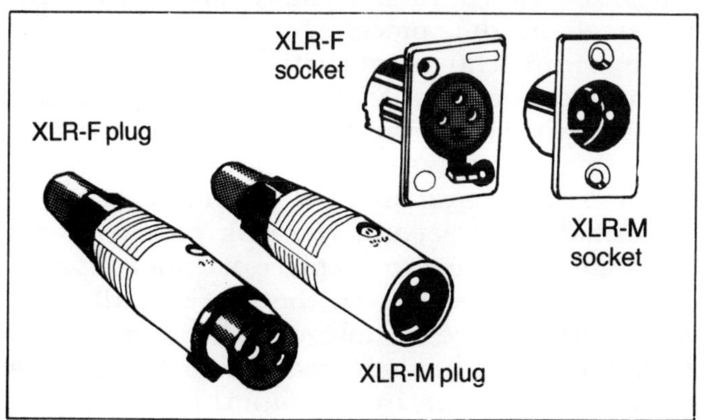

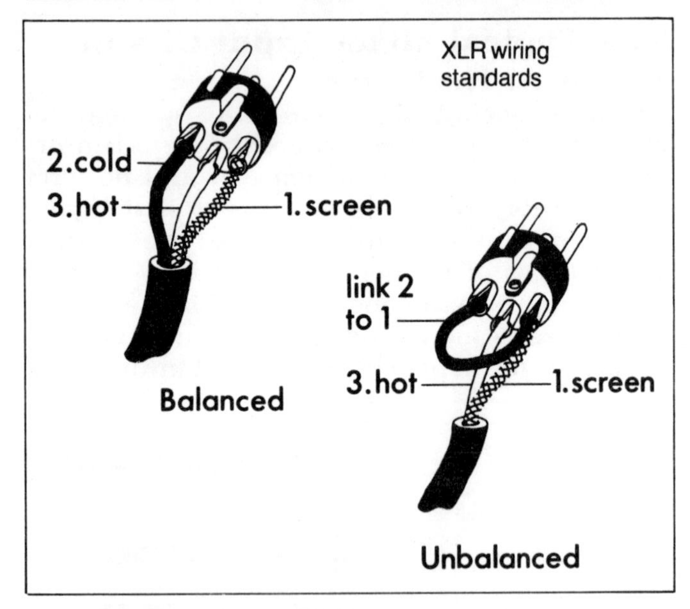

connections, as are phonos. XLRs are three core, which allows them to be wired balanced or unbalanced; this is the main reason – coupled with their ruggedness and reliability – why these have emerged as the most popular and most universally used connector. There are a couple of other XLR permutations such as the five pin type, which is sometimes found as a power conductor/connector on more professional desks.

Standards
Every connector usually has a small number of standards which are applied inflexibly to give the engineer – no matter where the equipment he's working on came from – as few problems as possible. However, wiring standards on XLRs are not, in a lot of cases, adhered to in the United States. The only real standard you should remember and work according to is: signals go *into* a female XLR and come *out* of a male XLR.

However, even this strongest of all universal connection standards has been ignored and reversed on some pieces of equipment of European origin. The usual British arrangement is for pin one of the XLR to be wired for the screen, pin two 'cold' (out of phase) and pin three 'hot' (in phase). The Americans tend to reverse the arrangement of pin one and two. In an unbalanced set up, you link pins two and one together, via a small piece of soldered wire. In nearly every desk on the market, all XLR mike inputs are balanced. After the signal from the mike has entered the socket it goes into a new section in the signal chain, which converts the balanced input signal into an unbalanced one, which then travels throughout the desk. On the whole, manufacturers utilize two different ways of conversion, the first of which is 'transformer inputting'. A transformer is put into the signal chain which has two inputs – hot and cold – and one output which is referenced to earth (or the system's working level). Then there are 'electronic inputs', which are more or less the same thing; they have a hot and a cold input which are referenced to themselves, which then gives out an unbalanced signal to the rest of the mixing desk. Neither of these systems is better than the other. But compactness is becoming more and more an important design criterion for even professional consoles; transformer type input conversion circuits are being dumped in favour of the less bulky electronic type. Transformer systems have also been accused of not relaying to the rest of the mixer *all* the signal a microphone can produce.

The transformers used in such a system also have to be of a generally high quality (and thus more expensive), as opposed to the latest bi-fet op-amps which are commonly used on electronic inputs. A badly built transformer input can also limit sharp transients coming in via the microphone, such as percussive guitar stabs, energetic drums or cymbals. Engineers measure a mixer's ability to relay transients such as these and call it the 'slew rate'. Even the cheapest of electronic input designs have good slew rates, where these rising signal peaks are passed through the input stage without attenuation or damping of any sort.

The Line Input Socket
As previously pointed out, line inputs usually employ the mono jack plug and socket system. The plug is made up of two parts – the tip and the sleeve. When inserted into the jack socket these make contact on two pieces of bent metal separated by plastic or sometimes a brown bakelite material. The tip carries the signal and the sleeve is connected to the screen or braid of the connection cable. Empty jack plugs of reasonable quality – with a plastic lead shell – can be bought for about 50¢; the sockets vary between 40¢ and 65-75¢. This compares favourably with the usually quite expensive XLR system, which varies from $2-$5 or so for a plug, and about $1.50 (give or take 50-60¢) for a reasonable quality XLR

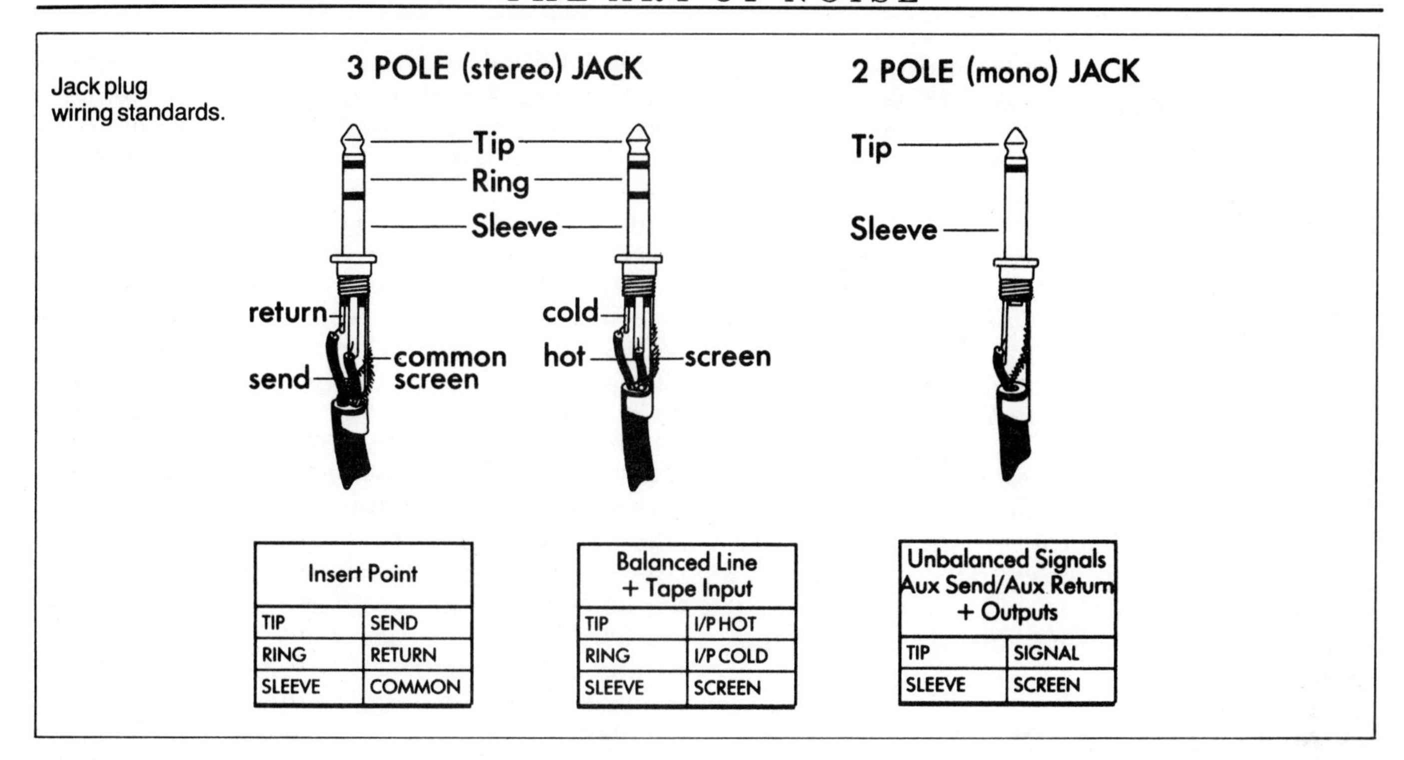

Insert Point	
TIP	SEND
RING	RETURN
SLEEVE	COMMON

Balanced Line + Tape Input	
TIP	I/P HOT
RING	I/P COLD
SLEEVE	SCREEN

Unbalanced Signals Aux Send/Aux Return + Outputs	
TIP	SIGNAL
SLEEVE	SCREEN

Jack plug wiring standards.

socket. Two of the leading makes of XLR connectors are Neutrik and Switchcraft. Some cheaper Japanese models have appeared recently which are just as good.

A basic line input socket also takes the shape of a phono; it utilizes almost identical wiring arrangements and is a little cheaper in general for manufacturers to install. When buying phono plugs to make up your own leads, make sure you get the sensible tag type which doesn't require you to spend boring and and blisteringly painful hours chucking blobs of molten solder down the pin shaft, via a minute hole. Excellent 'professional' quality phonos have been available recently which use brass or even gold-plated contacts. This might seem excessive, but if you can afford a decent quality batch of connectors, then buy them. Save them for those crucial connections, such as between mixer output and amplifier or mixer output and 2-T machine.

Section B: Mike/Line Selector, Gain Pot and Pad

Mixers do not utilise breakpoint connection systems on their line inputs; this means that connecting a jack to the line input socket will not automatically terminate the signal coming from the mike XLR socket and vice versa. This is because a lot of people plug direct to the appropriate sockets on a patchbay if they are doing recording sessions; it would be impractical to swap connectors whenever it is necessary to change input channel sources. Once the plugs have been installed in the relative sockets and connected to the back of the patchbay the back of the mixer, which is usually inaccessible in a small studio, can be totally forgotten about, except for maintenance. All of this means that there is going to be some need for a mike/line input signal selector which manufacturers usually install next in the signal chain.

The next most common feature on a basic input channel is the pad switch; this takes the form of a buffer circuit and is designed to cut down by anything from 10dB to more usually 20dB any over-energetic input signals. Some synthesizers are notorious for pushing out a signal which is far too strong for the average line input and, on the older varieties, there is little or no *gain* control of the output. It's worth emphasizing a point about signal to noise performances of input channels. Almost without exception, the best results occur when you're putting almost maximum signal through the i/p ch. without causing distortion, without limiting the amount of transient headroom available and without causing peak distortion. The same principle must be applied to getting the best noise-free performance from tape recorders. The more signal you lay down on tape, the further the quietest signal is from the noise floor. Manufacturers recommend that the gain pot (which is really a small amplifier) should be somewhere in the 40-80 per cent position, and the fader in an 80 per cent maximum position which affords plenty of movement in either direction. Using the pad control, gain pot and fader it is possible to achieve excellent results, making systems hiss unnoticeable even on cheap equipment. The noise reduction section has a fuller description of the actual sequences involved. On some poor quality gain pot circuits, it's better not to turn the pots up at all and to combat noisy input by amplifiers by relying on external quieter forms of gain or volume increase. Unfortunately you may also have to have your faders right up full blast most of the time, but they are the quietest form of gain on 99.9 per cent of all desks.

Section C: The Typical EQ

In recording, there are three main types of equalization (bass and treble cut or boost) used. Shelved EQ is a fixed frequency variety that only gives the user the opportunity to lift or cut a certain frequency in the spectrum; it leaves the rest of the signal to pass unchanged, either through to the next part of the EQ section or onto the following part of the input channel. A variation on this is graphic EQ in which the frequency spectrum is represented in ascending bands. Each 'band' has its own slider; this is centre detented at the 'flat position', which is where the signal in that band passes through without alteration. By altering each slider, you can emphasize a particular frequency band. The best types of graphic equalizer are the sort which have small rather than large gaps between each adjustment band. A ten band graphic equalizer is more crude than a thirty-one band graphic. For a ten band unit to cover the whole frequency range perhaps from 40Hz to 17kHz, there have to be more 'holes', for example there'll probably be a gap between 8K and 10K, with all the signal between these two adjustable bands going through with no way of changing it. A thirty-one band graphic in 1/3rd octave steps; this allows a greater amount of control and detail to be added or taken away across the frequency spectrum.

Finally, there is 'parametric' EQ. This is most commonly found on mixers, rather than graphic EQ which is available on the whole in separate rack-mounting units. More expensive desks have 'full' parametric EQ from bass to treble, but usually, as you can see from our diagram of a basic mixer i/p ch, it is used in conjunction with shelved frequencies. A parametric section takes the form of a sweep filter, which utilises two pots. The first pinpoints a desired frequency within a limited range of frequencies. A typical mid-sweep parametric EQ arrangement will have a bottom end starting at 600Hz and end at 10kHz where the treble shelving control will take over. The second pot in this arrangement has a centre position which denotes a 'flat' or unaltered setting. This allows the signal to pass through this frequency band without any cut or boost of the selected frequency. Turning this pot anti-clockwise will decrease the selected frequency by anything from 0.1dB to -12dB, and turning it clockwise will emphasize the pre-selected frequency by anything from 0.1dB to +12dB.

Nine times out of ten, it is the mid range frequencies entering a desk which need trimming. Thus manufacturers, if they are to include a parametric section to the EQ part of the i/p ch., will feature a general sweep filter based on the rather large range I've used as an example above.

It is called 'sweep' filtering because graphic and parametric types of EQ allow the user to pinpoint a single frequency and adjust that, whilst leaving the rest of the signal frequency content unchanged. The 'sweep' part of it comes from a technique which many engineers use when adjusting the tonal content of an incoming signal. The first step is usually to decide whether the input signal is lacking or overemphasizing a particular frequency. You simply turn the cut/boost pot related to the suspect frequency range to maximum or minimum, and then 'sweep' up and down the frequency range with the filter pot until the undesirable frequency is greatly boosted or cut. Once you've found it, you then decide how much strengthening or weakening of that particular frequency the overall sound requires.

EQ Techniques

When it comes to using microphones, EQ sections must first and foremost be used to tighten, punctuate or slightly trim the mike signal. EQ is *not* there to make up for bad microphones or bad microphone technique. It's always best to start with all the tone controls flat at the centre position and get closest to your desired sound by moving the microphone, or trying different types of mikes. Only then, if there is still something lacking in the tonal balance of the sound and you've tried every practical 'front-end' alternative, resort to using your EQ section.

An accurate parametric or graphic, which has little overlap on adjacent frequencies can be used to great effect to reduce annoyances such as camera whirr and low level traffic rumble. However, I would generally recommend the judicious use of a noise gate which will be explored in much greater detail when it comes to the Processing and FX chapter.

As always there are no hard and fast rules, and when recording synthesizers or other direct injected instruments I relish turning

INSTRUMENT	BOOSTING	CUTTING	OTHER COMMENTS
Piano	Bassy at 120Hz Metalic at 5K	Rotten at 1 or 2K Bassy at 300Hz	Use two mikes as minimum. Uprights should have the front soundboard removed
Human Voice	Good at 4K-8K Clear and concise above 3K. Ful and Bassy at 200-400Hz	Sssss-sibilant at 12K. Telephone type sound at 1K. Popping B's and P's below 90Hz	Watch out for phase cancellation when using more than three vocal mikes
Acoustic Guitar	Metallic at 5K. Very strong at 125-135Hz	Rotten at 2-3.5K. Boomy and undefined at 185-230Hz	Best with cardioid or hyper cardioid mikes
Electric Guitar	Funky and clear at 3.5K. Bassy at 120Hz	Dull below 90Hz. Metallic at 5K	Place mike within 12ins of speaker in amp for full sound. 2ft or more away from cab will result in a thinner, warmer sound
Electric Bass	Bassy and Boomy at 90Hz and below. Slappish at 4K	Rotten at 1K. Warm and Bassy at 20Hz	Use of a plectrum will result in a more metallic, attack-ish sound
Cymbals	Metallic at 6K	Rotten at 1K	May not agree with certain misaligned noise reduction units.
Bass Drum	Beater impact at 4K±. Solid at 90-125Hz	Boomy below 80Hz	Damping of the impact head may produce a more claustrophobic sound
Snare Drum	Bassy and full at 125Hz. Deep and boomy at 80Hz	Bad at 1K	One of the hardest sounds to capture on tape to everyone's liking
Toms	Stick impact at 4K. Strong and pumpy at 75-225Hz	Boomy at 300-350Hz	Plastic, clear heads give a snappier sound than the thick, white batter heads which can be wooley
Strings	Good at 8-10K. Sibilant at 125K. Strong and bassy at 300-400Hz		Difficult to record
Horns	Cutting at 8K. Strong and bassy at 125-350Hz	Nasal at 1K	Listen to Prokoviev's Romeo & Juliet for perfect brass representation

sounds inside out by experimenting with in-line or outboard EQ units. Synths with some added 60Hz can be considerably thickened up; saxophones can be made thin and wiry (not to mention annoyingly cutting) if you boost the 1K frequency and reduce all the bass end power.

Use the chart on EQing as a rough guide. Experiment (preferably not during an expensive session) as much as you can and really get to know the capabilities of your mixer's EQ section. Dull and lifeless noises can suddenly come to life.

An EQ bypass switch can be tremendously helpful in some cases, so that you can flick between the Frankenstein sounds you may have created with your EQing and the untouched, virginal signal. However, this shouldn't be made into a major purchasing criterion. Look for a powerful and creative EQ section on any desk you consider before starting to wonder how to bypass it.

Single output drum machines such as the Roland TR606 and the excellent Yamaha RX15 can sound much thicker and punchier with the right sort and amount of EQ. However, these machines send out a huge range of frequencies through just one or two outputs, so a graphic equalizer is usually a more flexible and direct way of adjusting the individual tonal ingredients which go to make up the overall sound. For those about to start an outboard collection, a twenty-seven or thirty-one band graphic of good noise performance should be high on the shopping list.

Even if a graphic is not available, taking the mono output and phones output of, say, the TR606 and giving them each an i/p ch. and then adjusting one to emphasize the highs and the other to bring out the lows and then combining them carefully can be a reasonable alternative. This could theoretically create phase problems, which is something I'll be dealing with later on. If the emphasized frequencies on the separate channels overlap in any way, they may create a thick wedge of frequencies which are hard to fit into the mix; this is known as 'un-musical EQing'.

EQ sections are also placed in the signal chain so as to affect the amount of signal entering the following electronics. Adding large amounts of bass and treble boost is more than likely to cause overload and distortion if you've already set the signal level up according to section B. Most mixers have overload LEDs which are line up in slightly different ways. For example, the Trident VFM series requires the LEDs on the i/p channels to flicker on the loudest transients entering the desk; on a Dynamix PMR you have to turn the gain pot down if an LED flashes.

Section D: Auxiliaries

As can be seen from the diagram, our basic i/p ch. has just two auxiliaries: one pre and the other post fader. These pots are auxiliary send controls which route internally to their respective master outputs (jack) on the back of the mixer. This in turn can be used to feed the input on any piece or pieces of outboard, or on an amplifier feeding a headphone splitter-box which cans are plugged into, so the musicians can monitor the 'aux-mix' during overdubs. This function usually has a dedicated aux send on each i/p ch. and is called 'foldback', but there is nothing to stop you using foldback aux send pots for FX feeding.

When you turn an aux pot up, an internal parallel feed off the signal coming through that particular input gets routed to the master aux output. There is one master output for each aux send group. So a mixer which has six auxiliaries on each i/p ch will have six master aux outputs or busses as they are sometimes called.

An aux send pot which is pre fader will send a clone of the signal coming through that particular i/p ch. to its intended aux group master output, regardless of whether that channel's fader is open or closed. This means that, if you are using some of the pre fader aux sends to feed a reverb unit, even when the direct signal is taken away from the mix by closing the faders down, the 'wet' or reverberated signal will still be heard via the dedicated aux return busses or another i/p ch.

A post fader aux send pot will have its feed affected by the position of the fader(s) on any of the i/p channels utilizing it. In other words, at the end of a mix when you close down the faders on these particular channels, the aux send feed is also taken from the post fade aux group master output on the back of the mixer, and all processing effects or musicians have the signal die on them with the closing down of the faders. Post fader auxiliaries are therefore not very good for effects which require reverb or delay to be left at the end of a mix after the direct signal has gone.

As it is sometimes necessary, on recording sessions which are tight for time, to practise mixes during final overdubs on the tracks which have been successfully put onto the multitrack, it is usually best to feed headphone amplifiers (and ultimately the musicians on the session) with pre fade auxiliaries; this is why dedicated foldback pots in the aux section of most mixers are generally pre fade.

FX in the Recording Chain

Unless you are working on anything less than 24-T, recording FX on the same tracks as their originating signals is the only way you are going to save tracks and create thick, intricate textures without investing large sums in FX units. Even if you do have many outboard pieces of equipment, the average desk will not have a large enough auxiliary system to cope with the inevitable demands you are sometimes going to make upon it.

Older professional engineers will occasionally argue that the only way to have maximum flexibility on any mix is to record FX on separate tracks; then, if it's decided a certain effect is not required in the mix, all they have to do is pull down the corresponding fader(s) and forget that they were ever recorded. There are even harder extremists around, who believe that it is not worth recording *any* FX unless you are absolutely forced to.

There is a case for recording FX on separate tracks; I do this when working on 48-T, but without unnecessarily burning up valuable tracks. Even with 46 tracks available, I put FX to tape with their originating signals sharing the same track(s). If you come up with a brilliant, complicated FX combination and the performer creating the originating signal is able to *play* with the resulting effect, then *record it*. In today's world of complicated digital reverb units which incorporate feedback, first reflection control and pre delay, and with the equally devious DDLs, it's practically impossible to recreate FX accurately on mixdown that were apparent the previous day without spending lots of time and energy dumping the FX data onto cassette or writing down the control settings. Create and constructively follow your instincts, experiment purposefully; if you find something inspired, record it then and there.

On smaller formats, it is possible to build up quite extensive recorded FX by bringing required tape return signals back through the aux circuits and sending these newly created effects to the track you are about to do a fresh overdub on, probably using a different instrument. The drawback of this technique is that the levels of the fresh overdub and the resulting secondary FX are permanently linked together for mixdown, but clever planning is essential even on formats as big as 24-T; this way of creating multi image textures with just one or two pieces of outboard can result in very rich, full tracks of sound.

Reverb

To get the best from every reverb unit it is necessary to make sure that you are inputting the optimum signal. Most advanced springs and all the digital reverbs have input signal LEDs which tell you how much is being received. Some reverbs have limiters which control the input signal from overloading and prevent distortion.

Reverb is the single most essential effect you will ever have to buy and should be your first priority. Reverb, used conventionally, is there to give instruments such as synthesizers, electronic percussion and electric guitars an ambience or a point in space where their sounds originate from. Acoustic instruments are always perceived by the ear as having their ambience from the surrounding they're in as an integral part of the sound. This is why accurate synthesis of sounds is such a difficult thing to achieve, as there is always an ambience to be considered and recreated before the sound is even close to being convincing. This is why some synth patches take on a new dimension of realism in the studio when it's decided to add reverb. When I'm creating new sounds, especially on something complex like the PPG 2.3, I always have the output going through a reverb that sounds like a normal room. The sounds have the disadvantage of relying on that particular reverb sound to give them their original program realism, but it is much better than programming with no ambience effect at all. There is a negative side to relying on reverb for injecting ambience into a program, as it all means that little bit more data has to be saved; however, with the new MIDI DDLs and reverbs it's only a matter of time before some bright manufacturer will be able to produce save and load software which is suitable for both effect unit *and* synth.

To understand auxiliary arrangements in desks, think of aux circuits as mixers within mixers. The more auxiliaries contained on the i/p channels, the more aux mixes you can send out from the desk. But why have more than one or two auxiliary systems in a desk? On a full recording session where you're recording overdubs while taping perhaps a guitarist and drummer together, each musician might require to hear in his cans something completely different from the musician involved in the same overdub. Drummers usually require a great deal more level in their cans than a singer for example; this is surely a good enough reason on its own for having two aux systems, so that they can be fed to independent headphone amps or independent channel stereo. Secondly, to achieve different textures to the sound, you may need to send incoming signals to several FX units simultaneously, while isolating one particular incoming signal and sending that to a different place.

Auxiliary master outputs are usually fed to a patchbay where they can be paralleled and *then* fed to outboard equipment. Indeed, as I've suggested, auxiliary and FX patching are – in the small studio – the only reasons why I'd recommend including a patching system in the set-up at all.

In a full session, with several musicians involved in each overdub simultaneously, each requiring different 'off-tape' balances in their cans, having a well-thought out aux system on your desk is essential. It's like doing two, three, four or maybe even more mixes all at once, keeping each performer happy and juggling with the aux master outputs.

A good engineer can switch his mind from one internal aux mix to the other and still keep the session bubbling along without spending too much time acquiring the right patch. Many desk manufacturers include a PFL (Post or Pre Fade Listen) or AFL (After Fade Listen – the same as Post Fade) switch for each of the auxiliary master busses; when pressed they cut across the monitors to the exclusion of every other signal the desk is pushing out. They reveal what that particular aux group sounds like, providing a quick dipstick for the engineer to judge what sort of balance he's sending to the musician's headphones or the outboard.

Auxiliary Return Alternatives

As I've mentioned, auxiliary master busses have send as well as return connections which receive the signal back into the console, ready to be routed and placed in the stereo picture. Unfortunately, on lower priced mixers, these aux returns have no independent EQ of their own, and it is usually necessary to trim or 'sweeten' the returned signal from outboard units with some tonal sharpening or damping.

To combat the lack of control in this area, rather than using the aux master returns, it's more common – unless short on input channels – to bring the output of the last piece of outboard in the chain or the returned outboard signal from the patchbay into a spare input channel, where various tonal adjustments can be made using the in line EQ. This results in all the routing flexibility you could want.

When adopting the above procedure on aux originated returns, never turn the same aux send up on the receiving i/p channel that is being used to route the desired signals out of the desk in the first place; a feedback loop will be set up which will result in howling whistles and screams across the monitoring system. If the wrong aux send on a channel is fed to the musician's cans it could result in serious ear damage.

Foldback Amplification and Techniques

Not many sub sixteen track studios I've visited have more than one headphone amplifier for two very sound reasons. Firstly, it is rare that an overdub session requires a selection of performers to play together who need a wholly different mix from one another in their respective cans. Secondly, many mixers used at this level only obviously designate one aux group to be used for foldback and when setting up a small studio it never occurs to many uninitiated home recordists to think about the number of headphone amps and feed circuits they should install.

If you are a solo recordist, then much of what has been said about 'full' sessions has been irrelevant; you'll be more interested in how to make the best use of the aux circuits in your mixer for FX feeding and return signals.

If you are planning to take on sessions

involving a more or less standard selection of instrumentalists, it may be worth acquiring a secondary headphone amplifier.

The Rolls Royce of headphone amps – even though its specification allows it to do ideal stereo powering – is the Quad 303. Resembling a gun metal green house brick, this amp can be found, more than any other, powering headphone feeds in studios across the globe. Any clean two channel amplifier will do the job; 80 per cent of the hifi amps on the market would be adequate and it is important to remember that each side can be used independently to give two can feed circuits before it's necessary to worry about getting another amplifier in. Mono amps such as the Quad 50 may seem extravagant, but do offer total isolation between signals and make hook up a little more simple.

The next step is to take the feed from the speaker out(s) on the amp and split it via a box with as many sockets on as the number of pairs of cans you feel necessary. The splitter box must be of high quality and be capable of taking the wattage being given out by the can amp. To the exclusion of all other splitter boxes (bar the professional, expensive types used in pro studios), the Accessit 8 way split box can be recommended; this has isolated jack outputs, so that if one shorts out it doesn't affect the other cans being fed from the other sockets. There is an input jack at each end for connecting series of these excellent boxes together.

Using single channel employment independently within a stereo amp will result, if wired conventionally, in only one-sided powering of the cans in the studio. This is common for vocalists, who require to hear their own voices, rather than the mike signal going to the desk, being sent back through the foldback to their cans. Dual terminal soldering – bonding two signal paths together in the plug on each set of cans – will result in direct mono feeding on both sides; this is the accepted studio practice on headphone monitoring. Some mixing desks have wiring permutations which will require always checking the spec before you go and buy your foldback amp(s), to make sure that the levels match not only between amp and mixer, but also between split box and amp and split box and cans (which do vary remarkably from model to model).

Headphones and Volume in the Studio

The maximum feed anyone should stick into the cans, except possibly for deaf heavy metal drummers, is twenty-five watts. Closed type headphones should be used to the exclusion of 'open' types and 'micros'. These, even at low wattage, tend to leak over microphones and after doing several overdubs can all go to contribute quite a bit of annoying 'spill' at the beginning and end of tracks, which makes the final mixdown more difficult.

The sound in a musician's cans affects the performance in the same way as different sounds on a synth dictate the feel and style of what is finally composed on that instrument. It is extremely important that the sound is not overly harsh or thin, or, going towards the other extreme, lacking in treble and drowning the listener in bass. So it is essential, especially when utilising a Quad 303, to have a pre-amp with volume and correction tone controls to make up for any deficiency in the signal being pushed out to the back of the desk. The Quad 34 is therefore the ideal candidate for this job. The beauty of owning a Quad 303/34 system is that you could use it for record playback when foldback is not required.

In a large studio, headphone access points (or cue points, as they are sometimes referred to) are generally evenly placed along the walls to make the most of cable lengths. In a one room studio, in which through-the-monitors listening is the rule, the Accessit splitter box with headphones fitted with ordinary cable lengths should be fine; however you can buy extension cables, some of which even have 'Y' type splitters on the end. Coiled extension leads are usually less of a tangle and hassle than having a vast quantity of straight cable to add to the usual array of spaghetti that accumulates on the floor during the average session.

So, some final foldback tips:

1. Don't waste money on a too powerful amp for cans.
2. Go for low impedance (± 8ohm) cans that will produce healthy volume levels from small amps.
3. Go for comfortable closed type headphones with padded headbands which will not create premature baldness in studio clients!
4. Always store your headphones and foldback cable(s) neatly when not in use.
5. Always give the musicians the benefit of the

doubt – don't expect them to listen to can signals which you yourself couldn't work with.

Section E: The Pan and Routing System
The next link in the chain after the aux/foldback circuits is the Pan pot. This control derives its name from its ability to sweep or

Recording Chain BASICS

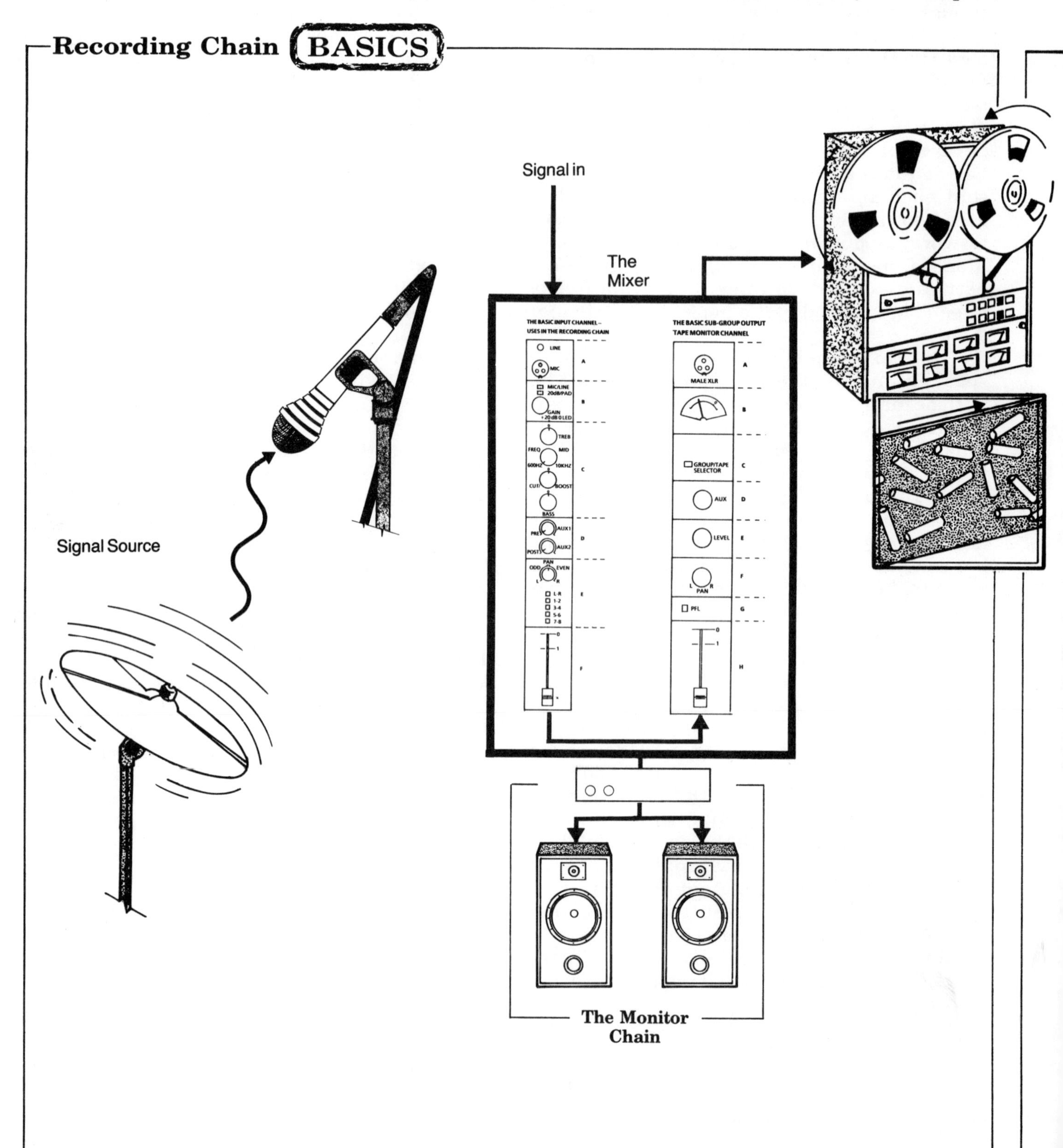

pan the incoming signal anywhere in the stereo field, from hard left through centre (mono) to hard right. Its practical workings are identical to those of the 'balance' control found on all HiFi amps.

However, the pan pot is not usually used in its stereo context until mixdown, where off tape and/or outboard signals are fed into the

Mixdown Chain BASICS

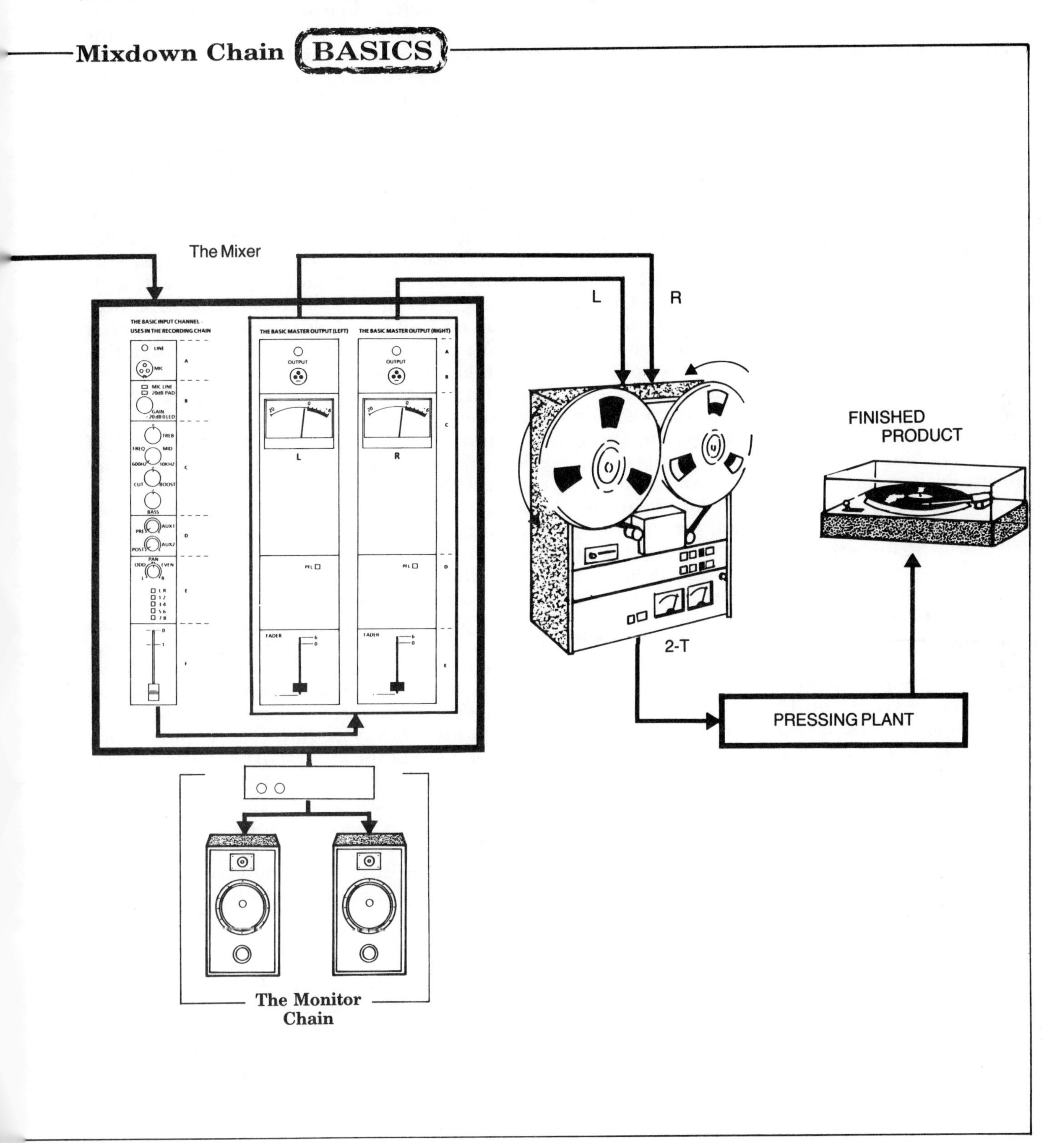

i/p channels. Its function in the recording chain is to route the incoming signal into one, some or all of the sub group outputs that send the feed to the multitrack machine.

The pan system on desks needs to be 'selected' via the second half of the routing system; until this is done, there is no internal electronics to translate its position to the rest of the electronics. The first of these selectors is usually the master L-R left and right switch, which relays the pan pot's position to the master left and right outputs and also the stereo monitor out sockets to the back of the desk. This is the most common way of relating stereo positioning of an input channel signal when it comes to final mixdown. This will be covered later in 'The Mixdown Chain'.

The pan pot's use in The Recording Chain is to act as the mediator and primary selector for the next set of switches in the routing matrix. These are alternately twin numbered switches which are sided 'odd' and 'even' (see the diagram). On a four way group output desk there would be two of these selectors; there would be four selectors on an eight group output desk, eight on a sixteen, and so on.

When the pan pot is positioned in the centre and you have depressed, for instance, selector 7-8, sub groups seven and eight will receive the signal from that particular i/p channel. When the pan pot is turned to the left – or the 'odd' side – it will cut the signal away from sub group eight, which is the 'even' side. You have to take care, when using this form of routing, to avoid 'leaks' when you're feeding two or more tracks on the multitrack at the same time. Leakage from one sub group to another is counteracted by taking care to turn the pan pot *full* left or *full* right when you do not wish an input signal to be sent to more than one track on the multitrack.

Routing systems can seem strange; what I've described and what appears in our diagram is the most common of all routing matrixes employed by manufacturers. Some desks have much more simple but hugely more expensive systems; the console inputs have in-line electronics where the sub grouped and/or tape return is handled via the same or alternative fader, all on the *same* input channel. Like the aux system(s), look upon routing as a mixer within a mixer.

Section F: The Input Channel Fader

As was mentioned in relation to section B, the fader is the means to adjust the level of the incoming signal not only to the sub-group output (this should be set to an optimum level so as to get the best possible result from the multitrack) but also the level control for that channel on mixdown, with the routing going straight to left and right master busses and onto the 2-T machine.

The fader is usually one of two types: either carbon or plastic conductive. The plastic one is usually the more expensive of the two for manufacturers to install, but it does have major advantages over the carbon or 'Alps' type. Plastic conductive faders are less susceptible to wear and do not allow dust, grit, grime, gravel or any of those strange things which you find in a fader runner on servicing to affect the audio signal, as carbon varieties do which usually takes the form of nasty crackling and 'dead spots' along the travel of the fader.

Penny & Giles are the most popular of plastic faders and appear on every desk of any reputation. Alps faders on the other hand, only cost a couple of bucks or so to replace; they should take quite a fair amount of use and last a reasonable time.

As faders are the 'human interface' between engineer and the music coming through the console, it is important that they are calibrated to give even and accurate volume input control. 'Long Throw' faders which have a travel of 100mm or more are usually best at giving you a smooth incremental control on each channel. Many manufacturers put output levels on each of the faders; in practice, however, your ears are the final judges of instrument and/or vocal balance, and the sub group or main 2-T output meters can be monitored for signs of overload.

Nine times out of ten the correct position for an input channel fader to be in is around 60-75 per cent. This allows you enough level gain 'headroom' for attaining real-time volume increase during a mixdown period. But as pointed out in section B, a fader when sending a signal to a sub group output (ie, one whose transients dictate level fluctuation(s)) may have to be placed in the 100 per cent position, as the gain pot may introduce too much noise into the signal chain, and the fader is usually the quietest form of gain.

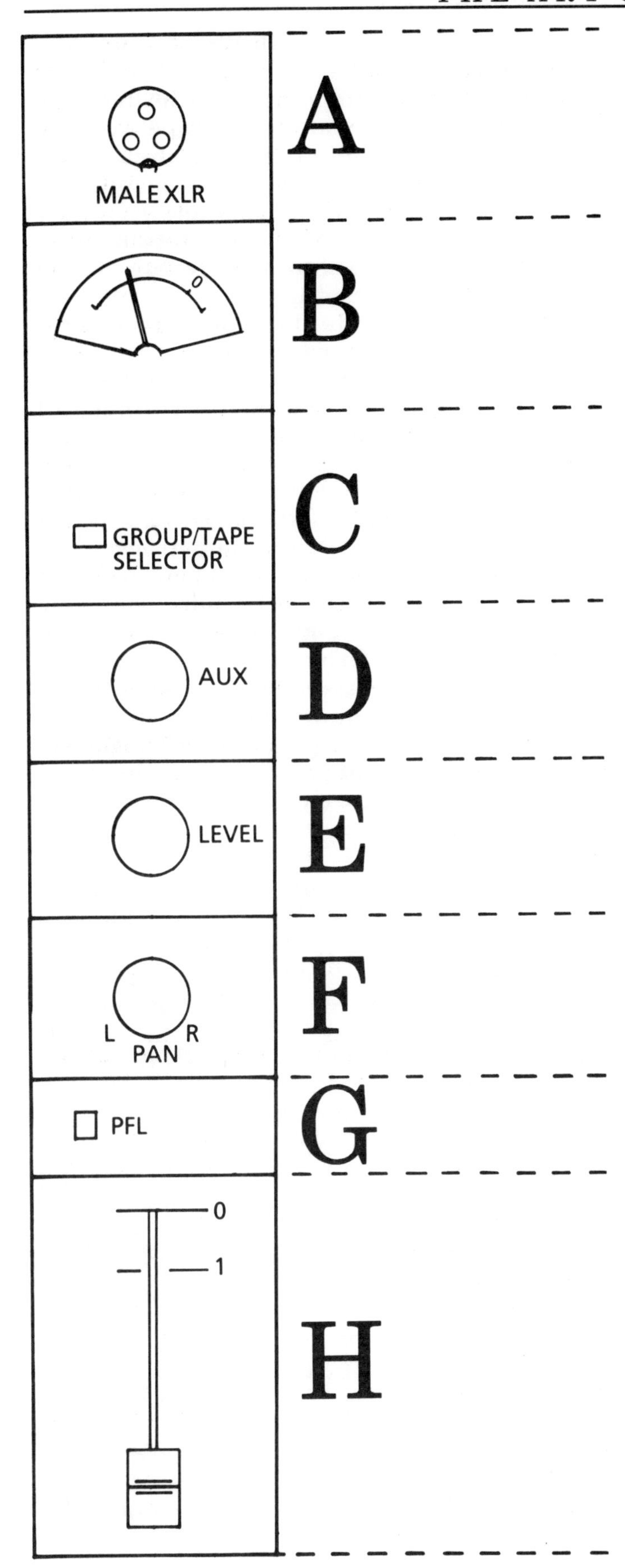

The Typical Sub Group Output

The heading of this part may seem misleading, because, as you'll see from the 'Basics' section, the sub group output channel on many mixers also acts as a 'tape monitor' channel for each track of the multitrack. This is usually arranged in a chronological/relative way, with sub gp. o/p ch. 1 also being tape monitor channel 1. For economy, certain manufacturers have in the past 'piggy-backed' tape monitor inputs on the gp. o/p section. So you might have a desk with just (at first glance) four group output channels; each channel, however, has dual function switching so that they can be used to feed an eight track machine. Similarly, this means that there have to be eight tape monitors too – and these also are usually cascaded on top of one another.

There is rarely on budget desks anything more than level and stereo positioning controls for tape return signal paths. These are more than usually seen by manufacturers as a 'during session' rough mix facility so as not to encroach on the number of input channels available. The main theory is that, when all tracks have been recorded, the leads can be switched around, either at the back of the desk or on the patchbay, and mixed through the input channels, gaining the benefits of second EQ options, auxiliaries and much improved gain trimming facilities.

If you are using a mixer with a very basic sub group tape monitor selection of channels, listening to what is coming off the multitrack will require a little more imagination and foresight. Without EQ trimming and enough auxiliaries to enhance or sweeten the sound, you can get a *very* rough-sounding, dry, almost desolate representation of what has been laid down in the session so far.

Once you have mastered the Monitormix syndrome you can really call yourself an engineer. The usual technique is to start (once you have your first track down) with the monitor level control at just above minimum and then gradually introduce the sound into the monitors.

Section A: The Inputs

Usually the sub group output socket is a male XLR. It is from this point that you connect your leads to the inputs on the multitrack. The tape monitor inputs are usually line level jack sockets (mono).

Section B: The Meter
The next link in the chain is the meter, which is usually one of two popular kinds – either LED (Light Emitting Diode) or VU (Volume Unit); both of these measure the volume or amplitude of an incoming or outgoing signal.

The legending of the meters produced by a couple of manufacturers is so bizarre that it isn't possible to go into any 'standard' forms of legending in any great detail. However, any meter is usually split into two parts, the majority of the ballistic range is 'safe' and at a marked point termed universally as 'Nought VU' (though never universally, *accurately* practised) is the point where the safe area, meets the red or 'caution' area of the scale. This section of any meter – if the needle is straying in too often and too far – usually means that overload or distortion is going to be evident on transients.

However, as owners of compact multi-tracker or dbx'd multitrack machines will perhaps find, meters can become little more than decoration. You must always let your ears be the judge and never be afraid to do short test recordings if you suspect that the signal which is reading just right on your output meter (peaking at nought VU), may not be strong enough to combat tape noise – or on the other hand if you never seem to be straying into the red area, but your recordings are distorting on transients – you obviously have to disregard the metering system as far as that track is concerned and experiment. 'Good' home recording levels, after all, are those which produce the best end result and do not harm the machinery.

Section C: The Output/Input Selector
Fairly self-explanatory. This control does a very similar job to the mike/line selector which was mentioned earlier.

Section D: The Aux Pot
This aux system usually has its own master output and return, and is not usually associated in any way with the input channel auxiliary circuits. The sub group output aux circuit is very useful for processing gangs of input signals on feed to the multitrack. This can not only save aux send circuits from being used on the inputs, but can actually save the number of patches being involved at the same time, making the whole operation of processing signals being fed to the multitrack less complicated.

It is important to point out that, because the channels in the sub group/tape monitor section *are* dual function, the aux circuit does have to be carefully thought about before use. Be prepared to chop and change, as many engineers prefer to use the aux on tape returns for adding a little subliminal reverb to the overall rough mix picture, to avoid the dry, edgy effect due to the lack of return parameters available for sweetening.

This makeshift sweetening is not possible to do by using the sub group aux circuits on full sessions with more than one musician involved – as the most logical thing to use these auxiliaries for is to send to the cue amp each of the tape return signals, so that musicians can hear what is coming off the multitrack. Now this might sound like good common sense but if you *have* returned all the outputs from your multitrack into line inputs sending cues to the performers is going to be slightly more complicated and involved – it may also mean restricting yourself in the number of auxs you have available for processing, as it may be impractical due to all sorts of problems and hitches to 'split feed' off an aux circuit both cue amplifiers *and* FX.

Section E: The Level Pot
This allows you to set the desired balance between tape return signals while recording a session. All of these level pots are internally routed (like everything else, except the aux and f/back signal paths) to the master monitor output which feeds the amp driving the monitors.

Striking the correct balance between what is being sent to the multitrack and what is coming back is one of *the* major keys to getting a session running smoothly. It is important to explain to uninitiated performers that what they're hearing during a session is only rough. The vital thing is that any return signal should be good quality. You should continually ask yourself if you've recorded your signal(s) at the optimum level on tape so as to combat noise, rather than worrying too much about tonal characteristics. What is coming back should be clean, clear cut, undistorted and (if you're using noise reduction) not suffering from breathing effects due to there not being enough signal sent to the NR unit for the system to get a firm grip on the transients and average amplitude content.

Many people initially make the mistake of recording signals at the level they want them to finally appear in the mix. The theory is that mixdown is easier, as all they have to do is just leave all the faders in one position during playback and everything will mix itself. The only time this sort of recording technique works is using totally professional equipment, with a multitrack tape speed of no less than 30ips. Not one of the multitracks featured in this book would be suitable for this kind of recording, as hiss of varying levels would be audible on the majority of tracks recorded at below optimum level. However, many mixdowns, especially on formats of eight tracks and below, will require very little finger work. If a lot of group bounces have been done, where signals have all been ganged from adjacent or non-adjacent tracks on to a single one and had their relative levels altered as for the final visualised mix when all the tracks are complete and come to be mixed, the bounce tracks (or sub mix tracks) just stay at a fairly static level and let their transient qualities produce the light and shade necessary to make any piece of music interesting. This will be dealt with in greater detail later on.

Section F: The Pan Pot

This pan pot enables a sub group output signal to be placed into the stereo field when feeding the multitrack; this gives an idea of how the mix will sound. This also applies when using the channels as tape returns. Some institutionalized engineers have the illogical habit of panning hard right and hard left alternately on any channels being used as tape returns. This leaves no doubt as to which signal is going and which signal is coming, but it destroys any delicate textures which rely on their stereo placing. This antediluvian madness also has the side effect of blowing up speakers, should a couple of loud tracks happen to fall both on the left or both on the right. This is rare, however, and safeguards in systems should prevent this. This form of mixing should have gone out with valve radio and shouldn't ever be employed.

Section G: The PFL Switch

This is a feature which goes under a number of different titles, one of the most common being 'Solo'. When depressed, all signals except those passing through that single channel are cut from the master left and right monitor output(s). This is very useful as signal quality on tape returns can be checked one at a time.

Even if you have done a test recording, always listen right the way through any tracks freshly laid down, using the solo on that tape return channel intermittently. It's the safest way of continually monitoring quality. There is, though, a line to be drawn between chucking it all in and re-recording the track or ignoring any small quality losses which now and again appear. It's surprising what naughty bits you can get away with when it's all been mixed and mastered!

Section H: The Fader

This fader is the last level control for any signals going to the multitrack. It has to be set at a level relative to what the channel meter is reading and what the multitrack meter is reading. But what your ears tell you is happening when you've done a quick test recording and played it back off tape, is the most important thing.

Multitrack BASICS

However many tracks the multitrack machine has, what it does is basically the same, whether it is a 30ips 24-T or a Tascam 144 compact multitracker. There are, however, a couple of facilities which really do differentiate multitrack machines, the first of which is tape speed and width types.

The golden rule is that, as far as analogue machines are concerned, the wider the tape and the faster it travels

across the heads, the better the quality. This is obviously relative, however. Two inch tape is generally a good quality format, but if you cram more than twenty-four tracks onto it, the signal bandwidth is going to be put under a lot of strain. The physics of the thing is that the more emulsion passing the heads both linearly and width wise, the more the information being recorded will be spread over the magnetic particles contained in the tape emulsion.

The professional standard speed for both multitracks and mastering machines is fifteen inches per second – that's about eight and a half miles per hour. Many studios prefer to run their 24-Ts at 30ips, which does give much improved signal quality. For the budget conscious studio, however, running any machine faster than 15ips will create much higher tape bills, and is generally only done in the most professional end of the market. Noise Reduction enables machines offering large numbers of tracks to be run on very small width tapes at 15ips; Fostex of Japan have become world leaders in this field, producing widely used multitrack recorders that offer a good number of tracks, with low running costs.

Multitrack Connections

For the average domestic machine the chassis mounting phono type connector is used. The most common lead harness combination used in a home recording system is (for 8-T) eight XLR-F plugs going into eight phonos. The return version is eight phonos into eight jack plugs (mono).

Budget 16-T & 24-T machines will sometimes employ a multi-connector which is a much cheaper alternative. The most expensive system employs an XLR connector for every track input and output.

Apart from the down-market Fostex and Tascam machines, most multitrack machines employ large spools with large scale hub fittings. These measure 10.5 inches in diameter; the hub fittings lock onto the single spindle amateur type spikes which are normally found on all machines (awaiting to be used with large hubs), except the hugely expensive, usually European, 24-Ts.

Track Bouncing

Track bouncing is a technique employed when you are forced into recording many things on a multitrack machine with limited numbers of tracks available. Bouncing, however, is not something which is only practised in amateur studios. I myself have, on a couple of occasions while working with two 24-T machines synced together to provide 46 audio tracks, been forced into a situation where I've had to mix several tracks down onto a stereo pair, in order to use these tracks again for something else.

As you'll see from the diagrams, track bouncing can be done even on compact multitrackers. However there are many machines which, due to the way they have had their replay and monitor signal paths arranged in relation to other input electronics, will not allow you to bounce a track onto an *adjacent* one; these types of machine do force you to plan more carefully.

It's important to stick to some sort of plan or track sheet. There are some examples suitable for varying machine formats on the following pages.

Good track planning or track placing will ensure that you are fully familiar with the piece when it comes to mixdown and that, when sharing tracks, you put instruments together which are recorded at similar levels to each other, so that you don't have to make massive fader position adjustments. Good track placing will also minimize the chances of losing a whole title due to tape damage.

The equipment will become second nature if you work out a routine way of going about things. This doesn't mean recording instruments in a set order as the musical composition will dictate that.What it *does* mean is allocating certain tracks for particular things, whatever type of music you happen to be recording.

Engineers who were born during the second world war and who look at you with a blank expression should you mention MIDI in their presence will tell you that you must always record the bass guitar on track one, the drums on the next track(s) and so on, working across the tape until you get to the vocals, reserving track 24 (if you're working on 24-T), or the last track, for any sync pulse which has to be recorded. This may sound reasonable enough; however, while laying a sync pulse down on the last track may be easy to remember, it does put all the information recorded on that track at risk from possible damage during winding and/or storage. If a wound tape is going to have something spilt on it, the outer upfacing track is going to be worst hit.

Even when working on professional Otaris and Studers, I always place anything as crucial and important to the music as the click track at least two tracks in from the edge. If only very slight creasing of the tape edge should occur, the whole track around the point of damage usually has to be edited or even re-recorded. Outer tape tacks should always be reserved for unimportant things such as minor FX. Anything crucial to the piece should be recorded as near to the centre of the tape as possible.

I was involved in a session not long ago, where lemonade had been spilt all over one side of a wound tape and allowed to become partially dry. When it came to adding the finishing touches to the tracks and mixing them, you could hear this funny clicking noise as all the layers of tape were prised from each other as they went from the feed spool to the take-up spool. Luckily, the only tracks affected were the two outer ones which were carrying the odd reverb and delay signal. As we mixed the track and thick spots of half-dried lemonade were dragged over the heads (very naughty and not recommended), the reverb and delay on some instruments died away and then re-appeared a little later, making the instruments alter in perspective. It's an effect which I now employ but using conventional recording techniques. Even in the heyday of punk rock it was rare to find direct violation of the multitrack tape being employed for dramatic effect, although I was on a session where someone vomited all over the newly completed and as yet uncopied master tapes, but that, as they say, is another story!

The diagram illustrating 'the ten track bounce' for the portastudio can be used with any multitrack machine. 10cc's 'I'm Not In Love' is a classic example of the sort of thick vocal textures which can be created by employing carefully planned track bouncing on an eight track and upwards. When working on eight track, I rarely have a percussion track going that isn't bounced somewhere along the line. Modern technology has decreased the number of bounces I do now, as usually one of the first things I lay down is a click track from the drum machine; ultimately I end up running many things 'off-sync' or 'wild' when doing overdubs and final mixes. This form of recording is changing the face of professional techniques as well. Many keyboard orientated clients are now reverting back to 24-T format or maybe even 16-T, simply because the use of Fairlights, PPG Waveterm Systems, Yamaha QX1s and Roland MSQ700s offers 'digital keyboard data recording' facilities only a common sync is needed, which most digital drum machines now produce. Once this common sync or click track has been laid down, practically everything, except acoustic instruments and vocals, can wait to be committed to tape until mixdown, when all signals are sent to the mastering machine.

Using this sort of technology in combination with track bouncing techniques, it is possible to create huge sounds and very 'full' textures on quality eight track set-ups. Although the musical hardware costs more, we are not spending as much as would have been necessary six or seven years ago on recording equipment. Instead of having to own a 24-T to attain complicated textures, it's feasible to work on eight track with a set-up as simple as, say, a Yamaha RX15 drum machine (which is synced to tape); then, via MIDI, we can use a keyboard data recorder such as the MSQ100 together with three Casio CZ101s, all of which costs less than $3,000.

There is economy in technology!

Multitrack Pitch Control

Many multitrack recorders, including some compact multitrackers, have a pitch control. This is a pot which decreases and increases tape speed, usually by a small percentage. The most common pitch change is ±10%, although some professional machines are capable of a range ±50%. It is called a pitch control because music has to be played back at the speed it was originally recorded at for it to stay in the same octave and key range. Record a flute at 15ips and play it back at 7.5ips, and it'll have dropped a whole octave in pitch.

Some cassette and bad quality (usually ancient) multitracks will sometimes stretch the tape over a long period of time, and successive overdubs (where the tape is being stretched more and more) create small pitch variations. Even though your instruments haven't gone out of tune, when you come to lay

down an overdub with a piece played by the same synth perhaps five hours earlier, it may be a quarter semitone or even a whole tone down from where it was originally recorded. A pitch control will minimize the effect by allowing you to tweak the speed up or down slightly to compensate. But fortunately this situation is rare, and pitch controls are usually employed to create weird and wonderful 'real-time' whole tone time slips. The opening sounds to Japan's 'Ghosts' is a good example of the sort of pitch variations one can achieve by just slurring and tweaking the speed of the multitrack while in record.

It is not wise on budget multitracks to run a machine all the time on full varispeed (another term to describe pitch) attempting to improve the s/n ratio, as their wow & flutter figures (see glossary) would deteriorate considerably.

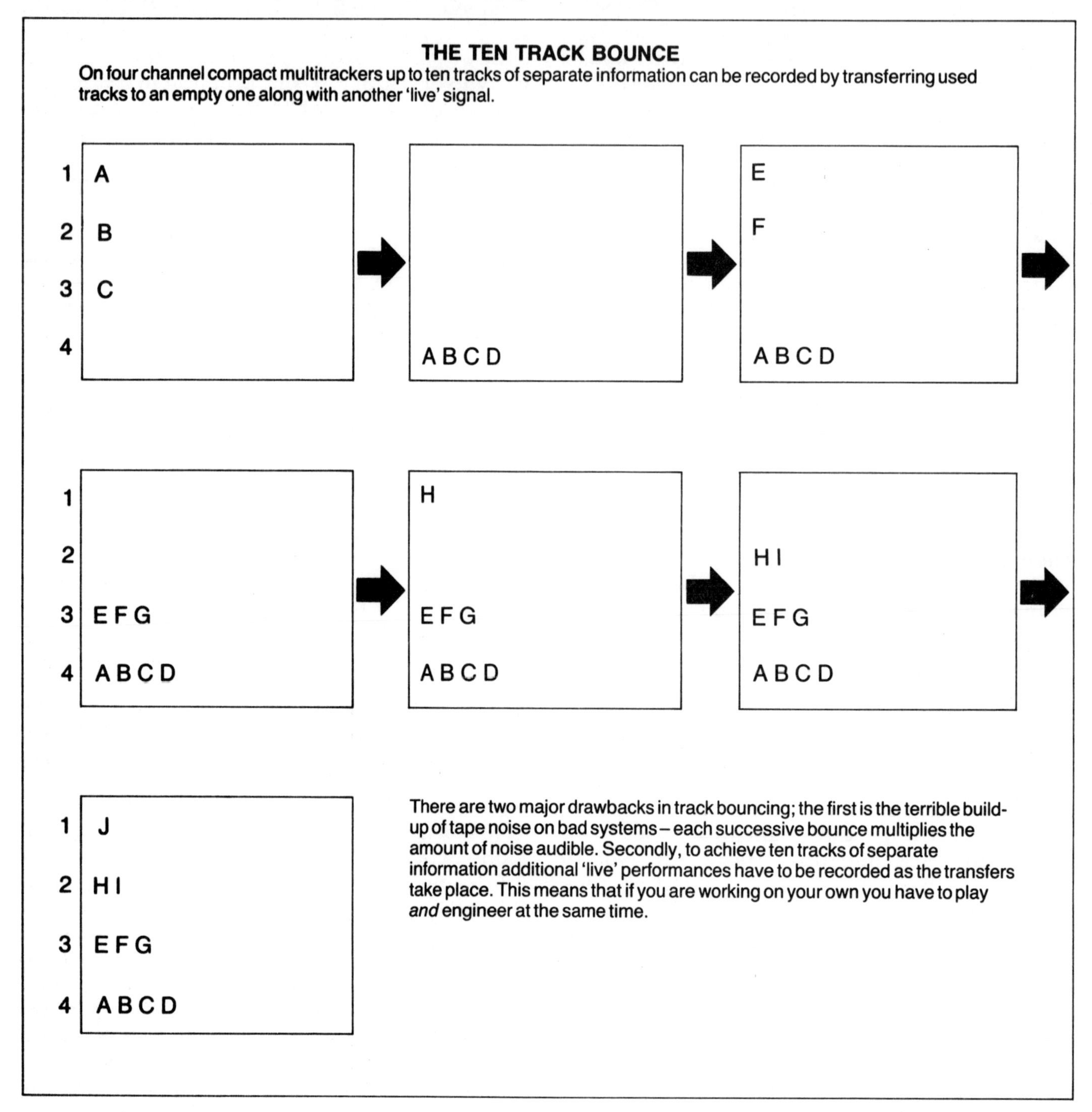
THE TEN TRACK BOUNCE
On four channel compact multitrackers up to ten tracks of separate information can be recorded by transferring used tracks to an empty one along with another 'live' signal.
1 A
2 B
3 C
4
ABCD
E
F
ABCD
1
2
3 EFG
4 ABCD
H
EFG
ABCD
HI
EFG
ABCD
1 J
2 HI
3 EFG
4 ABCD
There are two major drawbacks in track bouncing; the first is the terrible build-up of tape noise on bad systems – each successive bounce multiplies the amount of noise audible. Secondly, to achieve ten tracks of separate information additional 'live' performances have to be recorded as the transfers take place. This means that if you are working on your own you have to play and engineer at the same time.

The Mixdown Chain

THE multitrack machine marks the half-way point between the two chains of operation involved in making a recording. The mixdown chain is the transition from music being separate tracks on a multitrack to becoming the final master. This part of the proceedings usually involves the outboard equipment a lot more, and things such as phase (which the human ear is very insensitive to) have to be taken into account if your finished master is to be used for record production.

The first step is to select the Monitor or Replay head on your multitrack, as this will nearly always have a better frequency response than the dual function record/sync head which you've been using during the session. On a good multitrack (and if your ears are in perfect condition) you should hear a little extra high frequency content entering the sound. On a bad or dirty multitrack you'll probably hear quite a marked difference on nearly everything. This is one of the perils of having dirty heads, and you may find that what you've recorded is lacking tonally in certain areas, or that some sounds have been recorded far too harshly. It's your fault for not regularly cleaning the heads and some tracks may have to be re-recorded.

Mixing

Whether you return your tape outputs into line inputs or just use the tape returns is up to you. Personally, I always re-patch and zero all the input channels involved in the final mixdown. Certain tracks will be louder than others in the composition and that means that the core of the music will sort itself out. Nine times out of ten it is the position and relative level of FX and background sounds which give a mix that 'completed' feel. In this section I'd like to pass on a few tricks of the trade and talk about the psychological as well as practical ways to deal with a mix.

It is important in composing music and in mixing it, that you constantly use contrasts to highlight areas of the work, so that the listener is guided through but also surprised. Very dense, busy passages and tracks of music can be made to sound open and barren by good mixing technique. By using solo switching, it is possible to re-arrange compositions. Soft sounds can be made to appear hard, aggressive and loud and vice versa.

Contrasts
Hard – Soft
Loud – Quiet
Dense – Sparse
Foreground – Background

The last contrast can be achieved by the use of good microphone technique and application of reverb. In a mix where everything is reverberated, anything you want to stick out you have dry. This works the other way round too, a good example being Peter Gabriel's third album. Having reverb or not really does govern a particular track's place in perspective. So many of the demos I get sent in by bands have just added either a lot of reverb to create depth or distance and very little for a sound to appear close; these effects have been implemented *without* really listening to the mix and trying to evaluate the effects they've created. Natural reverb tends to have two major properties. Reverb at high frequencies tends to decay a lot quicker than at others, and distant reverb is usually characterized by a gradual loss of low frequencies.

There are several ways of re-creating the above effects, which if judiciously used in a mix make the perspective that much more realistic. To achieve quicker reverb decay at high frequencies, run your input signal into *two* input channels; EQ one with bass and mid range emphasis, and the second with full low and mid cut and treble boost. Feed the bass EQd signal to the reverb at the desired level, but feed the high tone signal at a lesser input level. Most spring units will give a shorter decay on the weaker signal, but if this doesn't result in realism use a second reverb unit. To achieve the second natural characteristic have more wet than dry signal in the mix and reduce the bass content on both.

Only experimentation with mike placing and reverb units will open the doors of perspective creation and control. It is an art which only a handful of record producers and retiring stalwarts at the BBC have. I have yet to meet a fellow engineer who has actually bothered to *understand* perspective. It may be necessary to get rid of room ambience on a track; the only really effective way of doing this is by gating the track extremely tightly so as to completely cut out any flutter echoes and/or reverb in between strums of a guitar, thuds of a drum or

A TYPICAL 8-TRACK PLAN SHEET

TRACK TITLE:		DATE:	ENGINEER:
PRODUCER:	STUDIO:		BOUNCE DETAILS
1			
2			
3			
4			
5			
6			
7			
8			
COMMENTS:			SHEET No:
TAPE SPEED: i.p.s	JOB No:	COMPLETION DATE:	

8-T track plan sheet HRH Virgin

A TYPICAL 16-TRACK PLAN SHEET

TRACK TITLE:	DATE:	ENGINEER:	
PRODUCER:	STUDIO:		

1	2	3	4	5	6	7	8
9	10	11	12	13	14	15	16

COMMENTS:			
TAPE SPEED: i.p.s	JOB No:	COMPLETION DATE:	SHEET No:

16-T track plan sheet HRH Virgin

chords on a piano. You may have to cancel the room ambience on sounds which linger and would have their decays and sustains murdered by the gate(s) closing. This will mean splitting your track into two and inserting it into separate input channels. Use EQ to pinpoint the main ambience frequency, and cut by as much as you can without ruining the tone or the texture of the sound. Gate this channel as described above and allow the second to ring on with a much less lenient EQ setting, so that more of the reverb or ambience frequencies are cut from the sound. The end result will be that the sound will usually be a bit thinner than you would have hoped (but compression will help a little), and your instrument(s) will appear to change tone as the first channel gets gated off and the second, thinner tone, rings on. This effect can be further manipulated by setting a slower close time on the gate and/or putting an attack control such as Boss's Slow Gear in line on the second input, to make the transition from one to the other more controlled and to take the second, thinner tone away from underneath the first.

A mistake in perspective made with mike positioning may turn out to be impossible to reverse, but perfection is impossible and perseverance is the name of the game.

Stereo Placing

One engineer I know squinted at my eight track and said, 'You can't have stereo on eight track, can you?' His experiences maintaining equipment on sixteen, twenty-four and forty-eight track sessions had educated him in the uneconomical, flamboyant professional way of achieving a large stereo picture. This isn't necessarily wrong – just a little inflexible. Dave Stewart and Annie Lennox of the Eurythmics recorded *Sweet Dreams* on a Tascam 38, and it won the award for best Compact Disc of its year. No one would accuse that album of lacking in 'stereo'.

If stereo means 'in two ears', on eight track you only can record four stereo pairs. However, using sync and MIDI layered keyboard techniques, it is possible to create, even on four track, detailed and complex sound images which are using the stereo sound stage to the full. Most people, even professionals, are astonished when I tell them that some of my TV and radio ads were recorded on eight track. The less experienced of them ask how so many things are going on with so few tracks; the more initiated stare for a few seconds and nod their heads, aware that working on small format is a lot more demanding than having the luxury of twenty-four or forty-six tracks. They realize that they shouldn't take things for granted, and go away determined to stretch their native formats further.

But there *are* limits to how much you can stick onto a two track tape and through a pair of speakers without getting the sound muddled. Gating, clever horizontal plane or, most importantly, calculated stereo technique is the best way to achieve clarity.

The first rule is that high frequencies are much more directional than low frequencies; those below 1kHz have wavelengths so long (usually about 10 to 14 inches) that they tend to bend around the head and therefore enter both ears at the same time, no matter whether they are right or left of centre in the sound stage. To compensate for this, I filter off the frequencies on signals which are lower than 1kHz, and put them through a phaser with the depth control set to about 10 per cent and on the slowest possible sweep setting. It's not possible to hear the phaser, but you will be able to hear whether the low frequency sounds are coming from left or right. I'm not sure of the theory behind this, but it does work.

For track economy reasons, I usually record the main drum track on just one track and run synced percussion on mixdown and during overdubs. The bass drum and snare should for the main part of any track be centre positioned. I tend to spread toms and other percussion across the picture as if you were playing a kit.

I've recently added to my equipment two stereo simulators which give the listener an expanded picture of sound from single track or mono recordings. These are extremely useful units which at times give the added flexibility to record vocals, which previously would have occupied two tracks, on just one.

Another golden rule, when spreading the sounds from left to right, is never to allow instruments which contain large amounts of the same frequencies to sit on top of each other and enter the same ear simultaneously. This results in 'thick spots' which are difficult to disperse and can only be alleviated (if you *do* have to have them on top of each other) by setting one further away in perspective than the other.

Never be afraid of starkly contrasting the positions of instruments and vocals, for example by sticking one cymbal hard right and the hi hat hard left. On headphones, this may sound too disjointed and unnatural, but it is an interesting effect and can be used to great dramatic effect. I always recommend the lead vocals should be placed centre stage, with any reverb and/or delay fills panning from side to side during mixdown.

Another common mistake when mixing is that the only 'action' you perceive happening *during* a mix is one effect now and again travelling from hard left to hard right. This is valid enough but is becoming a major cliché, especially on disco 12 inchers. Try to plan a vibrant choreography of horizontal plane or stereo movement in tracks which will benefit from it. Some tracks such as Phil Collins's 'This Must Be Love' from the L.P. *Face Value* and Sade's 'Your Love Is King' will *not* benefit from more than a little casual action panning, whereas Frankie's 'Relax' and 'Two Tribes' and the average east coast American rock song like Bryan Adams's 'Run to You' were enhanced by on beat pan scanning.

The Phil Collins and Sade tracks mentioned are good examples of how the stereo positioning in these tracks mix themselves. The drums in Phil's track are well placed, with toms and a wood block making full use of both sides of the soundscape. 'Your Love Is King', which was produced by Robin Millar, seems to be filled with air; the spaces left by the musicians in the composition are almost subliminally filled with a reverb derived from one of the MET valve plates, with a very small amount of pre-delay added and the sound stretched by using a long delay. The result is uncommonly smooth and very professional. This is an effect which cannot easily be accomplished by spring reverbs at the budget end of the market, and is unattainable through digital reverb techniques (with the exception of the Klark Teknik DN780) because of their inherent clinical processing. This is discussed further in the 'FX in the Mixdown Chain' section.

Vertical positioning is something I've only recently started to explore. It is possible to create a movement in the vertical plane from bottom to top and vice versa by sweeping an emphasized filter between 12.5kHz and 5.8kHz. However, this is only apparent in broadband signals such as cymbal crashes or perhaps the more clangy PPG sounds. Theoretically, stereo is not a medium which will enable signal placing on the vertical plane, let alone defined up and down movements, but that doesn't mean you shouldn't attempt it. So far I've only occasionally been able to create a strong vertical plane placement and movement in mixes. Too often it is an effect that you have to ask listeners to watch out for, otherwise they wouldn't notice it. Close field monitoring and headphone listening seem to be the two most successful ways of listening to vertical plane positioning in mixes rather than on small bookshelf hifi speakers. On a recent session we were monitoring via the huge Urei 815 speakers in an Eastlaked control room; the effect was not as defined but did seem more expanded.

The 'Doppler' effect is a curious phenomenon which we have all heard at one time or another. It is the term used to describe the fall in pitch in sounds which move away into the distance, such as the fall in pitch of a car's engine as it speeds away.

Studio equipment has been around for years that can synthesize the Doppler effect. It is best used on mixes where there are no clashing harmonies or chromatic relationships. Adding more reverb and taking away from the mix the direct signal, while dropping the pitch via a harmonizer, coupled with taking the whole thing's volume down gradually (as the fall in pitch in real life is linked to the speed and distance the object is going), will produce stunningly real movement. But the fall in pitch will always clash with any of the other harmonic/scaled content of a composition; unless you are working in a more experimental field, the discordances produced make the effect virtually unusable, except at the beginnings or ends of pieces, or where there is room for disjointed harmonic relationships. I don't know any recordings which have either intentionally or accidentally recreated the Doppler effect. The closest example I can think of is the ending of Mike Oldfield's track 'Five Miles Out'; although lacking in reverb techniques, it does make an interesting end to a superb single.

The Use of EQ in the Mixdown Chain

EQing a tape return is very different from

EQing a live signal source going to tape. If your multitrack has recorded everything faithfully and you were able to create the right tonal content *before* it was committed to multitrack, then on mixdown your EQ setting should be more or less 'flat' (with all the knobs in the central position).

EQ should be used as an overall trimming facility, either to add anything to the sound which may have been lost once committed to tape, or as a way of adding tonal variation into sounds which couldn't be achieved before being sent to the multitrack. This is called 'Double EQing'; on the more expensive desks, you can even send the input signals through two EQ sections before tape, and then do the same thing on return. But it's rare on domestic equipment to be able to double EQ *before* multitrack, unless you invest in expensive outboard EQ.

Double EQing can produce great tonal differences, so that a double EQd signal will be difficult to fit into the mix; a compromise will have to be sought to stop the isolated sound(s) from creating a disjointed feel to the final mix.

Very few people use EQ to the full; they don't experiment and utilize it to the extent they will a digital reverb or delay line. John Foxx, on his album *The Garden*, uses EQ very successfully; this not only allows him to make mono signals into stereo by clever use of parametric and graphic filtering, but also to create massive changes in tone to certain sounds.

FX in the Mixdown Chain

If you have followed the guidelines in the section 'FX in the Recording Chain' and you are recording contemporary music, you will probably have a fair number of FX coming off the multitrack, depending on the sounds or atmosphere you're trying to create. Always treat recorded FX as a part of the sounds they are linked to. Too many uninitiated engineers try to make the most of a delay effect on tape by boosting its volume above the originating signal and throwing the whole thing out of context. Highlighting FX, rather than the originating signal, is a fine effect in itself and can be used to create both delicate and powerful sound images; for example, in The Rolling Stones's 'Under Cover', they often bring the reverb signals to the foreground and allow it to override and takeover the mix on drum and rest beats. The effect is rather like a thunder after the initial crack of lightning.

The more you become used to different FX and units which produce them, the more it's possible to detect and analyse what is going on on records. Listen not only to the music and lyrics but the sounds which go to make them up, and listen for any use of reverb or delay FX. Try to work out how unorthodox, abstract acoustic sounds were created. It is only by constant dedication that one becomes a good musician or engineer. Try to combine multilayer listening with practical analytical practices, always thinking which equipment and processes could recreate both the natural and recorded sounds you hear all the time.

I won't dwell on the role of FX in the mixdown chain for fear of inhibiting novices from experimenting by laying down too many rules. Experimentation is the key to originality, and financial success in the contemporary music field lies in commercially implementing your originality.

Mastering a Track

Once you have gone through the track a few times and are sure of what to do and where, it is time to have a go for real. It is as necessary to rehearse doing a multitrack mix, as it is as much a performance as playing an instrument part. Rehearse until you feel confident that you know all your cue points for changing levels, adjusting EQ and producing 'movement' in the stereo field. But do not overrehearse, or you may kill off spontaneous ideas; they become stale through constant repetition, your ears tire of them and they begin to sound 'different'.

The element of slight uncertainty will keep that added spark of originality. Nevertheless, although you will develop your own individual style of mastering a track, there is a sequence which must be adhered to on 2-T, as on the multitrack, so that committing a song onto a mastering machine becomes second nature.

Some producers will leave all mixes until all the songs in a session have been recorded when they go back to the first title they recorded and mix that. The main advantage of this is that your ears are fresh to the sounds on the song when you come to mix; however, by the time the whole thing has been played through three or four times to reset the controls on the desk and rehearsed a couple of

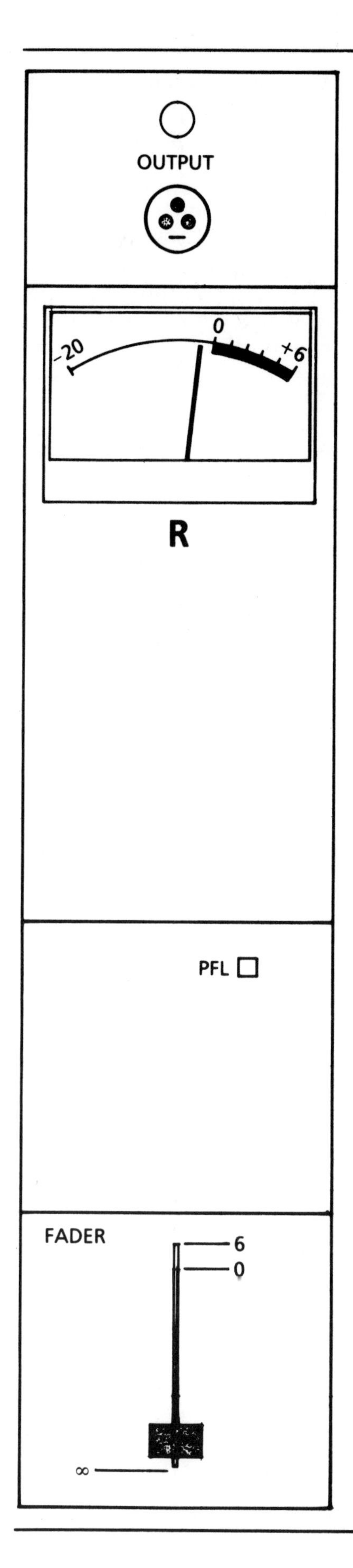

The right-hand side of a typical master output section.

times, it can often (even if you haven't listened to it for a couple of weeks) sound stale.

It's better to rehearse to the point explained above, taking detailed notes and relating them directly to the track sheet(s), together with taking full advantage of the multitrack's tape counter, and then go away leaving the desk untouched and ready to do the mix. I'd perhaps leave it the best part of a day, avoiding too much drink, drugs or sleep. I'll return, double check that the mastering machine is on record and load a fresh tape. Then referring to my notes whenever I feel uncertain, I playback the master on headphones and the monitors at probably the loudest I'd ever monitored the track. If it sounded good on mixdown and on playback and didn't have too many technical faults, I'll master it again just to see if I could improve it, transfer it to cassette, put it into my Walkman and ask a few selected friends which take they preferred. If they say there is no difference, I usually use the first mix as the master.

So much for the actual process of laying down a master take. Let's go back to how you monitor the 2-T through your speakers after completion. There is a socket on the back of most mixers which is termed 2-T monitor input and is frequently a stereo jack input. Tip and ring are left and right signals respectively, and the sleeve is common ground. This input is internally routed to a switch (see diagram) which is usually in the master aux foldback monitor channel. This switch cuts all extraneous signals from entering the monitor chain but allows the 2-T input. Slightly more advanced desks sometimes have a volume pot relating to this input. Really professional desks have standard left and right separate inputs which range between XLR or phono sockets.

If you have a mixer with no 2-T input, then the next best alternative is linking the outputs of your mastering machine into two spare input channels. DO NOT make the mistake of EQing the 2-T returns, as the EQ *must* be flat for you to make a good evaluation of the tonal balance held in the mix. Make sure that you are not inadvertently sending the 2-T return to any FX which may still be on-line after the mix. Analyse the result in the way suggested earlier, never taking the decision to repeat the mixdown because of a minor error, without first playing it to someone who hasn't heard a completed mix. The worst thing about modern recording on multitrack is that most of the time everyone involved has heard the song so many times that it's forgotten that their perception is far superior to that of someone who is listening to the final mix for the first time. You hear things in the mix only because you know they are there; minor background noises or occasional bum notes by the musicians are hardly ever noticed by the vast majority of listeners.

A final guideline on mastering is never to erase any takes unless they are definitely unusable. Keep everything, as you never know when a catastrophe may occur, such as the master multitrack tape being destroyed, which will stop you from ever mastering the thing again. If you have a reasonably decent take, keep it until you come up with something better. Before you embark on any mixdown on a tape which has had other things mastered on it, always check that you are not going to wipe something which you wanted to save by confirming that the tape is blank by fast forwarding and re-winding.

SECTION THREE

Digital Recording

Digital Recording

COMPACT disc players (or 'C.D.' as it is known by the hippest of gramophone record fanatics) is certainly causing some unforeseen headaches; however, it is offering the sort of clarity and quality which no one expected would ever be possible in the home.

Putting audio into a digital code and then transferring that code onto a tape or chip medium and re-converting the signal back into music via the same digital processor is the key to any 'digital' system. Digital has become a byword for some manufacturers; Roland, Sequential Circuits and perhaps more noticeably Yamaha have all mastered digital chip technology in the synth field and made it both user-friendly and cheap.

As far as mastering and multitrack machines are concerned, there has been a much more cautious approach, yet the grappling with new materials and design theories has been just as competitive and fervent. New chips specifically designed to store digitally

Genesis: a band who have eagerly accepted digital recording technology.

One of the first and most prominent musicians to pick up on the benefits offered by digital mastering was Phil Collins. Pictured here at The Farm in Surrey, the studio which he's put together with the two other members of the band Genesis, Tony Banks and Mike Rutherford. The control room was designed and built by Andy Munroe, whose company is affiliated to the Turnkey organization in London.

encoded sound are coming out all the time. There are a few people involved in digital recording, such as JVC, Mitsubishi, 3M (with their 32-T multitrack) and, most notably, Philips and Sony, who are responsible more than the others for creating the Compact Disc. Sony is gaining the edge when it comes to cramming as many facilities as possible onto ½″ tape. The Sony PCM3324 24-T multitrack recorder has become something of an industry standard since its launch.

Processing the Signal

Before we go into the details of the new digital technology it would be a good idea to briefly go over how 85 per cent of professional recordings are still made – via analogue means.

Conventional analogue recording works on the principle of having a tape coated with a magnetic substance. This tape is then used to store electrical impulses as variations in the field of the magnetic coating. The electrical impulses are derived from natural air vibrations (sound) passing into a microphone. There are of course other means, such as direct injection. When played, the tape passes magnetic heads which reconvert the electrical impulses. You then amplify these and feed them into loudspeakers, which complete the cycle by converting the signals they receive back into air vibrations (sound) via a moving cone.

In digital recording, a digital processor converts audio, or analogue signals, into a series of binary pulses. It takes small amounts of the signal it's being fed with, analyses the sound in terms of the frequencies it contains, and converts it into pulses of 'ons' and 'offs' or 1s and 0s. The number of times per second that

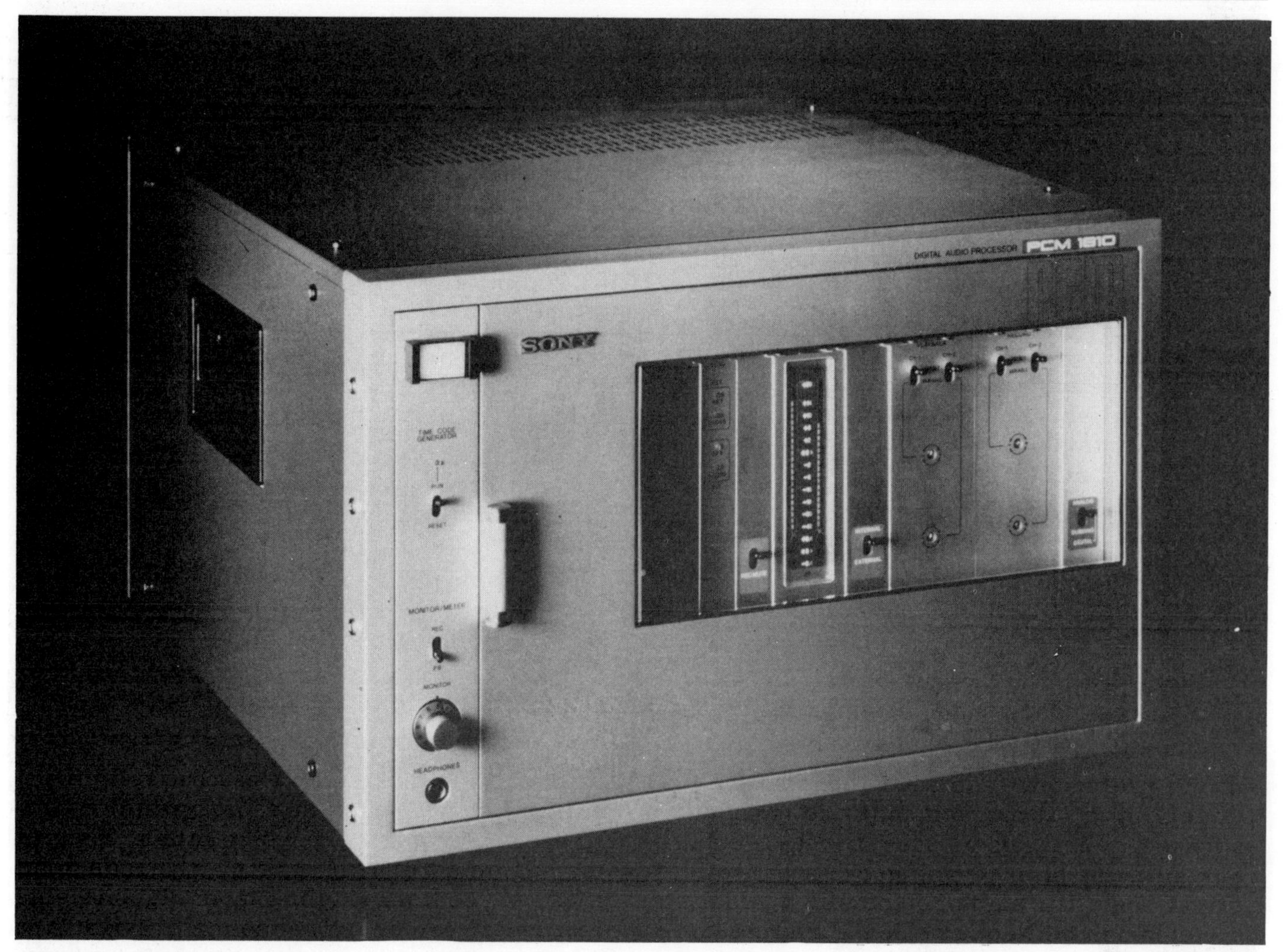

The Sony 1610 digital processor – recently superseded by the 1630. Both these units are designed for mastering onto U-matic VCRs.

the digital processor changes the audio signal into a binary pulse is governed by the very highest signal needed. Humans can rarely hear above 16-17kHz. Just to be on the safe side, though, most audio equipment works up to 20kHz; this means that to get an accurate signal it must be sampled at least at twice this rate of frequency, and this is usually 40-50kHz. This has been termed the 'sampling frequency'.

As mentioned before, the language used in digital processing is binary 1 or 0. Every pulse is divided into a series of vertical steps, which convey to the memory of the processor the exact height of each pulse. The more steps you have, the more accurately the system will be able to recreate a pulse of the correct height when reading or playing back the information from digital tape or disc. A professional digital set-up will usually use anything between 16,000 and 65,000 steps, depending on the number of bits that the processor can handle. 16,000 steps will need 14 bits and will produce a signal corresponding to a noise ratio of 84 decibels, while 65,000 steps will need 16 bits and can give a noise ratio of 96 decibels.

Hardware

There are quite a few kinds of digital processors around, for use with Sony and JVC's professional three-quarter-inch (U-matic) video cassette recorders and for the conversion of analogue to digital in the production of compact discs from quarter inch analogue masters (hence the arrival in your local record shop of compact discs from recordings made before digital recording was a twinkle in a research department's eye!). The state-of-the-art processor (at the moment) is the Sony PCM 1610,

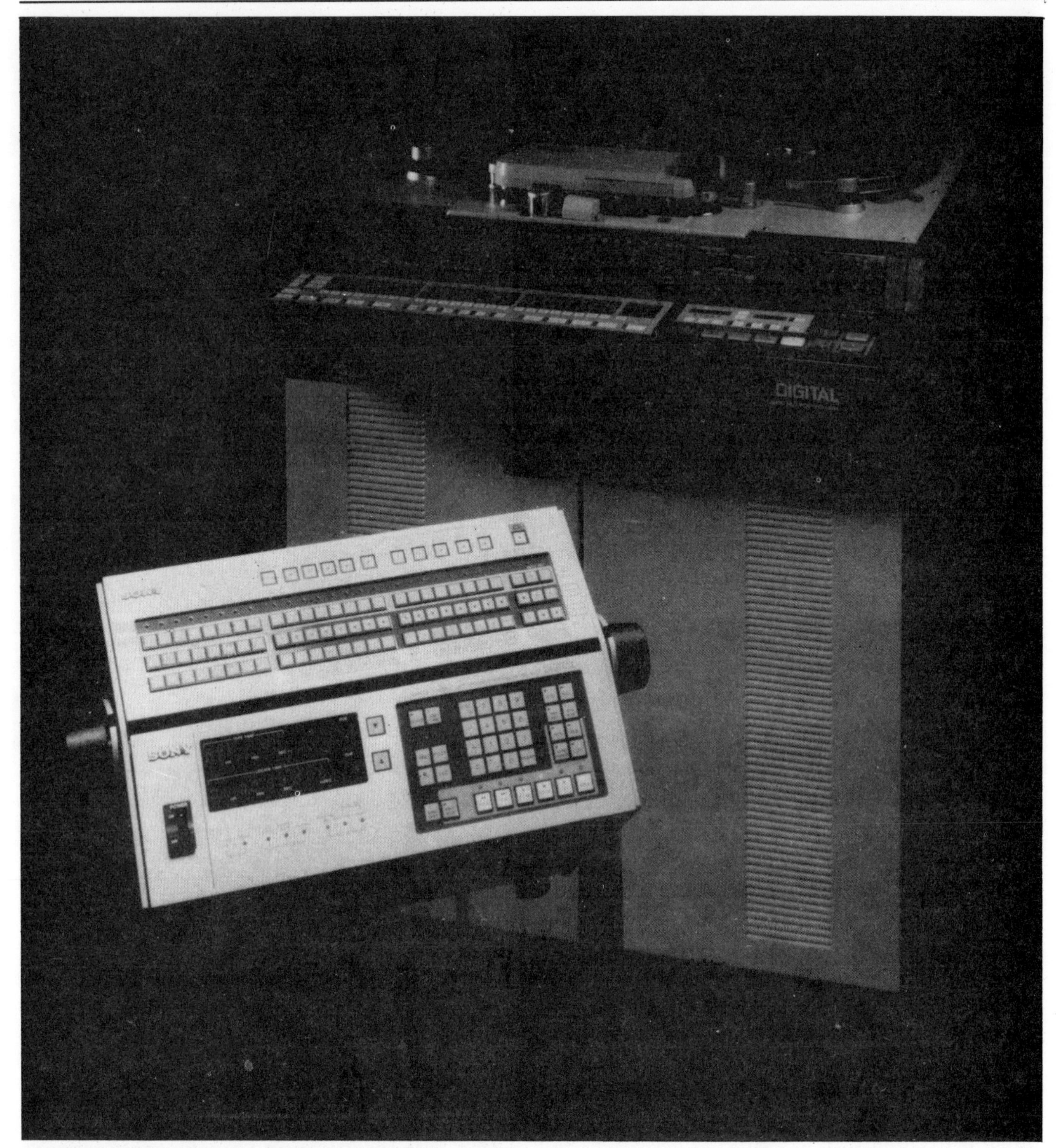

The Sony PCM 332424-T digital multitrack – a snip at around $175,000.

which is used widely in video and audio production houses throughout the world. Among its many features is a built-in SMPTE time code generator which allows you to locate the programme contents precisely on the tape.

Multitrack digital, however, is where most interest is shown nowadays, due to the fact that, because of the digital technology at the sound engineer's fingertips and the recent introduction of compact discs, the recorded material stays in digital form right the way through the chain to where you – the consumer

– play it on your HiFi. Several multitrack recorders are available. The 3M machine from America, mentioned before, uses one-inch digital tape running at 45ips and can record up to 32 tracks. However, the machine which has really made a big impact is the Sony PCM 3324 machine; this uses half-inch tape running at 30 inches per second and contains not only 24 digital tracks, but also a control track, an external data track *and* two analogue audio tracks for normal recording.

The PCM 3324 uses Sony's own brand of half-inch tape on 14 inch spools. It has switchable sampling rates – 44.1kHz at 66.5 cm/s and 48Hz at 72.38cm/s – and all the features you expect to find on a top quality 2-inch 24-track recorder, including punch in and punch out facility and remote control.

CLUE – A Computer Logging and Editing system – this is a package designed and developed by HHB in London that allows Sony's low-cost processors to be used as effective, professional mastering systems. It allows the user to pinpoint edit marks and switch into playback or record from PAL or NTSC video cassette digital masters, frame by frame.

The Digital Mixer

The mixing desk hasn't been neglected either, in the quest for a fully digital recording system. You may think that having a digital desk is going too far, as the current breed of high tech consoles are so advanced and noise free that digital multi-tracking and mastering machines are all you need to produce the ultimate in sound recording.

The first thing that springs to mind when comparing a digital desk to a standard one is size. The entire desk can be operated from just a couple of faders, equalizers and other switches, as the desk's operations and control functions are all assignable to every track of the tape machine. A colour video monitoring system is used by the engineer to display the required information. Another interesting advantage is the ability to have a small remote control unit that can control 85% of the desk's

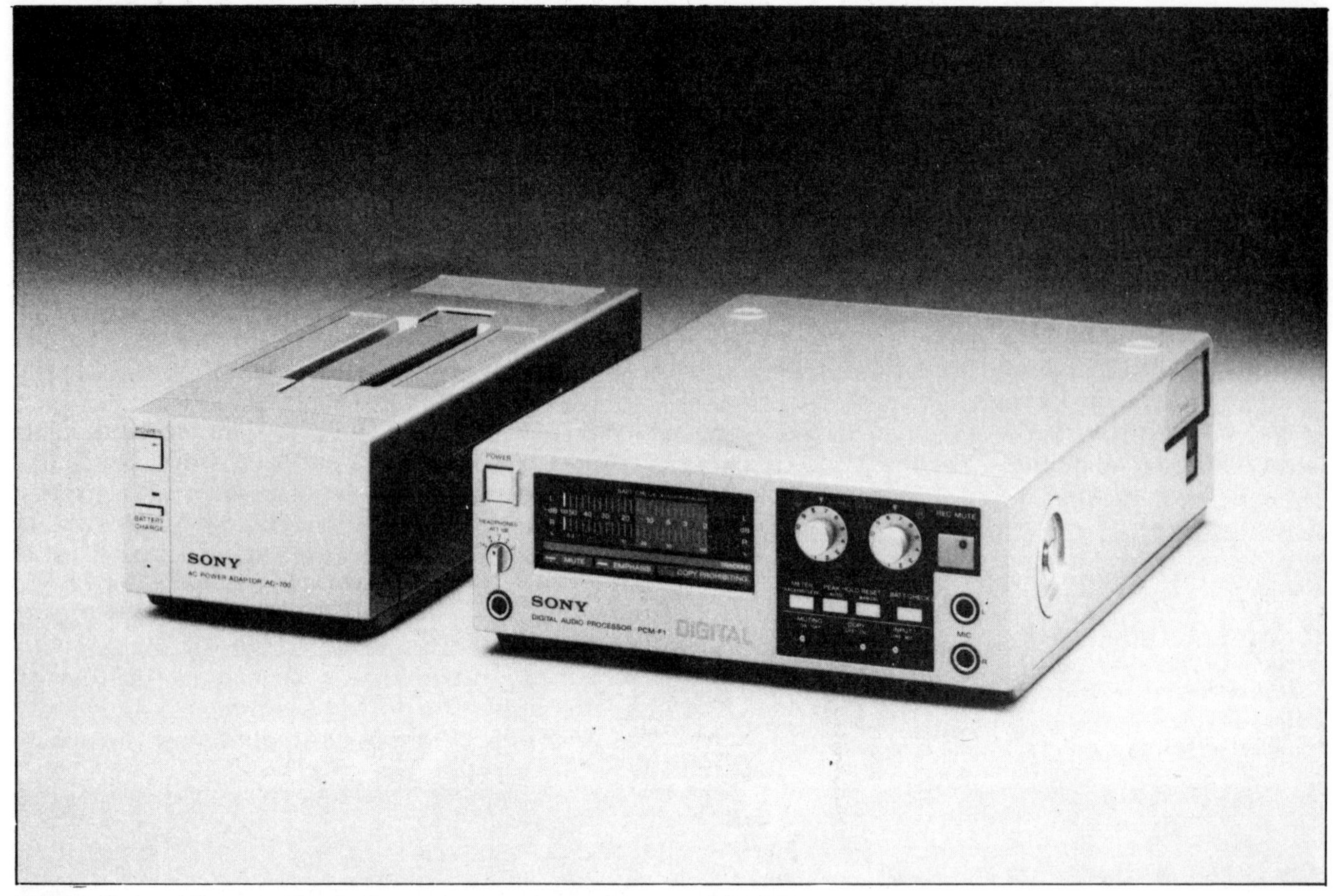

The most popular of all 2-T digital processors – the Sony PCM F1.

functions through a single fibre optic cable. This comes in handy for people who work alone on recording projects and who need to change desk controls while playing instruments. Data storage and automation during mixdown can all be stored on a floppy disc and the scope for expansion in the field of digital mixing is incredible.

Leaving the world of pro-recording, it's time to mention the fact that you don't have to be super rich to go in for digital multitracking. The Sony PCM F1 digital processor enables you, with the use of two Betamax video recorders, to do digital track sound on sound recording. One of the great advantages of recording in digital is that you can make huge numbers of copies without any audible degradation. This means that, with some good monitors and a decent mixing desk, it's quite possible to produce fantastic results for around fifteen hundred quid.

The ability to make countless copies before the signal deteriorates significantly is a big plus in favour of any form of digital recording. This amazing achievement is due mainly to the fact that the binary pulses (numbers, not magnetic variations in an emulsion) are recorded at levels well above the residual noise level and well below the saturation level; therefore, because you haven't got the limitations set by normal analogue recording on magnetic tape with magnetic heads, a much improved dynamic range (around 90dB) can be attained. Digital editing can be a problem, but using the equipment Sony are marketing makes it virtually effortless. When editing using their DAE 1100 digital audio editor and two of their U-Matic VCRs, you gain the extra advantage of not physically having to change, splice or cut the tape at all. However, in all fairness it must be pointed out that any recording system employing tape as a recording medium will now and again fall foul of tape drop-outs. When tape has a momentary loss of coating during playback or recording on digital equipment, this is heard as a short 'hole' in the sound. To safeguard this happening, error correction systems have been developed that

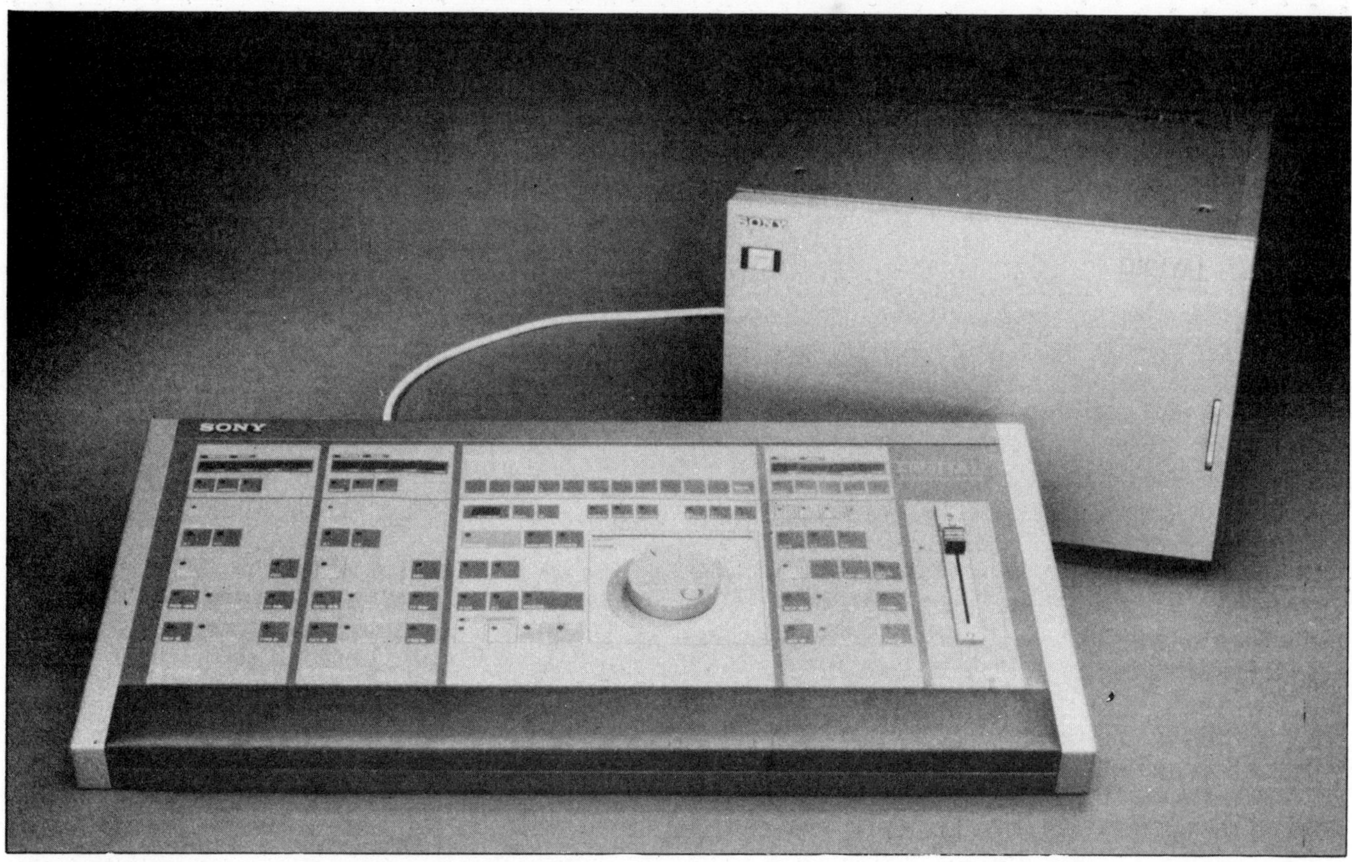

Enabling the user to do complex edits without physical splicing of the tape, the Sony DAE 1100 editor has become somewhat of an industry standard.

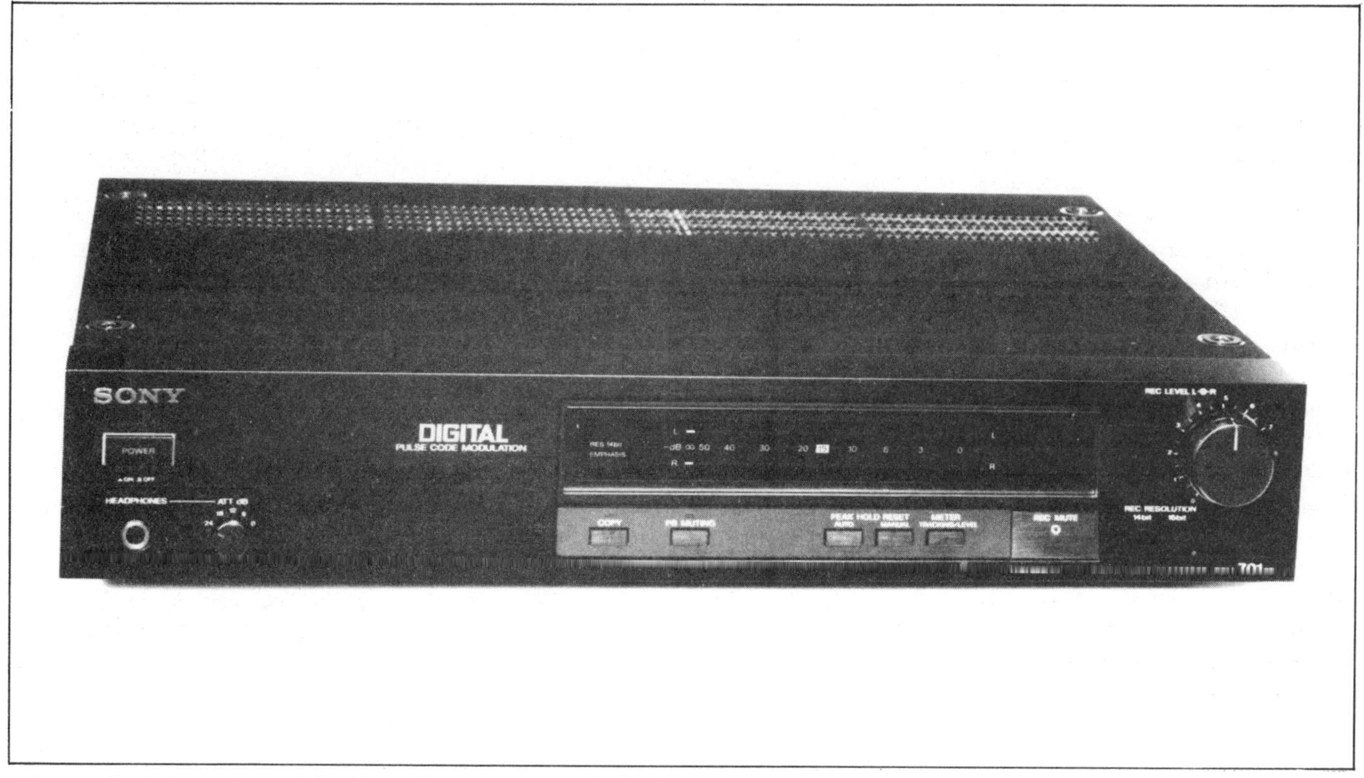

The updated version of the F1 – the Sony 701ES digital processor.

SPECIFICATIONS FOR SONY PCM F1 AND PCM 701ES DIGITAL AUDIO PROCESSORS

Common Specifications

System:	PCM Encoder & Decoder
Number of channels:	Two PCM channels
Modulation system:	Pulse Code Modulation Using PAL/SECAM or NTSC video format
Coding format:	EIAJ standard (14 bit) & 16 bit
Sampling frequency:	44.1kHz
Quantization:	14 or 16 bit linear
Emphasis:	Pre-emphasis (in recording): fixed ON De-emphasis (in playback); automatically switched (by detection of relevant code)
Emphasis time constants:	Pre-emphasis 50usec De-emphasis 15usec
Error correction:	Error correction and concealment effected by CRCC and parity checks.
Frequency response:	10-20,000 Hz +/− 0.5dB
Dynamic range:	90dB (16 bit mode) 86dB (14 bit mode)
Harmonic distortion:	0.005% (16 bit mode) 0.007% (14 bit mode)
Channel separation:	80dB
Wow and Flutter:	Below measurable limits

Input and output specifications

	PCM F1	PCM 701ES
Mike Inputs	2 × 1/4″ jacks	NONE
– Impedance	Low imp. mikes	
– Minimum level	-65dB	
Line Inputs	Phono (RCA pin)	sockets
– Reference level	-10dB	50 kilohms
– Impedance	40 kilohms	
Video Input	Phono (RCA pin)	socket
– Reference level	1 volt p-p	
– Impedance	75 ohms	
Line Outputs	Phono (RCA pin)	sockets
– Reference level	-10dB	
– Impedance	75 ohms	
Headphone output	1/4″ jack socket	
– Reference level	-24 to -48 dB	
– Impedance	For lo-imp phones	
– Attenuation	5 steps: 24, 18, 12, 6, 0 dB	
Power requirements:	110/120 VAC 60 Hz (AC 700 adaptor supplied) or/ 12 VDC (NP1 ni-cad battery) or/	110/120 VAC
Power consumption:	17 watts (DC)	40 watts
Dimensions (w/d/h)	8.5×3.25×12.25″ (PCM-F1)215×80×305 mm 4.25×3.25×12.25″ (AC700) 107×80×305 mm (not inc. projections)	17×3.25×15″ 430×80×375 mm (not inc. projs.)
Weight:	4kg/8lb 13oz (PCM F1) 3.2kg/7lb 13oz (AC700)	8.5kg/18lb 12oz
Supplied accessories:	AC700 power adaptor VMC110C video adaptor shoulder strap 2 × BNC to phono leads 2 × dual phono to phono leads	

fill in the 'holes' so that you no longer notice them. These systems are now so advanced that physical splicing and editing of digital tape is possible without the joins being audible.

Coming back to digital desks, it's also possible using the floppy disk to program from an external source the onboard compressors (for instance) to sound like any other compressors on the market by just feeding their characteristics into the control system. This is just the tip of the iceberg, and I'm sure that it'll be possible to feed in 'phantom' FX derived from analysing the characteristics of various digital systems. With Lexicon, Ursa Major and AMS wanting big money for their digital FX units, a desk with the capability to mimic the FX they can create will easily earn its living – especially in a busy recording studio where time is (lots of) money.

With such a vast subject as this, it's not really possible to cover every aspect, especially with so many new developments. All the digital recordings I've heard have been pure and, in a couple of cases, almost impossible to distinguish from the original sound. Not having the extra worry of noise reduction on multitrack, and still being able to bounce several tracks together without getting dreadful amounts of hiss or pumping, is like a dream come true. The quality is stunning. Even though the prices being asked for the pro equipment make you go dizzy, there's nothing stopping the average person from getting involved at home. So, get out there and start buying Sony PCM F1s and CD players – the world will never sound the same again!

SECTION FOUR

Talking Heads

INTERVIEW
Brian Eno

Brian Eno is perhaps the most diverse of the many talents which go to combine today's contemporary music scene. In the second quarter of 1984, he finished producing U2's hit album, *The Unforgettable Fire*, his first involvement in rock music for a long time. Since his departure from Roxy Music he has evolved a style so diverse that it defies definition. However, there is a common thread running through all Eno albums, a thread that is as much to do with the actual music as it is with the atmospheric pauses which punctuate the music.

Brian cannot be classed as a home recordist. He is as much a home visionary as a dabbler with the Suzuki Omnichord must be. His experiences in recording studios, working with such people as Robert Fripp, David Bowie and Talking Heads guitarist/vocalist David Byrne, have led him to an entirely individual set of opinions on studio practices and recording techniques.

To understand some of his philosophies on studio practices, it is also important to consider his attitude towards musical instruments; while reading this interview, especially when Brian is discussing the techniques used on the U2 album, you may come to the conclusion that recording can not only be approached and executed in a variety of ways, but is also an art form.

I begin with a query as to what musical instruments he owns, and why? . . .

"I own a Suzuki Omnichord. I like that a lot. I own a Pro One, I got that because it enables me to play Arabic solos. It has that arpeggiate feature, which I can play Arabic solos on. . . I like Arabic music a lot and I can play it on that. . ."

Is that the sole reason why you bought the Pro One — not because it was a mono version of the Prophet-5?

"I don't like the Prophet-5. . . I like the Pro One though. I've also got a Casio 202. . ." (Interrupting the interview, I withdrew from my bag a Casio PT-80 which I had taken to carrying around with me.) I said I particularly liked the PT-80 because it structures everything you write into it in an orthodox way and allows no room for mistakes, good for experimenting. "Yes, I like that one too . . . I really like the sounds on the 202, I'd say that there were about 15 good sounds on the 202." I described the Casio CT6000 to him and the conversation came round to FM. "Speaking of FM, I have been playing a DX7 a lot, I don't own one but the studio I work in in Canada has one."

Is this the place near Ontario?

"Yes, it's in a town called Hamilton – it's a 24-track, it's called Grant Avenue, it has an MCI desk, no total recall or automation though – just a good ol' honest desk! As far as electronic instruments go that's all I've got – apart from an old Farfisa organ – it used to belong to Pink Floyd."

As far as electronic musical instruments are concerned, what are you going to buy next – now that you've been playing a DX7, are you going to buy one?

"No, I've got my own programs stored on two RAM cartridges – the studio has the keyboard so I just turn up with my little RAM."

So there's nothing definite you'd like to acquire?

"No. I'm not that interested in buying instruments really – I don't have anywhere to live, I'm only staying in a hotel in Paris. I have two instruments which I love, one is a copy of a 1957 Stratocaster, a Fernandez copy, it's a *brilliant* instrument, beautiful guitar, which Bob Quine, Lou Reed's guitar player, selected

for me in New York. He'd already bought three or four Fernandez guitars himself, he's a Stratocaster fan.

"A Fernandez copy costs the same as a brand new Stratocaster, but they are *perfect* copies – they do a '53, a '57 and a '61 and I have the '57. It's an absolutely identical copy, you can't get a '57 Strat now that sounds good for less than $1500."

Why does this instrument appeal to you so much? Is it the tones that come from the pick-ups for instance?

"It's just a totally inspiring instrument – that's all I look for in instruments. Even if they only make one sound . . . if when I pick it up I find myself doing things that I like, then that's an instrument I want. That's why I've never got into things like Fairlights and Synclaviers and all of those sort of things."

What are your opinions on a keyboard that costs $55,000?

"I think they're . . . boring! I'm just not

thrilled by them you know. I mean I can appreciate the beauty of the technical feat that they represent, but as *instruments* they bore me. The other instrument I have that I love is an old fretless bass guitar that I bought in '76 or '77. It was a fretted guitar but somebody had taken the frets out. I went into a music store one day and said I was looking for a fretless bass and the guy said: 'Oh, well . . . sorry we haven't got any.' Anyway, another guy who was in the store said he'd got one in the back of his car! He was just a customer, so I went out to his car and there was this bass guitar which I bought on the spot for $50! It's called an Ansonia, it's a copy of a Gibson I think, a *Japanese* copy of a Gibson, but it's just an *inspiring* instrument and I love it. I always come up with good things on that instrument."

Have you tried a Wal fretless bass? They have a sort of dry, biting tone to them – Jaco Pastaurious uses one.

"I haven't ever tried a Wal. I'm not into bite much in basses, the type of bass playing I like is the kind you get in South African music or in reggae or in old soul records where the bass is very definitely a *bass*, it's a big, *deep* sound. I'm sort of pretty anti-lead bass at the moment. . ."

You don't like Stanley Clarke then?

"He's just about the antithesis of what I like, he's at the other extreme!"

In the past, I believe you've lectured in the States on the subject of using the recording studio as an instrument in itself – do you look upon different studios as different instruments, in the same way as a Steinway is different from a Bösendorfer?

"Very definitely, yes. Since my work is so dependent on studios and since it couldn't exist without them, it's not the kind of thing that could be done in any other way – it's work which is really *born* of a studio like a piano concerto is *born* of a piano. And my work is born from whichever studio I happen to be working in. Normally I turn up at a studio without any instruments at all and I just start using what's lying around."

Is this when you're producing or just doing your own work?

"Both! I walk in and I see that they've got this and they've got one of them and I say to myself: 'Well, they haven't got one of them so I won't be doing that sort of thing'. So the studio very definitely is like an instrument and learning about it takes a little while . . . finding what the strength and sound of that instrument is takes a little time."

Have you ever, or do you ever plan to record in a digital studio?

"I'm interested in digital recording for the most boring technical reason, which is that a lot of my music is very quiet and the lack of background hiss you get in a digital studio set-up really makes quite a big difference. I very often work by making a piece out of a number of very quiet elements and then I'll take a section of that and loop it or something and that'll become the basis for another piece, so within one piece there might be 60 or 70 generations of tape hiss because I'm always collaging from other pieces. Hiss doesn't bother me too much most of the time, but it does put a limit on how far I can go when I'm doing things like I've just described.

"So that's one of the main reasons I'd be interested in digital recording. The thing I don't like about it at the moment is that for me one of the most important things is having a wide range of speed change available. I don't know of a digital multitrack machine that can give more than about 15 per cent and that's just not enough for me.

"I work in a very wide range of speeds. Recently I was doing a piece where I was using within the piece from 45ips to 3ips, so I was recording and playing back at all different speeds. Then I will frequently mix at a completely different speed from what most of it was recorded at."

What happens as far as the harmonies are concerned when you're recording at different speeds within a track?

"Well, it all works out OK. I have all of my mathematics worked out on lots of different charts so if I want to go up by an octave and a flat fifth for example, I just run along two rows on the corresponding chart and it gives the speed at which I'll be able to achieve the harmony I want – as long as the multitrack is accurate, then you're OK."

What sort of multitrack machines have you been working on?

"Well, in Canada we have an MCI which has a very wide range and a good readout and it's reliable at all sorts of speeds, it's a very good machine, I like the MCI a lot. The MCI 2-track is also a lovely machine. The other multitrack machines I've worked on recently are Studers which are *beautiful* machines technically – they were A80s. At Windmill, I was working on an Otari MTR90 mkII 24-track machine, great machines but they have one serious problem, very, very stupid, and that's the fact that you can't bounce onto adjacent tracks. I bounce a hell of a lot on a 24-track doing sub-mixes as I go along and it's awful because it forces you to plan ahead all the time and slows down how fast you can get things completed.

"Also on the 24-track, if you're bouncing on tracks that are very far apart on the tape, then you do tend to run into problems of azimuth and phasing, which I really noticed when I was doing the U2 album. It's a very demanding thing for a tape recorder – very demanding to actually expect phase to be maintained at high frequencies over a gap that big. So what I try to do is bounce down to two tracks which are close together and which are preferably in the centre of the tape. You see, what I often do now, if I'm working on a track which isn't finished but sounds really good and has something going with the treatments that I like, is run that mix onto two tracks of the 24 and then in the future I can alter that mix, obviously by adding in more of the original individual tracks that are there, but also by *subtracting* them by putting the original out of phase. So, say that I've put too much bass in a 24-track mix, well I've still got the original bass on a discrete channel so I just switch it out of phase and feed it in to cancel it – this is my new style of mixing!"

Amazing, is it *total* cancellation?

"It's very close – actually, sometimes it is total. It depends on the frequencies, but it's good enough to make a very significant decrease in the level of something, and one of the very interesting things about that is that if you'd had a treatment on the original thing – say some digital reverb or delay, or whatever – you're still left with the echo, for example. All you've done is cancel the original signal and you can't cancel the echo, so you have to be aware of the likelihood of that happening when you start using this method . . ."

Did you use what you've just described on *The Pearl*?

"I can't remember whether I used it specifically on that record, but I know I got the same effect – I just went about it a different way. That phase cancellation technique was something I just developed because I've noticed so often in mixing that in working on a track, because I use treatments so much, in very complicated ways, like I'll be sending something into a Prime Time and then sending one of the two outs into an AMS for a pitch change and the other into a digital reverb, then sending that reverb to another pitch changer . . . these sorts of routes are just too *involved* to ever be able to recreate, so I think: well . . . down it goes, onto the 24-track! It always used to be a problem to subtract from these 24-track mixes, but now I have very good control over almost everything by putting things out of phase!"

If there had been as many synths around as there are today when you recorded *Here Come the Warm Jets* and your earlier albums, do you think they would have *sounded* different?

"That's a good question . . . I wonder . . . Because, as you probably know, there is a *vast* quantity of synths available now and all other forms of equipment . . . Well, I'm not all that interested in equipment as you have probably realized from the scant amount that I own (laughs). If I find a couple of things that I like I am very happy with them, and I'll just work with *them*.

"For instance, one thing I loved on those early albums is an old guitar I used to have called a Starway which I bought for $15 in Portsmouth fourteen years ago – no *sixteen* years ago! Anyway this guitar had strings on it when I got it and I never changed them for years and years, it was a sort of policy never to change them because I used it with an old fuzz box – a Project Wem Fuzz Box . . . Good Lord, we're going back some! Anyway, to get the best fuzz sound – for me anyway – you need to feed in a sound which contains no or few harmonics, then you get really excellent fuzz sounds – it doesn't sound like fuzz guitar any more; it's like some other new instrument."

It sounds very synthy – I was always under the impression that the sound you've just described was done on a Minimoog or something similar.

". . . I suppose it does sound synthy, yes, a pure, soft sort of middle frequency sound. It was one of the most important sounds in those earlier albums. It was the sound I kept working with and returning to . . . I never had a Minimoog at *that* time, I didn't get a Minimoog until about . . . 1976."

What did you think of it?

"Well I'd always resisted them before because the sounds I'd heard from them were so *disgusting*, because you've got to remember that when I started playing with synthesizers what people meant when they said 'synthesizer' was weeeeeaaaaa*rrrrrnnzzzzz*! EMS's and the like, just those awful sounds."

I seem to remember seeing an old film of you with Roxy, I think it was the *Old Grey Whistle Test* or something similar, and you were playing what seemed to be an ARP2600. Is that right?

"No, I'll tell you what that was, it was actually an EMS VCS3 synthesizer built into a unit that I designed. With Roxy you see, a lot of the time I was taking live instruments and feeding them into the synthesizer and treating them, so what I had was the basic synthesizer with some extra bits to help me . . . they are quite rough though, those early synths."

Is there anything *not* available on the electronic musical instrument market, that you'd like to see become available?

"I'd like to see a turn around in synthesizer design away from synthesizers that can do more and more, to making synthesizers that can do one or maybe two things extremely well . . ."

Something like an extended and professional version of the Omnichord?

"Yes, something like that, that can do very specific sounds – like a Fender Stratocaster guitar, which has maybe three basic sounds, with a bit of variation on the tone control – *but* they're fabulous sounds, they are inspiring *sounds* and each one has a lot of character. It's *character* that I want from instruments, and character means a lot of different things, it means notes responding differently from one another. Notes in different positions respond differently too, when played in different positions on the instrument etc. One thing I would really like to see in synthesizers again – do you remember the Yamaha . . .?"

CS80?

"No – oh *that's* a *great* instrument! What a great synthesizer! I love it, in fact I'm part owner in one. I *love* that synthesizer – I'm a big fan of Yamaha's equipment in general. Anyway, I think it's the CS60 had a function that enabled you to wobble the note by touch. It's exactly how you would introduce bending on a string if you played the cello or guitar – it's such a great idea, ever since then, whenever I'm playing any keyboard instrument, I'm always wobbling the keys and expecting the sound to react like the Yamaha. I really miss that."

So you're a fan of touch sensitivity then . . .?

"Oh yes!"

Studio Lay-out

What advice would you give to someone if they wanted to start up their own studio on a limited budget?

I've got lots of advice for them! First of all, forget about anything you've ever seen in recording studios – find a room you *like* to be in, totally regardless of its acoustic properties. You of course have to worry about it if you intend to record orchestras, but that's understandable. Just start in a place you like being in, that's the most important thing, and then think of what you want to do – you're not going to need 73 microphones or six square miles of space – think of whether you're going to work out in the studio or in the control room. I do nearly all my work in the control room so my studio – if I had one – would have a very small *studio*, maybe just about the size of a small kitchen, and then it would have a big control room – a big *comfortable* control room – room for lots of instruments."

Is that why you prefer working in the studio in Hamilton?

"Yes, it's the control room size and because the engineer there is really keyed in to this way of thinking. The partition between the control room and the studio I would make removable, maybe like a concertina screen of glass or whatever, so that they could be one room if you wished. I would have the console on wheels so *it* could move. You'd have to make arrangements for all of the wiring to give a bit of leeway.

"I'd have monitors like you do usually but then I'd have other pairs of monitors, so that when you sit at the back of the room, or you're sitting at the end of the desk (you don't want to hear the sound *all* from one speaker, just because you don't happen to be sitting in the right place) I'd have it so that you could just switch from one set of monitors to another, to suit your needs. You could even choose which set of monitors you want to work on for one day and then change for the next."

So you'd use different types and makes of

speakers?

"Oh yeah – I really get a thrill out of switching from speakers to speakers! On the U2 record I did, I mixed most of it on a ghetto-blaster . . ."

You mean you fed the outputs of the SSL 4000E into the ghetto-blaster?

"I found it the most reliable thing in the studio. I found that if I was mixing on the big speakers – they were JBLs – they were very transparent, deep sounding speakers, very clean and toppy . . . I found that when I did mixes on those and then laid them on my ghetto-blaster, which after all is what half the population is going to listen on – the results sounded cloudy and 'thick' – they sounded very dense."

What on earth did you do about judging the stereo image?

"Well, I did switch back to the big speakers occasionally. I wouldn't do a *complete* judgement just using the ghetto-blaster – but it was the ghetto-blaster that I took most of my readings by and did most of the mixing on, and I found that listening to the ghetto-blaster made me work much harder, for achieving greater clarity and depth in the mix. That sense of depth is something you almost automatically get on those big speakers – you hear echoes and a lot of bass extension; when you come to translate that into small speakers, that's all *gone*, so you have to work a lot harder and it's very demanding mixing on a ghetto-blaster. You have to really work to make things sound good on one."

I can't wait to hear this album now!

"It's a beautiful record, I'm really pleased with it . . ."

Is it rock?

"Yeah . . . I guess so, yeah . . ."

And did you enjoy going back to rock?

"Yes, I did – I *really* enjoyed the whole experience. U2 are a great band and they are great people. They are such nice people, it was a real pleasure to work with them."

Were they actually there when you were mixing it or did you like to mix it alone?

"Oh no, it was free entry. They were sometimes there and sometimes not. At one time we had two studios going at the same time. Windmill – the studio in Ireland that we used – had another studio along the road and we did some stuff in there using a little AHB mixer. It was quite refreshing after the SSL, and it was great to be able to chop and change desks and equipment." ■ **C.E.**

INTERVIEW

Katrina Bihari

Since this interview was done, Katrina has adopted the name Zsa Zsa.

If women in rock are still something of a novelty, female producers, programmers and engineers are virtually non-existent, not so much an endangered as a mythical species. Katrina Bihari is, of course, the exception that proves the rule. Not only is she the owner of the first Prophet-5 synthesizer to enter the UK but she runs her own 16-track facility to boot. She also has a background Virna Lindt can only dream about.

"I was born in Budapest but my parents come from that rather notorious place, Transylvania. Anyway, I lived in Hungary until I was sixteen but somehow – I don't know why – I didn't become totally indoctrinated."

And then you came to England?

"Yes, I defected or, as it's called in Hungary, deserted. I can't go back, as I'm a British citizen anyway now."

After travelling the world, assimilating different cultures and music, Katrina has settled in London. With the costs involved in setting up a studio, she has Suffered For Her Art, going without essentials to help pay for the equipment until the all-important record deal comes along. Her flat is littered with instruments including percussion, violins, guitars, flute, and an out-of-tune upright piano.

"I'm a multi-instrumentalist, but a master of none. Most of the time I lay down guide-tracks and get really good musicians in to do the final take. The musicians are the most important thing, *then* comes the gear."

For Katrina, the music comes before the hardware. For her, the studio is an important addition to her musical armoury but no more so than any other instrument, however humble.

"To me, the studio is a musical instrument and I evaluate it as such. Synthesizers, mixers and so on are often very sophisticated. Lots of work and thought goes into their design and in the right hands they're fantastic instruments but no more than, say, a talking drum is. In its own way it took just as much genius to put that together."

Katrina is quite old-fashioned in her songwriting, continuing the time-honoured tradition of starting with a lyric.

"It can be just an idea or feeling. My original transcripts for a song are sometimes ten pages long! Having said that, the lyrics I'm proudest of are those that are shortest but say the most, so I throw away line after line."

The melody's next, worked out either on her acoustic guitar or piano. Only then does she move into the studio, which occupies the whole of her second bedroom. An RSD Studiomaster 20-8-2 (16-8-2 with expander module) mixing console, Fostex B-16 multitrack and Revox master are the mainstay of her recording gear, a Quad 303 amplifier and Auratones providing the monitoring set-up. Main instruments are the Sequential Prophet-5 and a newly acquired Greengate DS3 sampler and Apple IIe computer.

"At first, I only had two cassette machines and used to bounce. Later, I got my first multi-track, a Teac A3440. From there it was a Fostex A-8 and eventually the B-16. I want to gain a foothold in the music industry and to do that I've got to be on the frontier of new developments, so as soon as the Fostex 16-track came out I had to get one in order to be on the frontline.

"I've always tried to buy things before they become popular, and sell them before they lose their popularity, which means I have to look ahead to see what the next thing to come on the market will be. For instance, my first synthesizer was a Roland SH-2 monophonic and later when I sold it to get a polyphonic, I got the same amount of money that I bought it for."

David Vorhaus, of *White Noise* fame, sold Katrina the Prophet-5 when he upgraded to a Fairlight CMI and PPG. It's one of the originals with SSM semiconductors which Sequential changed over to Curtis with the Rev. 3.

"I phoned David and said 'Can I come round and talk to you and learn from you?' I was very lucky as the SSM 5s have got a much better sound than the later ones although it does have tuning problems. Of all the analogue synthesizers, I think only the Prophet and the Jupiter 8 are going to stay."

Katrina's most recent purchase is a Greengate DS3. Following her policy of keeping up with musical instrument trends, she had to say goodbye to her Drumulator and Yamaha DX7.

"The Drumulator was a good instrument but I got bored with the sound. The DX7 was not one of my favourites because it is not a user-friendly instrument. I loved the sounds on it but somehow I never got into programming it properly. I like the sound of digital synthesizers but with the Prophet there is physical interaction. With the DX7 I felt I was doing brain surgery without having taken the course."

The Greengate DS3 sampling system is based around the ever-popular Apple IIe. Katrina bought it as the first 'Poor (wo)man's Fairlight', mainly intending to use it to sample and sequence her own drum sounds. She says it's a great machine slightly spoilt by its documentation.

"It's very difficult to use at the moment, mainly because of the manual. I've made myself a complete pest and I ring up Greengate up to ten times a day and say 'This is not working! What do I do?' and some poor person at the other end of the line has to sit down and take me through the steps. But I'm sure it'll be great once I've familiarised myself with it. Meanwhile, I look forward to the day when Greengate write a proper manual. I might offer to do it for them!"

Have you come up with any interesting samples?

"Yes – by accident! I sampled my electric guitar and I clipped the beginning of the sound, so I didn't get the actual attack of the guitar. But when I played it back I found I had a new sound. It sounds like an organ but you hear the strings in it as well."

A lot of people will think a 16-T home studio a little, shall we say *excessive*.

"I don't believe in making demos. What I'm trying to make here are masters. Sixteen-track is essential for me because I don't like the feeling that I'm making a demo. It might sound funny from a person surrounded by all this gear but I maintain that there is no music without feeling and I can't get that feeling if I think 'This is a demo.'

"My whole aim all along the line has been to come up to mastering quality and as I'm not a

rich person I've had to build up gradually. A couple of producers I've spoken to have assured me that the masters I've done here can be transferred to 24-track, so the original feeling that went into the music can be captured and the whole thing 'prettied' up. I don't have an expensive microphone, only a Shure SM58, so anything recorded with a microphone will need to be re-recorded."

Whilst being reasonably content with her Fostex B-16, which apart from a few overheating problems, has performed well, Katrina does not dispute that it was the only 16-track on the market she could afford. "Obviously I'd prefer a 2" model," she says.

Once the guide-tracks are laid down on a recording, Katrina goes round to the local 24-track studio, Addis Ababa, to lure back any unsuspecting session musician to overdub and add a professional touch to the proceedings.

"Whenever I meet a good musician I literally drag them back here and get them to play on my music which you could never do if you were having to book a studio. With a home studio you can capture spontaneous expression. I have played with some wonderful musicians such as people from Sunny Ade's and Fela Kuti's bands who were only 'passing through town', which you can't do unless you have your own recording facilities. When people stop thinking about home recording equipment as sub-standard demo machinery, they will be getting somewhere."

Due to the high initial cost of getting into 16-T, Katrina has little in the way of outboard gear – no compressors, noise gates or DDLs. Indeed her only effect, providing both reverb and echo, is an old Roland RE-301 Chorus Echo, which shares a shelf with an Aiwa cassette deck. These are all luxuries she can ill afford at the moment. She'd prefer professional equipment, Drawmer gates rather than Accessit, AMS rather than Boss. All these can be added when she bounces up to 24-track but for the moment, she records everything 'dry'. The important thing, she insists, is not to economise on tape. Katrina only uses Ampex GM.

One of her better decisions on the equipment front is her RSD 20-8-2 mixing desk. It's linked to a custom-made 76-input patchbay.

"I'm really pleased I made this choice. The RSD has made my set-up much more flexible. It's got two inputs on every channel plus an effects in and out which is very helpful. It means I can have the outputs from the B-16 in the mixer – bypassing the patchbay – and yet at the same time use the same channel for other incoming sounds, like a drum machine, just by switching between the inputs. I had an M&A desk before and that only had one input per channel – it was chaos! It's also very easy to use. I can use it blindfolded now."

Despite her obvious abilities as engineer and producer, Katrina plays down that side of her music. Recording is purely a necessary evil, she maintains.

"I'm not a very technical person. All along the way I knew that machinery was there and that I needed to use it, but it's never been for the sake of being able to operate the machines; it's been for the sake of the music. When you're making music and getting carried away with ideas, you shouldn't have to think about the technicalities."

Having progressed from cassette bouncing, four track, eight track and now sixteen, she has a pearl of wisdom to conclude with.

"Of course! There has been this great explosion of home recording but most people have only thought of it as demos. I've heard stuff made on a four-track cassette machine that sounds better than stuff done in a 24-track studio. It's a question of attitude. Be professional – it could be the stepping stone to greater things." ■

Sam Hearnton

INTERVIEW

Hans Joachim Roedelius

Despite his dislike of travelling in general and having a phobia of flying, Hans Joachim Roedelius' record company, as it was then, EG, managed to persuade him to spend a few days in the UK last summer to promote his latest album, *Gift of the Moment*. He seemed unruffled by his cross-channel trip, so we began by discussing modern equipment technology and the equipment he used on *Gift of the Moment*.

"This record is almost totally done using acoustic instruments. I play grand piano, accordion, acoustic guitar and electric guitar and bass and I used the vocoder (Roland Vocoder Plus) and a Korg Poly 61. The vocoder is a beautiful instrument, wonderful . . ."

Surprisingly he seemed unaware of the advances which have recently fundamentally changed the electronic instrument scene, such as MIDI. He enthused over the Korg MS20 synthesizer, a piece of equipment which Roedelius has relied upon greatly in the past. "I bought an MS20 for 9,000 Austrian schillings in 1980, that's $500; it's a pity there is no second-hand market in my country . . ."

So the new album isn't electronic, but it does stand as being probably *the* most successful attempt at integrating electronically produced sounds with acoustic instruments. In a sense this is a project which is a *true* Roedelius record, but also is the product of a collaboration in music with two other musicians – cellist Arjen Uittenbogaard and Tjitse Letterie on violin. Roedelius is no stranger to collaborations – having worked with Cluster, Harmonia, Brian Eno, Holger Czukay, Conrad Schnitzler and Peter Baumann.

Roedelius felt that Cluster outlived its natural life-span. "Cluster should have stopped with *Sowiesoso* – that was a great album – we should have stopped there.

"Each album has its own parts which when put together go to make an overall feeling or mood . . ."

Shutting yourself away in an open room, with the lights out in the middle of the night, wearing headphones, is a great way of feeling *After the Heat* and *Gift of the Moment*. For Roedelius, commerciality has never been a consideration. "I've never worried about the music being able to sell well. I know people who *have* worried and tried to put the music second to popularity; for instance, Peter Baumann has tried it since *Transharmonic Nights*, but I do not worry." It shows, as there *are* what some would term as self-indulgent chunks in Roedelius' music, like the *Selbstportrait* series of records for one, but the music has never been mismanaged or forcefully moulded into something which is designed for the market.

The Home Approach

How do you approach recording?

"I have a grand piano at home and the basic album tracks were recorded there using a Revox A77 in stereo at 7½ips. I made sure I got 'space' on the tape, then I went into the studio in Rotterdam and transferred the stereo recording onto one track of the 4-track (the album was done on 4-track with dbx), and then I started adding to the music using the different instruments."

To many of us this sort of technology would only be employed in our bedrooms for recording "demos" ready for the day when someone will pay for you to go into a 24-track or 48-track studio to record the material "properly". *Gift of the Moment* thrives and nourishes itself on the limitations of such a facility. Roedelius seems to pull all he can out of even the simplest of sounds and come up with something sounding so good that you can *hear* that nothing else is needed.

At the top of Roedelius' shopping list is a Mellotron and then ultimately his own multitrack set-up. "It would be ideal for me to work at home. For me, the best music comes from unexpected moments which I could capture at home," he comments. Is there anything that particularly inspires him to write? "I find looking at the colour green helps. But the most important thing is to be free from outside noises and terrible distractions, like traffic noise." He's aware of the problems of Mellotrons, such as transporting them, but is still keen to have one. His friend Edgar Froese offered him one recently for 500 marks.

The Future

He assured me that he wouldn't be working with Brian Eno or Moebius again, but he is planning some material with a saxophonist called Alexander Czjzek who has released two albums.

Joachim (as he likes to be called) was glad to leave Sky Records. "They never did any promotion, no public relations even! The boss just had the records pressed up and waited to see if they sold – it was all by chance. I asked him once how he felt about the music and he said he didn't even like it!

"A ballet group in Vienna have asked me to start thinking about composing some music for them to perform to at an open-air festival in Italy. There will be fireworks and the music should go along with them. I won't be playing there though. I want to play live, but just with a piano – I'm a pianist now!"

Much can be learned from the approach Roedelius takes to recording. It *is* possible to release records from four-track. More importantly, he shows that if the music is good, it can transcend any form of reproduction. ■ C.E.

INTERVIEW

Derek Bramble

For a relatively unknown producer to be rung up out of the blue by David Bowie with the offer of co-producing his new album might seem like winning the pools. But that's exactly what happened to Derek Bramble. Not surprisingly, Derek accepted the Bowie summons, and the results can be heard on the LP *Tonight* (which included Bowie's recent single 'Loving the Alien').

In the first quarter of this year, Derek began to install new equipment properly at his home studio. Being co-producer on a Bowie album has enabled Derek to splash out on above average equipment. His outboard department is better equipped than many 24-T studios I've visited in London, but while his approach is one of confidence in new technology he treats his home studio as strictly exactly that: a *home studio*.

We started by discussing his multitrack equipment. "I've got two Fostex B16s, synchronised with the Applied Microsystems ICON. I bought all the gear from HHB in London. I find that a 32-T system allows me a lot of flexibility." And what about your mixer? "I've got a TAC Matchless with a 26:8:2 configuration." So when you use the multitrack system to full capacity (30 tracks), where do you bring back the last four tape returns? Do you submix? "No, I just stick them up the auxiliaries, works absolutely fine, I've got enough control."

How big is your studio? "It's no bigger than about 10′ × 10′ . . ." Do you have a separate room for isolating vocals? "Not really, whatever happens will usually all happen in here."

Staying more or less at the 'front end' of his studio, I asked him what makes he uses. "I've got an AKG Tube, it's great, really clear, but I want to get a Neumann U87, they're really good . . ." What about instruments? "I've got an Emu-2, which I think is really quite flexible and good quality. I've got a few drum machines such as a Yamaha RX11." Did you buy that knowing that a hotrod is available to give you separate outs on the RX15? "I knew that could be done but the extra two hundred quid or whatever it is didn't really seem like more than the hassle of getting a 15 doctored. I've also got two Roland machines, the TR808 which is all analogue and the claps are pretty useful. It doesn't sound anything like a drumkit, and if you look at it as a sound box in its own right, it's brilliant. The other Roland machine I have is the new TR727, which I think is quite punchy, and I've got an Oberheim DMX, which is sharp and powerful. I've got interchangeable voice cards for it." He has one of Oberheim's electronic kit bass drum cards. "A real stunner, so much bite and crack to it," he says.

Derek has an expansive collection of outboard equipment. "I've got plenty of digital reverb such as the Yamaha Rev-1. Storing your presets in the remote is a good idea as you don't have to mess around lugging the whole unit to a studio. The Yamaha is a well-designed piece of gear and I've just got the Klark Teknik DN780, which has added density reverberation software. The reverb you can get out of it is extraordinarily realistic, and it sounds very 'musical', it has a reasonable amount of pre-delay too."

Pre-delay on digital reverbs is an essential part to the sound as it allows you to create a Phil Collins drum sound as long as you have the right sort of drum sound to put through the unit. Derek has the MXRO1a, with remote and reverse reverb FX software. The combination of the DMX through the MXRO1a using a sound with a lot of pre-delay gets amazing drum sounds rather like having a Phil Collins preset that you can always call up.

Derek has a Bel BD80 DDL, which he uses for sampling, although he prefers using his Emu-2. "Having the Emu-2 around I tend to always do my sampling on there, the Bel is good, but the Emulator is dedicated and more flexible.

Rather than concentrating on more 'noticeable' FX, I asked Derek about compressors. "The compressors I use are the Drawmers which are very good, although you just can't get that bite at the beginning. I've got the new Yamaha dual compressor/limiter (the GC2020), it's much better than the Drawmers for getting that tightness at the beginning. I like it a lot, very cracky.

"I have two dual expanders from Drawmer and two dual noise gates too. I've also got a valve Allen & Heath compressor, and have just got the Spanner! I like that a lot, it's great to use and can create amazing images. I've also got three pieces of Roland Rack Series gear, the SDE 3000 and the Dimension D, together with the rack mounting vocoder."

Finally, I asked him what monitors he uses and what he masters onto. "I've got a wonderful pair of Westlake monitors. They are really nice, lovely units and run off an HH amp." The V500? "No, not quite that powerful, I've got the V200. For mastering, I use the Sony 701ES."

Mr Bramble's home studio is a peculiar and unique mixture of truly professional equipment with not so professional equipment such as the Fostex B16s. However, after speaking to Derek and listening again to a B16 master, I came to the conclusion that there are many quality thresholds in the recording game, not one major one. If you are permanently listening to bad quality cassettes, suddenly one rough open-reel 7½ips master can be sheer bliss.

I find cramming 16 tracks onto half-inch a contradiction to basic magnetic tape theory. Hopefully we will *all* learn how to accept and embrace new technology. With luck, better, cheaper equipment will come out, and it won't be necessary to book into a B16-T studio with reservations about the sound quality. ■ C.E.

INTERVIEW

Paul Gomersall

Paul Gomersall is a success. In two short years he has worked his way up from manning the night desk at Sarm East to tape-opping and co-engineering credits on two of 1984's biggest albums, Frankie's *Pleasure Dome* and Wham!'s *Make It Big,* as well as with several smaller bands like Cabaret Voltaire and The Damned. His work doesn't seem to have brought him any great riches though. Apart from the gold disc upon the wall he received for his work on 'Wake Me Up Before You GoGo', there are few clues in Paul's flat as to how he makes his living.

Part of the old school of engineers, Paul makes little pretence to being a musician – "I can do the standard five chords on the guitar," he deadpans. However, with a diploma in Electronics For The Music Industry and an interest in electronics and sound since he was ten, he knows desks and outboard gear inside out. He's now freelance and has his own eight-track set-up and MIDI system about which he can be scathing. It's hard to be positive about a Fostex 350 after an SSL.

"I don't even find it adequate," he moans. "For starters, it's only got eight inputs and you've got eight tracks on the tape, so if you want to put echo or any FX on while you're recording – which I do a lot because it saves hassles when you're mixing – you've got to have it in a mode in which you can't monitor. This is because the monitor knobs double as an echo send, so you've got to keep unplugging things from your patchbay in order to hear things and record on another track.

"Also, when it comes to mixing, it's a drag as well, because you've got two busses and if you plug anything into a buss it just goes hard left or hard right. They should have had some facility to pan from the busses."

For the Fostex A8 he is, however, full of praise.

"The noise reduction on it is great, a lot better than the dbx which was on my Teac 244 which I used to have. That used to bounce up and down with the hi-hat, which was horrible!

"The only problem I've had with the A8 was with a click track (which I usually put on track eight). On one tape it kept jumping out of sync. I always use Ampex Grand Master – it definitely wasn't the tape."

Do you find only being able to record on four tracks at any one time a problem?

"I did once have a heavy metal band in the kitchen. It *was* then, but nearly all my stuff is multitracked so, no, it's no problem really." Paul enthuses about the sound quality of his kitchen, even if having a heavy metal band in there might sound like something out of The Young Ones.

"The kitchen is like the studio area and the living room is the control room. I usually mike up drums and so on in the kitchen – it's got a great sound. Everything else I D.I., sometimes via a D.I. box."

Like all engineers, Paul has definite preferences about microphones.

"I've got a C-ducer strip mike which I never use, a Beyer Dynamic cheapo M300C and two PZMs, which are good and cheap, aren't they? They're very bright. You can gaffa tape them to a wall! I've tried doing vocals through PZMs but they don't sound hard enough. Normally, I try the PZM and the Beyer just to see what sounds best. But coming back to the PZMs, for $40 they're a dead giveaway, even if you can't exactly prance around on stage with them. They'd look silly hanging from a coat hanger, wouldn't they?"

Paul's FX rack includes a Powertran DDL

and MCS-1 sampler, and an Accessit rack with the reverb, compressor and noise gate. The Powertran was self-built.

"The MCS-1 took about two days to build and as soon as I switched it on, it worked first time. When I bought it, it was the only sampler for the price but there's quite a few faults with it. You can't edit sounds internally for instance, that's why I have to do it on an old Akai 4000DS. But then, anyone who's buying one shouldn't expect an Emulator or a Fairlight. It's only monophonic, anyway, but it's good at what it does. I've always used sound effect records and just flown them in off the cassette deck but with a sampler you can get the right pitch. It makes things a lot easier."

Is the Powertran DDL still useful?

"Let's just say it took about three months to get working! Maybe it was my fault, because I didn't have proper equipment to test it with, but the major reason was that the sockets they provided with it were awful and there were IC pins that just weren't being connected. In the end, I hand-soldered in a lot of the ICs, including the memory ICs where the main problem was. But that said, the Powertran is a good unit. It does FX you can't do on Korgs and things. When you press one of the switches on top, it goes instantly into that new delay time. Whereas, on most DDLs you've got incrementor systems and you've got to pass through possibly four different steps before you get to the setting you want.

"The LFO is supposed to run at 10Khz and 4Khz which is totally unmusical, so I've lined it up so that it runs at 10Khz and 5Khz. When you press that button, it doubles the delay time, which sounds great."

Paul seemed less than impressed by the Accessit rack.

"The reverb's okay, as long as you don't overload it – then it starts making *horrible* noises. The noise gate is just there to fill up the rack, really – it's noisier than the noise! It's got slow release times and it's really bad. The compressor is also a bit noisy. Does the job I suppose."

So why buy the Accessits if you're not very keen on them?

"Because they're cheap! The nearest thing to these are the Rebis modules which are twice the price. (Not quite true, check out the Vesta rack – ed.) I bought the Accessit stuff when I had my Portastudio and when you first buy things price has got as much to do with it as quality. I could have made the units myself but I couldn't find decent circuits, so if there's anyone out there with a decent compressor circuit get in touch."

Paul's happier with his MIDI system despite difficulties with his speech synthesizer.

"I've got a ZX Spectrum with Micon MIDI Interface and software and that controls the MCS-1, the Juno 106, a Casio CZ-101, a Roland TR909 and a MC-202. I've also got a Currah Speech Synthesizer for the Sinclair. It's really funny, you have to spell everything phonetically. You can spend half an hour getting it to say 'fuck'!

"I got the TR909 because it was cheap and the first drum machine with MIDI (along with the Drumtracks). Also, the TR707 wasn't out then! It's really good at controlling things and you can hook almost anything into it. You can MIDI it, trigger from it and, although the actual sounds aren't that great, they're good for an analogue. I don't regret buying it."

What about the Juno and Casio?

"Well, *I* like the Juno 'fizz' (Paul's word for the Juno's distinctive filter). The Juno 60 had it as well. It's just a good, cheap all-rounder, at the time the cheapest synth with MIDI. Can't say much about the Casio as I've only just got it. It sounds brilliant, though."

Paul's a great believer in the virtues of buying second-hand.

"Everything except the CZ-101 and the MCS-1 was second-hand. I got the Juno for $650 and it was only six months old – it was probably ripped off! Buying S/H, you save a bit of money and if you're lucky it's still under guarantee. It's the best way to start. If you buy something new, it depreciates straight away."

The last time I saw Paul (he lives on the floor above mine) was just after he had got back from China with Wham! He's now decided to opt for a life of luxury. Now that he's working most of the time in top studios he no longer feels he can work on semi-pro gear; he say he's going to flog his whole system and buy some 'creature comforts' instead. I got his '909 for $350. He's right. It does pay to buy second hand. ■

Sam Hearnton

INTERVIEW

Dave Cunningham

David Cunningham is a typical example of how varied and untypical your average home studio and owner is. His face is unknown to us, but his invention of the Flying Lizards brought us a single ('Money') which is still memorable, even though it appeared in the quagmire of partial post-punk.

He is an informed man, acquainted with the works of experimentalists like John Cage, an element which is present in nearly all his recordings. Mr. Cunningham has the knowledge and experience to draw parallels between the avant-garde Stockhausen pieces and modern day NYC-based scratch music.

The employment of tape loops and tape delay techniques is partly responsible for the way his studio is, but he looks upon it as an instrument in itself, seeing through the apparent untidiness as only an owner can, describing the set-up as *organic*. As much can be learned from the list of equipment as the interview itself . . .

I suppose I should have expected to find David Cunningham's studio in an art complex. In between a woman with dyed red hair and a hippy and 'meaningful' sculptures lies the Flying Lizard's lair, a veritable fortress amongst a middle-class shanty town. Security is always a major obsession with the working musician, but Cunningham's studio has a solid metal door *four inches thick*. David, a bespectacled silver-haired man, explains. Apparently the whole collection of buildings used to be a meat pie factory and David's studio was the icehouse, hence the Fort Knox like door. A quick look inside confirms this. Most of the meat hooks are still present, only where the cow (and, no doubt, horse) carcasses used to hang, now dangle tape loops, jack plugs, cannons – even a soldering iron. There's still a strong odour of dried blood too . . .

The Flying Lizards have recently reappeared with a new LP, *Top Ten,* which was preceded by a typically idiosyncratic reworking of the James Brown classic, 'Sex Machine'. But reptiles are just one side to David Cunningham. More recently, he's been working with long-time Peter Greenaway collaborator, Michael Nyman, on an eight-minute piece for Channel 4. He also produced Nyman's critically acclaimed soundtrack for Greenaway's *The Draughtsman's Contract*. Nyman is only the latest recipient of Cunningham's production skills. Inspired by punk, in 1976 he became involved with Wayne/Jayne County and The Electric Chairs and was elected to try his hand at production 'because I couldn't play an instrument'. From the advance he received for that LP he bought a secondhand Teac A3340 and moved into his current premises with the intention of starting his own studio. An album with This Heat followed, by which time he was beginning to find his way around the mixing desk. His first interest in recording became apparent a few years earlier when he was at art college. There students were encouraged to make use of the fledgling sound department's under-used reel-to-reels. David ingratiated himself until he was in the enviable position of being able to take home all eight of the tape recorders at weekends. At the time he was listening to a lot of John Cage's music and, inspired by this, spent his time making tape loops of odd noises for each of the machines, playing them back at different speeds out of phase, and most of all, out of sync.

"I soon realized (at art college) that everyone could draw better than I could so I got interested in graphic art and calligraphy. It was then that I found out I could get machines to draw for me and I applied the same principles to my music."

David's interest in tape manipulation has stayed with him and he is one of the few producers in this country who still uses tape loops.

His studio is more like a fifties picture of the Radiophonic Workshop than the hi-tech studios of today. He has about seven reel-to-reels, everything from an eight track to old recorders that are so decrepit they're utterly unrecognizable. Obviously a man who throws nothing away.

His only synthesizers are an SCI Prophet-5 and, more interestingly, an EMS Synthi AKS. "I got the Prophet because I'd mucked about on a mate's and it was the only one I knew how to work." The AKS he got seven years ago but minus its keyboard. He finds its external input useful for treating sounds. "It's got a built in VC springline reverb and ring modulator. It's really nasty but good for that element of roughness."

Absolutely everything in the studio goes direct into a patchbay rather than the Soundtracs 16-8-16 mixer, even the Linn Drum. His effects range from a few Rebis modules to an Ibanez HD1000 DDL, MXR Graphic Equaliser, and Electro Harmonix Instant Replay unit. There are also about five cheap and noisy effects pedals. Monitoring is via a pair of the ubiquitous Auratones whilst his latest purchase, a Sony PCM F1, has relegated his Revox B77 to the role of tape echo. The Sony is "a very neat little video machine. Betamax is much better than VHS because you can freeze frame upon frame which is great for me because I like working with pictures. It's brilliant for outdoor work too – it's lighter than a Uher and when you add a camera it's a video!"

The A3340 has been kept so that David can remix old masters recorded on it but in fact "it hasn't worked properly since the art critic from the *Guardian* dropped it."

Reptile Success

'Summertime Blues' was the first Flying Lizards single. This was recorded on the Teac in '76 and "I played it to Virgin that year but they rejected it. Then a friend of mine who had a tape of it played it to someone he knew at Virgin in 1978 and what wasn't acceptable two years earlier they suddenly wanted to release. I got a 'phone call one day and they offered me a one-off single deal.

"At the time I was sweeping floors in an art gallery and I didn't want to mess up my big chance so I persuaded them to make it a two single deal."

The rest is, as they say, minor history. That second single was a weird version of Berry Gordy's 'Money' with neurotic female vocal. However, despite the Top Five success of that single, Virgin's head of A&R dropped the Flying Lizards unceremoniously the following year. David doesn't blame them.

"They were too soft on me . . . They gave me a very self-indulgent deal and basically had to release whatever I gave them. I would have benefited from a stricter confine, something more disciplined. 'Money' was very much a fluke, I didn't plan it, but it was how I thought one could make a record. The problem was, I didn't know how to make another except by doing the same thing and I didn't want to do that because I knew I wouldn't learn anything. What I really needed was a long time to learn but, unfortunately, because of my contract with Virgin, I was instead forced into knocking an album out very, very quickly. When they dropped me I just gave up working with pop music. It was too much like a rat race."

David spent the next two years building his studio, living frugally on the money he made from the Lizards' debut.

The Studio

"I make music year in, year out, 80 per cent being awful and you need to allow yourself time for that wastage rate. That's why my home studio exists, it takes me ages working in proper studios because if you want to do anything at all unusual with the equipment (interfacing), they're generally not equipped to do it quickly."

Cunningham's studio is the direct result of the last eight years, learning, failing, the occasional success and the generosity of that latest benefactory to the arts, Channel 4, for whom he has done a number of TV soundtracks.

More recently, *Top Ten,* the Flying Lizards' LP has emerged on Statik.

Most of the recordings on it were started in 1981 but only recently finished. As the title suggests, there are ten tracks; all of them cover versions, ranging from Little Richard to Leonard Cohen, but all done in that inimitable Lizards style.

Accusation No. 1.

David Cunningham, you are too clever for your own good.

"No. If I was really clever, I'd get a shit hot manager and do what Trevor Horn does. Having said that, there was talk of me doing something with Bucks Fizz!"

You're joking! After all, they're strictly Andy Hill's creation . . .

"Well, he suggested it. I quite like the idea of doing it actually – it would help me get a wider vocabulary."

Which brings us onto . . . *Accusation No. 2.*

You think that what you are doing is art.

"No! What I'm doing isn't art – it has an art content. The Flying Lizards stuff is definitely pop – informed pop."

Ah, but that's the problem. It's too informed for its own good. Is it an elaborate joke?

"I suppose so, but that's not something I'd specifically apply to what I do. You can hear musical jokes in Beethoven. Some of Chopin's more vigorous piano pieces really remind me of Chico Marx's piano playing. Take the Sex Pistols. They were a great rock'n'roll group and yet a lot of the stuff they did was nonsense. That's the charm of it. Even in Dachau people made jokes."

Talking of 'serious' music, how did you get involved with Mr. Nyman?

"I work with Michael because (a) I think he is a genius and (b) I'm going to make tons and tons of money from him. No, really, the main reason was to get an education. I was sick of pop music."

Your music is a strange combination of minimalism and rock'n'roll. It's very calculated.

"Oh yes! The idea of the calculated pop record is the most interesting of all, don't you agree? Pop records can only be hybrids these days. In fact, they always have been. White man sings the blues and all that."

I've heard a lot of the stuff you've written yourself and it's good. Why do you persist in doing destructive cover versions?

"It's the record companies! They're always thinking of excuses to do cover versions. The major record buying age group nowadays are all grown-up Leonard Cohen fans with money, mortgages and professional jobs and they're all tired of waiting for the new Roxy album. So the record companies think 'Let's do a Leonard Cohen song only with a disco beat, they go for that these days.' It's putting together elements which theoretically make the wonderful hit record but in fact make the most obnoxious hybrid you've ever heard. That's what I do."

I would say that Robin Scott's 'Pop Musik' is the ultimate calculated pop record.

"Yes, I agree, but he's got fine calculation down to a T whereas my calculations are incredibly rough, mine are statistics. Kind of averages. Like, when I recorded 'Summertime Blues', it was only remembered, I hadn't heard the original in years!"■ **Sam Hearnton**

INTERVIEW
Mike Lindup

Mike Lindup is keyboardist/vocalist with Level 42. Although he is used to using expensive modern equipment in a professional studio, he still finds it useful to have home recording gear.

"It's said that there is nothing worse than a really good demo," says Mike. "But that was not my criterion for buying the Tascam 244 portastudio (it was my financial situation). I feel that although 4-T is limiting, and sometimes frustrating, it is enough for the basic idea.

"I tend to use keyboards and drum machine only, and a basic Beyer mike for vocals, percussion or real drums. My flat is pretty small and well damped (carpets, curtains etc), so if I need reverb or echo, I usually use a Roland Space Echo 301. One of the main benefits from the portastudio is that recording onto tape cassettes is very convenient, due to the availability, quality and ease of storage."

Mark King, centre, also has an extensive home recording set-up.

SECTION FIVE

MIDI/Synth

MIDI/Synth

Synths, Samplers and Studios

Since the introduction, in 1979, of the Fairlight, more and more recording has been taking place exclusively in the control room; any soundproofed studio areas are there for drums and vocals and usually nothing more – but you've heard this all before.

Basically, any hi-tech synthesizer (it doesn't have to be a $50,000 sampling system), can make life that little bit easier in *any* studio, enabling you to create vocal chorus type sounds, flutes, muted and interval related brass sections, cellos and even piano type noises synthetically, without any of the time-consuming and awkward miking techniques needed to commit these instruments to tape properly. A good programmable preset polyphonic synth – even if you don't play yourself – is a valued studio asset nowadays, mainly because it is something which, for the exact reasons outlined above, attracts more customers. Indeed many keyboards (namely, the Yamaha DX7, Prophet 5, EMU E-II, Fairlight, Roland JP8 and PPG Wave system) over the last two or so years have become accepted 'favourites' amongst contemporary studio clients and are recognised as being desirable items to include on your studio's rate card, listed in line (and indeed in seniority) to outboard equipment, monitors and microphones.

God's gift of MIDI has made the acquisition of a synthesizer an even more favoured (and urgent) item on the shopping list. Expander modules are particularly desirable objects; some rack away nicely and become part of the 'outboard' facilities. But to come back to my original point, it is a sampling keyboard more than any prog. poly which will have the greatest effect on the popularity (and layout) of your studio. Until recently, a sampling unit worthy of a mention on your rate card would have cost you £3,500 upwards (for a second-hand EMU E-I). But with the introduction of the excellent Ensoniq Mirage and the promise of a similar priced keyboard from SCI, sampling — and the sounds it offers studio clients — has been put within the reach of many, many studio owners.

Two other sampling systems are available at the reasonable, sub $3,000 mark: the Akai MIDI sampler (which is rack mountable) and the British Greengate DS3 (which you can hear about in the Zsa Zsa interview). These two systems are (in their own ways) more flexible than the Mirage, but have the disadvantage of not coming in completely self-contained units. This is a problem because the majority of small studios have control rooms only capable of fitting in three and no more people (with the gear of course) – not counting a computer, disk drives and a separate keyboard; in addition, for live work, a 'scattered' peripheral-based system can be a nightmare. Computers and disk drives do not travel well, unless specifically built for punishment, such as the Winchesters being manufactured for the Synclavier. A scattered system is also more difficult to 'sell' when you want to re-coup your investment via daily hire fees. People like a unit which they can just plug in; they'd rather not spend the extra half hour or so at your place receiving a lecture on the connections and management procedures for all the separate bits.

But there is an important point to be made here: a synth and/or a sampler are items which must be sought *after* you've got all your major bits of recording equipment. Too much haste in acquiring one of these extraordinarily useful items may result in you having somewhat of an 'unbalanced' facility. Don't try to run before you can walk.

The Rosetti 12-T Studio Package

Typical of the many software packages being made available which utilise MIDI, the Rosetti 12-T studio software offers huge advantages to anyone who uses MIDI equipment on multitrack – or for that matter, on stage. The title is more or less self explanatory, as it offers twelve 'tracks' each capable of storing polyphonic keyboard data, all syncable to your multitrack. It runs on the popular Commodore 64 and is disk based. One of the more sensible features is its compatability with non-MIDI drum machines, offering a standard sync pulse system. There is also another piece of additional software, called the Sequence Chain (RMS 27C), which is designed to organise and file songs composed or 'recorded' using the 12-T package.

I've gone into the sort of jiggery-pokery one can get up to using software systems like this before. If you were to utilise the system's facilities to the full, using an eight track, it would be possible to have *nineteen* first generation signals coming into your desk on mixdown (that's including the seven tracks left on your multitrack after the sync pulse has been gobbled).

The software is designed to be run through the Rosetti interface (RMS 2H), and retails for roughly $195. A 48K Spectrum and Apple computer version is also available.

Perhaps the most exciting of all the software developments currently being executed is the Rosetti Score Writer, which will convert your songs recorded on the 12-T studio package into staves and dots. It is hailed as being an intelligent system too, so that the idiosyncracies employed when scoring brass sections (interval-related note and chord groupings in reference to the other parts of the music) are automatically adopted so that real life eating, sleeping, breathing and living brass players can play the score with little or no adaptation whatsoever.

The only reservation I have about the Score Writer is that if it is designed to work on a dot matrix, the printer will probably cost more to buy than the computer and software that's controlling it! Cheap dot matrix printers are fine for everyday word processing tasks, but for accurate hard copy of a score, which (who knows?) may be required to be read by an orchestra, the print resolution may be too low. I hope Rosetti are thinking along the lines of having the hard copy facility control a plotter as an alternative. However, the cost may still be prohibitive and only wealthy individuals will be able to have the luxury of either a high resolution dot matrix printer or plotter as part of their system full-time.

The Yamaha CX5M System

Perhaps the most promising and also disappointing of all Yamaha products, the CX5 to this date (end of spring '85) still has not made the splash it should have simply because it is an (MSX) computer with a built-in DX9 voice board and no product compatible or well thought out software to run on it.

Product compatible software, what's that? It's simply a term I use when I'm on the subject of the thoughtlessness which has dominated the software development for the CX5 – Yamaha have not made available any soft or hardware options which allow you to input MIDI data from an external keyboard. The flimsy remote keyboards which one is still being forced to purchase to input pitch data and the sluggish, non-friendly, note-by-note sequencing has held back this otherwise excellent product from world domination.

However, EMR are rumoured to have cracked the shell in writing some external MIDI input software which makes the CX5 controllable from any MIDI keyboard – but this is still not available. The realtime sequencing software has also been a target of my criticisms in the past, that too should be well and truly sorted out once one or two of the many independent software packages are on the market. Yamaha's realtime CX5 package is a little unwieldy to say the very least.

But the major drawback from a recording point of view is the lack of separate user assignable outputs on the hardware – clearly there is still some more production line investment needed in Japan for the CX5 to be used properly as a studio instrument. Any Page R type software utilising the multi-assignable voice card is worthless other than for demos if you can't separately EQ and process each faction.

So, surely there must be a lesson to be learnt here for studio owners: obviously new technology is creating advanced and expensive facilities for little outlay, isn't computer data recording the most cost effective way of increasing your studio's facilities in terms of the number of tracks available? And if you have a leaning towards profiting from your studio, isn't a data recording system linked to a high quality printer or plotter going to attract more customers than say another graphic and digital delay?

I think it is blatantly obvious that this new data recording software is going to have a marked effect on the facilities being offered by domestic and professional studios alike. This new technology may be the turning point which I've been predicting for quite some time. For about the last year I've been expecting the sales of professional equipment to deteriorate, as the gulf between studio investment and record sales profits grows bigger and bigger. But who knows? The eager investment which has seen more million pound plus facilities spring up over the last two years than in any other part of British industry may continue.

After all, many predicted that the Fairlight would have a dramatic effect on the amount of studio time being booked by established clients – it did, but *positively!* Re-syncing Page R to itself has, in the last three years, been perhaps the most widespread reason for sessions to go into expensive overtime!

Roland JX8P: Profile
Price: $1,695

Designed with the same semi-modular approach as the JX3P (now discontinued), the Roland JX8P is a full-size polyphonic touch-sensitive synthesizer. It has an accompanying programmer unit called the PG800.

First impressions are that this is quite a responsive instrument, with sound-creating possibilities similar to those of the JX3P. The design is classically simple, bearing a great resemblance to that of the hugely popular Yamaha DX7.

In short, the JX8P is a totally credible instrument, offering nice touch-sensitivity and good looks at a price that has really helped to bring the cost of purely analogue straightforward synths down below $2,000.

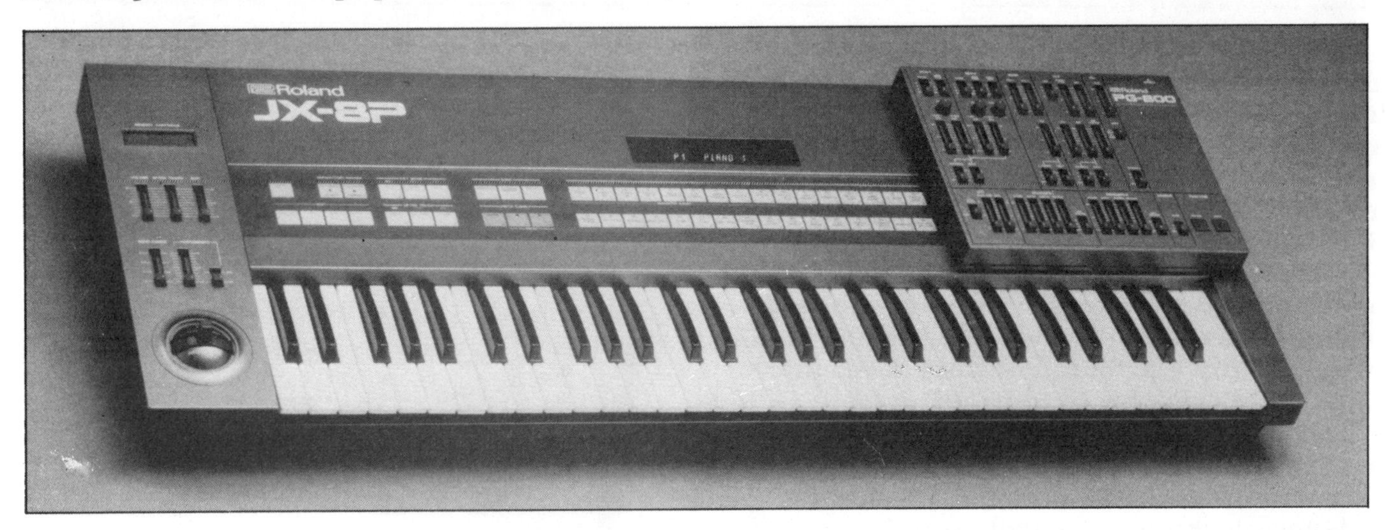

Roland JX3P: Review (incorporating PG200 Profile)
Price: JX3P: $1,395 +/– (second hand) PG200: $500 +/–

The JX3P is my all-time favourite Roland synthesizer. Its tones and sound-creating possibilities do not strike you immediately: its lack of a separate envelope for the filter and its piggy-back programmer (though you can edit

and store sounds without one) give it an unprepossessing appearance – but switch it on and call up the 'church bells' factory preset (one of 64 on-board un-erasable sounds), and anyone listening would swear you'd sneaked Salisbury Cathedral into your bedroom!

After a year with one of these, you should have built up an impressive library of sounds, including metallic twangs and clangs, modulated strings and many classic synth sounds – the JX3P is capable of them all.

The MIDI on earlier models are a little half-baked; even on the newer ones you can't edit sounds while using the MIDI outputs!

A good-looking – if a trifle fragile – synthesizer, the JX3P from Roland represents an astounding value-for-money step in synth design. If you're sharp, you'll be able to buy one of these for around $750 second-hand. A real sonic bargain.

64 un-erasable factory presets (which can be edited), 64 user definable patches, step-time sequencer with limited overdub facilities, 5 octave keyboard . . . the Roland JX3P, a real advance in synth design.

The Roland PG200: accompanying programmer unit (to bypass the DACS circuitry) for use with the JX3P and the new MIDI guitar synth from Roland.

Siel System: Review

Name a six-voice polyphonic synthesiser which has programmable presets, noise generator, MIDI and is touch sensitive that you could go out and buy for under a grand?

The Answer: The Siel DK600 Keyboard.

The Italian Siel company have seen fit to make some innovative amendments/improvements to the Opera 6 keyboard, which as it stood offered comprehensive features at a very reasonable price. The most notable improvement Siel have made is to the casing and selector switches. This, together with the slightly different colour combination, has in their view brought the Opera 6 right up to date with current design trends.

As far as the gubbins are concerned, the re-styled keyboard features full Poly Mode on the MIDI connection(s) which enables the user to give subsequent slave keyboards each their own channel numbers, which opens the floodgates when it comes to definable multi-timbral sequencing. There is now a four-way intensity setting on the touch sensitivity side of things which can give amazing control over the ADSR and/or just the Attack of each note. And finally, the third major mode is the floating

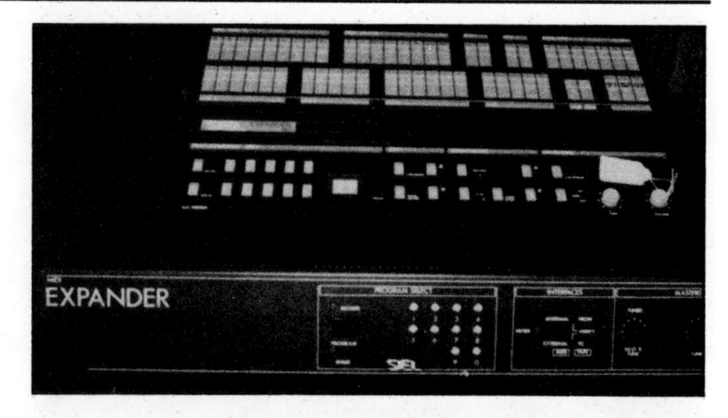

The non-bitimbric DK80 expander (the EX80) sits on top of the DK600's expander.

MIDI key-split function which is designed for when a slave is being used. The player can define where the split comes on the keyboard and what information is then transmitted to the slave. This means that say the top two octaves could be the Opera voicing, then the remainder of the keyboard would control the slave keyboard. Thus, if you were using a six-voice slave unit, such as the JX3P or Siel's own excellent MIDI Expander, you would have six-voice polyphony on the top *and* bottom of the split point – 12 voice control really makes a huge difference on long, sustained runs and

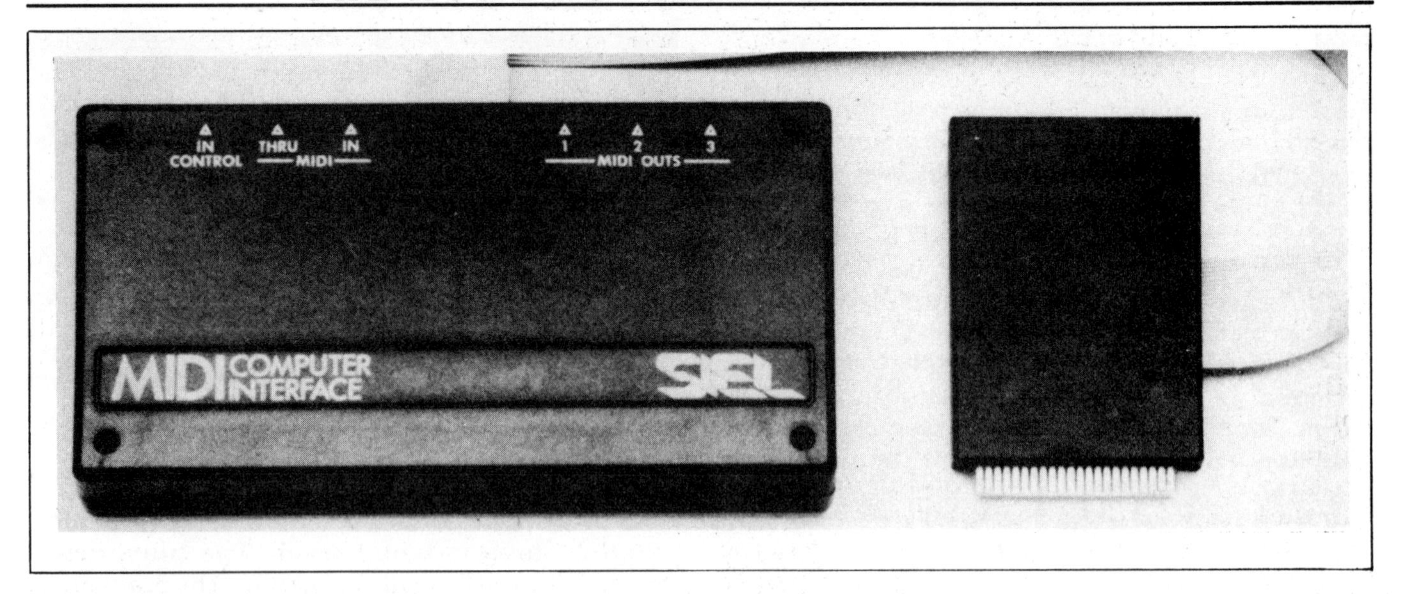

The Siel computer interface: versions are available for Commodore, Acorn and Sinclair computers.

gives the textures more readily associated with the DX keyboards (which are 16-note polyphonics).

At a mere $1,295 it puts other similarly priced polys in the shade.

But turning the old Opera into the DK600 isn't the only thing Siel have been involved with as they've produced a cunningly clever Computer Interface – the Siel MCI – and some very good sequencer orientated software which will run (by the time you read this) with all the major home micros, including the Spectrum 48K, BBC-B, Acorn Electron and Commodore CBM64 and SX64.

Perhaps even more remarkably, the interface is only $150 and comes with a free software package called *Live Sequencer* which if sold on its own should cost $35 retail.

The interface is a simple affair to set up. It has three MIDI out ports, one in, one thru and a 5-pin DIN clock in. Connection to whichever computer you're using is verified – if correct – by a small LED.

Centering on the software cassette you get with the interface first, it's basically a straightforward, menu-driven Realtime sequencer program with no overdubbing facility, but it does have a six-way memory and does remember patch changes and keyboard velocity information all within one track of polyphonic information.

Page one is the menu and it looks like this: 1. – Play, 2. – Playback, 3. – Load from Tape, 4. – Save on Tape, 5. – Correct time, 6. – Refrain.

As can be seen, much of the functioning in this software is self-explanatory. PLAY is the menu command that you input when you put a piece of music into the memory. The CORRECT TIME mode is an auto time correct option which when poked into operation runs through the inputted information, works out the amount of memory used and sets this against the amount of time the piece of music lasts for. After doing this, it uses an equation that ultimately gives every step an allocated beat length. I know this sounds a little complicated, but in practice it works beautifully and I

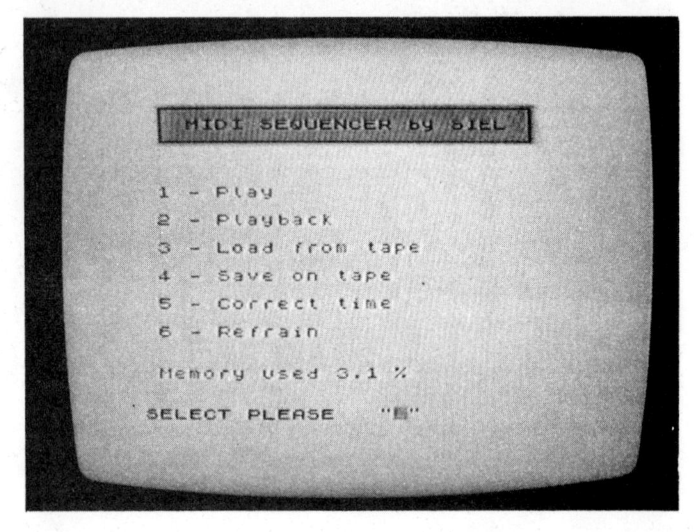

The graphics on all Siel's packages are clear and concise. This main menu screen is typical of their 'no-fuss' approach.

came across none of the time correction glitches that you find on many other pieces of software – even some DDM's of over a thousand pounds have auto-correction faults – and this software comes free with the interface.

The available memory space is displayed on your monitor in the form of a percentage, with 0 being nothing and 100% obviously meaning you've reached full capacity. The memory is very large and at suitable throttle a piece utilising all 100% would last about half an hour!

The REFRAIN mode is just a loop function which you punch in when you want the inputted information to loop around. I would've liked to have seen this particular function a little more versatile with maybe screen definable break points – but it's obvious that this program is designed as a composer's notepad more than anything else and I feel should be looked upon as introductory.

The Siel Multitrack – Composer package: Profile

This is an altogether more versatile and 'professional' package whose main aim is to offer multi-layered/timbral sequencing (overdubbing) to anyone with the right gear. I had the system rigged up to a Commodore SX64 portable computer and the software was on five-and-a-quarter-inch floppy disk.

What it basically offers is a composing package with the capacity to record 9,000 notes or pauses which are divided into six channels of 1,533 steps each. The program will also remember patch changing in mid sequence. You can program each event with a different dynamic value, there are 127 different steps with 1=min and 127=max. All information has to be inputted using the QWERTY keyboard.

As far as signature allocation is concerned, just about any time group can be programmed in. A full note in 4/4 is equal to 96 – and can be divided into any length from one to 96, offering every conceivable differential. The function keys on the Commodore correspond to the following musical values: fl=2/4:48, f3=1/4:24, f5=1/8:12, f7=1/16:6.

Staccato and Legato can be easily inputted on a QWERTY keyboard using different parameter values. The tempo is variable between 40 and 210 pulses per quarter minute(!) During playback a video clock shows the

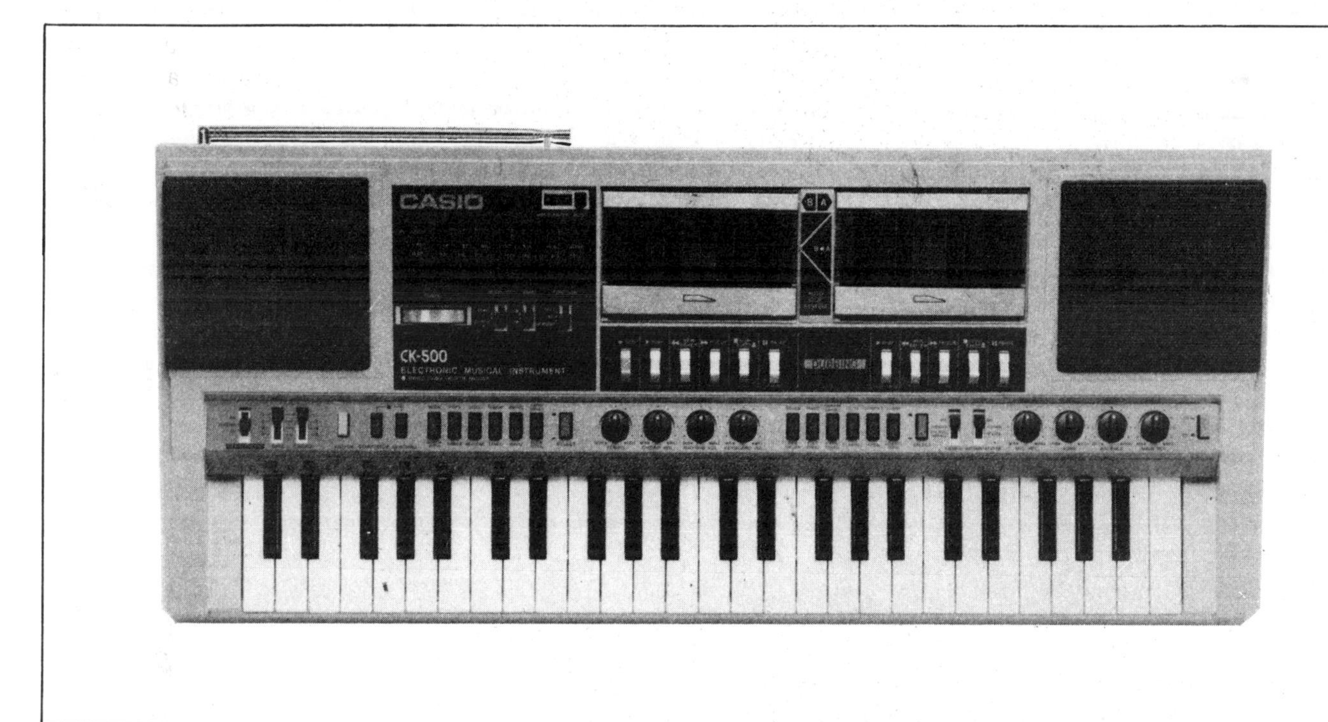

Casio CK500: Sound-on-sound recording, polyphonic presets and Jimmy Young – all included in what is perhaps the most original and eccentric item in this book.

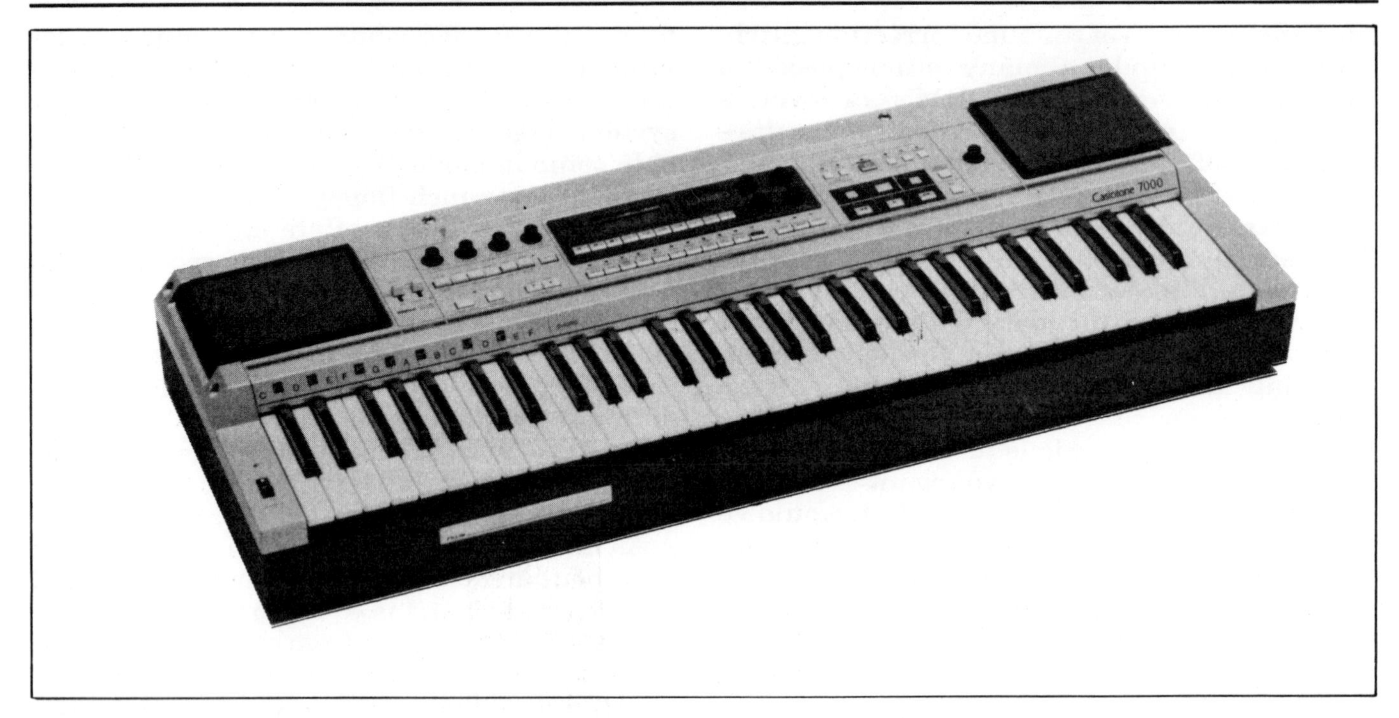

The Casio CT7000: digital real-time bounce-over recording in a package betrayed by its sounds.

length of the piece in minutes and seconds.

Similar to the *Live Sequencer* package, the CMP1.1 software is menu driven with the primary menu offering three modes:

C Composer, M MIDI Control, D Disk Operation.

As the software is also available in cassette form, the last section applies to cassette dump and load operations too. There are basically four major control commands; L=Load, S=Save, R=Rename and Sc=Scratch. As you can see, it's quite straightforward with the main commands being abbreviated.

Before going further, I feel it's important to point out that although inputting information from a computer's keyboard isn't particularly easy for many musicians, after a short while the processes of calling up the channels and allocating each key on the synth's keyboard with a number and its chromatic letter gets ingrained into your brain, and I guarantee after just a short while you'll happily be banging off Czulkayzy's *Basque Sonata in B minor* within a few minutes.

Vince Hill – Siel's technical consultant and general trouble-shooter-come-operations consultant played a couple of demos – one of which he'd programmed in himself – that left me speechless. Like all new technology, if you're not willing to invest time and effort into programming you'll get nothing at the end of it. It appeared to me that using a multi channel/multi Timbral set up, then about 15 minutes slog at the QWERTY would produce about a minute (on average tempo) of music at the other end, which is very reasonable.

Returning to the primary menu: the MIDI control offers three levels of MIDI operating.

OMNI mode is for relaying information on channel one of the 16 MIDI channels, to keyboards that are unable to receive on any other such as the DX's. This means that only layering information from one or all of the composer's channels can be transmitted.

Poly Mode is more or less the opposite of Omni mode. It allows you to give each synth module a designated MIDI channel and thus make each one correspond to one, some, or all of the sequencer channels. This is where the God-given amazing multi channel/multi timbral MIDI functions come into the proceedings, enabling the user to produce incredibly complex patterns of music and/or sounds.

Mono Mode enables the sequencer to make the most of a six voice (or any other poly) synth which has a poly timbric capability, i.e. this means you could have six mono lines each with different presets being run simultaneously from the DK600.

It's impossible to go into all the intricacies of

the 'composer language', but it's all based on allocation of sequencer channel and then inputting the information by using the chromatic letter of the required note. Its exact position on the keyboard is then shown by a number.

The editing functions are amazingly simple to execute and are mastered in no time at all. To help matters, there's a NEW command that completely wipes the entire memory.

Linking the system to a drum machine for synchronisation is quite simple in playback mode, the program sends out a sync frequency on 1/24. This is accessed via MIDI out ports on the back of the interface.

So, overall, the Siel system offers an unparalleled value for money and really should be checked out if you're seriously thinking of making music.

N.B. Siel are offering the external updates on all existing Opera 6 keyboards on the market free of charge.

Sycologic AMI: Review

First of all, the Sycologic AMI is rack mountable. Secondly, all the patch locations appear on the front panel – except for the MIDI out port. This means that once you've installed your DIN lead you can stick it in a rack and more or less forget about the back panel when it comes to interfacing.

Using the Sycologic AMI, anyone with equipment incorporating standard one volt per octave CV's (control voltages) and gates can control MIDI instruments. Making full use of the AMI's different control modes will also enable you to transmit from your analogue synth not only pitch and dynamic information but also program changes, modulation parameters and sync codes over any pre-assigned MIDI channel(s). However, it's essential to point out that your non-MIDI synth has to have these control and sensing functions itself in order for the information to be translated into MIDI. In other words, for there to be any dynamic information transmitted, dynamics have to be apparent in the first place.

A Roland SH 101 only sends out pitch and gate, it has no dynamic sensing or accent facilities on it. However, the SH101's excellent little big brother the MC202 has dynamic control on sequencing, therefore, a sequence composed on the MC202 (or any other piece of 1V/Oct. equipment with accent or dynamic control) utilising this facility to the full will have (if wished) all this information transmitted to a MIDI keyboard. However, it all then depends on the MIDI keyboard itself. If you have a MIDI keyboard which has no dynamic sensing or accent allocation, then the information cannot be translated and then duly acted upon.

Ken McAlpine, who designed the unit, had it

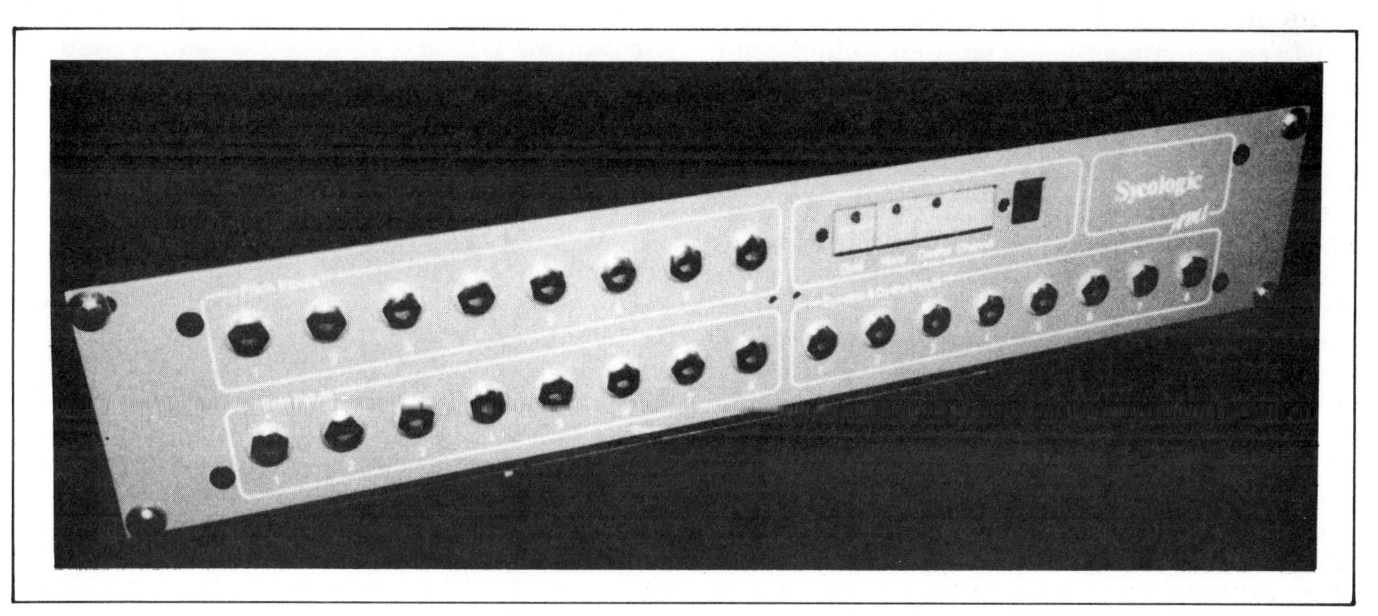

Sycologic AMI

Casio's first serious attempt at conquering the professional keyboard market – the phase distortion based CZ5000. Sonically no different from the CZ101 – which is a quarter of the price – it remains to be seen whether this captures the imagination of the prospective market.

rigged up to a Roland MC4 and Yamaha DX7, with a Juno 106 also being used. He made no secret of the fact that the unit had been designed with the MC4 and DX7 in mind. But after a while I realised that it would be of as much use to a person with the aforementioned set-up as it would to someone using just an SH101 and a JX3P. Its huge range of possibilities makes its applications almost limitless. In short, a unit such as this enables your whole keyboard set-up to talk to itself, and that can never be a bad thing.

Mode Arrangements

On power-up, the unit is in its normal mode which is the Poly mode, which means you have eight CV's, eight gates and eight dynamics going out on channel one of the MIDI. This means that you can have control of up to eight voices polyphonically from say a Juno 60 or any other non-MIDI poly. Again, if you only have a 4-note poly, you can only have four-note chords played on the MIDI slave and vice versa. When it comes to putting an eight-note poly into JX3P for instance, you'll lose two notes because the JX3P can't handle more than six notes at a time. More to the point though, you'd have to have each of the voice modules in your analogue synth modified so that you could have CV and gate outs fitted for each one. A headache in no uncertain terms! However, if the keyboard-to-keyboard facility is important to you, then it would probably be a sound investment, letting the Sycologic AMI do the rest once the sockets had been fitted, although this will mean that you will still only have analogue to MIDI control and not the other way round. If your poly is already fitted with an MPU, such as a Z80 or 6502, then it would probably be a better idea to have the actual keyboard itself MIDIfied, which will enable full function crosstalk to ensue.

So, we learn our first lesson, and that is that the AMI is undoubtedly designed for interfacing *sequencing* equipment to MIDI equipment rather than anything else.

The design concept behind the poly mode on the AMI is to cater for polyphonic multibus sequencers such as the MC4 and MC8. It's interesting to note then, that major manufacturers have ultimately decided to kill off their old analogue sequencers (with digital memory) in favour of producing complete MIDI master control units such as the Yamaha QX1 and the Roland MSQ700 and 100 machines. Personally, I feel their decision to commit themselves completely to a MIDI system as far as poly sequencing is concerned was made due

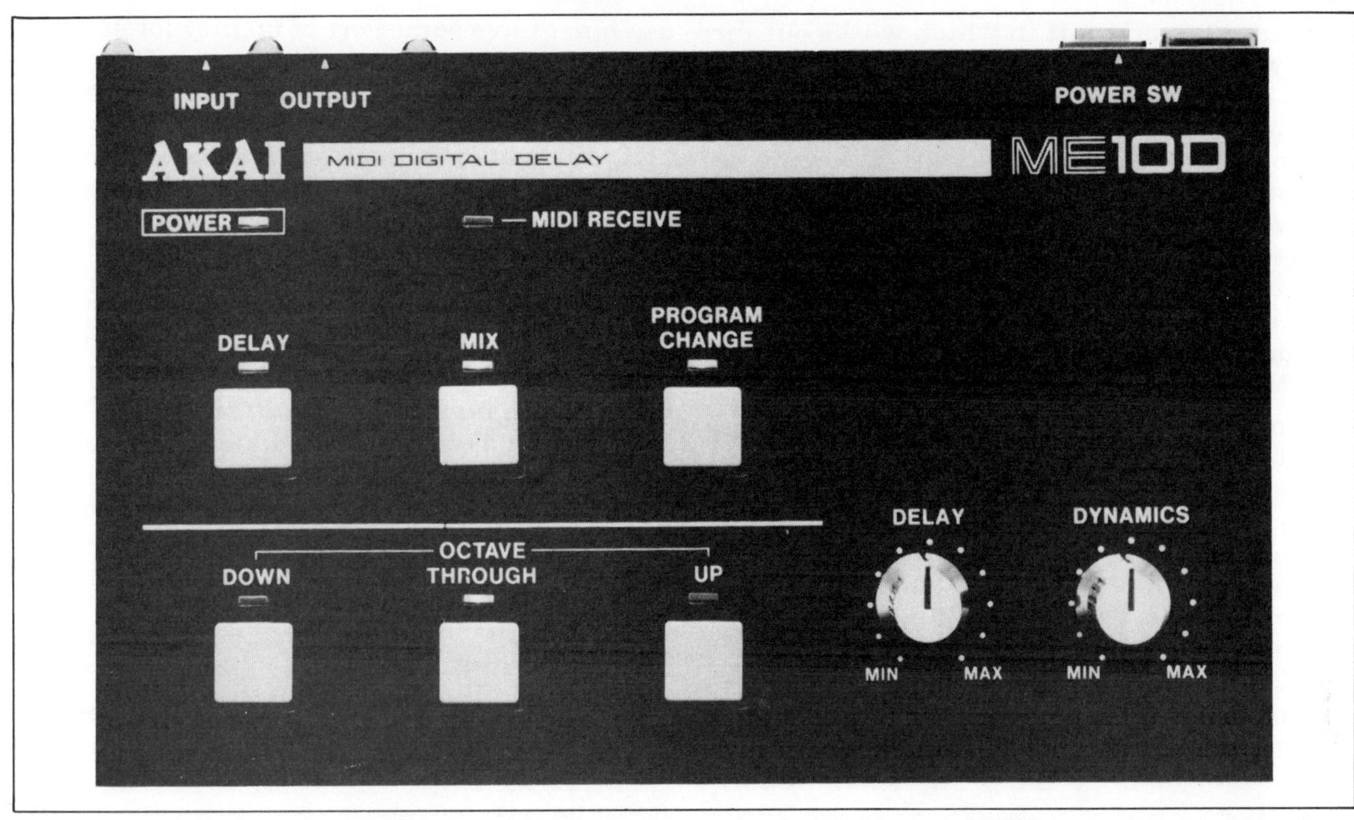

The revolutionary Akai MIDI digital delay pips many larger, more MIDI-conscious companies at the post.

to the problems caused by manufacturing equipment designed a good few years ago. There's a lot less inside an MSQ than there is inside an MC4. New technology has really not only brought about a revolution in musical instruments themselves, but in the ways they are *prôduced* too.

Anyone who's thinking of buying an AMI for their MC4 had better start saving their pennies for lots and lots of mini-jack to normal ¼″ jack (what the AMI takes) leads. I'm not that keen on mini jacks and was pleased to see that Syco had decided to go for the most common of all connectors.

Dual mode gives you control of four voices polyphonically on each of two MIDI channels. This means that you could have multi-timbral sequencing using an MC4 and two MIDI keyboards. Or alternatively, utilising all the channels on an MC8 you could have two 4-note polyphonic sequences each playing a different MIDI keyboard.

The Mono mode on the AMI enables you to control one voice monophonically on each of eight MIDI channels. This means that, using one voice of a poly keyboard, you could run a sequence and use the remaining voices to play over it polyphonically. Or, more to the point, it enables you to have eight monophonic sequences going, each controlling a different keyboard via its user-defined MIDI channel. For me, this is the true meaning of MIDI. Having eight completely different sounds going at the same time, playing independently of each other, has got to be heard to be believed. Of course, to do this you'd have to have up to eight MIDI keyboards, or four with split keyboard facility and independent channel assign for each sound – but it's worth it!

In Dynamic mode, eight CV's allow dynamic information to be added to note events in accordance with the operating mode. If no voltage is present a default value is transmitted. Put into English, this means the eight channels free for dynamic allocation may or may not have dynamics going through them at any one time. Unlike some systems, if a dynamic connection is made and the event is not accented then no information will be relayed. The Sycologic, however, has an 'intelligence factor' built in which works out for itself whether dynamics are being transmitted or not when the appropriate connections have been made. All the factors previously discussed in this review apply when it comes to transmitting dynamics, and it's important that you have dynamics location points and sockets on your analogue sequencer.

Control Mode enables you, when using the AMI in Poly or Mono operating modes, to transmit the following via MIDI on any definable MIDI channel from one to eight:

1. Common Dynamics
2. Patch Change
3. Pitch Bend
4. Modulation
5. After Touch
6. Yamaha DX Volume
7. Yamaha DX Portamento
8. Yamaha DX Breath Control

This means that you can adjust the parameters of any of the above simply by adjusting the same controls on the master analogue synth. Remember, the synth or sequencer you use *must* have some sort of facility for storing information such as patch changes. The number you input will correspond to the patch you end up with on the MIDI synth.

If your sequencer has facilities for it, you can control on separate events the amount of modulation and/or after touch (when inputting sequencer information from the keyboard), Portamento and Amplitude if you have a DX7.

When working in the Control mode and operating the system in Dual mode, the following controls may be transmitted via MIDI:
1. Common Dynamics, 2. Patch Change, 3. Pitch Bend, 4. Modulation.

Again, the same rules apply depending on the memory facilities of whatever analogue sequencer you're using.

That Sync-ing Feeling

The normal sync pulse output of the AMI is set at 24b.p.q.n. (beats per quarter note) which is roughly the standard of most drum machines.

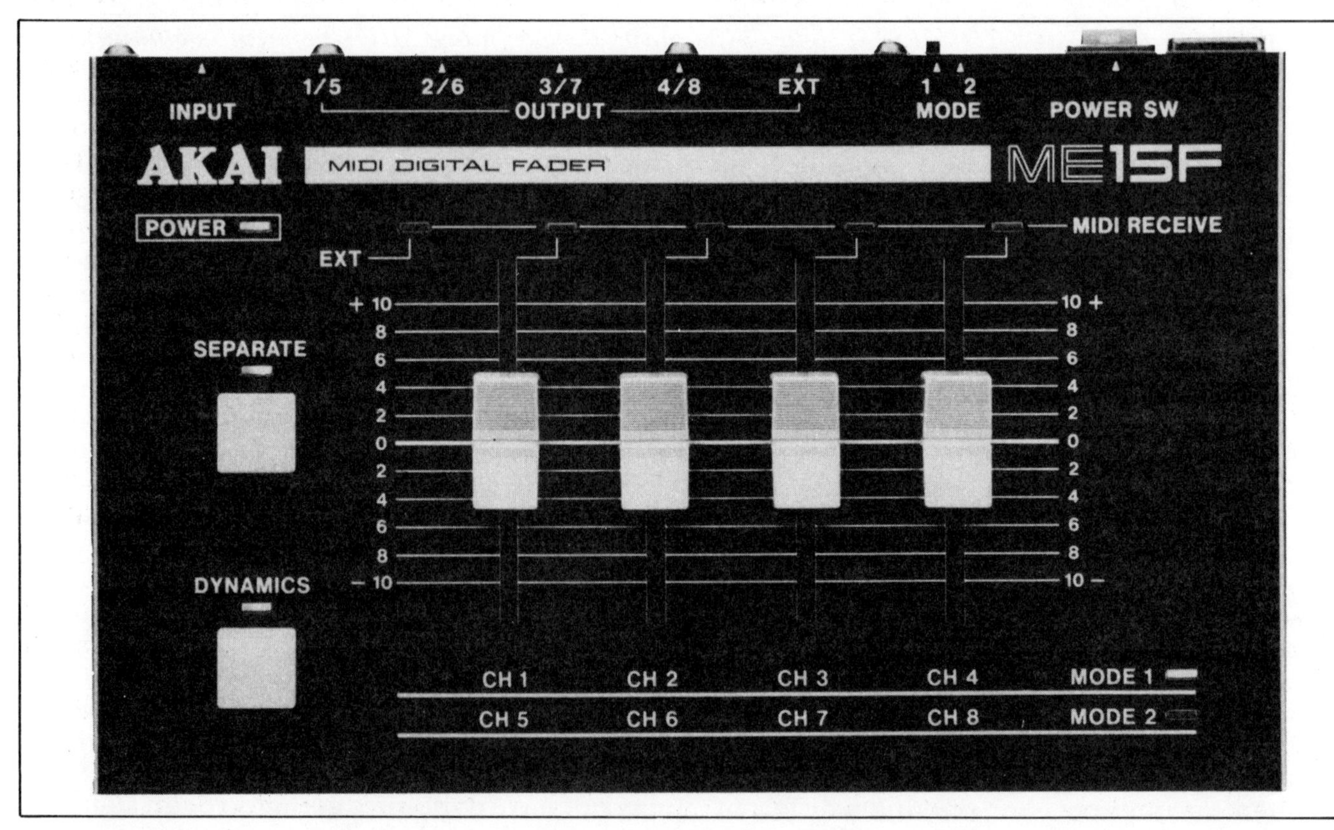

As is the case with the other Akai units mentioned, very little information was available at the time of going to press. However, it does look as if this unit is going to bring automated fader control within the reach of anyone with a MIDI sequencer and tape machine. What would be the possibilities if it were linked to the new Fostex MIDI sync unit?

However, it's been seen fit to let the user define the b.p.q.n. himself and alternative settings are available which are 48 and 96. This means that you can sync the AMI to just about any well-known brand of drum machine, which is good news indeed. The AMI is also intelligent when it comes to knowing when things have stopped. It's been built with a sensor circuit which, if receiving no incoming signal for 500ms, tells itself that the song is over and shuts down transmissions accordingly. This can have drawbacks on stage, but as we all know interfaces are the sort of thing that are used to their greatest potential in the studio.

So basically, as far as syncing is concerned, the AMI is extremely easy to use and the two jack inputs on the back are simple to understand. The start/stop one is calibrated and designed for operation with the Roland sync system and sends out all the necessary information in a gate that will tell the slave equipment exactly what's happening when it comes to starting and stopping. However, when you're using Oberheim, Linn and E-Mu machines, only the clock input is required as they can tell what's going on without the additional information.

Finally, when it comes to setting up the whole system with your sequencer, drum machine and keyboards, there are two trimmer pots on the front panel for adjusting the complete offset and the exact volt per octave setting.

So, not to put too fine a point on it, the AMI is just about the only serious choice when it comes to analogue to MIDI interfacing and its enormous capacity and flexibility is unrivalled.

Another enormous advantage of the system is that it's software dependent, which means with a bit of chopping and changing with the EPROMS contained, it can be made to perform all sorts of different tasks.

The greatest pull about the AMI is that it's extremely easy to use and I promise that after spending an afternoon using it you'll wonder how you ever managed without one. It's tricky to get to grips with the ins and outs of MIDI at first, but anyone who's bothered will tell you that it's the future and all the hard work reading up on the subject is well worth it.

The E-mu Drumulator: Review

The E-mu Systems' Drumulator was one of the first digital drum machines to smash the $1,000 barrier though it only just made it, with an SRP of $745. Also, this unit was perhaps the first digital to be widely available throughout the country. Being first doesn't always mean a product will be best of course, and the Drumulator missed out on some industry developments which have revolutionised the business – one of which being MIDI. Because things progress so quickly and new ways are adopted so readily in the electronic music field, certain products which lack important, recent features are usually shunned and die a thousand deaths. Luckily, this fate hasn't befallen the Drumulator, as it possesses other features that the market desires in its own particular price range. Having said this though, I sincerely believe that if the Drumulator had been released later than it was and still didn't have a MIDI port, this – coupled with the fact that it didn't have a very large song memory to begin with – would have undoubtedly stopped the unit from doing anything in this country at all.

However, now that there has been a chip update to increase its memory and new sound chips have been devised, the Drumulator lives quite happily next to the MIDI equipped

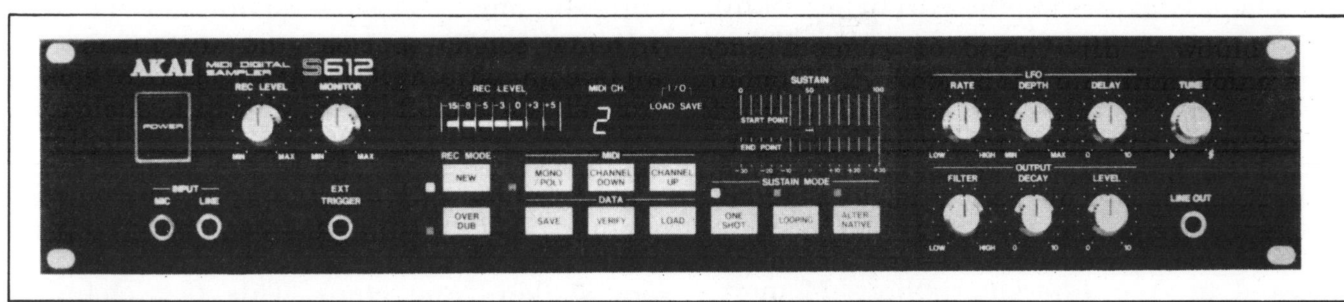

The Akai MIDI sampler is, on the face of it, extremely good value for money. However, the need for two disk-drives and a controlling keyboard bumps up the cost to bring it into the same price range as the Ensoniq Mirage.

The Classic E-mu Systems Inc Drumulator.

machines that followed not far behind. The machine employs a form of DACS (digital access control system), and many of the buttons have dual function capability, some with four commands. It has an LED display and a multi-function slider. Only four drum sounds can be programmed at any one time, which is fine for 99% of most applications – but the odd 1%, like Samba beats and Beguine rhythms require command of about seven or so different drum timbres all at once, to get the right flow and feel. Anyhow, once you've partly written the rhythm, going as far as you can using the first four drum sounds (bass, snare and open and closed hi hat seem to be the best four to start with), you then re-assign a different sound to each button until the rhythm is complete. The Drumulator has exceedingly good editing facilities which make adjustments to patterns after they've been written very easy. For people who haven't got the knack of putting the information in just right, there's an auto correct facility which moves 'hits' that are between beats to the nearest one. This operation usually kills all intentional off-beats stone dead – either that or 'correcting' what 'human' feel there is.

The sounds on the Drumulator are very good, especially the snare and toms. There are basically 12 separate sounds which can be accented to give different timbres. Memory allocation is 64K, and this is about average. Tempo is variable from 40 to 240 beats per minute.

Although, as I mentioned earlier, the Drumulator doesn't include MIDI in its spec sheet, other backpanel ports have been provided, including several phono sockets which, for the home recordist and the professional recording engineer is heaven and hell respectively! One of these phonos is a clock/cas out port, which will drive most popular sequencers (1 volt/oct.) at six beats per quarter note. However, the Drumulator doesn't provide the 10 volt level which certain sequencers (the Roland TB303, for example) need to tell them when to stop/start and reset. Most arpeggiators are no problem though, and the hefty manual gives pages of advice on various interfacing. The Drumulator can also sync to its own pulse code off tape, which is essential for studio recording nowadays.

The Drumulator is a good machine, which can be relied upon to come up with good sounds and to behave itself on stage too. If it had MIDI and tuning flexibility, it would be a great machine. Emulator II? Drumulator II too, please!

The Oberheim DX: Review

Like the Drumulator, the Oberheim DX has the curse of being thrust upon the professional recording/performing market without MIDI and with a price tag of just under a thousand quid. Still, I won't beat about the shrub – let's get straight on with it.

First of all, the Oberheim DX has a tuning facility for each of its six channels, which considerably increases the number of sounds you can produce with the unit. For instance, a deeply pitched crash and tom struck together will do a very good impersonation of a large Chinese gong. The same applies to open hi hats, which when detuned can pass for a second or third cymbal, albeit rather strange. The bass, snare and cymbal channels each contain three variations on the same sound – soft, medium and loud (volume). The remaining channels are: toms high, medium and low; hi hat closed, open and accent; and finally, the last channel is called perc and has two different shakers and claps. This last channel represents one of my biggest grumbles about the DX – who needs two different kinds of shaker for Christ's sake? A cowbell would be

For my money, the DX's bigger brother, the DMX, is the best machine of its kind – a powerful monster.

much more useful.

The DX has a 64K memory and the samples are very good. I couldn't work out whether all the toms had been tuned and committed to memory from the same sample. I would say that with only 64K to muck around with, the three variations are taken from just the one sample, though of course I could be mistaken. The DX uses realtime programming and there's a built-in metronome waiting for you.

Each of the instrument channels has a volume slider, which you can use to fade-in and fade-out certain instruments – this has several advantages when recording and doing live work. I must point out that the DX's tuning ability isn't assigned, or for that matter, assignable to separate instruments within a channel – the pot on the back panel to each channel tunes all the samples contained therein annoying, eh?

Control layout is very good and the design features the same graphics as the rest of the Oberheim range. Internal and external construction is nice and solid, with those inevitable 'real simulated wood' cheek panels. Each group channel has got its own output, which isn't the way it should be, but at least the sounds – except on channel 6 – are in the same tone field, even though getting a decent EQ on a high and low tom through the same input channel on a mixer isn't easy at all – time for the old graphic!

The DX can do any time signature, including swing for which it has a function dedicated button. All program information and editing is done via the ten digit numerical keypad to the right of the front panel. You can keep tabs on what's going on inside by calling up information to be displayed in the LED display.

Like the Drumulator, the DX has the accuracy settings which 'move' beats which are slightly out to the nearest one. The DX has eight programmable accuracy settings which can be individually selected between programming different voices. For example, if you want a bass drum on every beat, then you'd record it using a very low correction setting, making sure it doesn't get 'moved' – however a hi hat pattern using triplets will probably require you to use the highest setting so that it is positioned correctly on top of the previously recorded pattern. The DX has a 'quantize' control which handles this.

The Oberheim DX offers good quality sounds and reasonable versatility in a well constructed box. For me, the toms and the bass were the best samples, though they all deserved an award for crispness. Taking into account that it can sync to its own tape pulse, the DX is a unit which I would highly recommend you try out before spending any cash.

The Hammond DPM 48: Review

You wouldn't think Hammond were the kind of people who make a habit of releasing something aimed at the semi/pro end of the market would you? Well, they have. Only thing is, it's not a semi-pro or pro price tag – just $1,200. The Hammond DPM-48 is a handsome beast with an impressive list of specs to match. It has all the usual features that you find on a digital drum machine, such as LED display, numerical key pad and 'tap' buttons for each instrument – and the layout and design are superb. It claims to have 22 separately recorded drum sounds and with 84K of memory – which is, on average, at least 20K above the rest of the competition – who's arguing?

Without boring you to tears going through the sounds one by one, I'll give you a brief guided tour of this particular department. You've got four differently pitched toms although you can only play two at a time due to the time sharing principle. These sounds seem to suffer from slight quantization noise, but it's nothing that can't be got rid of in the mix. There are three variations of bass drum available, three snares (all good), hi-hat closed, hi-hat open and accent, a very strange clap, two cabasas, rim shot and a couple of agogos (yes – agogos!). As I said, the toms are quite dirty in comparison to the rest of the sounds which are very crisp and 'edgy'. I wouldn't class any of the sounds as unusable – and I think at this price the selection is amazing.

Programming can be done in real time or in a step mode, which is very handy. Editing too is also very easy and quick to do. Having a colour coded display of buttons is extremely helpful when you're getting to know the machine. It has the usual programming form of turning patterns in chains to form songs. You can store up to 48 patterns with 32 events in each one. You can program any time signature you want and there's a button which divides a beat into either a 1/2, 1/3, 1/4, 1/6, 1/8, 1/12, 1/16, 1/24 and 1/32 – demi-semi quaver. You can also determine on what step you wish a measure to end. To make things easier, it has a built-in metronome. You've also got a main tempo knob with fine tune beside it – very good.

The DPM-48 doesn't have cassette dump facilities but you can put all the information stored in the machine onto an ultra reliable RAM-pack. However, this can only store 2K and therefore the DPM-48 will only give you access to three songs at a time, so having a library of RAM-packs is essential, though you need to turn the machine off when changing and this could be a headache on stage.

The Hammond has grouped outputs for voices – eight of them – and at this price, I'm not complaining! It also has the din sync in/out sockets that Roland and Korg have used in the past. There is a 12 pin 'D' type connector as a trigger input – does the MXR have these too? You can also have footswitch control of the run/stop button and also a rhythm break footswitch can be attached to the back panel for 'lengthening' songs – rather like the Drumulator. Each sub group out has its own volume slider and there are also mono, stereo and headphone sockets.

I cannot be certain whether or not the 22 sounds are all definitely separate samples but in any event, the DPM-48 delivers the goods all the way. A larger memory update would be nice to see in the future, for machine and RAM-pack alike! At this sort of price, I have no grumbles and it certainly is great value for money – well done Hammond!

Drumtraks: Review

The Drumtraks is one of the newest MIDI equipped digital machines on the market. It should cost around $1,295 and is being promoted by SCI along with the MIDI Six-Trak polyphonic keyboard. The control layout is very good, and has the same styling as the rest of the Sequential Circuits products, ie the Prophet 5, 10 and 600. The controls are made up of 15 large scale black plastic 'hit' buttons assigned to each of the 13 sounds and two for run/stop and accent respectively. It also has four rotary knobs and seven smaller scale push buttons. In the centre of the front panel you have the numerical key pad and LED display.

The Drumtraks has 13 sounds and in comparison with other units on the market in this price range, it doesn't initially look like value for money. However, the Drumtraks has a programmable tuning facility which will enable the user to program different pitches of the same sample within the same pattern – the toms for instance are tunable over 15 increments (as are the rest of the voices) so you can incorporate a fill in a pattern using just one of the tom buttons that will sound like someone hitting 15 toms in series! This feature is incredibly useful and gives the unit a big advantage over the rest of the competition. The individual volume of each sample is also programmable, which gives you the ability to program echo effects using gradually fading increments in volume as the sample repeatedly appears. There is also an independent accent control for each voice which adds further to the 'feels' which can be created on this machine.

The Drumtraks uses the now very common digital access control system, (DACS) – or at least a form of it. Each drum sound is edited by depressing the instrument button and rotating the required knob – the LED display gives you all the information you need to make the right adjustments. Programmed volume and tuning changes take up space in the memory, so to stop you from running out of space while putting your masterpiece together, the red LED display shows a percentage of what memory you have left. The overall memory capacity is 3289 events. You can program up to 100 measures, in any time signature, and then compose 100 songs using any combination of measures. The Drumtraks has a back up memory system, which uses a battery that they claim has a ten year life.

The sounds are good, with the toms and the claps being very lifelike indeed. If you detune the claps you get what some people call 'gorilla' claps, which are commonly used on disco records. Although there are two tom buttons, there is in fact only one tom sample inside the Drumtraks. This means they both have the same tuning ranges, which is a bit silly really. The toms are the CS head type, Afro sound, which seems to be the most widely used tom sound nowadays. The tambourine is very weak – but then again, it is a very fair representation of the Salvation Army's favourite instrument. I like the Phil Spector tambourine sound – full of guts! The sounds that the Drumtraks can produce are clean and extremely useful – I'd say that they were better on average than the Oberheim DX.

Interfacing the Drumtraks using the MIDI is very easy. One way to speed up the real time programming of the Drumtraks is to link it to a velocity sensitive keyboard such as the Prophet T8 or Roland's new MKB1000. This means that you're able to control the tuning and amplitude of every beat quickly and easily, without having to stop and re-tune instruments in the record mode to get variations. Of course, soon there will be pad controllers for MIDI equipped machines. One of the other silly things on the Drumtraks is that it has grouped outputs, similar to the DX from Oberheim. On the back panel you have just six separate jack outputs for the sounds. Ch. 1 is the bass drum, Ch. 2 = snare and rim shot, Ch. 3 = the two toms, Ch. 4 = crash and ride cymbals, Ch. 5 = open and closed hi hat and finally, Ch. 6 is for tambourine, cabasa, cowbell and aforementioned claps. It can conveniently sync to its own tape click and also has an audio out jack.

The biggest advantage with the Drumtraks is that it will take Linn chips – so you can swap sounds at will. I'm going to buy one!

Yamaha DX 1 FM Keyboard: Review

In case you haven't heard, Syco Systems have thrown away their prestige image and have developed their premises in Conduit Place to such an extent that they practically own one side of it! Nevertheless, they are still stocking the elite of the electronic instrument world and, as such, are now selling the Yamaha DX 1 FM keyboard. I must say, that I was hoping that the DX 1 was going to be as powerful as the Synclavier and be of a fully 'open-ended' design concept, but after just two or three minutes, it was apparent that the DX 1 isn't (and probably won't be) as powerful as the aforementioned yanky job.

The attempted comparison is well founded, as New England Digital – the makers of the Synclavier – are actually manufacturing the FM side of it under licence from Yamaha, and (at the time of writing) are about to launch a new 'resynthesis' package for the Synclavier which will allow the system to listen to and analyse any sound fed into it, and then match all of the sounds' parameters and thus create an FM generated version which has remarkable similarities to the original.

The DX 1 is really just two DX 7's in one box, with a wooden weighted keyboard, and has been primarily designed as a performance-orientated machine. I know that sounds a bit off-the-cuff, but it's technically accurate. Oh, by the way, it costs $10,900.

In my infinite wisdom, I thought I'd best start this review by putting FM into simple terms, as I don't think anybody's actually had

Close-up of the parameter display panel on the DX1.

The Yamaha DX1 – a good-looking keyboard.

the sense to do this. I haven't come across more than a handful of dealers yet who actually *understand* how to program a DX keyboard. If they can't tell you, then it's left to me to explain, isn't it?

First of all, Yamaha have gone for a few oddball ideas when it comes to naming the actual sections that make up an FM keyboard, they've also numbered some of the parameters in a contradictory way.

Here we go then. . .(virtuosos on the 7 & 9 can skip this bit – go on, impress your friends!)

Operators
These are sine wave generators. They are *not* to be thought of as voltage or digitally controlled efforts found on normal synths.

Algorithm
The patterns in which the operators are linked. There are 6 operators on the DX 1 and these can be linked up in 32 different ways. Each of these algorithms is suited for different particular sounds.

Frequency Modulation
Sound-creating on a normal synthesiser usually means first selecting a waveform and then processing it through various sections of the synth – a filter to cut out unwanted harmonics, an envelope shaper to cut up the waveform into the desired pattern (ADSR) – and so on. To cut a long story short, on normal synths, 9 times out of 10, you start with a full, raw waveform and cut chunks out of it until you are happy. This, ultimately, is subtractive.

The world's most hip synth, the Yamaha DX7, relaying MIDI data to the monstrous QX1 sequencer.

Therefore, in direct comparison one could look upon FM synthesis as additive, using operators to modulate each other and so produce completely new, totally different waveforms. This is where the algorithms come in – they offer 32 different ways of making the operators act upon each other, For example, operators 1, 2 & 3 could be set to modulate 4, 5 & 6, culminating in an almighty noise, as the combining of the first three's outputs using different intervals and envelopes is already a complex waveform, and when this is transferred over to the remaining three and used to modulate *their* waveforms an extremely complex sound is produced.

Envelopes
The envelope functions on the DX 1 are totally different from the ADSR types on normal synths. EG rate 1 is the time it takes for the

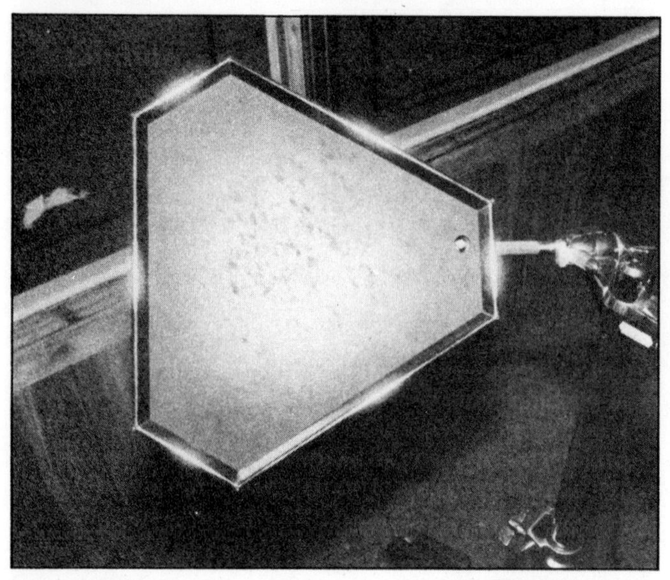

One of the pads to the electronic UP K27D kit. A serious contender for anyone's money.

note to rise in volume from the initial key being depressed. EG level 1 is the volume it climbs to. Similarly, this is how decay, sustain and release are controlled. All good so far, eh? Well, depending on what algorithm you choose, the envelope functions can have enormous impact on the sounds produced. If, for instance, you had operators 1 & 2 modulating 3 & 4 which were then made to modulate 5 & 6 but the attack times for each couple were set differently so that the first two had an attack time that was very fast, the second couple had an attack that was slower and the third couple was set even slower, then the operators would come into effect in stages – the first pair, then the second and finally, the third – BUT, because they were modulating each other, as each pair came into earshot, the sound would change and dive from one sound angle to another, leaving you speechless! So, the envelope functions on FM keyboards have an enormous amount to do with creating sound – much more so than on normal synths.

Just to recap on what I mentioned earlier, the DX 1 has exactly the same voice generating sections and capacity as the DX 7. Its forte is in the fact that it can layer sounds in a 'performance memory' mode which will remember your selections and, of course, that it has a wooden weighted keyboard.

Design and constructionwise, the DX 1, in my opinion, is simply the best looking and most impressive keyboard on the market. It's hand-made by the Japs, and they've made a brilliant job of it. The DX 1 has the usual envelope and algorithm diagrams on the front panel, but the greatest advantage is that along with the illuminated LCD readout, red LEDs in smart windows have been provided to give you 'up to the second' information on the actual algorithm being used – this is an enormous advantage, as practically all the vital information is immediately available. As you've probably gathered, FM isn't as straightforward as some dealers would have you believe: 'Oh it's so straightforward, we didn't think it was worth going through the manual and setting up our own sounds. . .' is a comment I heard from one dealer when confronted by an eager punter wanting to know why wherever he went, all he ever heard were factory presets on the DX's. Dealers like that should be hung, drawn and quartered for lying – Yamaha have gone to great lengths to 'educate' their dealers in the delights of FM, so if you come across a rogue shop assistant, don't take no for an answer, there should be no excuse.

Still, getting back to the design, I was pretty convinced that although the front panel information was very useful, it was there for the sake of it. Let me explain – the new Yamaha equipment is all MIDI and, as such, is interfaceable with computers, namely, the Yamaha CX 5 (though no doubt computer interfaces for many, many models are on their way), therefore, all relevant information stored in a DX keyboard can be displayed in glowing colour on any handy TV set. I know some of you are questioning this logic, but I assure you that computers and colour televisions are no longer untransportable boxes full of red-hot valves and are completely roadworthy in this day and age. After all, Tangerine Dream have been doing it for years!

The performance memory is undoubtedly the best selling point, with the capacity to remember a large number of combinations of any two presets, the balance between them, the definable split point on the keyboard (if used) – in fact all the vital information. The DX 1 can take two ROM packs at a time, which are the same as the ones used on the DX 7. You can combine, or layer two presets from the same ROM cartridge or have one from each. You can program how the breath controller

The Mirage's control layout is devilishly simple. To the left of the keyboard is one of the Ensoniq formatted disks which have proved difficult to obtain.

The popular Ensoniq Mirage offers three times as many features as the E-mu 1 at a third of the latter's original RRP.

affects the sounds. You can have it so that on a brass/orchestra setting, the orchestra comes in when you do a bit of judicial puffing! The DX 1 can also have its programmable modulation modes *simultaneously* controlled from the wheel and from a rocker foot pedal inserted on the back panel.

As DX 7 owners should have discovered, touch sensitivity properly assigned to presets can make all the difference, and the DX 1's touch sensitivity is multi-assignable, doing everything from making sounds louder when pressure is increased, to bringing in a second preset. It's interesting to see that when two sounds are layered together, no compromise is struck in the generating of them, you always have the full, original number of operators being controlled by the same algorithm, unlike the analogue synths that usually trade in polyphony and/or the number of oscillators available when layering of sounds is selected. This is where FM *wins*!

The Sounds

The sounds on the DX 1 at Syco were the best sounds that I've heard from an FM keyboard, rich in character and frighteningly realistic, with some making me wonder whether Yamaha have encoded digital samples onto the ROM packs – they were *that* convincing! The stringed instruments were particularly good, with amazing cello quartets and ensembles. Using the breath controller, a great deal of expression could be injected into sounds – especially brass solos.

There was a good jungle preset, complete with a touch sensitive roaring lion and screeching monkeys – very eerie! All the usual metallic blocks and bowed saws were there, in fact, they took up most of the memory. Phil Nicholas whizzed through most of the cartridges, jumping from trombones to Fender Rhodes pianos with split second timing. One preset was meant to be a Hammond organ going through a Lesley cabinet that was distorting! It just sounded like a muggy casio to me, but to organ freaks everywhere it might bring reminiscent tears to their eyes! A demonstration of the performance memory, detailing how easy it was to skip from combination to combination, was brought about when Phil called up a setting that had a great sounding violin on the left of the keyboard and a rather 'over-bowed' scratchy effort on the upper. 'Take the left as being the teacher and the right as the young beginner. . .' I stood bemused as he played a little ditty, the upper keyboard had been tuned out so as to emulate the efforts of a student protegé. 'Two weeks later. . .' (and a change of preset) the student had become better, more in tune and the bowing action much improved (*what am I talking about?*) Anyhow, it was an interesting concept and put the message across, albeit very strangely!

Getting back to sounds (and this is the nitty gritty of this review) FM synthesis isn't an end in itself. FM keyboards, because of the very way they are programmed, will never have their full potential realised by their owners. I know many DX owners and all they've ever really come up with are Casio type weedy poly noises and a few excellent percussion sounds. As an engineer friend of mine once said, when commenting on the uses to which the bands he works with put the DX 7 & 9s: 'They just hit them now and again, the closest they get to really *playing* them is in conjunction with an analogue keyboard via MIDI. . . they don't go 'waaazzzz''

I'm afraid this is all very true. Many professionals who I've seen using a DX (other than for pose value) have got pathetic sounds from them, a genuine case of being used (and originally purchased, no doubt) because they *are* FM keyboards, or *are* digital!

FM keyboards are capable of producing amazing sounds that no conventional analogue synth could ever create. But FM won't sound mellow or washy, or as some term it – 'warm'. It's true that the FM keyboards are capable of producing clean and precise percussive effects, but, that perhaps is the root of the trouble – the fact that all FM sounds *are* clean and *are* precise, indeed 'clinical' is the best word to use. Music played entirely on FM keyboards *is* clinical, too sharp in timbre, too hard in transience.

The new E-mu Systems SP12 sampling drum machine. An amazingly powerful unit which is certain to become an industry standard.

Counterpoint is the main ingredient of any interesting sound (or composition). Only FM mixed with analogue can achieve this. In music, 'light & shade' is the ultimate aim.

And Finally, As The Sun Sets. . .

So where does the Yamaha DX 1 fit in? What niche are they trying to fill? Looked upon rationally, I can only see the DX 1 being the sort of keyboard that is bought by musicians who are *told* by their accountants to buy it – they just *have* to spend the money, or see the tax man have it.

Personally, I'd rather have two DX 7s, MIDI'd together; a computer such as the Yamaha CX 5 (which includes a DX 9 voice card and event generator), a portable colour TV for display of aforementioned information and a touch sensitive, wooden weighted, external MIDI keyboard controller – all of this still only comes to $4,800 and, subtracted from the asking price of the DX 1, still leaves you enough money to buy a van to put it all in!

I suppose, though, that there are die-hards among you who will no doubt cast an admiring eye over those wooden piano keys and say, 'Ah, but it's a *professional's* keyboard. . .' But who the hell are they talking about? Surely today's professionals were never *all* born and bred pushing wooden keys down. People like Depeche Mode, Ultravox, and Vince Clark have all begun and continued to play in a sea of sprung loaded plastic keyboards. The days when a piano was the best piece of furniture in the average working class parlour are well and truly gone. A lot of today's professionals started on plastic and therefore, on the whole, are happy to stick with plastic, or at the very least, tend to use both mediums together. Because it's wood – it ain't always good!

The DX 1's future looks promising, as it will have enormous chic appeal for many months to come – that is, until something else comes along to steal the limelight and the tax deductable revenues!

SECTION SIX

Profiles and Reviews

Compact Multitrackers

Fostex 250 Compact Multitracker: Review
Price: $995

The similarities between the Fostex 250 and the Tascam 244 are exceptional: they extend not only to facilities, construction quality and control layout, but also to sound quality.

It is possible to record on all four tracks simultaneously and the pitch control stretches to +/− 10%. According to the literature, the EQ section has a shelved bass response with +/− 12dB at 100Hz but, strangely, the machine fascia indicates 300Hz. After only an hour or two of use, I cannot say which it is; in order to be sure, I'll have to stick a clear tone down one of the input channels and reference the EQ band against an oscillator. The treble is a peaking-type response with +/− 12dB at 4kHz.

The master left and right fader is ganged, which is limiting. Each of the four input channels has an auxiliary circuit. Standard jack (all-level) sockets are fitted to each input channel, and all main tape inputs and outputs are phono. Fostex have included a useful bi-feed two-output headphone circuit. The transport is very smooth and the return-to-zero feature would be welcome on any multi-track. The mixer is configured in a peculiar way – the Fostex way! It is very similar to the 350 mixer – not surprising, as the 250 mixer section was the prototype for the 350. But, all in all, the control layout is easy to get on with and the illuminated VUs a pleasure to work with.

Dolby C noise reduction was brand new on the scene when Fostex adopted it for the 250. As I've already said, there's really nothing in it when it comes to choosing between the Tascam 244 and this machine. You can do clean, punchy, almost noise-free demos. Because of the four-channel facilities, it's possible to do the maximum ten-track-bounce on the 250, and this results in the same sort of noise level as on the 244 – annoying, but passable if you record *everything* at optimum level.

I like the 250 as much as the 244 – which is quite a lot. Look at the 250, look at its price, listen to it and, who knows, you might end up buying it!

Specifications
Mike/Line Input (× 4)
Mike impedance 10kohms or less
Input impedance 50kohms
Nominal input level Mike: -60dBV (1mV)
Line: -10dBV (0.3V)
4 Chan Rec In (× 4)
Input impedance 20kohms
Nominal input level -10dBV (0.3V)
Aux In (× 2)
Input impedance 20kohms
Nominal input level -10dBV (0.3V)
Aux Send/Monmix out
Output load impedance 10kohms or more
Nominal output level -10dBV (0.3V)
Direct Out (× 4)
Output load impedance 10kohms or more
Nominal output level -10dBV (0.3V)
Tape Cue Out (× 4)
Output load impedance 10kohms or more
Nominal output level -10dBV (0.3V)
Headphone Output (stereo)
Load impedance 8ohms or more (4ohms minimum)
Maximum output 100mW at 8ohms
Equalizer
4kHz Variable ± 12dB, peaking
100Hz Variable ±12dB, shelving
Recording Tape Standard cassette, C-60 or C-90, high bias type (TDK SA, MAXELL XL-II or equivalent)
Record Tracks 4 track simultaneous, one direction (Special format)
Record Channels 4 simultaneous, with Dolby** NR Type C in encode mode throughout (encode/decode switchable)
Reproduce Channels 4 simultaneous, with Dolby** NR Type C in decode mode throughout (encode/decode switchable)
Tape Speed 3¼ips (9.5cm/s) ± 1%
Pitch Control ±10%
Recording Time 22 min. for C-90, 15 min. for C-60
Heads 4 track record/reproduce (Permalloy) 4 track erase (ferrite)
Motors One FG servo-controlled DC capstan motor and one DC reel motor.
Fast Wind Time 80 seconds typ. for C-60
Frequency Response
Mixer section 20Hz-20kHz ±1dB
Recorder section 20Hz-18kHz (40Hz-14kHz +2dB, -3dB at 0 VU)
THD
Mixer section Better than 0.05% at 1kHz nominal level
Recorder section 1.5% at 315Hz, 0 VU level (overall)
Signal-To-Noise Ratio
Mixer section Overall 75dB wtd.
Recorder section 71dB wtd.
Crosstalk
Mixer section 65dB at 1kHz
Recorder section 45dB at 1kHz
Erasure 70dB at 1kHz
Power requirements 120V AC, 60Hz, 35W*
Dimensions 3⅛ H × 17″ W × 14″ D 80mm H × 430mm W × 355mm D
Weight Net 19lbs (8.5Kg)

Fostex X-15 Compact Multitracker: Review
Price: $495

With the launch of the new A-80, 450 mixer and A-20, in the summer of 1985, the Fostex Corporation of Japan is the only manufacturer that can rightfully be credited for overturning accepted traditions, in the semi-pro audio industry – no other has even come close.

The 'baba multitrackah', as it is affec-

PROFILES AND REVIEWS

tionately known to mixer-madmen around the world, was the first of its kind – a *portable* compact multitracker. Running at standard cassette speed of 1⅞ips, with Dolby B noise reduction (non-switchable) *and* capable of running off batteries, it really created a new category overnight. Someone had obviously realized that small, portable, self-accompanying keyboards would one day need a multitrack facility!

As usual, you are able to record only two tracks at a time, mixing to final master being done via a gain and pan pot for each tape channel. EQ is a simple shelved type bass and treble arrangement which is ganged across the stereo output for final trimming and sweetening. It has to be said that this is not as flexible as the Porta One from Tascam, but I found that as each overdub was EQd before recording and then EQd again on mixdown – albeit over a mix – the tonal control available was much the same on both machines. Having only two input channels rules out bouncing tracks to produce more than 7 separate takes. There is no auxiliary circuit on this machine, and all in-line FX devices have to be types with a direct FX balance pot and output. The only alternative is to record the track and take its direct output either into a mixer that has an auxiliary circuit, or straight into an FX de-

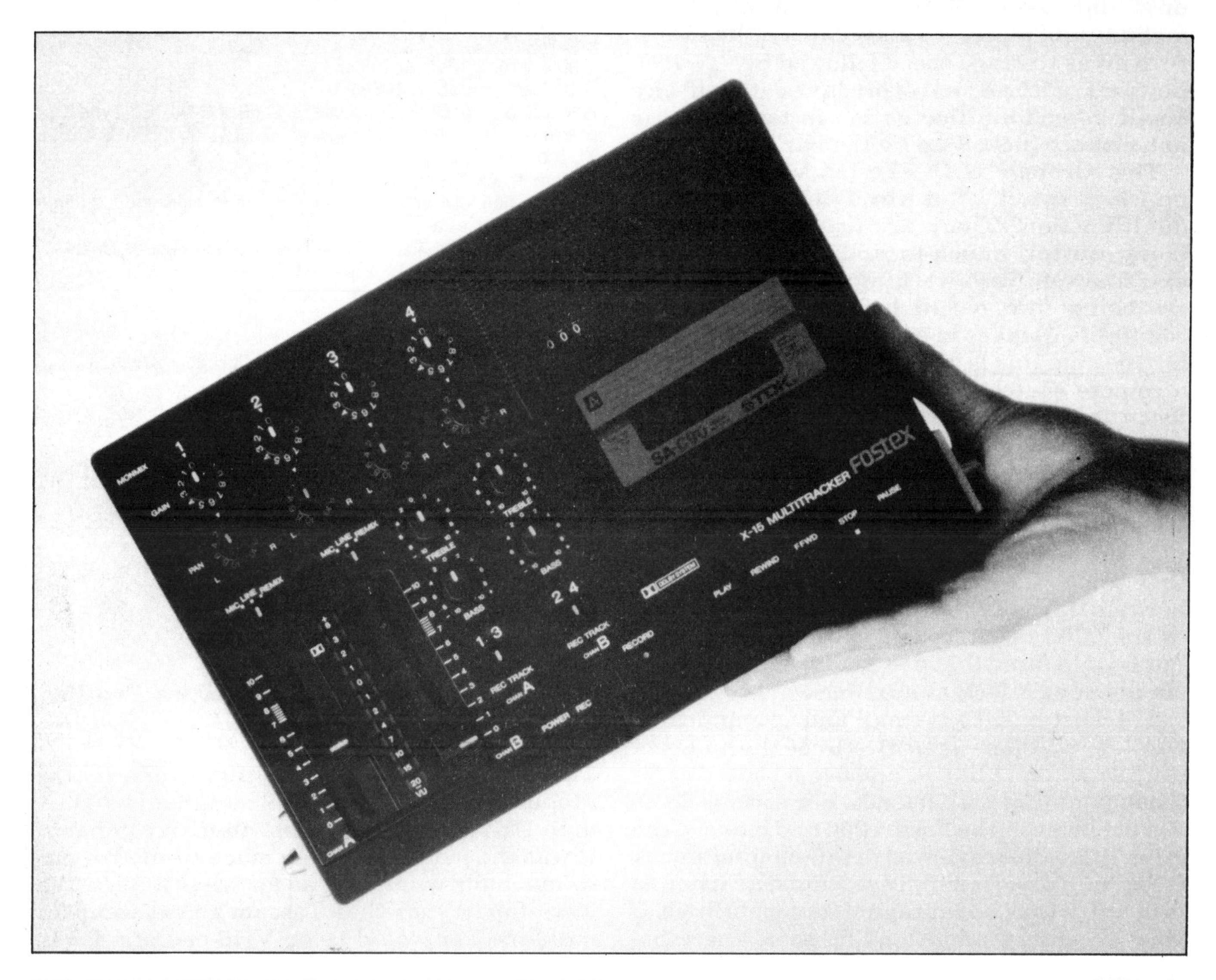

vice, and then return it into a spare input channel. Basically, if you want to achieve solid and reliably flexible processing on your demos, buying the X-15 may turn out to be a false economy owing to the need for an external mixer.

Having normal tape speed and only Dolby B, the poor old X-15 is a peg or two down in the quality stakes. However, if you record things properly – at optimum levels – the quality from the X-15 can be as good as from the Porta One.

Overall design is pretty impressive and construction appears to be extremely well-tooled. The old wow and flutter on my friend's unit did seem alarming on a couple of meandering pieces we played (even the literature gives the tape speed followed by +/−1%); however, with normal everyday beat stuff, any small-to-medium fluctuation in tape speed is not usually picked up by the ear.

The 'Orange' is the Fostex version of the punch-in switch – but why didn't they make it dual-function? There are *two* sockets for remote control, punch-in and punch-*out!* It is extremely difficult working transport buttons, switching into record before overdubbing a couple of mistakes in a track; your hands must be free, and this is what gave rise to the idea of a remote switch that can be operated by the foot – or whatever! Because you cannot use two remotes simultaneously on the X-15, you have to drop yourself into a track and play your way out of it. If there are no gaps or rests, you simply do not have time to hit the stop switch!

X-15s can be picked up for under £250; at this price, they are undeniably an all-time bargain. If you're considering something nearer the £300 mark, consider what I have said, but bear in mind that a mixer may be needed to supplement a lack of auxiliaries.

The Fostex X-15 is small and economical to run – the Volkswagen Beetle of the compact multitrackers! I like it, and use it occasionally when jamming with friends. For serious demo work, however, the Fostex 250 and many of the other machines reviewed in this chapter knock it for six. To use it simply as a musical notepad is to fail to take advantage of its capabilities. If your recording ambitions fit somewhere between the two, the Fostex X-15 must be treated as a serious contender for your money.

Specifications
Mike Input (×2)
Mike impedance 10kΩ or less
Mike input level -50dBV (3mV)
Line Input (×2)
Line input impedance 20kΩ
Line input level -20dBV (0.1V)
Line Output (Stereo)
Output load impedance 10kΩ or more (5kΩ min)
Output level -20dBV (0.1V)
Tape Output (×4)
Output load impedance 10kΩ or more (5kΩ min)
Output level -10dBV (0.3V)
Headphone Output (Stereo)
Output load impedance 8Ω–40Ω
Max. output level 100mW
Equalizer (×2)
Treble Vari. ±12dB at 10kHz
Bass Vari. ±12dB at 100Hz
Recording Tape Compact cassette, C-60 or C-90, IEC Type II for use at high bias position (CrO_2) and 70µs EQ. (TDK SA, MAXELL XL-II or equivalent)
Record Track 4 track, one direction
Record Channel 4 with Dolby NR type B in encode mode, records up to 2 tracks at a time
Playback Channel 4 with Dolby NR type B in decode mode
Tape Speed 4.8cm/s (1⅞ ips) ±1%
Pitch Control ±15% of normal tape speed
Recording Time 30 min. for C-60
Wow and Flutter ±0.1% peak, weighted IEC/ANSI
Frequency Response 40Hz-12.5kHz ±3dB at −10VU
T.H.D. 1.5% at 1kHz, 0VU
S/N 60dB weighted, 50dB unweighted
Crosstalk 40dB at 1kHz
Erasure 70dB at 1kHz
Power Requirements 11-15V, DC 350mA max.
Dimensions 75 × 290 × 195mm (3 × 11½ × 7¾ in)
w/Battery pack 75 × 290 × 230mm (3 × 11½ × 9 in)
Weight 2.1kg (4.6lbs)
w/Battery pack 2.9kg (6.4lbs)

Tascam 388 8-T Recorder/Mixer: Profile
Price: $3,995

The 388 was one of the highlights of a recent product launch given in Birmingham by Harman UK, Tascam's UK distribution company. It was the most surprising machine of all – not so much for what it is, as for what it isn't. We were fairly sure that Tascam's next compact multitracker would be on VHS or Beta. I was absolutely stunned when I realized that it shared the same format as the hugely popular Fostex A-8, having eight tracks on quarter inch tape.

This machine is exceptionally well-tooled. The pre-production sample has very attractive colour-coding and a handsome transparent door which hooks on to lugs, allowing it to be shut over the transport recess where the 7″ spools drag along at a modest 7½ips. The noise reduction system used is dbx; the S/N ratio stated in the preliminary literature is 90dB – if it *is* 90dB, I take my hat off to them. But I suspect that this machine's performance can, at the very outside, be only slightly better than that of the A-8. In fact, it's arguable whether this machine can even get within 5dB of the dodgy S/N ratio figure of the A-8, which goes at 15ips.

The mixer section boasts an 8:8:2 format, with eight input channels which can be routed to any one or all eight PGM output buses. There are two FX return systems and a comprehensive monitor section. Each input channel offers either balanced XLR or ¼″ line inputs, 'access' send and return feed-off circuit, and quite a powerful three-band parametric EQ section.

The 388 incorporates many 'professional' features, including a realtime minute and second counter, SMPTE compatibility – which it is hoped, will make the machine popular with A/V companies – and a special, if a trifle untoward, tape-load facility designed to prevent accidental tape run-off from the feed spool. This has the disadvantage of cutting the machine's transport into 'stop' when you get within two or three minutes of the end of the tape. All right on the drawing board, but disastrous if you're nearing the end of a masterpiece and it cuts out in the middle of a mind-blowing, unrepeatable guitar solo!

Other features include compatibility with the rather extensive AQ65 Autolocater, which was originally designed for use with the new MS16 16-T machine; also, much more in line with tradition, a facility that allows the 388 to accept the simpler and easier-to-handle RC71 remote and the all-essential RC30P punch-in/out remote switch.

The 388 is not only burdened by a fundamentally low performance tape system but also weighed down by a suggested retail price of around $4,000! My comment is that hybrid machines should have hybrid price tags, *not* professional ones.

I don't want to condemn it out of hand before I've had the chance to use it; there is undoubtedly a market for compact multitrackers that can sync with video and offer reasonably good recording quality. But this market, although quite rich, is not big. *Marketing* is the bottom line here; unless the world distributors recognize, develop and cultivate the new market which has only just emerged, they may as well not bother to import even one 388. There have been rumours that it is to be targeted at the upper end of the domestic recording semi/pro musician market – if so, I wish the distributors luck! No musician, un-

PROFILES AND REVIEWS

less his space is severely restricted at home, is likely to choose a 388 in preference to, say, a Tascam ½″ 8-T small mixer and noise reduction system; if he shops around carefully, this will actually work out feature-for-feature *cheaper* than the 388. And how many musicians *at home* need SMPTE anyway?

For the 388 to be successful in hitting the semi/pro higher end of the domestic musician market, its price *has* to be lower than that of a modest 8-T & mixer package. But it *does* have SMPTE and the main market is out there waiting for it. It is a facility which should immediately appeal to companies requiring in-house, no-fuss multitracking that can be linked to video. Just as we were going to press, I heard that Tascam were increasing the 388's tape speed to 15ips, putting it in line with the Fostex A80. This will improve sound quality, but it doesn't change any of my main criticisms.

Preliminary Specifications:
19 cm/sec tape speed
3 motor, 2 head
Wow & Flutter: 0.05% WRMS
Overall Frequency Response: 35 Hz-15 kHz, + 3dB, -10 Vu
S/N Ratio: 90 dB w/dbx
THD: less than 1%
Dimensions (W × H × D): 837 × 219 × 641 mm
Weight: 38 kg

Tascam 234 Syncaset: Profile
Price: $949

I know very little about this machine and have had only two opportunities to audition it. Basically, it stands as a front-loading,

stripped-down version of the 244.

Running at 3¾ips, with dbx, the 234 is said to be capable of an s/n ratio of 95dB – a figure that, from experience, I'm inclined to dispute. Noise levels are, however, very low, and on the majority of recordings I made, noise was not audible. I'd put the figure closer to 70dB-80dB; even so, that's still very acceptable indeed.

The mixer section is not particularly comprehensive, offering no side-chain access for FX or, for that matter, any EQ. Cleverly, Tascam have seen fit to include a headphones amplifier – something they should have had in the 244, as most HiFi headphones are too high in impedance terms to get anything near a suitable level from the 244.

In short, the 234 Syncaset offers basic 4-T facilities, capable of the ten-track-bounce. Rack-mountable and very stylish, the 234 surely merits serious consideration if you are intent on using a separate mixing desk – and if you agree with the price.

234 Specifications
Track format: 4-track, 4-channel
Tape Speed: 9.5 cm/sec
Wow & Flutter: ± 0.06% peak, weighted
Frequency Response: 40-14,000 Hz ± 3dB (0 VU)
S/N Ratio: 95dB (dbx IN, weighted)
Dimensions (W × H × D): 482 × 147 × 357 mm
Weight: 9.8 kg

Audio Technica AT-RMX64 Compact Multitracker: Profile
Price: $1,595

Audio Technica are renowned for their good quality, value-for-money microphones. It was

PROFILES AND REVIEWS

a complete surprise to me – and to many others – that they should launch into the 4-T compact multitracker market. The AT-RMX64 sells at a price that means it must be looked upon as a *serious* investment by any home recordist. As in the case of the Tascam 246, the high price reflects the production cost of the expanded – in compact multitracker terms – mixer section, which boasts six inputs instead of the usual four.

Each input channel has two-band sweepable EQ, two auxiliary sends, mike/line selection and trim, together with a rather clever solo facility, which one rarely sees on budget mixers in any format.

The AT-RMX64 is a good-looker and built to very high standards. It has switchable speeds of 1⅞ and 3¾ips. Why not a 4-T compact multitracker that goes at 7½ips? The technology is there. Cassette shells are known to be capable of 7½ips and more – 80% of all commercially-available, pre-recorded material is copied at somewhere in the region of 10 times normal cassette speed!

Sound quality looks quite promising, with a maximum s/n ratio of 68dB with Dolby C. Frequency response is 20Hz-18kHz, which is very good.

Sadly, I feel the extra money being asked for what is only a 4-T compact multitracker is for a choice of facilities that is out of touch with home recordists' needs. Why not a standard motor speed of 7½ips instead of dual speed switching? Why not *one* NR system instead of two? To charge a thousand pounds for what is potentially the same quality as a Fostex 250 is ridiculous – even if you *have* got two more input channels and expanded facilities.

Approaching a 'complete' multitracker, the AT-RMX64 is not a high-quality, value-for-money, professional one. As it stands, it looks good – but it could be so much better.

Mixer Specification

Mike Input Sensitivity (balanced) Max: +4 dBm (Pad -20 dB, Trim -40 dB)

PROFILES AND REVIEWS

Min: -55 dBm (Pad 0 dB, Trim 0 dB)
Mike Input Impedance 4,000 Ohms
Line Input Sensitivity (unbalanced) Max: +2 dBm (Pad -20 dB, Trim -40 dB)
Min: -54 dBm (Pad 0 dB, Trim 0 dB)
Line Input Impedance 33,000 Ohms
Aux Input Sensitivity +4 dBm
Aux input impedance 100,000 Ohms
Return Input Sensitivity +4 dBm (Return gain at max)
Send Output (send gain at max) +3.2 dBm (Post EQ/Fader) +4.6 dBm (Pre EQ/Fader)
Sub Output +2 dBm (Ch 1 & 2, Pan Center) +4 dBm (Ch 3 & 4, Pan Center)
Solo Output +4.6 dBm (Ch Solo) +2 dBm (Ch 1 & 2) +4 dBm (Ch 3 & 4)
Maximum Output +18 dBm
Headphone Output 1.2 Watts at 8 Ohms, 1 kHz (@ 0 VU with headphone gain at max)
Hum and Noise -122 dB equivalent input noise (Trim 0 dB, Pad 0 dB)
Total Harmonic Distortion Less than 0.05% (20 to 20,000 Hz)
Frequency Response 20 to 20,000 Hz ± 1.5 dB
Equalization Frequency Range 60 to 1,500 Hz (Low) 600 to 10,000 Hz (High)
Equalization Gain/Loss Range ± 15 dB

Recorder Specification
Tape Output Level +4 dBm
Tape Output Impedance 100 Ohms
Frequency Response (rec/play) 20 to 18,000 Hz (± 3 dB from 40 to 15,000 Hz)
Bias Frequency 85 kHz
Signal to Noise Ratio Dolby NR Off Dolby B On Dolby C On 55 dB 64 dB 68 dB
Total Harmonic Distortion Less than 1.5% at 0 VU/1 kHz
Channel Separation Better than 60 dB at 1 kHz
Peak Level Indicator +8dBm (+4 VU)
Tape Type Compact Cassette High Bias 70 μs EQ Type II
Tape Speed 1⅞ ips (4.75cm/sec) and 3¾ips (9.5cm/sec)
Track Format 4-track compatible with stereo 2-track
Pitch Control ±15%
Wow & Flutter 0.04% RMS (JIS-A)
Fast Wind/Rewind Time 80 seconds for C-60
Tape Counter 4 Digit LED
Motors 3 DC motors, direct drive servo-controlled capstan

General Specification
Dimensions 23.3″ wide, 20.4″ deep, 5.4″ high
Weight 48.5lbs
Power Requirements 120VAC, 60 Hz, 65 Watts

PROFILES AND REVIEWS

The Teczon Dub Multi 4×4 Compact Multitracker: Profile
Price: $695

I haven't, as yet, had the chance to audition this machine, but, on the face of it, it looks like a basic 1⅞ips compact multitracker with a pretty simple 4-channel mixer section. The EQ is shelved and there is no auxiliary circuit. Faders appear only for the master section, and all input channels have an input and output pot.

Teczon have incorporated a rec/punch-in switch on each channel, which is more than a little unconventional, but it does seem to be quite a logical arrangement.

I shall wait with baited breath to see what price the shops actually *do* charge for this little machine. Sound quality – it has an NR system – should be about the same as with the Tascam Porta One or Fostex X-15.

For this unit to do well in an already crowded market, the Teczon and any other subsequent 4-channel, 1⅞ips compact multitracker will have to break the $300 barrier.

Deck Specifications
Track format
4-channel and 4-track mixer and cassette tape recorder
Tape head configuration
Record/play tape head – 4 channel permalloy core × 1
Erase head – 4 channel ferrite core × 1
Tape formulation C-46, C-60, C-90
Motor Frequency Generated (FG type) servo DC motor × 1
Tape speed 4.8cm/sec ± 1%
Pitch control ±15%
Wow & Flutter 0.08% WRMS
Superior built in noise reduction system
Frequency response 40Hz – 12.5 KHz ±3dB (at -10VU)
Signal to noise ratio 60 dB (3% TDH level)
Total harmonic distortion 1.5% (1KHz 0VU)
Cross talk 45 dB (1KHz 0VU)
Erasure 70 dB (1KHz)
Noise reduction switch Push On

Track monitor switch Push on

Mixer Section
Mike Input -50 dBV (3 mV)/10Kohm × 4
Line Input -20 dBV (0.1V)/10Kohm × 4
Line output -10 dBV (0.3V)/1Kohm × 4
Headphone output
R. 100mW + L. 100mW/8 Ohm
EQ control high 10KHz ± 12dB × 4
EQ control low 100Hz ± 12dB × 4
Power supply
11V - 15V DC, 600 mA Max - Battery: SUM-2 × 10
Dimensions 350(W) × 103(H) × 250(D)mm
Weight 2.5 kg (battery with 3.3 kg)

The Tascam 244 Compact Multitracker: Review
Price: $895

This is the world's most famous and most popular portastudio. The 244 was developed and marketed soon after the 144 had got a firm grip on the international market.

In terms of sound quality, the 244 is little different from the Fostex 250 – you can make extremely good demos with this machine and attain all the treble and fidelity you could ever wish for.

The 244 uses a dbx noise-reduction system and you can certainly hear the difference when you compare it with a 144.

Each input channel, of which there are four, sports two-band parametric EQ and, interestingly, a channel on/off switch which allows unwanted signal noise from unused equipment plugged into the portastudio to be kept to an absolute minimum. A punch-in remote, the RC30P, is available; I strongly suggest you purchase one with the machine – you'll probably get it free or at any rate for a couple of quid less than if you bought it separately.

The 244 offers two headphone outputs on the front, though several users I know complain

frequently about the impedance of these outputs – they're too low in volume for your average HiFi cans. You can record on all four tracks simultaneously with the 244 which makes it suitable for recording live gigs. It has a reasonably simple auxiliary circuit for each input channel. The tape counter is a handy, large-scale, fluorescent type, and there is a return-to-zero facility – a godsend for home recordists who don't relish paying for a 'tape-op' just to push rewind and play/record switches!

The 244 is extremely well-tooled. It has three motors, one of which is dedicated entirely to moving the head assembly in and out of cassettes, thus ensuring that correct head alignment lasts as long as possible. The 244 also has four independent tape output jacks – essential if you wish to mix your demos with an external, perhaps more professional, mixer.

If everything is taken into consideration, the 244 is a bargain at its occasional knock-down offer price of around $550. However, as the norm is nearer the $600 mark, do consider buying the 244's smaller brother, the Porta One, and perhaps spending the difference on some FX. Sound quality apart, there are few things on the 244 that warrant the extra $300. You simply have to decide what quality your demos *need* to be.

Tascam 246 Compact Multitracker: Profile
Price: $1,395

As we all know design philosophy in the home recording market is quite baffling. Who would have expected Tascam to release a top-of-the-range, four-track compact multitracker and, at the same time, a $3,995 8-T portastudio?

The 246 is a de-luxe version of the 244. Instead of the customary four input channels, Tascam have seen fit to include six – still only just enough, though, for your average hot-rodded, effected and EQd drum machine.

Perhaps the most disappointing feature of

the 246 is its maximum tape speed of 3¾ips. True, it is switchable, but *down* instead of up! Surely they must realize that if they were to design a transport that would allow you to record at 7½ips on cassette, the quality attainable would seriously affect the multitrack market. Whoops – have I just stumbled on the reason they haven't done so? Well, I dare say Japanese business men like Rolls Royces as much as the rest of us!

Snipes and wheezes apart, the 246 offers a tight little mixer section, with multi-parametric EQ, mike/line trim pot, two effects circuits, stereo mixing buses and headphone monitoring.

The dbx is switchable and there is a digital tape counter. There are also full logic controls and a +/– 12% pitch control.

I don't want to get myself into too much hot water by discussing prices but, in my opinion, the 246 is only just about value for money when you consider that its sound quality is not much better than you can get on a 244.

Faster tape speeds mean better quality – on a four-track cassette with dbx, it would be near perfect. It's what the Cutec Octette is offering. The 246 is here. The MR808 *should be*. The prices are not going to be too dissimilar. With the Octette, you'll need a mixer – but, even so, you'll be into the 8-T bracket for around $100 more than you'd pay for the 246.

Well-built, bound to be reliable, from the stable that started compact multitracking. If you think the sound quality of the 244 is worthy of the extended features in the mixer section of the 246, then I can only recommend that you audition it and, if you are happy, buy it.

PROFILES AND REVIEWS

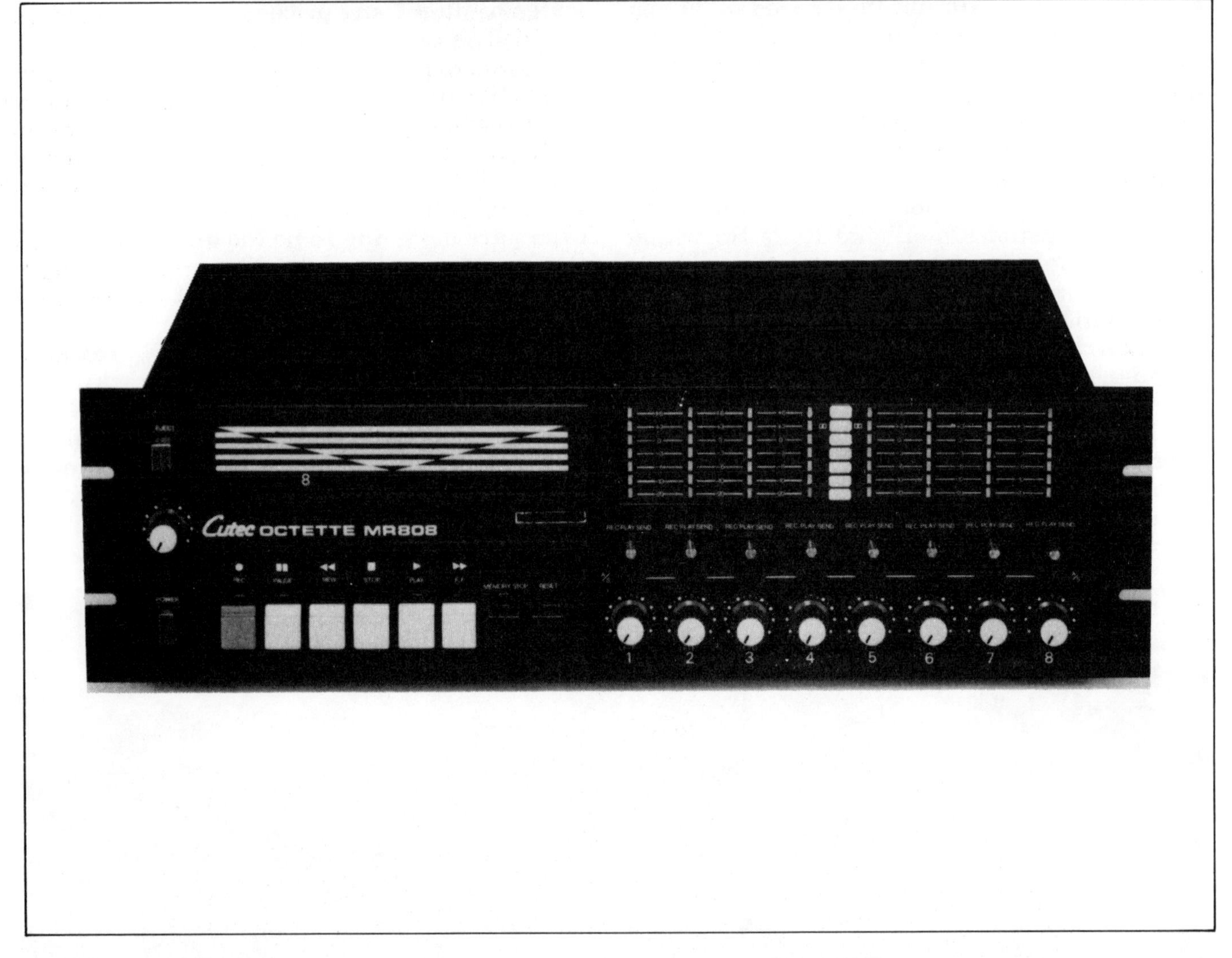

Cutec Octette MR808 8-T recorder: Profile
Price: $1,495

The Cutec Octette has been shrouded in mystery since its announcement over a year ago. I understand that the electronics have now been finalized and that, technically, all bugs have been ironed out of the system. So why is it that we're still in a pre-launch situation? The noise-reduction system, originally Dolby, is now dbx; although I approve of the switch, I have not yet fathomed the reason for it. The main problem, however, is that Cutec's *legal* obligations to the owners of the Betamax cassette patent still haven't been ratified.

This photograph is of a pre-production mock-up, designed to show retailers and punters around the world exactly what the final product will look like.

I was deeply disappointed when, in May 1985, Tascam unveiled their much-anticipated 8-T compact Multitracker. I was expecting it to be on VHS; it wasn't (see Profile) and this gave me plenty of food for thought. If Tascam can't get to grips with the legalities so that they can market an audio product using a video cassette format, *who can?*

It's obvious to me that the patent-holders must get together with the companies willing to develop the two popular video cassette formats for primarily audio purposes. Perhaps

if Cutec could design an extra circuit for the Octette, one that would necessitate the use of pre-formatted cassettes, they might be able to swing the deal their way by surrendering the sales and distribution of the formatted cassettes to the patent-holder – thus allowing them a cut of the *long-term* potential profits.

The Tascam 144 Compact Multitracker: Profile
Price: $495 (second hand)

This marvel is the grandpappy of all portastudios!

In terms of straight sound quality, the 144 is comparable to both the Fostex X-15 and the Porta One; this is largely owing to the fact that, although the 144 goes at the portastudio standard tape speed of 3¾ips, it unexpectedly sports Dolby B noise reduction.

You can record only two tracks at a time on this machine and I've repeatedly found that, if you use anything other than a TDK SA cassette, the treble and fidelity suffer.

The 144 can be a good buy second-hand – *if* you get it for under $500.

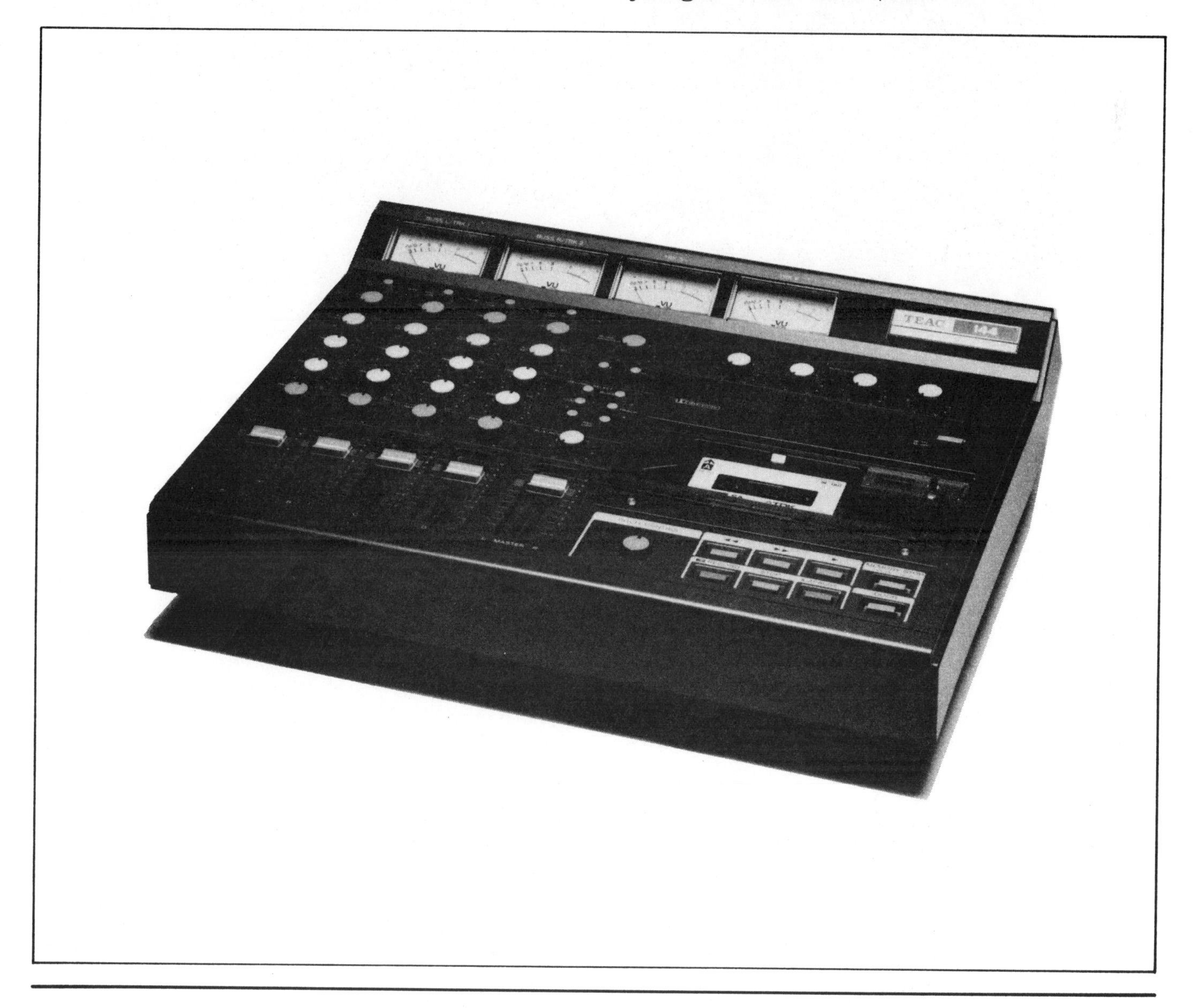

PROFILES AND REVIEWS

The Cutec MR404 Compact Multitracker: Profile
Price: $695

The MR404 has been designed by Cutec to replace the MR402d, their first foray into the compact multitracker market. Neither of these machines is as good to look at as the Tascam Porta One or the Fostex X-15; the sound quality, however, is better owing to the 3¾ ips tape speed. But is it sonically better than the 250 and 244, both of which have the same standard portastudio speed?

First impressions of the MR402d were extremely favourable but, on the whole, performance was slightly down compared with that of the 250 and 244. In track-bouncing situations, however, the MR402d was much better, the build up of tape noise not being so great.

So, it's swings and roundabouts! The difference in first-generation sound quality was not so apparent that it would stop me from buying the MR402d. I did, in fact, use only two types of cassette tape and, who knows, it could have been the brand that caused the very slight loss of detail. If your reason for wanting a portastudio is so that you can bounce around versions of the 1812 Overture using a Dr Rhythm and a Rolf Harris Stylophone, then the MR402d *has* to be your choice.

The 402d and 404 are both fairly basic; but, after all, isn't that the idea underlying *all* compact multitrackers? The one possible exception is the Akai MG1212, which has some excellent extra facilities. In the end, the deciding factor is really the price, and this is where the 402d and 404 score highly, being typically around $200-$300 cheaper than the 250 or the 244!

For no-nonsense multitracking on a tight budget, Cutec have done well with the MR402d and the new MR404 by cutting out features that are easily (and more economically) duplicated with auxiliary equipment – and by retaining all the essential workings of a compact multitracker that make it flexible and simple to use.

The Vesta MR1 Compact Multitracker: Profile
Price: $995

The Vesta MR1 is primarily a rack mounting, six-input portastudio which has only one real rival – the RSD Studio 4.

It boasts front *and* back line input sockets (jacks). Each can be filled with two signals and, through judicious use of the input trim and level facilities, it's possible to mix and balance two signals electronically on one input channel. Thus, effectively, it is a twelve-input mixer.

At $3\frac{3}{4}$ips, it runs at twice normal cassette speed and, by all appearances, seems an excellent machine. All components at the front end appear to be of uniform high standard with remote pause and remote punch-in/out, sensibly socketed on the front fascia – extremely good design practice.

With an 80dB S/N ratio, utilizing dbx noise reduction, the MR1 looks like amazing value for money, easily beating the Tascam 246.

For anyone planning to do a lot of live

PROFILES AND REVIEWS

recording, the MR1 *must* come at – or near – **the top of any** auditioning list. It's ideal **because all the input channels have independent** (or selected ganged) limiter circuits.

The following details are the manufacturer's preliminary specifications:

Rack mounting 5 unit high.
S/N ratio 80dB (w.dbx)
THD 0.05% @ 1k
Crosstalk (mixer section) 60dB @ 1k
2 head
2 motor
Tape speed: 3¾ips, w. +/– 12% varispeed
Wow & Flutter 0.04% NAB weighted
Mixer: 6ch, 12 input.

Tascam Porta One Compact Multitracker: Review
Price: $595

The Porta One is Tascam's answer to the Fostex X-15. It runs at normal cassette speed, with only two-track recording at any one time, a restriction that rules it out for recording live gigs in any great detail. This corner-cutting design concession was a policy also adopted by Fostex. It is price rather than facilities that sets these two machines apart, the Porta One costing typically around $100 more than its rival.

The Porta One is better built than the Fostex X-15, but the gap is not sufficiently great, in my opinion, to justify such a price difference. In many ways the standard of manufacture and design of the X-15 is as good as its Tascam rival. If Fostex are managing to make money out of the X-15 at the $450-$495 mark, why can't Tascam do the same? Naturally, manufacturers like to see as fast a return as possible on their investment which results, initially, in shop prices being a little on the high side. But as the product gets to the point of breaking even, shops and distributors start

cutting prices and introducing multiple discount deals. So, by the time you read this, the Porta One's price may well have dropped.

Except perhaps for its lack of auxiliary circuits on the input channels to link up outboard equipment – so that equipment without direct outputs, such as FX pedals, can be used – the Porta One is everything a basic compact multitracker should be. The noise-reduction system, as in all Tascam products, is dbx. The circuits are of very high quality and set up well. The dbx system does not like certain frequencies; most, however, were well-handled and were reproduced with as little over-compression/expansion as could be expected. With the tape running at normal speed – half that of the 244 and 250 – sound fidelity was not as good as it might have been.

The EQ system is nothing out of the ordinary, very much the same as on the 244, with shelving at around 100Hz for bass and 10kHz for treble, and each with a boost and cut range of 10dB. The main output fader is ganged which means you can't outbalance left with right at this stage, but have to do it in the mix – a silly option to take, considering the unorthodox methods the average portastudio user adopts when not properly familiar with the system. The VU meters are not illuminated when the unit is running from batteries unless switched in with a non-latching button. However, they all illuminate when you're using a power adaptor (11-15 volt) from the mains, with meters 1 and 2 acting as the main left and right meters for mixdown.

The four main inputs are unbalanced jack sockets, steering away, perhaps, from the norm of phonos. These inputs have been set up to receive just about everything under the sun; only low impedance and low output professional mikes might cause problems, though there should be enough torque on the trim pot to bring even the quietest mikes up to a workable level. This design policy entails the disregarding of mike/line input selectors and also, for that matter, pad switching.

The transport controls are more mechanical than electronic and engage little or no logic sensing. The record button is slaved to the play button, which on a compact multitracker is rather a silly thing to do, as it's easy to erase accidentally all or part of a potential masterpiece! The play and record buttons have been placed diametrically opposite each other; even so, this sort of design practice, although all right for domestic cassette recorders, should not be used for compact multitrackers.

Footswitch control of punch-in or drop-in is available and, a fantastic plus, the Japanese have made this facility a *two-way* thing. It's all very well dropping yourself into record to re-do a phrase or two but, when the music is syncopated and the tempo fast, you may not have an opportunity to reach for the stop button on the machine itself before another part begins.

Drop-ins created no nasty clicks or level 'bumps' – always a good point to bear in mind when you are recording quieter, more laid-back pieces.

On the whole, the unit was able to reproduce things quite well, with few of the dbx side effects coming into play. The Porta One gets my vote for being the best-to-look-at and the best-to-use portastudio on the market. Shame about the present price levels, but things may improve as its already astounding popularity grows. Tascam have something of a winner here – let's hope all this pays off one day and Tascam realize that the four-track one-way cassette format is *the* ideal medium for the domestic playback of quadrophonic!

Porta One Specifications
Track format: 4-track, 4-channel
Tape Speed: 4.8 cm/s 1⅞ips
Wow & Flutter: 0.05%, NAB weighted
Frequency Response: 40 hz-12.5 kHz, ±3 dB
S/N Ratio: 85 dB (weighted, with dbx)
Dimensions (W × H × D): 330 × 250 × 70mm
Weight: 3.0 kg without batteries, 3.5kg with batteries

Akai MG1212 Compact Multitracker: Profile
Price: $6,995

Seven thousand dollars for a portastudio! The reaction of many of us technical boffins in the music biz when we heard the price of the Akai MG1212 was one of incredulity.

PROFILES AND REVIEWS

Still, the MG1212 does offer a 12-channel mixer and a ½″ 14-T recorder in one devilishly good-looking package. 14-T? Well, the Akai is actually a 12-audio and 2-sync track format recorder – but, even so, it's strange! Akai have called their tape system 'Lambda' . . . don't ask me why. The extremely impressive transport control system can be slaved to another tape machine to an accuracy of one tenth of a second via one of the (edge) code tracks.

The Akai excels when it comes to recording quality. Everything I've heard done on one of these has been superb, owing a great deal to the use of dbx noise reduction which is switchable in/out. The tape speed is also switchable between 7½ips and 15ips, which is a very sensible choice – and very sensible of Akai to give *us* the choice in the first place! The signal-to-noise ratio is an unbelievable 94dB, matching Sony PCM domestic performance! Clearly not only its performance but also its facilities put it in a class of its own – very near the top! Every input channel has three-band sweep EQ, switchable pre/post auxiliaries, two-step pad and so on, and Akai has broken some interesting new ground with the head arrangement. The erase head splits the twelve separate paths across *two* heads, aligned so that each equally covers each track path.

Although I understand that the cassettes are Akai's own design and brand, I've heard that Beta cassettes can be used. (Mind you, the Akai 'MK' cassettes *do* look like Beta format.) The tape transport utilizes *optical* sensing – yet another step forward in uncharted waters. This does have the disadvantage, however, of sometimes inadvertently causing the transport to go into 'stop' mode if a bright light is angled over the cassette holder!

Perhaps one of the most amazing things

PROFILES AND REVIEWS

about this unit is that a computerized punch in/punch-out system has been built in; this allows locations to be entered in the memory via a multi-function keypad and the whole process becomes automatic!

The Akai is a bargain at under $7,500 – but only for the *right* sort of people. Few as yet know enough about this machine to make a solid judgement because the marketing in this country just hasn't been anywhere near as good as the product. I know *exactly* where the MG1212 would be most useful – in more or less the same situations as the Tascam 388. The Akai offers unrivalled functions, quality and flexibility in a handsome, superbly-crafted housing. The design is as clever as you can get, incorporating technology that we haven't seen in the multitrack field before.

Akai have made a superb assault on the serious music market. Their rack mounting sampler offers the only real competition to the Ensoniq Mirage – and *that* should go down in history, Akai's track record being firmly placed in HiFi and video! From nowhere, they have developed a revolutionary new multitrack system which far and away beats, in terms of quality, the performance quoted for Studers and Otaris. The recent introduction of MIDI FX/control units has really upset some large synth companies because they've been pipped at the post by Akai on things they should have had out at Frankfurt a year ago! However, the general public doesn't know about the MG1212, and the few who *are* in the know haven't got six grand to spend on one single item. That's you and me, folks!

For Akai to survive in the music recording market place, they must learn that potential professional studio owners will not be interested in offering clients multitrack time on a *cassette* system, and that only a handful of musicians can afford $7,000 for a home recording unit. But there *is* a market.

Yamaha MT44/D Compact Multitracker: Profile
Price: $535 +/– (not inclusive of mixer and rack etc.)

'D' is for digital. Yamaha introduced the

PROFILES AND REVIEWS

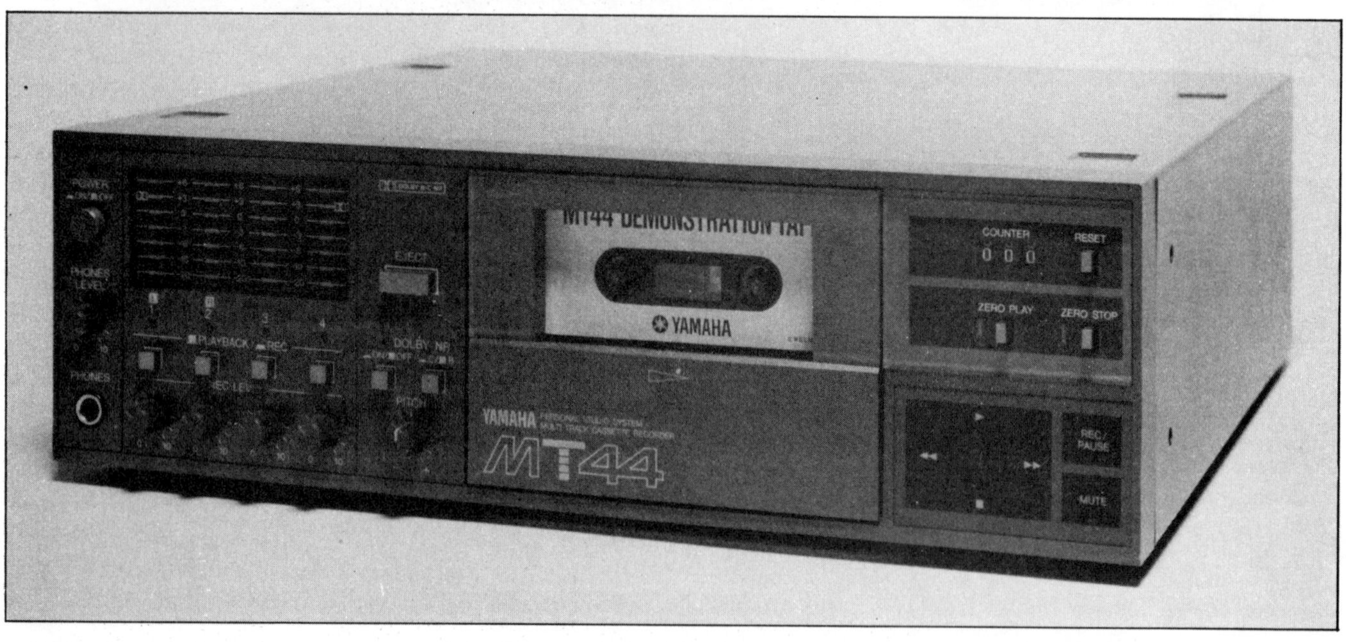

PROFILES AND REVIEWS

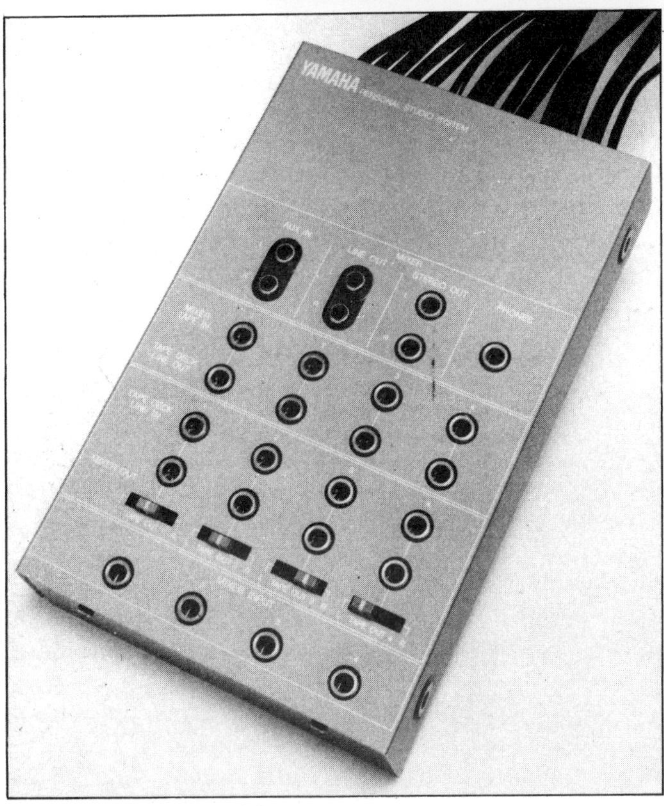

The dd DSS patchbay.

MT44D 4-T front loading compact multitracker together with a new mixer, the RM602, rack and patchbay in the first quarter of 1985. The new MT44 is much more hi-tech to look at and has new, red, fourteen-segment LED meters for each of the channels. Surprisingly, Yamaha have dropped the PSS (Professional Studio System) logo.

The old MT44 was a bargain. This new version, at $535, also has a lot going for it. But what are you *really* getting for your money? The MT44D's tape speed is only half that of the standard compact multitracker. Yamaha should have gone further in their improvements and really set this machine apart in terms of sound quality and gone for 3¾ips.

The MT44D is the only compact multitracker to give you a choice between Dolby B and Dolby C. The machine's S/N ratio, with the noise reduction switched out, is 55dB; with Dolby B it is 63dB – only slightly above the 'acceptable' level – and with Dolby C you get another 4dB improvement, bringing it up to 67dB. I'm not too sure why the decision was made to offer a choice between B and C; it is understandable on cassette machines – many people have Dolby B encoded cassettes – but can the same be said about *unmixed* Dolby B encoded 4-T cassette masters? I shall refrain, however, from criticizing a manufacturer for giving a choice of facilities – but there are choices and choices. The B/C option has no doubt increased the final price.

Sadly, apart from the new Teczon and Audio Technica unit, the Yamaha MT44D is the compact multitracker with which I am least familiar. Without the RM602, the MT44D is a very basic unit with no facility for mixing in FX on auxiliaries, only one headphone output, and no control over any sort of sweetening via an EQ circuit on playback.

The MT44D *does* have a good transport system, with LED counter and zero set facilities. There is also a 'rec mute' button which can be depressed during recording to give a period of silence on the appropriate channel(s) for as long as the button is held down. I must say this is the weirdest feature I've come across on any compact multitracker!

On the whole, the MT44D offers you the same sound quality as the Fostex X-15, and similar facilities. Like the X-15, it becomes a serious demo tool only when you've added a mixer to your home set-up. *Un*like the X-15, which is priced at around $495, the Yamaha MT44D costs $535.

Is looking more hi-tech worth the extra fifty bucks?

Open Reel Multitrackers

Otari 5050 BQ-II ¼″ 4-T open-reel recorder: Profile
Price: $3,425

Sadly, I heard recently that this machine is soon to be deleted from current stocks; I hope this isn't true, but this profile will hold as well for the second-hand buyer's market as it does for the new machines that are still around.

It has switchable speeds of 7½ips and 15ips, with a top s/n ratio of 66dB – which is quite good and easily on a par with the non-noise reduction quality attainable from the Fostex A4 and the Tascam 34.

PROFILES AND REVIEWS

The extra money being asked is to cover, developing and manufacturing an advanced transport system that is a lot better than that found on either the Fostex A4 or the Tascam 34. The deck plate on which all major components are mounted is of a die-cast construction, very strong and very solid.

This four-track machine from Otari is typical of the high-quality products made by this Japanese company.

The price could be prohibitive. The quality is not *that* much better than that of the equivalent ¼" 15ips machines, but the control facilities and smooth transport put this in a category of its own.

Otari also produce a 4-T ½" console version of this machine, the MX5050 MKIII/4, for an additional $1,000 or thereabouts. Running at 15ips, the ½" machine gives a s/n ratio of 70dB.

5050 BQ-II ¼" Four Channel Specifications
Transport
Tape Width and Channels: ¼" (6.3mm) tape, 4 channel
Tape Speeds: 15 and 7.5ips
Maximum Speed Deviation: ±0.2%
Reel Size: ¼" × 10½", NAB
Heads (4, in-line) Erase 1 & 3, 2 & 4, Record (four track) Reproduce (four track)
Motors: D.C. servo-controlled capstan motor, two induction reel motors
Rewind Time: Less than 90 seconds for 2400′ reel
Pitch Control: Variable within ±7%
Wow and Flutter: (NAB weighted) 15ips less than 0.06%, 7.5 ips, less than 0.08%
Electronics
Connectors: Line input and line output, standard three pin XL type type; mike, standard ¼" phone jack
Inputs: Line: unbalanced, bridging 50k ohms, isolation transformers optional mike: unbalanced 50k ohms
Outputs: Unbalanced, 40 ohms source impedance, +22 dB (ref. 0.775V) into 600 ohms or more, isolation transformers optional
Signal to Noise Ratio (3% Third Harmonic to noise floor, 30-18 kHz) 15ips (NAB) 66 dB unweighted, 7.5ips (NAB) 66 dB unweighted
Crosstalk: Less than 55dB at 1 kHz on adjacent tracks
Frequency Response: (Record/Reproduce) 15ips (0 VU): 30 to 20 kHz, ±2.0dB, 7.5ips (-10 VU): 20 to 18 kHz, ±2.0dB
Frequency Response: (Selective Reproduce) 15ips (0 VU): 50 to 18 kHz, ±3.0dB, 7.5ips (-10 VU): 30 to 12 kHz, ±3.0dB
Operating Level: 250 nWb/m, all measurements made with 3M #226 tape at operating level except where specified.
Distortion (1 kHz, 250 nWb/m) Less than 0.7% Third Harmonic
Test Oscillator Frequencies: Nominal 1kHz and 10kHz
Physical
Power Requirements: 100/117/220/240 V, ±10% 50/60 Hz single phase AC, 140 watts
Operating Environment: 40 to 104 degrees F (5 to 40C), 20 to 80% R.H.
Storage Environment: -5 to +113 degrees F (-20 to 45C) 10 to 80% R.H.
Mounting: Vinyl covered wood case; rack mounting kit and floor console (ZA-52L) optional
Standard Accessories: Reel hold down knobs, ¼" × 10½" empty NAB reel, operation manual and power cord
Optional Accessories: CB-102 remote transport control, ZA-52L roll-around pedestal, isolation transformers
Weight: 60lbs (27kg)

5050 Mark III/4 ½" Four Channel Specifications
Transport
Tape Width and Channels: ½" (12.7mm) tape, 4 channels
Tape Speeds: 15 and 7.5ips
Maximum Speed Deviation: ±0.2%
Reel Size ½" × 10½", NAB
Heads: (3, in-line) Erase (ferrite), Record, Reproduce (both hard permalloy)
Motors: D.C. servo-controlled capstan motor, two induction reel motors
Rewind Time: Less than 90 seconds for a 2,400′ reel
Pitch Control: Variable within ±7%
Wow and Flutter 15ips, 0.04%, 7.5ips, 0.06%
Electronics
Connectors: Line input and line output, standard three pin XL

PROFILES AND REVIEWS

type; mike, standard 1/4" phone jack
Inputs: Line: unbalanced, bridging 50k Ohms, isolation transformers optional mike: unbalanced 50 kOhms
Outputs: Unbalanced, 40 Ohms source impedance +21 dB (ref. 0.775V) into 600 Ohms or more, isolation transformers optional
Signal-to-Noise Ratio: (3% Third Harmonic to noise floor, 30-18 kHz) 15ips 70dB unweighted, 7.5ips 70dB unweighted
Equalization: NAB
Crosstalk: Less than 55dB at 1kHz on adjacent tracks
Frequency Response: (Record/Reproduce) 15ips (0 VU): 30 to 20 kHz, ±2.0dB, 7.5ips (-10 VU): 20 to 18 kHz, ±2.0dB
Frequency Response: (Selective Reproduce) 15ips (0 VU): 30 to 18 kHz, ±2.0dB, 7.5ips (-10 VU): 30 to 13 kHz, ±2.0 dB
Operating Level: 250 nWb/m
Distortion: (1kHz, 250 nWb/m) Less than 0.3% Third Harmonic (15ips)
Test Oscillator Frequencies: Nominal 1 kHz and 10 kHz
Test Conditions: As specified, using 3M #226 tape
Physical
Power Requirements: 100/117/220/240 V, ±10%, 50/60 Hz single phase AC, 140W
Operating Environment: 40 to 104 degrees F (5 to 40C), 20 to 80% R.H.
Storage Environment: -5 to +113 degrees F (-20 to 45C), 10 to 80% R.H.
Mounting: Tabletop console standard, rack mounting kit and floor console (ZA-52L) optional
Standard Accessories: Reel hold down knobs, 1/2" × 10 1/2" empty NAB reel, operation manual and power cord
Optional Accessories: CB-102 remote transport control, CB-116 Auto locator with six memories and tape time display (includes tape transport functions), ZA-52L roll-around pedestal, isolation transformers
Weight: 77lbs (35kg)

Tascam 34 4-T: Profile
Price: $1,795

At around $1,795, the Tascam is not exactly brilliant value for money. However, unlike the Fostex A4, it does offer large spool capability.

PROFILES AND REVIEWS

It uses ¼″ tape, and when it is switched to the higher of its speed options (15ips) its performance is almost identical to that of the 38.

I would not recommend the 34 to anyone seriously requiring high quality; however, with an added dbx unit, it can and does offer superb recording quality.

For further details I suggest you read the 38 Profile, which bears a good deal of relevance to the 34.

The Tascam A3440 was originally designed for domestic quadrophonic recording/listening, and the 34 is a descendant of that original ¼″ 4-T on large spools @ 15ips. However, I'd say that listening closely to one of the double-speed compact multitrackers and comparing it directly with a 34 with no NR system is something every potential 34 purchaser *must* do.

In early 1985 I heard that the 34 is being phased out in favour of the 34B which has built-in mike-and-line trim pots. This facility, again, is angled towards A/V production, and sadly the extra expense is put at the feet of those humble home recordists who want both 4-T and the quality of open-reel format.

Save the 34!!!

34B Specifications
Track Format: 4-track, 4-channel, 1/4″ tape
Reel Size: 10-1/2″
Tape Speeds: 38 and 19 cm/sec
Wow and Flutter (peak, weighted): ±0.06% at 38 cm/sec, ±0.09% at 19 cm/sec
Frequency Response (0 VU): 40 Hz-22 kHz, ±3 dB at 38 cm/sec.

40 Hz-16 kHz, ±3 dB at 19 cm/sec
S/N Ratio: 68 dB at 38 cm/sec, 66 dB at 19 cm/sec
THD: 0.8% (0 VU, 1 kHz)
Dimensions (W × H × D): 410 × 461 × 256 mm
Weight: 20 kg

Fostex A4 4-T: Profile
Price: $1,450

This machine closely follows the design principles underlying the Fostex A8. The A4, utilizing the open-reel 4-T standard ¼″ tape on 7″ spools, is strangely out of place in the Fostex open-reel multitrack line. Audio quality is extremely good, owing to the fully professional three-head motor system, though I think that the inclusion of integral noise reduction would have been more in line with Fostex's usual practice. Such an inclusion would have inaugurated a new category in the field of open-reel 4-T, and would almost certainly have given the A4 a head-start over its contemporaries.

The control layout is very well-defined and logically laid out. It works (like all domestic Fostex and Tascam equipment) at the unprofessional, unbalanced level of -10dBv. Interestingly, Fostex have given the A4 dual-speed capability, so that it can switch between 7½ips and 15ips. At 15ips, Fostex quote a 'full' frequency response of 40Hz-20kHz, and a signal-to-noise ratio of 63dB; this is an altogether odd figure, since at 15ips I would expect ¼″ 4-T to offer just over the 65dB mark – the noise figure Fostex quote is the same for both 7½ips *and* 15ips! There is an optional remote available: the 8030. The A4 also has a handy 'zero rtn' button.

The A4 is not a particularly sluggish machine to work with; it will fast wind a full spool of normal play tape through to the end within 2½ mins. It has a handy +/– 10% pitch control too. However, wow and flutter at 7½ips is a little shaky to say the least, at +/– 1%.

I would recommend the A4 to anyone who needs the flexibility of 4-T, but is aiming at a better than average quality on their demos. Having said this, I urge you *not* to buy *any* open-reel 4-T without first auditioning all of the double-speed compact multitrackers, such as the Fostex 250, the Tascam 244, and so on. The A4 is a reliable and good quality machine; for truly serious work, I'd have to recommend the employment of a noise-reduction system (perhaps Fostex's own 3040 Dolby C 4-channel unit), but even as it stands, the A4 offers very good value for money.

Specifications
Tape ¼ inch tape width, 1 mil base
Format 4 track 4 channel
Heads 4 track record, 4 track reproduce, 4 track erase
Reel Size 7 inch
Tape Speed 15 and 7½ips (38 and 19cm/s), ±0.5%
Pitch Control ±10%
Line Input -10dBV (0.3V) Impedance: 30kohms, unbalanced
Line Output -10dBV (0.3V) Load Impedance: 10kohms or higher, unbalanced
Record Level Calibration 0 VU referenced to 185nWb/m of tape flux
Equalization NAB (IEC available in Europe)
Wow & Flutter ±0.06% peak (IEC/ANSI), wtd, at 15ips
±0.10% peak (IEC/ANSI), wtd, at 7½ips
Fast Wind Time 130 seconds typ. for 1800 ft. of tape
Overall Freq. Response 40Hz-20kHz, ±3dB, at 15ips
40Hz-18kHz, ±3dB, at 7½ips
Signal-to-Noise Ratio (Sync/Reproduce) 63dB, wtd, at 15 and 7½ips, referenced to 1kHz, 3% THD level
THD Less than 1% at 1kHz, 0VU
Crosstalk (Reproduce) 50dB (at 1kHz)
Erasure Better than 70dB at 1kHz
Power Requirements 120V AC, 60Hz, 43W*
Dimensions 13½″ H × 14″ W × 6¾″ D 340mm H × 360mm W × 170mm D
Weight 29lbs (13Kg)

Fostex A8: Review
Price: $1,995

Wheezes of delight and institutionalized grumbles of '. . . it's not possible, won't sound any good – too hissy . . .' met the Fostex A8 prior to and during its launch. The fact that it had eight tracks on ¼″ tape was a total shock, and represented an inspired feat of research and development from Japan. Love it or hate it, the A8, at its minimally fluctuating price of around $1,995 *has* made open-reel multitracking more possible for less affluent home recordists than any other machine in the history of mankind (think about it!).

PROFILES AND REVIEWS

It boasted several features that left it uncomfortably somewhere between being a ramshackle, rough-and-ready home multitracker and being a serious contender for the small-studio owner's money – funds that were expected to realize a return. 7½" spools, running at 15ips, with Dolby noise reduction, and using *quarter inch tape* quite simply took the biscuit. Fostex will go down in history for their steely nerve in mixing professional and amateur features on an eight-track open-reel machine.

For me, a person all too much in love with 90dB+ S/N ratios, the A8 represents a cost-effective demo tool and nothing more. Bill Nelson is a famous A8 user and has indeed *released* products of his machine. The music is there, the tracks are there; however certain factors – the quality of sound in terms of

dynamic range, noise levels and the time restriction imposed (around 11-16 mins depending on tape thickness) by small spools running at a professional speed – convince me that a studio centred upon this machine will never create anything more than excellent quality *demos*.

Having eight tracks crammed on to ¼″ tape creates bad crosstalk figures, reduced tape band-width and consequently frequency band-width response and dynamic range. Noise figures without the Dolby switched on are not even worth printing. Noise figures with the Dolby employed are only marginally better than those you can get away with when using chrome cassettes on your HiFi deck.

The basic A8 is incapable of recording more than four tracks at any one time, which I think

PROFILES AND REVIEWS

is a perfectly reasonable limitation if a corner has to be cut. However, Fostex were not slow in picking up on possible new markets for the machine (e.g. those wishing to record live gigs) and introduced the A8LR with full-track recording. One of the less sensible ideas was the opting for 7½" spools. As I've already pointed out, this restricts you from developing any over long pieces of music, and as there are usually four or five tape-consuming false starts on any multitrack masters, you are forever worrying about whether there will be enough tape. Having small spools on multitrack is a bad idea – it almost eliminates the extra abilities of the A8LR. What PA engineer has time to change tapes six or seven times during one gig? Once or twice – maybe three times, but that is enough!

This said, the A8 is an agreeable and responsive gadget to use. The take-up spool speed is a little erratic, the transport can be very 'clunky' towards the end of reels, and the weight differential from reel to reel puts extra strain on the mechanism. The meters are nice and sharp, and the overall appearance will satisfy even the most uninformed observer that you are the proud owner of an eight-track recorder!

The A8 is definitely *not* a seven-days-a-week, fifty-two-weeks-a-year machine. It will not stand up to years of hammering in a busy studio. It is not a machine to impress clients, neither is it one that will allow you to charge full rates per hour in your studio, should you wish to make some money. But this is *not* an unfavourable review. The A8 machine *is* good, but never buy it on quality grounds alone; if you want to produce quality multitrack masters at home, which can be bounced on to a professional machine later on, the A8 will not give you competitive results. Owning an A8 will often mean re-recording *everything* should you get a recording contract.

If you are unable to find further sums of money stuffed down the back of bus seats, and you are *desperate* for eight tracks, then go ahead and buy the A8; there is really no other competition, for it is a breed of its own – perhaps barring Tascam's 388 eight-track portastudio – but there *are* some major differences.

A8s are brilliant at what they do. I certainly recommend that you audition one, even if your funds allow you to go further up market; what I find unsatisfactory (picking holes in equipment is part of my job) could well be acceptable to you. Fostex have made a winner – only a technical ignoramus could overlook that. When someone produces a machine that offers 32 tracks on ¼" tape, running at 7½ips and with no N.R., then I'll really pick some bones!

PROFILES AND REVIEWS

STOP PRESS:
New Fostex A8 and A2 launched at APRS, London, June 1985.

The new 2-T has centre-track capability and a new reinforced transport suitable for serious multi-sync environments. The new A8, like the new A2, has red LED meters and a striking black finish. Little is known about these machines, but rumours picked up are of an unwelcome sort. According to reliable sources, the old A8 is to be phased out completely in favour of the new 'A80'. The A80 is considerably more expensive than the old A8, mainly because of its SMPTE capability. This (as *someone* in Japan must realize) is a facility that is little understood and still less *used* by the vast majority of home recordists.

SMPTE on the A80 sets the machine firmly within the grips of A/V and/or video post-production houses – the sort of people who have the cash to buy this more expensive machine. As I see it now, there will no longer be an open-reel 8-T on the market for around $2,000. Does this mean Fostex have an 8-T compact multitracker up their skirts? If they have, they'd better hurry up! Not that the Tascam 388 is a threat, even at its new 'lower' price of $3,995; the challenger most likely to knock Fostex completely out of the value-for-money-open-reel-8-T market is the ½″ Tascam 38 8-T, which is always the subject of many dealer packages at favourable prices.

Save the A8!!!

Specifications
Tape ¼ inch tape width, 1 mil base
Format 8 track, 8 channel (4 channel record ×2, 8 channel reproduce)
Heads 8 track record/reproduce 8 track erase
Reel Size 7 inch
Tape Speed 15ips (38 cm/s), ±0.5%
Pitch Control ±10%
Line Input (×4) -10dBV (0.3V) Impedance: 15kohms, unbalanced
Line Output (×8) -10dBV (0.3V) Load impedance: 10kohms or higher, unbalanced
Record Level Calibration 0 VU referenced to 250nWb/m of tape flux
Equalization IEC (35 microsecs)
Wow & Flutter ±0.06% peak (IEC/ANSI) wtd.
Fast Wind Time 130 seconds typ. for 1800 ft. of tape
Overall Freq. Response 45Hz-18kHz, ±3dB
Signal-to-Noise Ratio 73dB wtd., referenced to 1kHz, 3% THD level
THD Less than 1% at 1kHz, 0 VU
Crosstalk (Reproduce) 45dB at 1kHz
Erasure Better than 70dB at 1kHz
Power Requirements 120V AC, 60Hz, 60W*
Dimensions 13½″ H × 14″ W × 6¾″ D 340mm H × 360mm W × 170mm D
Weights 29lbs (13Kg)

Soundcraft SCM 381 1″ 8-T: Profile
Price: $6,795

If you've managed to stagger past the price at the beginning of this profile, you are obviously someone who has a bit of cash handy and who knows a potentially good 8-T when he sees one – either that, or you're a dreamer! For the money, the Soundcraft 1″ 8-T does *not* offer any mind-blowing features or, for that matter, particularly amazing sound quality. With a signal-to-noise ratio of only 63dB at 15ips, the four thousand pounds or so you will have to pay for this machine seems hard to justify.

The 381 *does* have some pretty advanced features for an 8-T . . . it's up to you to decide whether the extra cash is money well spent. One of the best features is a varispeed of +10, -50%, which enables you to bring off some

really weird and wonderful sound FX and compositional cheats! There is a real-time red LED tape counter in minutes and seconds; the transport controls on the front panel can be removed and placed into a rugged if somewhat BBC-ish wooden cabinet and – via a reasonable stretch of multicore cable – can be used as a full-function remote/autolocater.

Connections on the rear panel take the form of standard jack sockets and a multiway Varelco connector port. XLRs can be fitted at additional cost.

I've had quite extensive experience of three of these machines, all of which were faulty – however, that is not a standard by which to judge *every* machine. They do tend to be a bit 'clunky' and ungraceful in operation, but that is only a minor quibble. Construction quality is very good – not excellent, but extremely commendable nevertheless and no doubt generally very reliable.

Do not be fooled anymore by anything to do with tape widths – just go straight for the noise figures and frequency response. I am mildly opposed to having eight tracks on anything narrower than ½″, even *with* noise reduction to aid a more professional result, but the Soundcraft, 3M, Skully, Brennell and Studer

PROFILES AND REVIEWS

1″ 8-Ts have gone too far the other way for my liking. Although, it is true, rigging a dbx system up to a 381 will result in better performance than that of a Tascam 38, the difference in performance will, because of the 38's excellent s/n ratio, be barely discernible to the human ear.

Certainly the improvements gained on a 1″ system, noise reduction or no noise reduction (and personally I think you *do* need a NR unit – even on 1″), are *not* worth forking out the extra $3,000 for.

The Soundcraft is good. 1″ 8-T is expensive to run. 1″ 8-T is *not* (at today's prices) value for money.

46.5 cms
55 cms
41 cms

Specifications
Format 8T 1″
Reel size 10.5″
Speed 38/76 cm/sec
Varispeed +10, -50%
Speed stability 0.1%
Wow + Flutter 0.03%
Start time 0.5sec
Wind time (700m) 100 sec
Power requirement 500VA
Voltage requirement 100/120/220/240 ±10%
Rec/rep freq resp +1, −2
Rec/Sync/Freq resp +1, −2
Rec/rep S/N 63dB
Rec/rep Xtalk 1kHZ −55dB
Rec/Sync Xtalk 1kHz −24db
Bias freq. 100kHz
I/P sensitivity −10 to +20 dBm, 10k input impedance
Output level −10 to +10 dBm @ OVU, +22dBm max @600R
Line o/p bandwidth (inc.sync mode) 24kHz
Sync line o/p b/w 16kHz
Audio connectors ¼″ Jack/Varelco multiway
Weight (unpacked) 34kg
Temperature 10°C to 30°C
Humidity less than 85%

Series 760 16-T & 24-T machines: Profile
1″ 16-T: SCM 761-16: $14,995
2″ 16-T: SCM 762-16: $20,995
24-T: SCM 762-24: $26,400

Soundcraft have never (or at any rate not yet) been lured into what is still relatively uncharted territory and crammed more than sixteen tracks on to 1″ tape. The SCM 761-16 is a large-scale 16-T featuring modular metering and calibration electronics and compatible with the 760 series (24-T capability) autolocator/remote.

Like the SCM 381 8-T, Varelco multiway

connectors are standard and XLRs can be fitted at extra cost. The 1″ format isn't an end in itself, but it may have the potential to be *twice* as good as a Fostex B16 – although things are never as simple as that. The s/n ratio quoted (and it's not clear whether it refers to 15ips or to 30ips, the two speeds available) is just 60dB – so there's definitely a case for adding an external noise-reduction unit.

These Soundcraft machines are extremely well constructed, utilizing full three-head/three-motor systems.

Bearing in mind the inevitable extra amount you will have to spend on noise reduction for this system to work at broadcast-quality levels, the SCM 761-16 may seem like a ridiculous purchase when compared with a

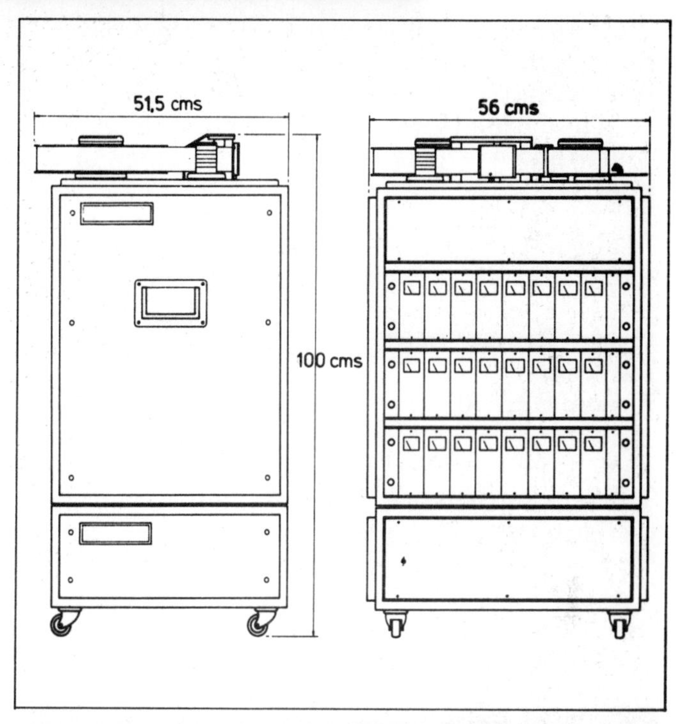

B16 or the new Aces SML 12-16. But this machine undeniably offers what is potentially much, much better quality in a more durable and professional housing.

The Soundcraft SCM 762-16 is a professional 2″ 16-T; having sixteen tracks on 2″ tape represents potentially the best possible multitrack analogue format. Personally, I've always felt that cramming twenty-four tracks on to 2″ tape is pushing it. I have, it is true, attained extremely good results on a 24-T (even at 15ips), but the extra tape width afforded to each track on the SCM 762-16 allows you improved dynamic range and frequency response. Like all the SCM recorder/reproducers, it gives you a varispeed option of +10, −50%. The transport on this machine is particularly silent, but unfortunately not very fast.

The s/n ratio is again just slightly above the 'acceptable' recording level, at 63dB. Noise reduction will have to be employed with this machine to facilitate completely noise-free performance.

Finally, the last multitrack Soundcraft product is the SCM 762-24 24-T, which is the third most popular machine in British studios (the first two being Studer and Otari). It has dual-speed capability, modular electronics, a 60dB s/n ratio, all I've told you about before; but perhaps the most appealing thing about this machine is its price tag – though the Aces machines are less than half the price of this one!

Open-Reel Multitrack: Tascam 38 8-T: Review
Price: $2,750

You have to spend quite a lot of money on a Tascam multitrack machine before you get a choice of running speeds; both the Tascam 80-8 (the grandpappy of all 8-T machines from Tascam) and the 38 run at 15ips on 10½″ large-hub spools, thereby fulfilling the optimum requirements.

The 38 has a (slightly) more impressive spec. sheet than the 80-8, from which the 38 was developed. However, before I investigate this machine more thoroughly, it must be understood that the durability of each of these two machines is quite different. The 38 is *not* a seven-days-a-week, fifty-two-weeks-a-year machine. Its ability to stand up to non-stop use in a busy studio is not as great as the 80-8's. Thus, when I reached the stage of wanting to buy an eight-track, I bought a second-hand 80-8 in preference to a 38, in spite of the latter's slightly superior performance.

Without the optional 8-channel noise-reduction unit which uses dbx, the 38 is, in my opinion, only slightly better than acceptable. Albums *have* been recorded on these machines *without* noise reduction (Mark Shreeve's excellent *Assassin* is just one example); *with* noise reduction, however, the 38 and the 80-8 produce almost digital, noise-free results.

The transport is 'clunk'-free and very smooth. The 38 has the basic control features, including a return-to-zero facility. Rewind and fast-forward functions are as snappy as those on any ½″ format machine I've seen. The ½″ format employed has now become standard in the industry, as has 1″ sixteen-track. I have no qualms about this format whatsoever; the tape width afforded to each track is enough (although only just) to give you (with dbx) the high quality I have described. The 38 works best with Ampex 456 Grand Master.

There is a basic remote available, the RC71; this leaves it up to you to select the tracks on which you want to record and to work the transport from the dual controls on the remote. Drop-ins are smooth and have no bumps or jumps to them. All inputs and outputs work at the domestic, non-professional level and are the chassis-mounting phono type.

I cannot fault the 38. Only its suspect durability in busy studios is grounds for any significant criticism. The durability is reflected in the price. If you are extra lucky, a kind dealer may throw in the matching 8-channel dbx noise-reduction unit at a generous discount when you buy a 38; this machine is the subject of more package deals and special offers than any other.

PROFILES AND REVIEWS

Even in the light of new developments in technology, a 38, with a dbx unit and small mixer, still gets my vote for being the best value-for-money system on the 8-T market. This position is bound to be strengthened now that Fostex have made the unwise decision to phase out the standard A8 in favour of the A80, which is much more expensive and offers more facilities than the average home recordist needs. The 'Stop Press' news that the price of Tascam's 388 8-T compact multitracker is being reduced to around $3,750 and the tape speed doubled to 15ips still doesn't threaten the 38's market. *Until* someone brings out an 8-T with comparable features and of comparable quality at less than the price of a 38, dbx unit and small mixer, the market is not going to alter in the slightest. If the 388 is to make a true dent in the market, it will have to retail for less than $3,000.

38 Specifications
Track Format: 8-track, 8-channel, ½″ tape
Reel Size: 10-½″
Tape Speed: 38 cm/sec
Wow and Flutter: 0.05%
Frequency Response: 40Hz-22kHz
S/N Ratio: 68 dB
THD: 0.8%, 0 VU 1kHz
Dimensions (W × H × D): 410 × 461 × 317mm
Weight: 27kg

Tascam 48 8-T: Profile
Price: $4,495

Cheaper than the Soundcraft 1″ (as one would expect), the Tascam 48 is a much more rugged and professional machine than the 38. I have none of the reservations I expressed in the 38 Profile. The 48 is truly a serious studio machine.

Its spec. does not differ much from the 38's; this is not because the 48 isn't much of an improvement, but because the 38 has achieved practically optimum performance from the ½″ format. Tascam decided to improve upon operational and transport control facilities rather than increase tape width. We have yet to see a 1″ 8-T from Tascam, and personally I don't think we ever will . . . they've achieved too much on ½″.

The 48 boasts SMPTE capability – the facility whereby a SMPTE code can be fed to the 48 and converted into information that in turn controls the transport, in terms of both speed and destination. This allows the 48 to be used for video post-production work and to be integrated into a code-driven A/V environment.

Other 'extras' include a (somewhat ill-positioned) return-to-zero button, a real-time LED counter and an integral edit block. There is also a programmable cue point which is handy for locating datum points within a piece of music. The 48 also has switchable speeds of 7½ips or 15ips; in terms of sound quality, with no noise reduction, the former choice is a waste of time.

The s/n ratio on this machine is pretty good: at 69dB, it is just 9dB above what is generally considered to be the acceptable level. Even so, this machine comes into its own only when used with a corresponding (and well set up) 8-channel noise-reduction unit. I think my comments regarding the 38's performance without noise reduction hold true with regard

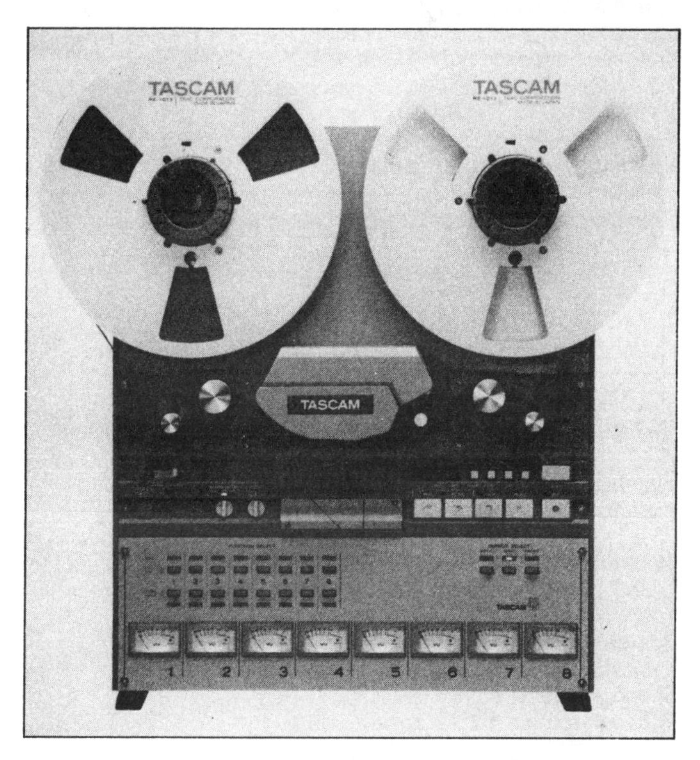

to both this machine, and, sadly, the Tascam 58, which has still more operational and transport facilities but shares the 48's s/n ratio of 69dB. For machines that run on ½″ tape at 15ips, Tascam have done as well as can be expected with both the 48 and the 58. Linked into a noise-reduction system, these 8-T machines offer incredible, articulate performance, with no noise audible whatsoever.

If you've decided to go for quality *and* 8-T, then any of the three Tascam ½″ machines, *with* noise reduction, will immediately please you. With noise reduction taken into account, the difference in quality between the 38 and 48 is extremely slight. SMPTE is certainly a handy facility. If you plan to use your home recordings in a professional environment, then the 48 and the 58 demand auditioning and further investigation. Any decision to buy a 48 as opposed to a 38 is one to be made on the basis of facilities – not of sound quality.

48 Specifications
Mechanical Characteristics
Tape: ½ inch, 1.5 mil, low noise, high output tape
Track Format: 8-track, 8 channel
Reel Size: 10-½″ NAB (large) Hub
Tape Speed: 15ips (38 cm/sec)
Speed Accuracy (2): ±0.2% deviation
Pitch Control: ±12%
Wow and Flutter (2): ±0.08% peak (DIN/IEC/ANSI weighted) ±0.12% peak (DIN/IEC/ANSI unweighted) 0.05% (NAB weighted) 0.07% (NAB unweighted)
Fast Wind Time: 120 seconds for 10-½″ reel, 2,400 feet
Spooling Wind Time: 400 seconds for 10-½″ reel, 2,400 feet
Start Time: Less than 0.8 sec to reach standard Wow and Flutter
Tape Drive System Capstan Motor: PLL (Phase Lock-Loop), DC, Direct Drive Capstan Motor Slotless, DC Reel Motor × 2
Head Configuration: 3 heads: erase, record/reproduce, reproduce
Tape Cue: Manual (slide lever) and automatic (RTZ and STC)
Motion Sensing: 0.5 sec ± 0.15 sec. delay time stop to next motion
Mounting: Standard 19-inch rack with optional RM-501
Remote Control: Basic transport function available with optional RC-71
Dimensions (W × H × D) 432 × 505 × 315.5 mm
Weight: 37kg

58 Specifications
Tape: ½ in, 1.5 mil, low noise, high output tape.
Track format: 8-track, 8-channel, track width 0.039 in (1.0mm)
Reel size: 10½ in (large) hub.
Tape speed: 15 in/s (38 cm/s)
Speed accuracy: ± 0.5% deviation
Pitch control: fine ±0.7% coarse ±15%
Wow and flutter: ±0.08% peak (DIN/IEC/ANSI weighted); ±0.12% peak (DIN/IEC/ANSI unweighted); 0.04% RMS (JIS/NAB weighted); 0.07% RMS (JIS/NAB unweighted)
Fast wind time: 120s for 10½ in reel, 2,400 ft.
Spooling wind time: 370 s for 10½ in reel, 2,400 ft.
Start time: >0.8s to reach standard wow and flutter.
Tape drive system: capstan motor FG (frequency generator), DC, direct drive motor. Reel motors – slotless DC motors.
Head configuration: three heads – erase, record and reproduce × 2
Tape cue: manual and automatic (RTZ and STC).
Motion sensing: 0.5s ± 0.15s delay time stop to next motion, tension sensing servo system.
Mounting: standard 19in rack with optional RM-500
Remoe control: full/basic functions available with optional RC-51/RC-50
Dimensions: 432 × 505 ×316mm (whd) 17 × 19⅞ × 12 7/16 in
Weight: 35kg (77 3/16lb)
Line input: Impedance 50k ohms unbalanced; mximum source impedance 2.5k ohms nominal input level -10dBV (0.3V); maximum input level +19 dBV (8.9V)
Line output: Impedance 500 ohms unbalanced; minimum load impedance 10k ohms; nominal load impedance 50k ohms; nominal output level -10dBV (0.3V); maximum output level +19dBV (8.9V)
Bias frequency: 150 kHz
Equalisation: Infinity + 35μs IEC standard
Record level calibration. 0 VU reference – 250 nWb/m tape flux level
Frequency response: record/reproduce 40Hz to 20kHz, ±3dB at 0 VU; 40 Hz to 20kHz, ±3dB at -10 VU; sync and reproduce 40Hz to 20kHz, ±3dB.
Total harmonic distortion: 0.8% at 0 VU, 1kHz, 250 nWb/m; 3% at 12 dB above 0 VU, 1,000 nWb/m.
Signal-to-noise ratio: at a reference of 1 kHz, at 12dB above 0 VU, 1,000 nWb/m –69dB A-weighted (NAB), 62dB unweighted; 107dB A-weighted (NAB) with dbx; 100 dB unweighted with dbx.
Adjacent channel crosstalk (overall): better than 50dB down at 1 kHz, 0 VU
Erasure: better than 70dB at 1 kHz, +10 VU reference
Headroom: record amplifier better than 26dB above 0 VU at 1 kHz. Reproduce amplifier better than 44 dB above 0 VU at 1 kHz
Connectors: line inputs and outputs – RCA jacks; remote control, accessory (ext sync) and dbx unit (control signal) multi-pin type connector
Power requirements: 100/120/220/240 VAC, 50/60 Hz, 180 W for general export model

Otari Model 5050 Mk III/8 ½″ 8-T open-reel recorder; Profile
Price: $5,295

This is the most expensive and (I'm happy to say) the best ½″ 8-T I've seen. It has many features that the Tascam 58 shares, but for my

PROFILES AND REVIEWS

money, I'd choose the Otari every time. The transport is extremely good, laid in a console, and the machine whizzes and breezes through tapes with no hint of any 'clunking' noises. Like the ¼″ & ½″ 4-T profiled earlier, the Mk3/8 (as I prefer to term it) has external sync capability so that you never have to bounce your home demos on to a professional machine for integrated mix-down. With these machines, you just switch them on to external sync, rig up a locking/transport system (such as the Applied Microsystems ICON) and away you go.

With no dbx, the s/n ratio will be around 68dB (at 15ips), which I think is pretty good, but for truly serious noise-free performance, noise reduction will have to be employed.

The construction of this unit gives you easy access to all calibration points.

This Otari is about as professional as you can get. If you want a sturdy, fully professional ½″ 8-T, this unit *has* to be considered.

5050 Mark III/8 ½″ Eight Channel Specifications

Transport

Tape Width and Channels: ½″ (12.7mm) tape, 8-channel
Tape Speeds: 15 and 7.5ips
Maximum Speed Deviation: ±0.2%
Reel Size: ½″×10½″, ±NAB
Heads: (3, in-line) Erase (ferrite), record/reproduce (both hard permalloy)
Motors: D.C. servo-controlled capstan motor, two induction reel motors
Rewind Time: Less than 90 seconds for 2400′ reel
Pitch Control: Variable within ±7%
Wow and Flutter: (NAB weighted) 15ips 0.06% 7.5ips 0.08%

Electronics

Connectors: Line input and line output, standard three pin XL type
Inputs: Unbalanced, bridging 50k ohms, isolation transformers optional
Outputs: Unbalanced, 40 ohms source impedance +21dB (ref. 0.775V) into 600 ohms or more, isolation transformers optional)
Signal to Noise Ratio: (3% Third Harmonic to noise floor, 30-18 kHz) 15ips (IEC), 68dB unweighted, 7.5ips (IEC), 67dB unweighted
Crosstalk: Less than 55dB at 1 kHZ on adjacent tracks
Frequency Response: (Record/Reproduce) 15ips (0 VU): 40 to 25 kHz ±2.0dB 7.5ips (-10 VU): 20 to 20 kHz ±2.0dB
Frequency Response: (Selective Reproduce) 15ips (0 VU): 40 to 15 kHz ±3.0dB 7.5ips (-10VU): 30 to 10kHz ±3.0dB
Operating Level: 250nWb/m, all measurements made with 3M #226 tape at operating level except where specified.
Distortion: (1 kHz, 250 nWb/m) Less than 0.7% third harmonic
Test Oscillator Frequencies: Nominal 1kHz and 10kHz

Physical

Power Requirements: 100/117/220/240V, ±10% 50/60 Hz single phase AC, 140 W
Operating Environment: 40 to 104 degrees F (5 to 40C) 20 to 80% R.H.
Storage Environment: -5 to ±113 degrees F (-20 to 45C) 10 to 80% R.H.
Mounting: Tabletop console standard, floor console (ZA-52L) optional
Standard Accessories: Reel hold down knobs, ½″×10½″ empty NAB reel, operation manual and power cord
Optional Accessories: CB-110 remote control (controls functions of transport, monitor electronics and tape timer), CB-102 remote control (controls transport only), ZA-52L roll-around pedestal, maintenance manual, isolation transformers.
Weight: 77lbs (35kg)

Aces ½″ 26-T, the SML 12-16; Profile Price: TBA

This new ½″ 16-T machine, from the Shrewsbury-based company Aces, really made an impression at the APRS this year.

The machine is obviously tooled and manufactured to a much more heavy-duty standard than the Fostex B16, and for my liking *has* to be more durable. In a console format, with head-mounted illuminated VUs, and channel-by-channel front access for calibration of Bias, Rec HF, Rec Level, P/B HF & P/B level, this Aces machine outstrips the B16 on console and electronics presentation alone.

Very few details are known about the SML 12-16, but it seems obvious that Aces are planning to market it at a price not too dissimilar to that of a B16. Integral 2:1 compansion noise reduction gives me the feeling that the sound quality on this more rugged machine will leave the B16 standing.

Aces also manufacture a 2″ 16-T (the TR16 – incredible value at around £6,000) which by all accounts is a very good quality machine. One version (the TR16A at £6,400) comes pre-wired to take another 8-channel record/reproduce calibration/metering set of electronics, which will turn it into a 24-T. The standard 24-T (the TR24) is also said to be of good audio quality, and retails for just £8,350.

PROFILES AND REVIEWS

Aces unfortunately get slated by salesmen more than any other manufacturer. Do not let this dissuade you from auditioning either the machines mentioned here or Aces' range of small and large consoles.

I know several Aces package owners and all of them admit to having had teething troubles – but no more than other package purchasers. Aces have a good service team who are not afraid of nipping out late on a Wednesday night to look at a customer's Bias level!

Don't expect faultless machinery, but remember you can rely on excellent after-sales service and modular electronics. I'm glad to say that Aces have retained their policy of providing good service with this new ½″ 16-T, which promises to be an absolute winner!

Open-Reel Multitrack Profile: the Fostex B16 16-T
Price: $5,900

This is the machine everybody anticipated when the A8 was released; as soon as the ¼″ 8-T was unveiled, every Tom, Dick and Harry who had any experience in the field of recording equipment immediately envisaged ½″ 16-T.

Most of what I had to say about the Fostex A8, with regard to construction and especially sound quality, holds true for the B16. Sound quality is abhorrent with the built-in noise reduction switched out, and the sonic performance of the B16, though highly acceptable to many, falls below professional broadcast standards.

The B16 is a versatile tool, having sync capability and an optional remote. For quite some time many dealers have been offering 32-T packages consisting of two B16s and the Applied Microsystems ICON sync and autolocate unit. Never have so many tracks been available for so little – around $13,000.

The B16 is not the fastest of multitracks I've used, the transport whizzing through tapes from destination to destination only as fast as

PROFILES AND REVIEWS

transports on other 16-Ts pulling 1″ or even 2″ tape. The transport controls are nicely laid out and legending is quite clear – bar the meters, which are reasonable LED types but are so crammed together that they can be a strain on your eyes, slowing down quick level checks during sessions. An overhead/console version of the B16 is available and I've used this too, but when the pressure is on and you've been up for nearly twenty-four hours solid, those meters still look just as jumbled and confusing – they are simply too close together for instant viewing. This means that a B16's levels can be accessed reliably in a short time only if the machine is beside the desk, and that is *exactly* the position I recommend.

On the face of it, the B16 looks like a dead-cert value-for-money 16-T. And it is. BUT it is not professional on its own, and is not as capable of day-in-day-out usage in a busy studio as some of the 1″ and 2″ 16-Ts you can buy for about the same amount.

Trendiness has certainly had a lot to do with the B16's popularity. Several owners I know would never (before the B16's introduction) have gone to the bank manager and got a loan for a 16-T set-up at home. There are quite a few Soundcraft, Tascam, ITAM and even Studer 16-Ts on the market for $6,000-$7,000, all of which offer potentially better quality performance and (depending on tape speed and noise reduction) are housed in a much more durable casing.

Specification
Tape speed: 15 in/s ±0.6%
Wow and flutter: CCIR unweighted ±0.12% weighted ±0.06%
Pitch control range: ±15%
Standard playback level (400 Hz): -10dBV ±0.5dB
Playback meter indication (400 Hz): 0 VU ± 1 VU
Playback signal to noise (noise reduction off): 47 dB unweighted 51 dB A-weighted
Input monitor level (400 Hz): -10 dBV ±0.5dB
Standard record/replay level with noise reduction on (400 Hz): -10dBV ±0.05dB
Record/replay meter indication with noise reduction on (400 Hz): 0 VU ±1 VU
Channel separation at 1 kHz: >40 dB
Record/replay signal to noise: noise reduction off 47 dB unweighted, 52 dB weighted

Erasure with noise reduction off: >70 dB
Adjacent channel erasure at 10 kHz: <1 dB with noise reduction off
Click level recorded on tape when switching record on/off: > -26 dBV
Bias leakage at line output: >-35 dBV.

Tascam MS16 1″ 16-T: Profile
Price: $9,995

Together with its matching AQ65 Autolocator, the brand new Tascam MS16 offers the 'ultimate' in 1″ 16-T format. Based very much on the 40- and 50-series transport, the MS16 has recently been introduced to supersede the 85-16B, which in any case always did have a bad wow and flutter performance. On the face of it, things haven't changed a great deal; the MS16s preliminary spec. suggests a wow and flutter reading of 1%; I hope this isn't correct.

Features include: SMPTE capability, -10dBV RCA inputs/outputs in *conjunction* with ±4dBm balanced sockets, varispeed of

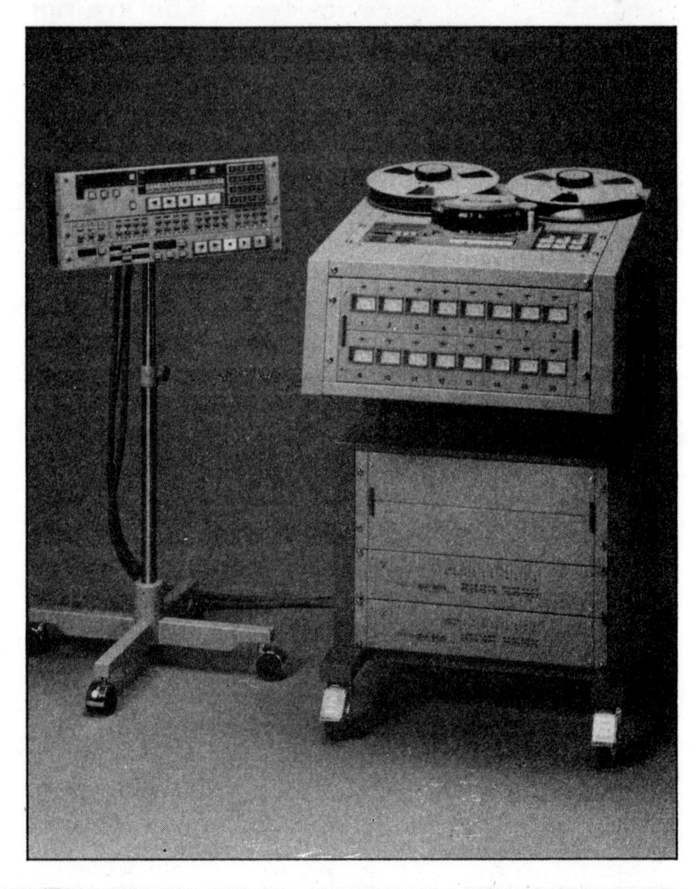

PROFILES AND REVIEWS

+/– 15%, optional 30ips tape speed, and the CS65 console rack which enables the MS16 to be positioned at virtually any angle.

Introducing dbx means that a staggering s/n ratio can be achieved – probably around the 90dB mark. With no noise reduction the figure is still reasonable, at 69dB. (Optional units: DX-8DS.)

With a suggested selling price of around $9,000+/–, the MS16 is to be considered a serious professional machine. I look forward to the day when I book into a studio and they have one of these in the corner!

Specifications
(Mechanical characteristcs)
Tape Format: 16 tracks, 1″ tape width
Reel size: 10-½″, NAB
Tape Speed: 38 cm/s
Speed Accuracy: ±0.2% deviation
Pitch Control: ±15%
Wow and Flutter 0.04% (NAB WTD) 0.07% (NAB UNWTD) ±0.08% peak (DIN/IEC/ANSI WTD) ±0.12% peak (DIN/IEC/ANSI UNWTD)
Fast Wind Time: 120 sec. for 2,400 feet
Spooling Wind Time: 370 sec. for 2,400 feet
Capstan Motor: PLL DC direct drive motor
Reel Motor: Slotless DC motor × 2
Head Configuration: 3-head; erase, rec/sync and reproduce
Dimensions (W×H×D): Transport; 482×459×310 mm Electronics; 482×192×321mm
Weight(net): Transport; 38kg Electronics; 16.5kg
(Electrical Characteristics)
Line Input: Balanced Input Impedance; 10 kohms Nominal Input Level; ±4 dBm Max. Input Level; ±28 dBm, Unbalanced Input Impedance; 50 kohms, Nominal Input Level; -10 dBV, Max. Input Level; ±18 dBV
Line Output: Balanced Output Impedance; 20 ohms, Nominal Output Level; ±4 dBm Max. Output Level; ±28 dBm, Unbalanced Output Impedance; 500 ohms, Nominal Output Level; -10 dBV, Max. Output Level; -10 dBV
Bias Frequency: 145 kHz
Equalization: IEC; 00 ± 35 µsec.
Record Level Calibration: 250 nWb/m
Power Consumption: 200 W
(Typical Performance)
Frequency Response: Record/Reproduce; 40Hz-20kHz, ±3 dB (0 VU), 40Hz-22kHz, ±2 dB (-10 VU), Sync Response: 40Hz-22kHz, ±2 dB (0 VU), 40Hz-22kHz, ±2 dB (-10 VU)
Total Harmonic Distortion: 0.8% at 0VU, 1 kHz 3% at 13 dB above OVU, 1kHz
Signal-to-Noise Ratio: (Reference 3% THD at 1 kHz) 69 dB (A WTD, NAB) 62 dB (UNWTD, DIN AUDIO)
Adjacent Channel Crosstalk: 55 dB at 1 kHz, 0 VU
Erasure: 70 dB at 1 kHz, ±10 VU
Record Amplifier Headroom: 28 dB above 0 VU at 1 kHz

Tascam 32/42 2-T Open Reel Machines: Profile

Price: (32) $1,495
Price: (42) $2,495

The Tascam 32 2-T ¼″ machine has become exceedingly popular recently, following its big brother, the 38 8-T, into use in many domestic and semi-pro situations.

As in the case of the Tascam 30-series, reservations about durability in a busy studio cloud this otherwise very favourable profile.

On the whole – and I know I'm being hard on Revox – the 32 is just as quiet, when running at 15ips, as a B77HS. Tascam have provided jack socket mike inputs on the front panel and the machine comes set up and ready for the unbalanced domestic level of -10dB.

The transport is decidedly smooth, though quite prone to kicking itself out when the

spools are exceptionally uneven with tape. To get the machine back to normal, I had to hand tension the take-up spool evenly where the tape idler/sensor had lost contact. Although this sounds serious, it didn't happen too often. However, it was a fault of which the 42 was also guilty.

There is an LED tape counter with return to zero and a reset button. The headblock is hinged. The 42 offers not only return to zero capability, but also one programmable cue point. The tape counter (LED) is also in minutes and seconds.

If you have serious demo work in mind, or need a hard-working, rugged 2-T, the Tascam 32 would come second to the Revox B77HS; neither's performance is comparable to that of any clear-cut winner, but the Revox has years

of European durability built into it. To be fair, though, the Tascam 32 is, on average, about $250-$300 cheaper.

The 42 is the machine from Tascam I always recommend when anyone asks me which is the best mastering machine – bearing in mind the cost – from this Japanese company. The 52 has more transport finesse and functions but the 42 has SMPTE capability and, although quite expensive, does offer all the right things in all the right places. However, certain prudent observers may find the Otari MX5050B-II ¼″ 2-T better value – it really all depends on your own personal needs.

The 32 is somewhat of a halfway house in terms of ergonomics. More expensive than the Fostex A2, with full-size reel capability, it is cheaper and less rugged than the B77HS. If

PROFILES AND REVIEWS

PROFILES AND REVIEWS

you want full-size reel capability and are *not* going to be wrestling with master editing every day, the Tascam 32 must be first choice for auditioning. If you need durability, then I shall have to recommend the B77HS; if you want advanced mastering facilities, then we're back to choosing the Tascam 42/Otari B-II.

Fostex A-2 2-T Open Reel: Profile
Price: $850

Illuminated VU meters (extended types) are the main feature on the fascia of this little machine from Fostex, my favourite from their A-series.

Like the A-8, the A-2 uses 7″ spools – this is a pity because multitrack small-spool machines are undoubtedly a pain in the neck for serious, long numbers, or for recording live gigs. Nobody likes changing tapes three or four times in one evening of recording. On a mastering machine, where the razor blade and splicing tape rule, small spools are more acceptable. Any really long numbers will only need transferring to a large-spool machine and, at most, one edit to cover the entire length of the track.

Most welcome on the A-2 is the return-to-zero facility on the transport. Varispeed is a

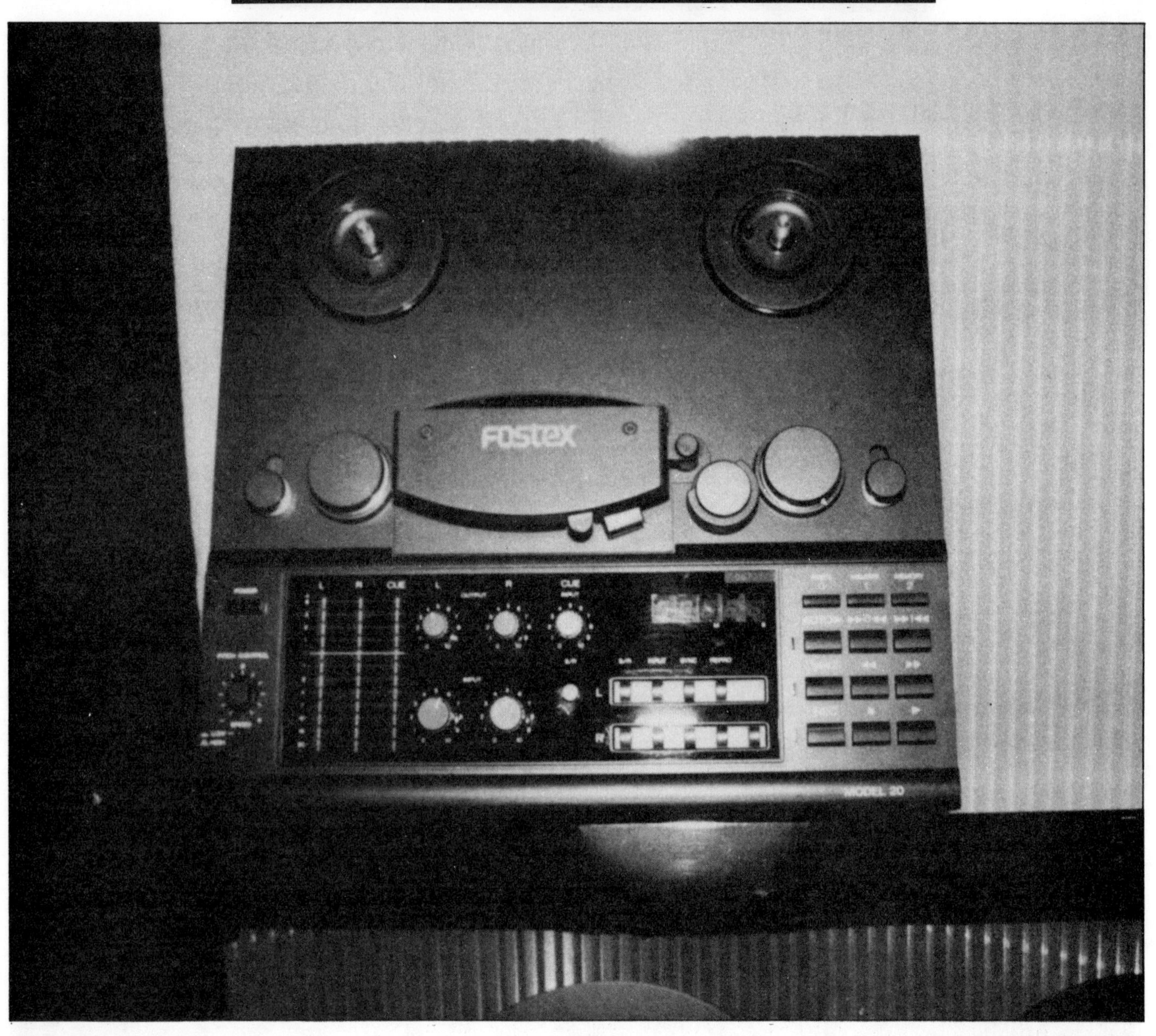

standard ± 10%.

I found the A-2 a lot quieter than many of the Revoxes I've mastered on to in the past, including the B77HS. Running at 15ips, you get pretty acceptable noise levels, provided you put optimum signal down. At 7.5ips, the Fostex A-2 just can't cope; the transport drags along and noise levels spoil any nuances in the music. For rough mixing and economy of tape, the slower speed is an option I'd rather have than not.

To return to the serious matter of transport, the literature says that the A-2 is suitable for sync work. However, the wow and flutter of this machine (1% at 7½ips) does hang a large question mark over the A-2's ability to do well in tight sync environments. (Happily, the new A-2 has a beefed-up transport which is much more constant and reliable.)

The price now being asked in some shops for a Fostex A-2 is something that I sincerely think you should investigate. It is rumoured that, like the A-8, the old A-2 is to be phased out in favour of the new version which has

PROFILES AND REVIEWS

facilities, once again, that 99% of home recordists do *not* need. Even if the final selling price is only a hundred pounds more, that's still a lot extra for your average home recordist to pay for a facility that will be used little – if at all.

Technical Specifications (A-2)
Tape: 1/4" tape width, 1 mil base
Format: 2 track, 2 channel
Heads: 2 track record, 2 track reproduce, 2 track erase
Reel Size: 7 inch
Tape Speed: 15 and 7½ips (38 and 19cm/s), ± 0.5%
Pitch Control: ± 10%
Line Input: -10dBV (0.3V)
Impedance: 30kohms, unbalanced
Line Output -10dBV (O.3V)
Load impedance: 10kohms or higher, unbalanced
Record Level Calibration: O VU referenced to 185nWb/m of tape flux
Equalization: NAB (IEC available in Europe)
Wow & Flutter: ± 0.06% peak (IEC/ANSI), wtd., at 15ips
± 0.10% peak (IEC/ANSI), wtd., at 7½ips
Fast Wind Time: 130 seconds typ. for 1800 ft. of tape
Overall Freq. Response: 40Hz-20kHz, ± 3dB, at 15ips
40Hz-18kHz, ± 3dB, at 7½ips
Signal-To-Noise Ratio (Sync/Reproduce): 65dB wtd., at 15 and 7½ips, referenced to 1kHz, 3% THD level
THD: Less than 1% at 1kHz, O VU
Crosstalk (Reproduce): 50dB (at 1kHz)
Erasure: Better than 70dB at 1kHz
Power Requirements: 120V, AC, 60Hz, 35W*
Dimensions: 13½" H × 14" W × 6¾" D 340mm H × 360mm W × 170mm D
Weight: 29 lbs (13Kg)

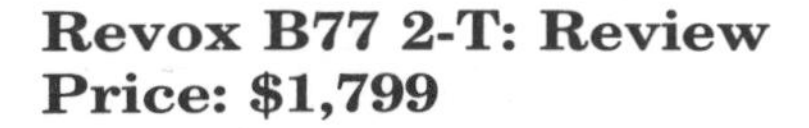

Revox B77 2-T: Review
Price: $1,799

The Ministry of Defence is the biggest UK customer for the Revox B77. Yes, the MODs (as we in the British Music press like to call them) are really into *home recording* – everybody else's, not their own!

I don't know of any other machine that has been brought out in so many versions. There is actually a B77 that goes at nearly cassette speed (2⅛ ips)! The standard machine found in studios is the B77HS (HS = High Speed ie 15ips max.)

The Revox has a reputation for durability and for components of a high, uniform quality and it offers quite reasonable facilities – nothing OTT. Studer, who own Revox, have usefully included an integral edit block and splicer. Varispeed is +/– 10%. Shop-bought B77s are usually lined up for Grand Master Ampex 456 tape and have their (phono) connections levelled to the domestic standard – although there are phono *and* XLR units around too.

I've always felt that I should be knocked out by the B77 performance – if the truth be known, the 1/4" 2-T format is a hissy one (even at 15 ips) and the B77 gives as near to optimum performance in this format as any machine costing less than $2,000.

Transport and operational controls are old-fashioned in design. The tape handling is quite smooth, and the lace-up time is minimized owing to the surprising lack of obstacles in the tape path. The VU meters are a little too sluggish for my liking – initial impressions led

PROFILES AND REVIEWS

me to believe that the LED peak indicators situated in each meter had been calibrated to a point that rendered them too insensitive.

Some people swear by the B77: Robert Fripp has recorded an album using nothing but two of them and a tape loop. I don't think they are particularly brilliant, but *not* having a Studer or Revox on my studio rate card is something I've avoided.

A heavy-duty version of the B77, model number PR99, can be purchased for just over $2,200. If offers many of the extras featured on the Otari B-II, but auditioning it revealed similar sonic performance to the B77. The Otari has, in my opinion, something of an edge on the PR99, but this is merely splitting hairs. The mastering quality from a B77, running at 15ips, is largely accepted by home recordists and cutting engineers alike. The B77 *and* the PR99 are both extremely well-crafted, sturdy, good-quality machines.

PROFILES AND REVIEWS

If you have the funds available, be sure to audition a Revox 77 or a PR99 *before* parting with a penny for a mastering machine.

Otari 5050B-II 2-T: Profile
Price: $2,295

The Otari MX5050 – I do wish they'd finally decide what to call their machines – offers unparalleled facilities for this sort of price. Its top speed is 15ips, although there is switching on the front panel down to 7½ ips; internally, you can make the machine run at maximum 7½ ips and minimum 3¾ips.

Quality of construction is very good, utilising XLR connectors and no phonos. Otari has even included a 1kHz/10kHz test oscillator to aid tape alignment. The meters are slightly-extended VU types, with red LED peaks. This machine, like all those in this section, is ideal for sound-on-sound recording (or S.O.S. as some BBC types prefer to call it!). The head-cover is hinged and has a fixed editing block. Varispeed is a useful, though not amazing, +/− 7%. Otari has also provided an edit button which puts the tape into contact with the heads, even out of motion, to aid chinagraph marking on the tape backing.

One of the best things about this machine is that there is a real time counter with hours as well as minutes and seconds; this is linked to a memory button which rewinds the tape to the programmed point. This is easier to use than the return-to-zero plus cue point system found on the Tascam 40 series machines.

This machine has a switchable output working level: +4dBm (pro)/-10dBm (domestic). It has two input choices: line (balanced 10Kohms) and mike (balanced -70 or -50 dBm switchable).

On the whole, I found this machine of better quality than the Revox B77 (15ips version). The reels were handled with a lot of efficiency and speed, and the memory system was as accurate as any I've come across.

At almost twice the price of a B77, while *not* twice as good, the Otari MX5050 is nevertheless worthy of a place in *any* studio control room. I am confident it can stand up to seven-day-a-week treatment and from a maintenance point of view it is really very good indeed.

Technical Specifications (5050 Mark III/2)
Transport
Tape Width and Channels: ¼″ (6.3mm) tape, 2 channel
Tape Speeds: 15 and 7.5 ips or 7.5 and 3.75 ips internally switchable speed pairs
Maximum Speed Deviation: ±0.2%
Reel Size: ¼″ × 5, 7 or 10.5″ EIA or NAB
Heads (4, in-line): Erase (half track), Play (quarter track), Record (half track), Play (half track)
Motors: D.C. servo-controlled capstan motor, two induction reel motors
Rewind Time: Less than 90 seconds for a 2,400′ reel
Pitch Control: Variable within ±7%
Wow and Flutter: 15 ips, less than 0.04%, 7.5 ips, less than 0.07%, 3.75 ips, less than 0.08%
Electronics
Connectors: Line input, Mike input and Line output: standard three pin XL type. Headphone: standard ¼″ phone jack
Inputs: Line = Active, balanced, 10 kOhms
Mike = Active, balanced, usable: 150 Ohms to 10 kOhms
Switchable 20 dB pad and mute
Outputs: Active, balanced 5 Ohms source impedance +27 dB (ref. 0.775 V) into 600 Ohms or more
Signal-To-Noise Ratio: (3% Third Harmonic to noise floor, 30-18kHz) NAB EQ: 15 ips 72 dB unweighted 7.5 ips 72 dB unweighted 3.75 ips 70 dB unweighted
Equalization: IEC or NAB, switchable
Crosstalk: Less than 55 dB at 1 kHz on adjacent track
Frequency Response: (Record/Reproduce) 15 ips (O VU): 25 Hz to 22 kHz ± 2.0 dB 7.5 ips (-10 VU): 20 Hz to 20 kHz ± 2.0 dB 3.75 ips (-20 VU): 20 Hz to 12 kHz ± 2.0 dB
Operating Level: 250 nWb/m
Distortion (1 kHz, 250 nWb/m): Less than 0.5% Third Harmonic (15 ips)
Test Oscillator Frequencies: Nominal 1 kHz and 10 kHz
Test Conditions: As specified, using 3M #226 tape
Physical
Power Requirements: 100/117/220/240 V, ±10%, 50/60 Hz single phase AC, 140 W
Operating Environment: 40 to 104 degrees F (5° to 40°C), 20 to 80% R.H.
Storage Environment: -5 to + 113 degrees F (-20° to +45°C), 10 to 80% R.H.
Mounting: Vinyl covered wood case; (RK-32) Rack mounting kit and (ZA-52L) Roll-around pedestal, optional
Standard Accessories: Reel hold down knobs, ¼″ × 10½″ empty NAB reel, operation manual and power cord
Optional Accessories: CB-116 Auto locator
CB-102 Remote transport control
ZA-52L Roll-around pedestal
ZA-53T Input isolation transformers
ZA-53S Output isolation transformers
RK-32 rack mount
Weight: 89 lbs. (40 kg) in shipping carton

Technical Specifications (5050B-II)
Transport
Tape Width and Channels: ¼″ (6.3mm) tape, ½ track 2 channel erase, record and reproduce ¼ track 2 channel reproduce
Tape Speed: 15 and 7.5 ips or 7.5 amd 3.75 ips, internally switchable speed pairs
Reel size: 10.5″ EIA or NAB, 5 or 7″ plastic
Reel Size Selector: 2 positions, 10.5″ or 5″/7″ reels
Speed Deviation: Less than ±0.2%
Pitch Control: Variable within ±7%
Wow and Flutter: (measured per NAB weighted) 15 ips less than 0.05% 7.5 ips less than 0.06% 3.75 ips less than 0.12%
Rewind Time: Less than 90 seconds for 2,400 ft. NAB reel
Head Configuration: 4 heads, ½ track erase, ¼ track reproduce, ½ track record and ½ track reproduce
Motors: Capstan: DC servo-controlled motor, direct drive Reels: Two induction torque motors
Transport Controls: Stop, Play, FF, RWD, Record, Edit, Cue, Pitch Control, Speed, Reel Size
Remote Controls: Stop, Play, FF, RWD, Record
Control Logic: TTL with motion sensing protection
Electronics
Connectors: Line Input, Mike input and Line output: standard three pin XLR type Headphone: standard ¼″ phone jack
Inputs: Line: Active, balanced, 10k ohms, Level: min. -15dBm, Max. input: + 30dBm Mike: Active, balanced Level: min. -70 or -50dBm switchable Applicable microphone: 150 ohms to 10k ohms
Outputs: Line: Active, balanced, 5 ohms source impedance Switchable level +4dBm or -10dBm, Max output: +27dBm (600 ohms impedance load) Headphone jack: – 24dBm, 8 ohms or higher impedance
Equalization: NAB or IEC standard, rear panel switchable, Recording equalization front panel adjustable
Signal to Noise Ratio: Unweighted 15 ips, 7.5 ips, 3.75ips, NAB 63dB, 65dB, 65dB, IEC 64dB, 63dB, 65dB, Measured with respect to a record level of 520nWb/m to biased tape noise when using 3M Scotch #226 tape.
Crosstalk: More than 55dB at 1kHz on adjacent tracks
Frequency Response: (overall record/reproduce) 15ips (0VU) 30 to 20,000Hz ±2.0dB 7.5ips (-10VU) 20 to 18,000Hz ±2.0dB 3.75 ips (-20VU) 20 to 10,000 Hz ±2.0dB
Record Level: Switchable, 185, 250 or 320mWb/m
Erase Effect: More than 75dB
Distortion: Less than 0.5% at 1kHz 250nWb/m
Bias Frequency: 133kHz
Test Oscillator Frequency: Nominal 1kHz and 10kHz
Physical
Power Requirements: 100/117/220/240V, ±10%, 50/60Hz single phase AC, 100 watts
Operating Environment: 5° to 40°C, 20 to 80% R.H.
Mounting: Vinyl covered wood case and floor console (ZA-52L) optional
Standard Accessories: Reel hold down knobs, ¼″ × 10½″ empty NAB reel, operation manual and power cord
Optional Accessories: CB-102 remote transport control. ZA-52L roll-around pedestal. Isolation transformers. DIN hub clamp adapter. Scissors.
Weight: 25kg (52 lbs)

Monitors

Fostex 6301 Personal (Self-Powered) Monitor: Profile
Price: $150 ea +/–
Scene: NED Synclavier Stand at the APRS 1985
Dave Whittaker: "Hello. I see you're looking at the Synclavier. The system on show today has full re-synthesis software and over 80% of all parameters are adjustable down to one hundredth of a Hertz. Would you like me to put on this Oscar Petersen demonstration? It uses a sample of a grand piano piece he played a year or so ago and which has recently been re-synthesized."
Punter: "Er . . . no, mate, it's all right. Just bung anything on so I can listen to those little speakers on top of the telly."

Oscar's dulcet notes ripple through the hum and bustle of the Kensington Exhibition Centre.
Punter: "Oh man! They are really, **really** amazin'!"

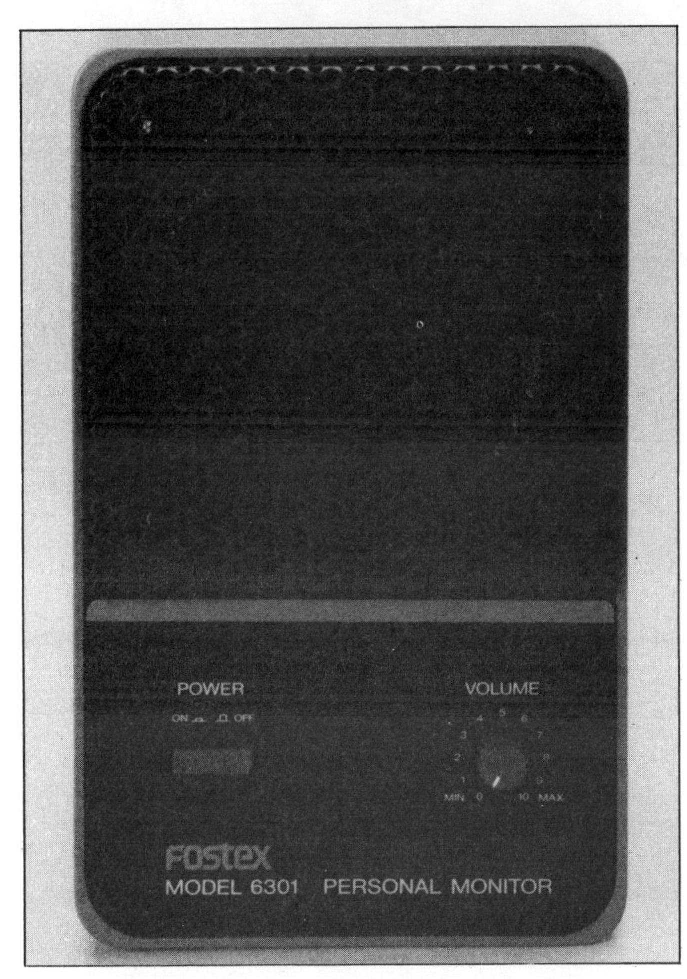

The above scenario is typical of the attention compact 6301 personal self-powered monitors from Fostex get at trade shows.

Working off AC only, each monitor has an on/off switch on the front panel and a gain control marked from 1 to 10. They weigh only about six pounds each and have a frequency response of between 80Hz and 13kHz – which really does rule them out for anything other than 'reference' monitoring. By putting these speakers into the signal chain, direct small speaker/large monitor comparisons can be made. But why make such comparisons? The reason is that most televisions have quite small speakers and AM or Medium Wave radio is mono; so, by introducing small speakers into the monitoring chain and switching into mono, you can tell what the finished product is going to sound like when played on either medium.

Personally, I think the only reliable form of reference monitoring is to do a rough mix on to cassette and play it on a Walkman – but you pays your money and you takes your choice!

These 6301 Personal Monitors are my favourite small speakers. They are lively and creditable. Each has an external speaker output rated at 10W into 8 ohms.

Buy them only for the above reasons – or maybe as car speakers!

Specifications
Speaker (Internal)
Type 10cm Full Range Single Cone
Impedance 4 ohms
Efficiency dB/W (1m) 84
Frequency Range 80Hz-13kHz
Amplifier (External Output Terminal)
Nominal Input Level -10dB (0.3V)
Output More Than 10W RMS (8 ohm load)
Response 20Hz-50kHz, OdB, -3dB
Distortion 0.05% (at 1W output)
Residual Noise -70dBv (0.3mV)
Min. Input Sensitivity 0.5V for max. output

Input Impedance 20k ohm
Power Requirements 120V 60Hz (USA/Canada) 33W
220V 50Hz (Europe) 33W
240V 50Hz (U.K./Australia) 33W
Dimensions 7-3/8″ × 4-3/4″ × 5″ (H,W,D)
188 × 120 × 118mm (H,W,D)
Weight 6 pounds 3.2kg

Quad Electrostatic Loudspeakers: Profile
Price: TBA

On the few occasions on which I have auditioned these speakers from Quad, the ESL63s have never failed to knock me out with their super realism, imaging and transparent

quality. If you've never heard Genesis' 'Blood on the Rooftops' through a pair of these at 100W, you have not yet lived!

Electrostatic loudspeaker technology is unfortunately taking a long time to get fully developed and this means that the ESL63s have not yet found their way into many studios. They are superb for all sorts of music and the price (which at first may seem ridiculous) soon becomes understandable once you've experienced the magic of pure, unadulterated, accurate monitoring.

Large – and most would consider, ungainly – the Quad electrostatic speakers look like square radar-like dishes and unfortunately cannot survive rough handling.

For what they offer, there is no comparison: what they promise, only time will tell.

Tannoy Little Red Monitors: Profile
Price: TBA

Misleadingly named, these Little Red Monitors are neither particularly little nor red! There are two versions – one with a 10″, the other with a 12″ dual concentric driver. Tannoy have included attenuating pots to the front baffle boards for treble energy (handy for dead control rooms) and roll-off.

These speakers are sharp and sparky, providing you drive them with a lot of clean power. They don't strike me as being particularly rugged, but I'm sure they will prove reliable.

Although they are good close-field monitors, I feel the Little Reds are too expensive for what they offer – quite a few times the price of a pair of Stratfords, but *not* proportionately better!

The Tannoy Little Red (third from left). Similar to the SRM10B, 12X & 15X, the Little Red has Tannoy's patented 'Syncsource' time alignment/compensation system: this employs a passive delay in the dual concentric drivers, designed to put all the frequencies out front in 'sync' with each other. Some may say that this is irrelevant due to modern miking techniques, but I say that, whatever the system (if any) used, Tannoy speakers are counted amongst the most accurate in the world.

PROFILES AND REVIEWS

Yamaha MS10 Powered Monitors: Profile
Price: $350

Although the word 'professional' appears on the front baffle of these speakers from Yamaha, any unit that is self-powered and has bass and treble controls is *not* professional.

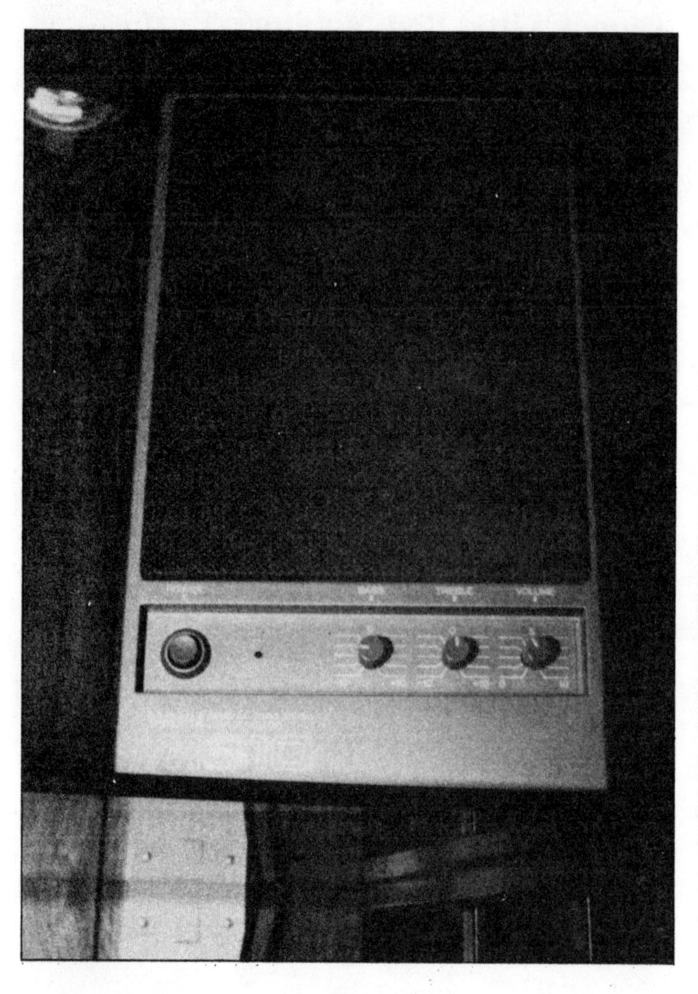

Designed more with the MT44 system in mind, these are a cheap – and certainly not a nasty – solution to certain monitoring problems. If you are a real 'notepad' compact multitracking musician, for example, these could save you the hassle of buying a main driver amp.

These Yamaha monitors should not be considered for anything approaching serious home sessions; they sound "boxy" and the construction is not of a standard that could produce remotely accurate broadcast quality.

Electro Voice EV Sentry 100A Monitors: Profile
Price: $255

These are the next step up from EV's Link series, of which the Link 7 2-way speakers have close field monitoring applications. As

there's little difference in price, however, I've decided to go for the accepted monitor range – the Sentry range – which I feel offers much better value for money.

The EV Sentry 100As are clean and sharp, although a lot of power is needed to get the best from them. A good 150Wp.c. only just gets them to the ticking-over stage; as the amp will cost more than usual, they could turn out to be a false economy. Not that I think the Sentry 100As are cheap – but you have to take into account the fact that they share a similar standing with speakers costing over the £450 mark.

The low frequency reproduction threshold is 45Hz, just 5Hz above the accepted professional low end capability. The speaker is made up from a 25W Super-dome tweeter and a single 8″ bass/mid driver.

All in all, the 100As offer the American version of the Celestion SL6 clarity, except in terms of true-to-life treble. Perhaps over-coloured, the 100As are great for rock music. Nowhere near as good value for money as the SL6s, but a serious contender for your money nonetheless.

Tannoy Stratford: Profile
Price: $199

Walk into any Our Price record shop and the chances are your brain will be seduced by a pair of Tannoy Stratfords (standard issue).

When it comes to a two-way speaker system, costing under $200. I have seen or heard no better. The Stratfords are crisp and concise, offering as much articulation and clarity in close field monitoring applications as any hardened home recordist could ever need.

The Stratfords aren't perfect, though – they never fool you into thinking that they are not there when your eyes are shut. The high-end treble still retains quite a bit of that old, mid-70s, sugary, HiFi quality. This has led less informed people to write Stratfords off as nothing more than accurate HiFi speakers. They most certainly are *not* that – not far from it, mind you – but they definitely aren't in the HiFi bracket.

Although standard connectors have been used, the enclosure seems a little flimsy, and the overall weight and ballast is not too great. Considering the price, the sensitivity figures are very good.

The HF driver is unusual in that it is fluid-cooled. The front baffle board has a ducted port which ensures clear reproduction in the lower-than-normal frequencies. Obviously they can't rival the 40Hz low thresholds of more professional monitors;

however, considering you can buy Stratfords for less than $150 in certain special offers, their low threshold of 53Hz is extremely commendable.

All in all, the Tannoy Stratford is very much the *typical* home recording monitor – it offers articulate, high SPLs with small amounts of amplification, in a medium-sized cabinet. Do not buy a pair of monitors without first auditioning the Stratfords. One retailer (Turnkey) calls them marvels. They are.

Rogers LS7: Review
Price: $500 +/–

Transparent (yes, see-through!) speaker cones are not my cup of tea. Rogers speakers have never really been aesthetically pleasing and their use of a polypropylene bass/mid driver – as in all the LS7 and studio 1 design considerations – has more to do with sound than with looks. Plastic has always offered a much more readily uniform consistency than paper in the manufacturing process. Paper also soaks up air moisture and can be more seriously damaged by sunlight.

Internal examination of the LS7 reveals a rather surprising approach to cabinet con-

struction and interior treatment. By dispensing with any form of bracing, Rogers have broken one of the major rules in enclosure design. If an enclosure is to be used for programme material exceeding 200W – and the LS7s are said to be able to handle between 200W and 300W PHC – bracing is the only way to attain solidity. What's more, the particle or chipboard used is not as thick as one would reasonably expect in a medium-sized speaker enclosure such as this. Damping is achieved by the stapling of strange bituminous panels over a large percentage of the internal wall area; this, coupled with what I think is an excessive amount of foam, not only poses a serious question about the cabinet rigidity, but also gives the LS7s an unnecessarily low sensitivity.

One of the nice things about the LS7s is that they are extremely easy to service; all the crossover components (the literature says there are thirteen but I could only find nine) are PCB mounted. Many monitors three times the price of the LS7s have no PCB mounting arrangements for the crossover components – it's a pity that this sort of design and construction policy was not carried over to the enclosure.

The usual 4mm terminal arrangement is found on the back of these speakers and to compensate for the fact that it is not recessed – and therefore can be more easily damaged – Rogers have used a thicker and more rugged type of connector.

The exterior veneer is not particularly inspiring and the grille, made from black woven plastic, has a nasty sheen to it.

Not being one to hold back the bad news, I have to say that, in my opinion, the LS7s are totally useless when it comes to handling any music which contains a bit of bite or power.

There was just no way I could play rock music through them at more than 75W without serious distortion. At 300W peak power, the LS7s became a joke. They staggered through the Power Station's 'Some Like It Hot'. Tony Thompson's drum work splattered and spluttered, and there was an awful sort of permanent 'boooommmmm' present on all the rock music I played.

I moved on to jazz and another problem appeared once Weather Report embarked on the quiet passages. The integration was not at all good. If I closed my eyes, the speakers just would not disappear and the treble seemed to have its own point in space.

Classical music (Radio 4) was handled well, except for the more boisterous passages of Beethoven and Bach. Again, once the amplifier had been pushed to its limits, and after I'd spent the best part of an hour controlling clipping, bass response was still messy and unco-ordinated.

These speakers are starkly flat and this leads me to the conclusion that, throughout the design process, Rogers must have had blinkers on. It's no good at all having flat speakers when they are incapable of handling anything but Radio 4 programme material.

The LS7s may be good for the BBC, who have influenced Rogers speaker designs for a long time; for me, they offer very little.

Technical Specifications (Rogers LS7)
Frequency Response: 55Hz-18KHz ± 3dB
Impedance: 8 ohms nominal
Sensitivity: 88dB @ 1m for 2.83 volts input
Maximum Sound Pressure Level: 107dBA (pair @ 2m)
Power Handling: 300 watts peak programme
200 watts continuous programme
Recommended Amplifier Power: 25-150 watts
Drive Units: Rogers 205mm cast chassis Polypropylene Copolymer coned Bass/Midrange driver with high flux magnet and ultra high temperature KAPTON voice coil system. Celestion 25mm Laser-developed soft dome tweeter.
Crossover: 13 precision elements crossing over @ 3KHz @ 18dB per octave
Bass Loading: Reflex to form a well-damped Quasi Butterworth 3rd order maximally flat alignment with a -3dB point @ 55Hz. (This filter function is formed by the combined interaction of the L.F. drive unit characteristics, cabinet volume and port dimensions).
Connectors: 4mm banana posts spaced @ 19mm
Recommended Placement: Stands minimum 35cm (14") high with loudspeakers angled inwards so that their axis crossing is just in front of the listener.
Cabinet: Medite (MDF board) critically damped. Selected veneers of Walnut, Teak or Black Ash. Black grille cloth.
Dimensions: 559 mm (22") high
273 mm (10.75") wide
280 mm (11") deep
Weight: 13.5 kg net (30 Lbs.)

Technical Specifications (Rogers Studio 1)
Frequency Response: 80Hz-20kHz ± 3dB

PROFILES AND REVIEWS

Impedance: 8 ohms nominal
Sensitivity: 85dB @ 1m for 2.83 volts input
Maximum Sound Pressure Level: 100dBA (pair @ 2m)
Power Handling: 200 watts peak programme
100 watts continuous programme
Recommended Amplifier Power: 15-100 watts
Drive Units: Rogers 125mm Polypropylene Copolymer coned Bass/Midrange driver fitted with ultra high temperature KAPTON voice coil system. SEAS 19mm synthetic dome tweeter with Ferro Fluid cooling and damping.
Crossover: 10 precision elements crossing over @ 4kHz @ 18dB per octave
Bass loading: Reflex to form a Quasi Butterworth 3rd order maximally flat alignment with a -3dB point @ 73Hz. (This filter function is formed by the combined interaction of the L.F. drive unit characteristics, cabinet volume and port dimensions).
Connectors: 4mm banana posts spaced @ 19mm
Recommended Placement: Stands minimum 50cm (19.5") high with loudspeakers angled inwards so that their axis crossing is just in front of the listener.
Cabinet: Medite (MDF board) critically damped. Selected veneers of Walnut, Teak, Black Ash or Rosewood. Black grille cloth.
Dimensions: 330 mm (13") high
191 mm (7.5") wide
165 mm (6.5") deep
Weight: 4.5 kg net (10 lbs)

Rogers Studio 1 Monitors: Review
Price: $595

The Rogers Studio 1 monitors differ from the

LS7s in that they employ a bextrene bass/mid cone and two *high*-range tweeters. Integrating three rather than two units is much more difficult and success depends on picking high-range units that complement each other sonically. It is also imperative that chosen crossover frequencies enter and leave the recipient driver's range with a generous amount of leeway. The first crossover point is at 3kHz and feeds into a Celestion 1300 driver. At 14kHz, we enter the second crossover point and the frequencies above this are handled by a KEF T27.

This arrangement has many merits, but also a number of disadvantages – one of which, concerning sound integration, has already been aired. Personally, I feel that good free standing medium-sized monitors (like the Studio 1s) are capable of articulate and accurate sound pictures with no need for a third high-range driver. Bass/mid cones are so advanced nowadays that each area of frequencies is easily attainable even with small amounts of amplification. A three driver system, especially in the case of the Studio 1s, is somewhat archaic in the light of recent cone developments (see the Celestion SL6 review).

The three-way split, so unavoidable in a three driver system, in conjunction with the use of a bextrene cone is probably responsible for the Studio 1s even lower sensitivity figure than the LS7s – 87.5dB SPL @ 1W @ 1m.

The Studio 1s have a removable back panel as Rogers have seen fit to mount the bass/mid driver on the rear of the front baffle board – a practice I haven't seen employed by major speaker manufacturers for a long time. On the pair I looked at, the back panel on the left speaker fitted less snugly than on the other. This is *very bad*. Sound gaps around the edges of panels on speaker enclosures can allow stray soundwaves, created by the cone's rarefaction, to leak out and cancel the legitimate soundwaves coming from the front of the cone.

Internal surfaces are treated in the same way as those of the LS7s. Bitumen-type panels are there to absorb resonant frequencies and seem to do a pretty good job of it.

Connections are via 4mm terminals and BBC spec. XLR-F sockets.

Bass handling was better than with the LS7s. You have to run well into the 300W mark to get high SPLs and this could make you run into clipping problems. Stereo imaging, for a pair of speakers costing this much, was totally unremarkable.

Rock music – in fact, anything with a bit of bite – again failed to stir the electronics or drivers into faithful, lively renditions. The strains of John Entwhistle and Keith Moon had the bass/mid cone getting closer and closer to shuddering point. For classical, non-boisterous stuff, they were certainly extremely flat and faithful. But, at the end of the day, I was not impressed.

Both the LS7s and Studio 1s need bags of amp power to attain high SPLs. In close monitoring situations, this is not too important, as even small transients in the music have improved impact at close quarters. Their range of clarity allows me to recommend them for home recording of classical music only.

Audition both these speakers very carefully.

Celestion SL6: Review
Price: $450

Celestion is an excellent British company with a first-rate track record. Jim Marshall has used their drive units exclusively in his amplification systems and, mainly thanks to the all-round performance and ruggedness of the drivers built by the Ipswich-based company, he has acquired an international reputation for quality.

I'm not going to beat about the bush – quite simply, the Celestion SL6s are *the* finest speakers I have ever heard. They are in the same class as Urei 815s – huge machines which cost a fortune and take up about twenty times the space! So what makes the Celestion SL6s as good as the giant Ureis? Well, both types of speaker have the same ability to make stereo come alive: 'stereo imaging' is the term used – to describe what is almost a religious experience. It occurs when sound is projected all around your head, with vertical sensations and a deep perspective drawing you closer to the music, and with the speakers just disappearing and turning transparent when you close your eyes.

The SL6s are the ultimate in near-field monitoring, offering the small-studio owner capabilities that were previously within the reach only of big-budget studios – and in extremely attractive, relatively small packages.

Designed by Allen Boothroyd, the exterior looks extremely professional. Celestion have employed advanced technology to optimalize the design and performance of the drive units in these speakers. Extremely involved measurements and observations were made possible at the design stage by a process called optical interferometry. This entails monitoring light-wave variations via a sync-pulsed strobe light, the light-wave frequencies and variations being reflected from the cone as it reacts to various audio frequencies. All clever stuff, but what matters to you and me is that these speakers are better for the R&D process that spawned them. Just ten minutes listening will confirm this.

The SL6s have a bass/mid driver and an aluminium dome tweeter. The sound that emanates from them, however, is not entirely due to this simple but hugely effective combination: the real wood enclosures incorporate infinite baffle design – one of the reasons why these speakers should be placed well away from walls if optimum results are to be achieved.

One minor complaint: the terminals at the back, although of very good quality, are slightly awkward flush-fitted binding post types.

At first glance you may shudder, if you understand these things, at the very bad sensitivity level: 82dB at 1W at 1 metre. The SL6s are only a tenth as loud as the Tannoy Stratfords or Electro Voice EV Sentry 100As. But, in practical terms, a sensitivity reading doesn't matter. You must allow your ear to be the judge in *all* cases. The SL6s, I can assure you, can be *loud*.

It's important to remember that these are close-field monitors – put 70W through them and your ears won't be splitting apart as is the case with some speakers. You will just experience loud, but safe, articulate, detailed music which can pump your chest with bass and transfer every single nuance of a cymbal crash. You will certainly require a stronger than usual amp – but that is nothing to worry about.

Unlike 90 per cent of the 'monitor' speakers on the market, the Celestion SL6s are capable of handling *every* type of music from classical to heavy metal, transferring and relaying *everything* to your ears. Even when your head is positioned close between the two at, say, a distance of less than three feet, sound integration between bass, mid and treble cannot be faulted. Each pair comes with its own personal trace, showing the frequency curve, and it is *not* the flattest one could buy at this price. However, the coloration that is present serves to enhance the sound; it is not there at certain frequencies, nor in any case in sufficient quantities, to put your final frequency content judgements at risk. Coloration, in a controlled and easily-identifiable format, is *not* impossible to work with: intimate relationships with the music you record and mix on speakers comes from *knowing* them, detail by detail.

The top-end exposed none of the unnatural sugary rawness some monitors possess – *all* high frequencies were dealt with beautifully. Articulation is the key word here – even at high SPLs where music criticisms are usually aired when a flaw has been heard for the first time.

When you are using the SL6s it is possible, owing to the clarity they possess, to find mistakes and tiny errors in the best-known of tracks. Jean-Michel Jarre's 'Oxygene Part 4', for instance, will never sound the same again – once you hear the mistakes on the Celestions, you remember they exist and, even when playing it on Walkman headphones, your brain annoyingly inserts them!

Power handling is relative to the amount of "twang thump jump" bass the programme material contains. If you're recording funk or rock, then 90W per channel should not be exceeded if you want to keep the speakers in perfect condition for a number of years. As far as classical music is concerned (but not the *1812 Overture*) 200W would not strain these marvellous little performers.

Only one record in a hundred is recorded in true stereo; if more people used their heads in combination with their ears, this shortcoming would all but disappear. I suggest that you sit in front of a pair of SL6s turned up to about 60W per channel on an amp with another 40W p.c. headroom (so as not to experience clipping), and play the compact disc version of Phil Collins's 'In the Air Tonight'. Superb!

For serious stereo work, the SL6s have no match at this price level. Seated with the mid-range unit pointing at your ears and the tweeters slightly above (the preferable arrangement, oddly enough, for these speakers), and spacing them about four and a half feet apart and with your head about three feet away, you'll find there is simply no equal.

Full of clarity, perhaps too truthful (although I approve of perfection), I cannot believe there are better speakers around. Well done, Celestion!

Technical Specifications
Dimensions: Height 370 mm/14.5″
Width: 200mm/8″
Depth: 255mm/10″
Effective internal volume: 12 litres/0.4 cubic feet
Impedance: 8 ohms
Amplifier requirements: 35-120 wats (Continuous rated sinewave output)
Sensitivity: 1 watt at 1 metre produces 82 dB SPL
Power rating: 100 watts programme
Crossover: 2.3 kHz second order high and low pass
Low frequency performance: -3 dB 75 Hz -6 dB 60 Hz
Weight (each): 7.7 kg/17 lbs

Celestion Ditton 100: Profile
Price: $125

A book on home recording would not be complete without mentioning the Celestion Ditton 100s. These little, inexpensive speakers are clear, defined and punchy. They excel in all types of programme material and, for the money, are impossible to beat. They do not have the really articulate magic of the SL6s but, after all, the technology is different and the latter cost on average $325 more!

These speakers closely compare in price and performance with the excellent Monitor Audio R252s. For me, the R252s have it, but the edge

PROFILES AND REVIEWS

is almost too small to define easily. Do not go any further into researching monitors without auditioning these Ditton 100s with a bit of Dire Straits. Sit close, shut your eyes and these speakers will all but disappear.

Celestion have done themselves proud with these lovelies; I find it difficult to believe that better can be achieved at the price.

Amplifiers

Amplifiers: A General Introduction

What constitutes a 'good' amplifier? First of all, and quite simply, an amplifier *cannot* be hallmarked good or bad on the basis of its power rating alone. Too many home recordists I meet are under the impression that any mega amp (600W upwards) *must* of necessity be good. This is garbage. Secondly, too much emphasis is put on amplifier usage rather than *quality*. I use what I feel is best for the job in hand, whether the manufacturers concerned recommend their amps for running P.A., for studio monitoring or for HiFi.

When you strip away the outside fascia and peripheral electronics, nearly all high-quality (and a lot of MOR amps) are basically designed around exactly the same circuit (MOSFET).

Overheating in modern day amplifiers is a rare occurrence. (No amp in any studio I've worked in has ever overheated.) If an amp *does* overheat, it is usually as a result of how it has been placed in the control room (eg, near a radiator in winter) and *not* because of a design fault. Nevertheless, many top-quality amps do have excellent cooling mechanisms: these rely on a fan system which either blows the hot air through a grille on the front cover or employs heat sinks (fins) that release their heat by

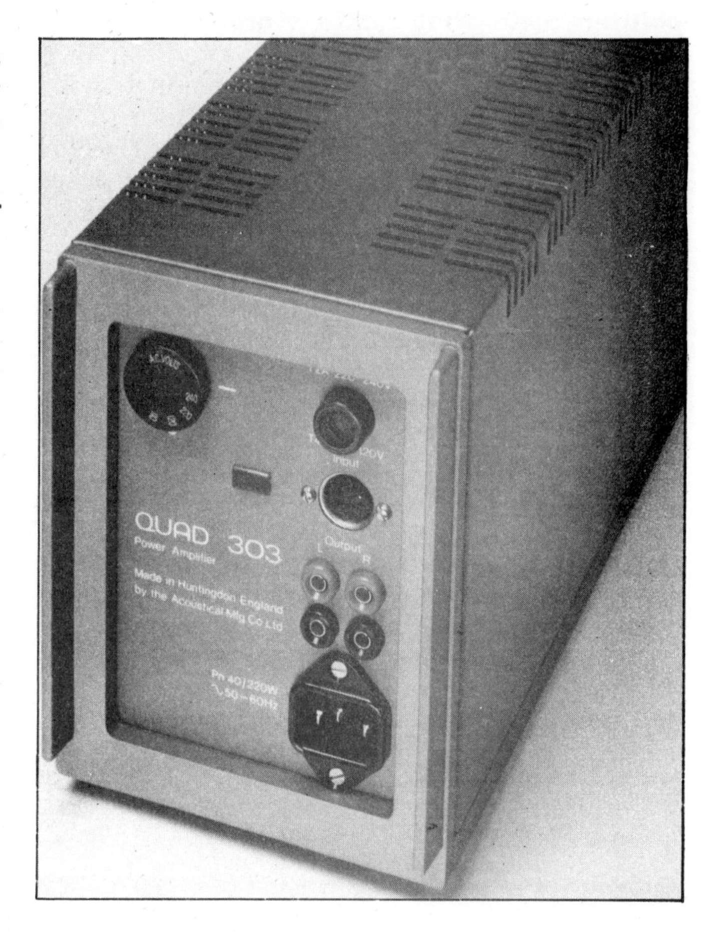

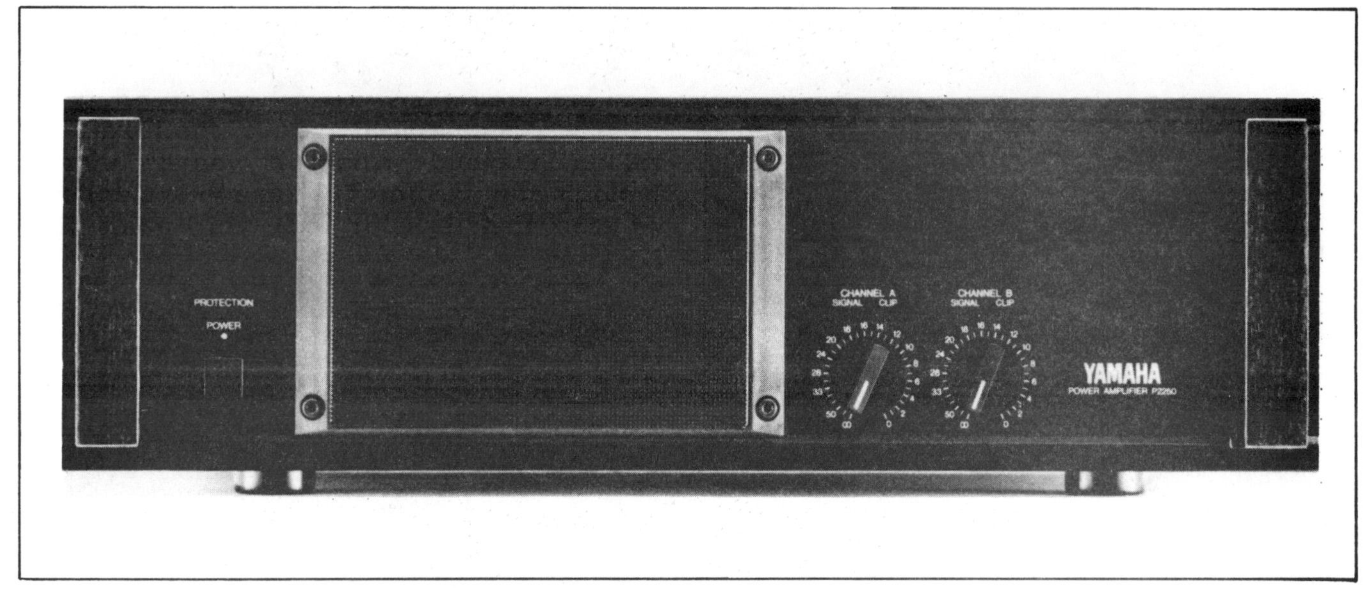

*Above right: The classic Quad 303. Bottom: One of the new Yamaha P series amps, sporting **a** front mounted ventilation grille.*

means of convection. I've already given some pointers as to what makes or breaks an amplifier. Just make sure you get an amplifier that does *not* exceed the power transience your monitors can handle. An amp I use for many things is the NAD 3020B. This is advertised as being a high-quality HiFi amp, but it is perfectly suitable for monitoring purposes – even though its power rating is only 30Wp.c. *Clean* amplifiers fool the ears into apparently hearing things a lot louder than they actually are; therefore 30W from a NAD 3020B into a pair of Tannoy Stratfords (whose sensitivity is quite high) is equivalent to the average '60Wp.c.' HiFi system.

There are more *good* amplifiers on the market suitable for a small studio than there are pages in this book. A new amplifier range is launched (on average, in this country) about once every three weeks. Amplifiers based around the accepted standard electronics circuit I've already mentioned are very easy to manufacture.

In short, look for the right power rating to suit your needs, look for an uncoloured, 'open'-sounding amp, look for one that is going to give you years of unquestionably loyal service.

Don't forget to use good-quality, monster-gauge mains cable when connecting your speakers. Bad wire will reduce clarity and speaker-response times.

You won't find as many units profiled here as in some of the other equipment sections. By referring to the basics covered in the first half of this book *and* to the Glossary of terms, you should be able to judge quite easily whether an amplifier warrants further investigation or not. A similar approach has been adopted in the microphone section.

Quad 405-2 & 303 Amplifier Profiles
Price: 405-2: $495
303: $250

Quad enjoy a revered, respected and envied reputation in the amplifier business for pro-

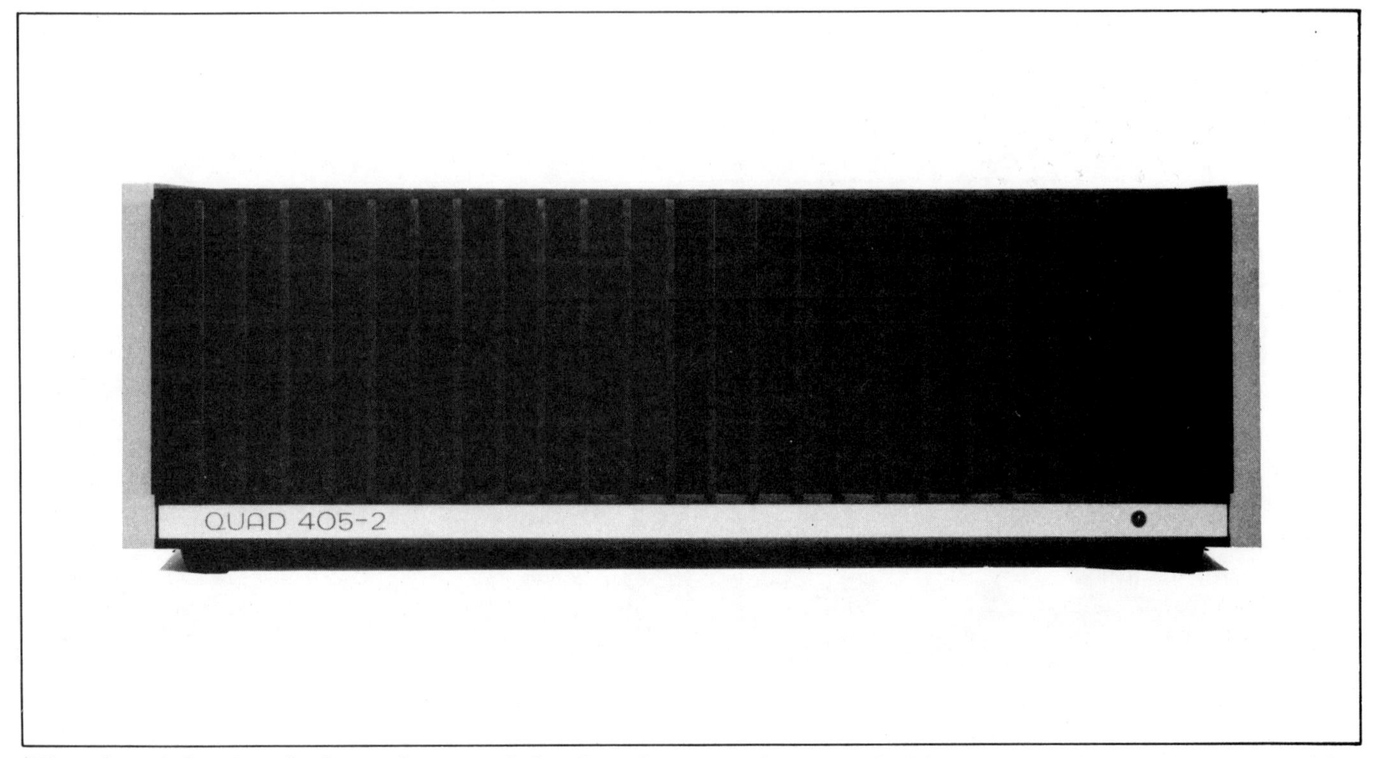

The classicly simple front fascia of the Quad 405-2. A remarkable amp and for a long time it's been the flagship from the Acoustical Manufacturing Company.

PROFILES AND REVIEWS

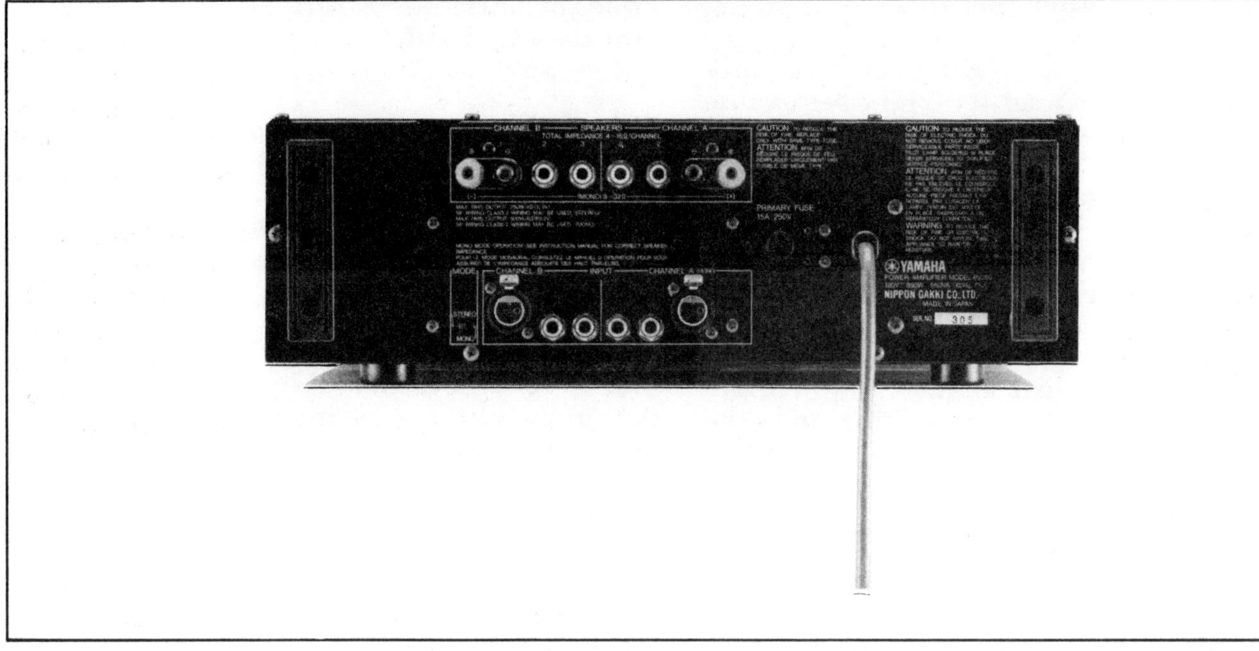

The back of a P series amp from Yamaha. Connections can either be made via jack or XLRs.

ducing extremely high-quality units – such as the 405-2 and 303 – at what I consider to be quite reasonable prices. On the current market it is difficult to find a 100Wp.c. amplifier suitable for studio purposes that costs less than $500, and as I have refused to feature amplifiers that exceed this price tag (regardless of how powerful they may be), the Quad 405-2 provides the perfect illustration of the fact that obtaining quality doesn't necessarily have to mean spending a *lot* of money.

I don't suggest you buy this amp unless you have a truly well-thought-out patchbay and mixer stereo buss, since apart from a power LED, the 405-2's front panel sports nothing more than a heat sink! Pushing out 100Wp.c. into 8ohms, the 405-2 is a classic of our day.

The 303

Also employing the Quad current-dumping technology, and offering 45W, the 303 is *the* ideal back-up amplifier, with a specification that at the time of its release was rivalled only by other Quad projects – and they hadn't even reached the public yet!

Basically, if you buy Quad amplifiers, you can't go wrong. Some incredible deals are being offered on both these amps and it is well worth paying the price for the pleasure of owning a piece of British technical heritage – let alone for the quality you receive in return for your money.

The new P series Yamaha amplifiers: Profile
Price: 2150: $545
2250: $695

Yamaha have made the clever move of producing smaller versions of their excellent top-line amps, which have found themselves in the world's best studios. In the new range – called the P series – there are two stereo models: the 2150 and 2250. These machines exceed the limits of this section in terms of both power output and (roughly speaking) price, but warrant a mention nevertheless because the circuitry used is scaled down from the excellent PG pro-end amps – which I consider to be the best amplifiers in the world.

Rack-mountable and smart in appearance, the P series looks set to start a new trend in small studios.

PROFILES AND REVIEWS

NAD 3020B: Profile
Price: $195

Offering 30Wp.c., the NAD 3020B is quite simply (next to the Quad 405-2) the best-value unit on the market. It oozes quality, looking smart and regal and featuring excellent-quality components both externally and internally.

This is a loud amp, giving you all the monitoring power you should ever require when working in close-field situations, in an average-sized room with monitors of medium to above-average sensitivity.

Many top-line studios are waking up to the fact that for around $200 the 3020B offers superb facilities and quality, and is ideal for powering reference monitors.

Audition one carefully on a decent pair of monitors (preferably the ones you are intending to buy – or have already bought). You will probably be amazed at the naturalness and the uncoloured operation it offers.

Tascam MH-40 Multi split-headphone amplifier: Profile
Price: $275

Offering a switchable rear-panel input selection of -20dB, -10dBm, 0dBu and +4dB, the MH-40 is a flexible and handy device, suitable for running four separate stereo/mono headphone feeds, with a master pan pot on the front panel. Rack-mountable, it is very good-looking and very handy, saving as it does hours of effort that it would take to put together a multi-feed fold-back system. The input signal (left and right) can be injected into two front-panel jack sockets or into two phono plugs on the back.

Output is 100mw into 8ohms – perhaps not the preferred running level for some engineers, but provided the output signal and impedance is loud enough for your headphones, you shouldn't encounter too many problems.

Mixers

Dynamix Mixers: Profile and Review

The D3000 range is Dynamix's top-liner; their PMR range (also sold under the 'Seck' name by Turnkey in London) follows behind, and at the bottom of the heap comes their range of 'into 2' mixers (ie. 6:2, 12:2 and so on).

The PMR

Probably more 8-T packages have been put together with the Dynamix PMR 16:8:2 than with any other unit. The desk has all the major features required for doing full back-line 8-T sessions. The mike/line gain amps are quite noisy and you have to work with your multi-rack, sticking down nothing except *optimum* levels (above the noise floor, but below saturation and distortion), so that on the tape-return channels (numbered 9-16) no extra gain needs to be added. If the pots *are* kept to the absolute minimum, relying on the quietest form of gain (with the fader at full tilt), the PMR offers outstanding overall quality.

The $1,750 or so being asked for the PMR 16:8:2 makes this unit quite a bargain.

D3000 Review

So you don't want to put a second mortgage on the hovel, but still have a good 8-track set-up

The Dynamix 16:16:2 D3000

with a decent mixer that can cope with lots of different applications? Come this way . . .

The D3000 series from Dynamix is a step up from the old PMR (Professional Multitrack Range) in more ways than one, and has started a little price war amongst its competitors – especially when it comes to the professional 8-track market. The range has some features which you wouldn't expect to find on even some of the more advanced desks, such as switchable ballistics on the LED meters, EQ bypass on every channel, P&G standard option, 4 auxiliaries and phase switching for all the inputs!

The 16:8:2 seems to offer good value for money; with an RRP of £2,420 it should be well within the means of anybody wishing to go into 8-track recording seriously. And so, after installing it in my studio over one lazy summer afternoon, we started to talk turkey (use it).

The first thing that hits you when you start using this desk is the fact that *all* of the control knobs and switches *and* the meters *and* all of the connectors are of uniform quality, which is very high. No compromises have been taken as far as construction is concerned, and it's clear that Dynamix take a lot of care with the assembly of these mixers.

The design is fully modular, but includes some interesting differences to the normal way of going about things. For a start, the fader modules are separate from the rest of the channel electronics; this means you don't have to worry about taking the *whole* channel out of the frame just to service the fader or, for example, to replace an LED in the control section. However, you wouldn't immediately

realize that the channels were in two different modules, as they've conveniently fitted a scribble strip where the modules join up. This not only hides the join, but is also the ideal place for making notes, since it's between the pan pot and the routing switches.

Most of the pots on the D3000 are fine click types, with centre detents. The spacing is excellent, as is the colour-coding of all the controls; this makes the mixer very easy to work with, as you can tell at a glance where each section lies – there's nothing worse than a mixer with cramped controls and no colour-coding. Thank God Dynamix have carried on their policies in this range.

Features

Starting with an input channel, running downwards, the first connector is the mike input which is the standard XLR-F; this is of reasonable quality and fitted all of my mikes well (unlike some other XLR sockets I've come across). It's wired in the conventional way, using pin 1 as screen, 2 as return, 3 as live and it's transformer balanced. Obviously it can be used with any form of dynamic mike which has a low impedance output, or with condenser mikes utilizing the standard 48 V phantom power supply. Next is the line out socket using a mono jack; this is a superb feature to have on a 16:8:2 and can obviously be used for many different applications, such as becoming another FX send for that particular channel. After that you have the independent mono jack insert return and send sockets – again this is quite an exceptional feature for a mixer of this price, as it means you don't have to make up sixteen stereo to two mono jack leads

A Dynamix 20:4:2 PMR desk

PROFILES AND REVIEWS

for the insert FX – excellent! Last of all in this section, you have the line in socket in the usual ¼″ jack configuration. This input is transformer balanced, but will accept a mono plug carrying an unbalanced signal; its high impedance will match to almost any line level input.

After the connections, there are four switch buttons with a peak red LED which shows when the pre-fade signal peaks at +20dBm (which is 2dB within clipping). The first of the buttons is for selecting the phantom power, the second is the usual mike (depressed) or line (up) selector, which also acts as a 20dB attenuator on the mike input if nothing is plugged into the line input socket. The third button is to select the 20dB pad which affects both mike and line inputs. The final button in this particular group is the selector to bring in reverse phase on both the mike and line inputs. This is designed to get rid of nasty 'dead spots' which are caused when you're using a selection of microphones and phase cancellation appears; again this is a feature which many more expensive mixers don't have as standard.

Moving slightly further down, we come to the first pot which as always is the gain control, this varies the gain of the input amplifier over a range of 30dB. The manufacturers recommend that it should be used in conjunction with the pad switch so that it is between 40%-80% of maximum; the input gain should be set as high as possible without causing the peak indicator to flash, so as to ensure the best possible distortion and signal-to-noise performance of the mixer – more of this later.

Next, we come to what is probably the most important feature of any mixer – the good old EQ section! In my opinion the EQ section on this D3000 is about the most powerful and accurate you're ever going to get on a mixer this size and at this price. It's a 4-band affair utilizing 6 pots. It consists of fixed frequency bass and treble with two parametric mid-range filters. The pots are fine click types with centre detents for easy zeroing; there's a handy EQ bypass switch too, which enables you to do A/B type comparisons on all the input signals – again an extremely useful feature to find on a mixer at this price. The EQ characteristics are as follows: Treble +/– 15dB at 12kHz – Shelving response, Mid 1+/– 15dB at 600Hz – to – 10kHz sweepable – Bell response, Mid 2+/– 15dB at 100Hz – to – 1kHz sweepable – Bell response, Bass +/– 15dB at 60Hz Bell response.

The next bit we come to is yet another (and I know you'll be sick and tired of hearing this) feature which you'll be hard pushed to find on any of its relatively priced competitors, which shows just how much forethought and planning has gone into this range of mixers – the independent send and return pots. The send pot controls how much of the signal from the socket on the back is sent to outboard equipment. Better still, Dynamix have then provided a return pot which determines the amount of straight or 'dry' signal that is left, as opposed to FX signal. This is a very simple arrangement – by turning the pot all the way clockwise you get just the processed signal, or by turning it all the other way, you're left with the unaffected signal. The centre detent denotes a 50%-50% mix, though of course you can have it in any proportion between 0% and 100%. An added bonus is the fact that you can use the return socket on the back as another line level input!

Coming down a bit further, we come to the auxiliaries, where you have at your disposal two pre-fade for use as foldback channels and two post fade for use as FX, though as we all know there are no steadfast rules to stick to.

Finally, at the bottom of every I/P channel you have the ever present pan pot, a portion of scribble strip (mentioned earlier) and the routing switches which take the form of the usual 'odd-and-even' arrangement, together with a red PFL and its accompanying LED indicator. The sub-group out sections have the same independent insert send and return sockets and controls, together with send pots that internally route the signal to aux 1 and/or 2. Also, there's the monitor level and pan pot, with the tape monitor selector. Basically, this is about the most control over sub out groups I've ever seen on a mixer costing under $6,000!

Last, but by no means least, we have the Output Modules and the Monitor Module. The former features the independent send and return controls for inserting FX into the signal path, an auxiliary return pot which receives from the sends on aux 2 and 3; the aux returns on these two master modules even have full routing capability, AFL *and* pan! The Monitor Module has all four of the aux outs, stereo tape in and stereo monitor out sockets, all the associated selectors, together with the four aux AFL pots. There's also a talkback selector. The stereo phones output and XLR-F connector for the talkback mike are situated on an adjacent panel; the talkback has its own independent routing system and can be sent to any or all of the auxiliaries.

Phew! Right, let's get down to the real nitty gritty!

On Trial

This is the important bit! I had the mixer in my studio for just over a couple of weeks; this meant we had it going through three completely different sessions, from beginning to mix-down. Because of the clear legending and good colour coding I knew where everything was within half an hour of setting it up. It exuded a sense of smoothness and there were no gremlins apparent at all. Gain amp hiss was audible with the pots all the way up – keeping them to minimum resulted in perfect recording conditions. The noise figures quoted aren't exactly stunning, being 69dB with all inputs routed at unity gain, but as in all things, it's the end product and ease of operation that counts; the D3000 scores highly on both these counts.

The metering is LED and you have a choice of ballistics – either PPI or VU; the switching is independent on all of the sub out groups and master O/Ps. Being an outboard freak, it didn't take me long to have all the auxiliaries and half the inserts stuffed full of compressors, gates, flangers, DDLs and a couple of stereo reverbs. On mix-down I never use dedicated aux returns, as bringing the FX output into an input channel gives you a lot more added flexibility and all the routing you could ever want. The EQ section did its job superbly; the sweepable mids were handy for turning synth and sax sounds alike inside out, and having 15dB of cut and lift on all four bands at hand was more than enough!

It brought tears to my eyes to see the mixer go. You tend to get attached to these sort of things – especially if they impress the clients!

All in all then, as far as the practical side of things went, it handled beautifully. Looking back on the sessions I did with the desk, and listening to the masters, it dawns on me that the D3000 has just about every important feature one could ever ask for when it comes to doing 8-track work.

Conclusions

There's no doubt in my mind that Dynamix have come up with a winner. Anyone looking for a serious 16:8:2 should most definitely not miss out on giving one of these a try before buying. It's a strange thing, but in this business there seems to be a sort of prejudice when it comes to products such as this which offer amazing value for money. Recently at the APRS I watched a couple of French-Canadian guys wandering around not bothering to look at any 16 buss desks if they were under £6,000! Certainly, when it comes to compromising facilities for a lower price, I'm the first to shout out aloud; however, I don't think anyone can argue seriously that Dynamix have cut corners on the number and type of facilities on this range of mixers to keep down prices.

Specification
Gain Mike Input (max) 64dB, Line Input (max) 44dB – Input amp only
Overall (max) 76dB Mike input to sub out
Noise Equivalent input noise -127Bv Ref 200 ohms
Output noise -96dBv Faders down
-69dBv All inputs routed unity gain
Crosstalk @ 40Hz-100dB, @ 1KHz-78dB, @10KHz-59dB – Measured at sub 3 output with sub 2 at + 20dBv
Input impedance
Mike input 600 ohms Balanced
Line Input ohms
Insert return ohms
Tape Return 47K ohms Unbalanced
Aux return 47K ohms Unbalanced
Output Impedance All outputs 470 ohms unbalanced
Distortion THD Better than 05% @ 1KHz
Meter Calibration
VU OVU = +4dBv RMS
PPI +4VU = +18dBv Peak
Headroom +22dBv or +18VU
Frequency Response
Mike Input 35Hz-35KHz -3dB points
Line inputs 35Hz-35KHz -3dB points
All others 10Hz-35KHz -3dB points

Ram Mixers RM18 Mega/RM16/RM10: Profile
Price: RM10: $995
RM16: $1,395
Mega: $2,795

The Mega is the top-line desk of the three Ram mixers. Having been designed mainly with the Fostex B16 in mind (like most of the new, 16 buss mixers), it has a total of eighteen input channels – sixteen of them dedicated to tape returns – and eight sub-group outputs. At well under $3,000, the Mega certainly does offer quite astounding value for money. The desk is fully modular; each input channel sports balanced mike inputs and phantom powering, four-band EQ (sweepable, low, mid and high), direct outputs (post-fader) to enable you to send more than eight tracks to a tape machine simultaneously, no less than six auxiliaries – and solo capability too.

The RM10 and the RM16 are less grand than the Mega, and retail for about $1,400 and $1,800 respectively. Slim and very portable, they incorporate every single feature a desk

should have for 8-T. They have the same split-monitoring system as the Soundcraft 200 series, and the meter bridge is made up of illuminated VUs.

All in all, the Ram desks offer better value for money than any other make of small mixer. The quality isn't so good that you can record something at any level you want, bring it back and get no systems hiss. Even on SSL desks, there's no point in testing the gain and trim circuits beyond their capabilities just for the fun of it!

There are rumours of a twenty-four buss Mega, something that would probably give all other small-mixer manufacturers a throbbing headache. The real question is: will there be a twenty-four buss D3000?

Soundtracs Mixers: Profile

Soundout Labs, who manufacture the popular Soundtracs mixers, won a Queen's award for industry last year and thoroughly deserved it.

I must confess that doing a session on a Soundtracs desk is a pleasure that has not so far befallen me. But I am familiar enough with them to realize that on the whole they offer decent value for money and are very reliable.

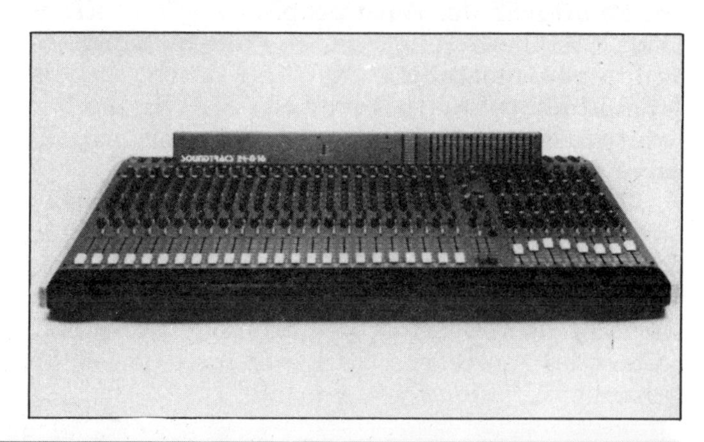

PROFILES AND REVIEWS

The CM4400 digital routing desk, with its integral RS232 computer port, is the most versatile of all the Soundtracs mixers, allowing you to expand your facilities by just plugging in extra modules. The software is self-updatable and thirty 'patches' can be stored in the desk's non-volatile memory.

Digital routing is becoming increasingly more affordable. With people like Soundtracs and AHB taking advantage of microtechnology in the construction of their desks, the big companies (namely Neve and SSL) will have to start looking at altogether much more expansive software/hardware packages.

The smaller Soundtracs desks are, on the whole, very good value for money, the 16:8:16 offering three-band EQ and direct post-fade outputs on each of the input channels. At around $4,400 or so, the Soundtracs 16:8:16 offers an impressive range of facilities at an almost ridiculously low price.

Seck mixers: Profile
Price: $2,495 (18:8:2)

Developed by Andy Bereza of Turnkey and the excellent Space Design company, these new-style Seck desks are a far cry from the old 16:8:2s that Turnkey recently stopped selling.

The bigger desks in the range are quite impressive, if somewhat unusual to look at. Since there is a healthy number of configurations in the range, there should be something to suit everybody. The overall design concept is of a budget in-line desk that is rugged and straightforward to use, and which will not break the purse-strings of the buyer. I'm happy to say that all these objectives have been successfully achieved.

The 18:8:2 is designed primarily for 16-T applications, having eight sub-group outputs and input channels that double as tape returns in true in-line fashion. Each input has electronically balanced mike and line inputs, going through a three-band (sweepable mid) EQ section. Insert points are provided on all in-

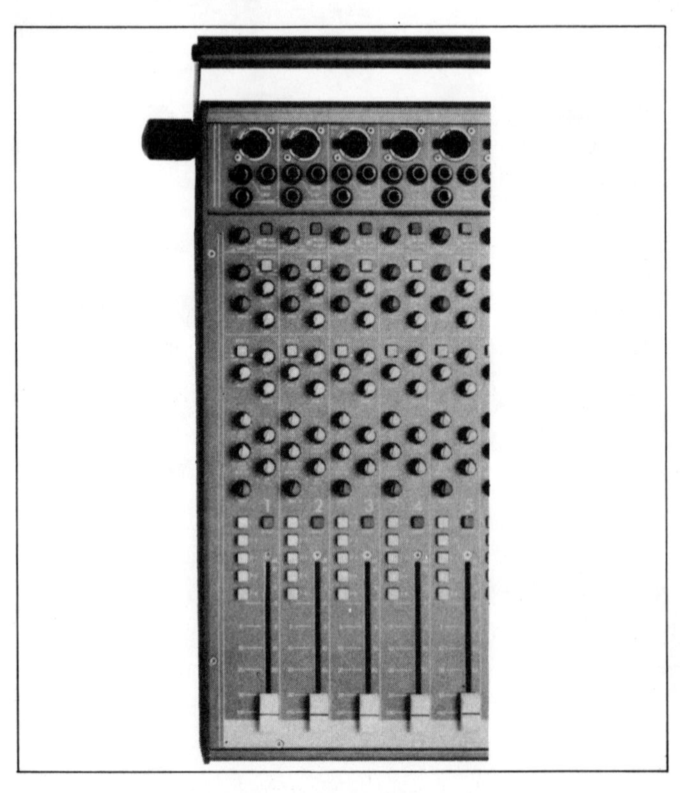

PROFILES AND REVIEWS

PROFILES AND REVIEWS

puts and there is a six-way (max.) auxiliary circuit.

The meters are top-mounted across the chassis and connectors. In short, all the consoles in the Seck range offer superb value for money – in extremely 'hip' casings!

Fostex MN15 Compressor/Mixer: Profile
Price: $75

It may be stretching the imagination a little to call this a 'mixer', as what it does has as much to do with compression as it has with combining several signals. It is neither rack-mountable nor foot-operated . . . just a smart little box of tricks that isn't designed to sit anywhere in particular.

This machine hasn't been designed with the discerning user in mind, and does tend to 'pump' and hiss a little – but it is far from being useless, even on serious sessions; you just have to be rather more careful.

There is no external control over compression attack, but the machine does have a modicum of adjustment for release. The compression ratio used is probably 2:1. It runs off the mains via an adaptor (9-15V).

With five phono inputs and one phono output, the MN15 is most useful for ganging FX devices together, and is an ideal pocket companion to the X-15.

Fostex 350: Profile
Price: $925

Undoubtedly one of the most popular mixers ever produced, the Fostex 350 is an 8:4:2 – though this is not immediately obvious at first glance. Sound quality can be somewhat hindered by systems noise via the gain/trim controls on the inputs, but on the whole this desk is pretty good value for money. However, it is worth noting that a certain amount of competition has arisen since the 350 first appeared with the tape machine around which it was designed, the Fostex A8. MTR, Prom-

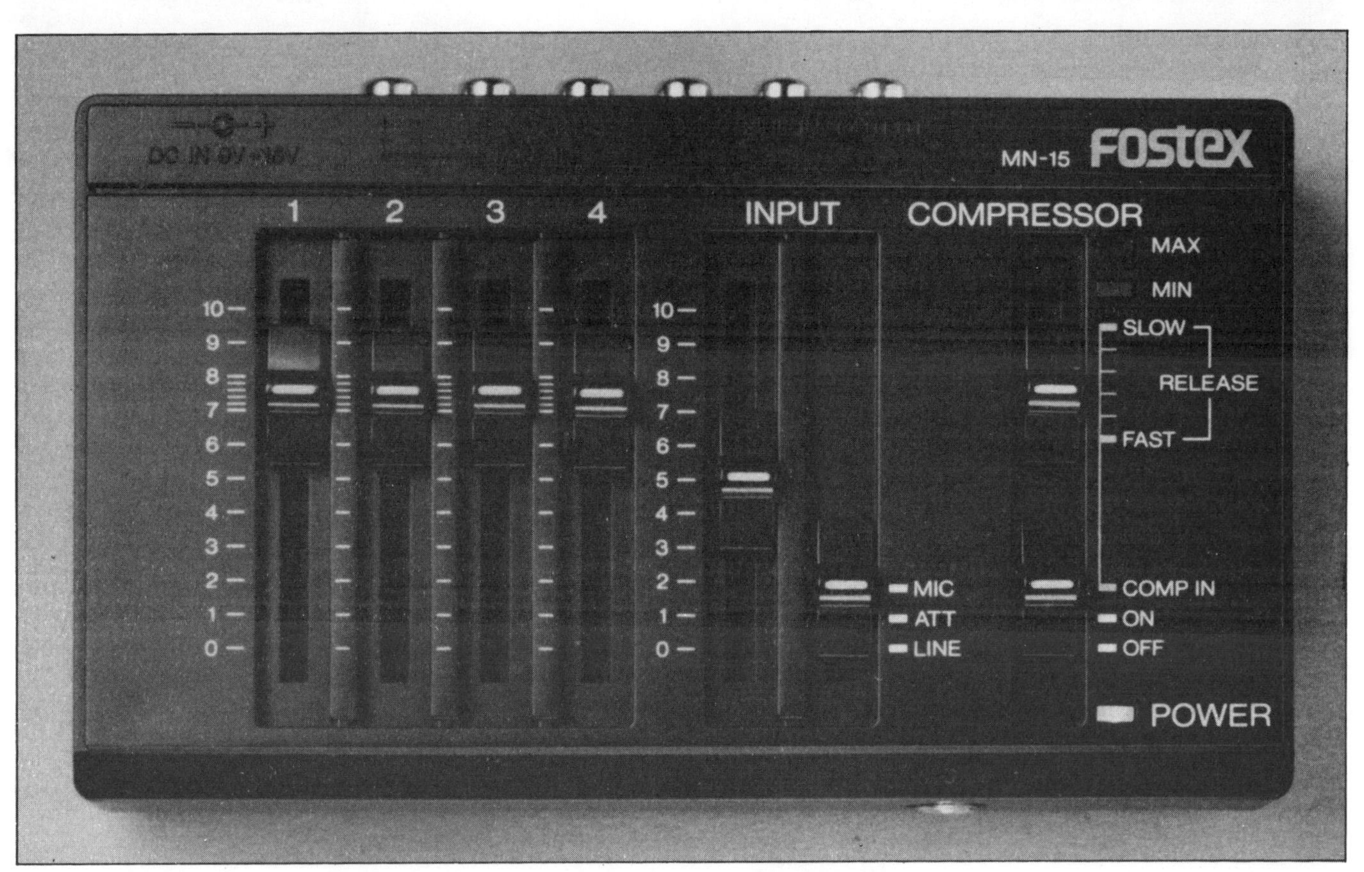

PROFILES AND REVIEWS

ark, Aces and RAM have all developed budget desks for the 8-T market and these should be investigated thoroughly before you purchase a 350.

Each channel is fitted with an all-purpose wide-ranging input socket, capable of taking most signals. The EQ is a two-band sweepable type and there is – strangely – a stereo(ish) auxiliary circuit which is switchable between pre- and post-fade.

Although the desk is manufactured so that only a maximum of four sub-group signals can be sent from that section at any one time, each input has an output that enables you to send a maximum of twelve tracks simultaneously to a multitrack. The lack of multi-auxiliaries is combatted by the inclusion of insert points on each channel for FX processing.

Costing somewhere in the region of $1,000 the 350 offers quite good value for money, but it is by no means exceptional. Sound quality, as I said earlier, can be a little dodgy, and I've heard strange cracks and whistles issuing from one unit belonging to a friend of mine. If you don't object to the strange pseudo-in-line design and if none of the similar (cheaper) desks appeals to you, then the Fostex 350 must be for you!

STOP PRESS:
A new Fostex 350 mixer, called the 450, has been launched at APRS. Little is known about this unit. It sports multi-segment LED metering and a solo facility on inputs and master sub-group outputs. The price looks likely to be a little higher – let's hope not too much higher!

PROFILES AND REVIEWS

Fostex Model 2050 Line Mixer: Profile
Price: $200

Designed exclusively for sub-mixing line-level and FX unit signals, this can be quite a life-saver in a complicated outboard environment. Sporting up to ten inputs (depending on usage) each with independent pan and gain, the 2050 is ideal for ganging FX outputs and inserting them via one of the mixer's outputs

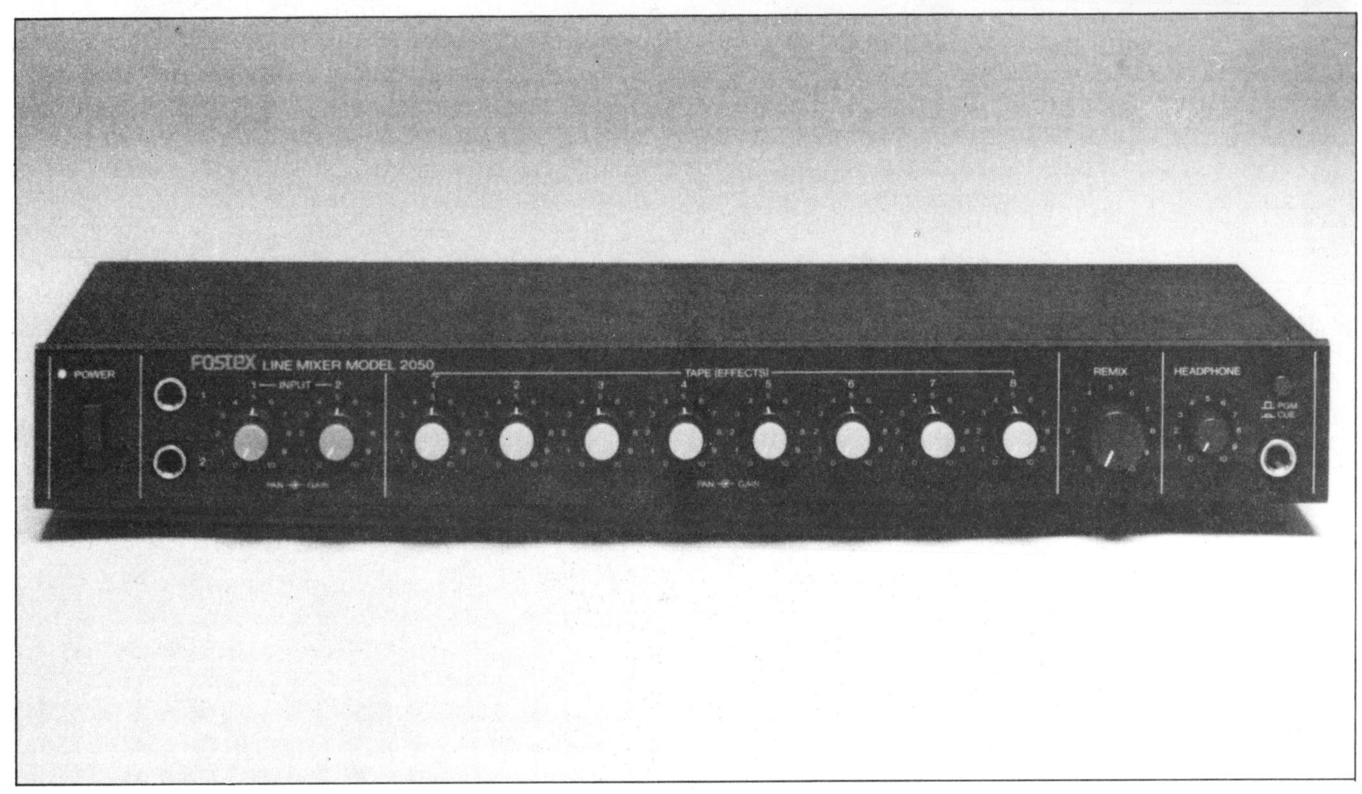

PROFILES AND REVIEWS

Boss and Roland mixers – easily the ***most***

PROFILES AND REVIEWS

popular and well regarded small mixers today

into a single input on the main mixer. Having a built-in headphone amplifier also increases this unit's flexibility, though it is not of sufficient strength or suitable design to be used as a serious fold-back centre.

I find it annoying to see Fostex charging extra for rack mount ears on this unit. It is a rack mixer and nothing more – only home organists stand things on top of mixing desks nowadays (including cups of putrid herbal tea) . . . I'd rather see Fostex get the hack-saw out than put my hand in my pocket for any more cash. The 2050 is reasonably clean and extremely useful. It has no clear-cut role in life, so it's up to you what you use it for. That's half the fun!

M200 desks from Tascam: Profile
Price: $1,095 (M208)
$1,695 (M216)

Extremely fresh on the market, the new M200 series is designed to replace the 30 series. Intended primarily for recording and PA applications (what other uses can you put a mixing desk to?), the M200 desks are quite slim and compact, and are available in two versions: an 8 input and 16 input. These desks unfortunately have no more than *four*-way sub-groups, but this is really a minor problem.

Each channel features three-band EQ (sweepable mid), fold-back send and insertion point.

The M208 is rack-mountable and can be fitted to any standard 19″ housing via a mounting kit at extra cost.

Specifications
Mike Input: XLR electronically balanced, -70 to +28 dBV/22.8 kohms
Line Input: ¼″ unbalanced, -50 to +35 dBV/22 kohms
Tape Return: RCA, -10 dBV/10 kohms
Effect Return: ¼″, 0 dBu/4.3 kohms
PGM Out: XLR unbalanced; 0 dBu/100 ohms
RCA; -10 dBV/490 ohms
Stereo Out: XLR unbalanced & ¼″, 0 dBu/100 ohms
Effect Out/FLB Out: ¼″, 0 dBu/100 ohms
Headphones Out: ¼″ TRS, 1.4W + 5W (8 ohms)
Frequency Response: 20 Hz-25 kHz, + 1.0 dB, -2.0 dB (Input to output nominal)
Equivalent Input Noise (150 ohms source): 130 dB(IHF-A), -128 dB (DIN AUDIO)
THD (20 Hz-20 kHz): Line input to any output; 0.025%
Dimensions (W × H × D) M216: 646 × 130 × 420mm. M-208: 438 × 130 × 420mm
Weight (net): M-216: 12kg. M-208: 8.5 kg.

Tascam M300 series desks: Profile
Price: $1,795 and up

These were launched at the same time as the smaller M200 desks from Tascam. The M300 series is a much more quality-conscious range, but still employs four-way sub-group outputs. Input sizes available are 8, 12 (strangely enough) and 20.

All inputs and outputs are suitable to be run at domestic working level and with +4dBm balanced equipment.

Interestingly, Tascam have designed these mixers so that they can be linked together to form an ever-expanding mixing unit.

Each input channel has three-band (two sweepable) EQ and dual auxiliary circuitry.

These mixers seem to offer quite reasonable value for money, the quality of their performance being on a par (so I've been told) with that of the Soundcraft 200 series mixers reviewed in this section. I should imagine the M320 20:4:2 will retail for no more than $2,500 though the exact price is as yet uncertain.

PROFILES AND REVIEWS

Specifications
Inputs – Mike: (-60 dBV)
Line: (-10 dBV)
Tape: (-10 dBV)
Effect RTN: (0 dBu)
Sub In: (-10 dBV)
Ext. In: (-10 dBV)
Insertion Receive: (-10 dBV)
T/B Mike In: (-50 dBV)
Outputs: -PGM Out: (+ 4 dBm & -10 dBV)
Stereo Out: (+ 4 dBm & -10 dBV)
Mono Out: (+ 4 dBm & 0 dBu)
Effect Out: (0 dBu & -10 dBV)
Aux Out: (0 dBu 7-10 dBV)
Monitor Out: (0 dBu)
Solo Out: (-10 dBV)
Direct Out: (-10 dBV)
Insertion Send: (-10 dBV)
Headphones: (1.5 W/ch. max)
Performance:
Frequency Response: 20Hz-30kHz, + 1dB-2dB
Equivalent Input Noise: 132 dB
Crosstalk: 70dB
THD: (20Hz-20kHz)

Dimensions (W × H × D):
M-320 - 992 × 220 × 692mm
M-312 - 720 × 220 × 692mm
M-308 - 584 × 220 × 692mm
Weight:
M-320 36kg.
M-312 - 26kg.
M-308 - 21kg.

Soundcraft Series 200 16:4:2 Desk: Review
Price: $2,495

When this Soundcraft desk was delivered to my studio I thought there was something wrong – the box seemed far too small. Could it really be a 16 into 4 into 2? After unpacking it and sitting it on top of my favourite combo (yes, it's *that* small!) I realized that Soundcraft

PROFILES AND REVIEWS

had achieved the impossible – quality components, a large number of features – all in all a very flexible mixer that's easy to use, but also very small.

I eagerly plugged it up to my synths and drum machine and put it through a Cutec driver amp into my monitors . . . I was won over within the first ten minutes – everything sounded so good! At first, especially if you're used to normal-sized desks, this Soundcraft feels very cramped to use, but it takes only a short while to get used to, and after that, going back to normal desks feels very strange – every knob seems too big!

As far as construction is concerned, this Soundcraft is hard to beat. Being built primarily for the road, there's no namby-pamby leatherette front panel – just hard metal, although since it is likely to stay in its flight case most of the time, it makes little difference anyway. It's of modular design, and all the input channels are easily lifted out of the frame: you just undo two screws and disconnect the internal electronics. The master module has the left and right faders and the four main sub-group faders, as well as all the main master rotaries. All the knobs and faders are of excellent quality; they all work very smoothly and there's no evidence of hit-and-miss construction design – everything has been well thought out and colour-coded. The back panel is laid out very well, considering that space is very tight; all the labelling all over this mixer is precise, easy to read and well positioned. Each input channel runs down thus: push-button selection of -20dB pad-and-line level input (for synths etc.), gain pot, four-band EQ, auxiliaries 1-4, routing push-button selection,

PROFILES AND REVIEWS

channel on/off button and PFL, followed by the channel fader which has a 100mm action.

All the series 200 desks have some very good features, which would be hard to find on desks fifty times the price. Although at first sight it looks like a normal 16:4:2, this particular desk is capable of 8-track monitoring via the four outputs without repatching. There's an excellent 'SUB' feature which routes the outputs of the group faders into the stereo buss, and causes the monitor channel above it to be routed into the corresponding sub-group. This means that you can fade out (or in) a whole group of instruments or vocals – together with their associated FX returns – on just one fader! This is an application for which large studios usually use only automated desks ($100,000 upwards).

As I mentioned, this desk is capable of full 8-track monitoring. It has a separate power supply which means that it doesn't hiss or hum at all; the S/N ratio exceeds 80dB. The EQ, although very simple, gives excellent results. Having built-in phantom power is also very handy. In fact, I would recommend this mixer to anybody wanting to set up an 8-track studio, even if they have no live usage in mind, because its performance is so clean and sharp.

Each channel has its own FX send-and-return insert and together with the four auxiliary sends this desk can be used for just about any job. The series 200 is even available

PROFILES AND REVIEWS

in a 19″ rack mounting version!

Although the price may initially make some people shudder, I assure you that every penny will be well spent. It's one of those machines that oozes quality! Soundcraft also produce more advanced desks: the 2400 & 1600 series consoles have found their way into many commercial and privately owned 24-T studios. For $25,000 or so, you get a healthy complement of features on either of two frame sizes in the 2400 series, one of which is the 24:16:2, with an optional 8-channel monitor module to bring back tape returns 17-24. I've used this desk and it's turned out to be inadequate for some complicated sessions, not allowing you enough input permutations to do *exactly* what you want. I favour the bigger of the two 2400 options, the 28:24:2. This still contains many of Soundcraft's 'unique' routing and/or muting features (all of which I find long-winded, gimmicky and pointless), but is a lot better to use, owing to the fact that there are a few extra inputs available.

The 2400 series is a clean and reliable desk. The patchbay is very comprehensive, and once you've gone through the desk and disregarded all the unnecessary peripheral electronics that Soundcraft insist on including in the spec. of their mixers, it becomes a fast and articulate tool to work with.

The 2400 series has recently been joined in the field by its in-line bigger brother, the TS24. This is a fairly straightforward, no-nonsense in-line console which can be purchased for around $38,000 – similar to the price of some other in-line consoles, but very reasonable value for money nevertheless.

Again some clumsiness of design is in evidence in the TS24. Soundcraft have termed some of the multi-feed/level inputs on the back 'instrument' sockets, capable of trimming a straight guitar output with no DI box. Most top-line desks are capable of this. Harrison consoles are known for their wide torque inputs, as are other less expensive desks.

The TS24 sports six auxiliaries per input channel, long-throw faders and four-band sweepable EQ with 'Q' controls for the mid bands. Metering is via LED and Soundcraft have invested in a moving fader automation system from the USA for the TS24.

The 600 . . .

On the other side of the 2400 is Soundcraft's next series of recording consoles up from the 200 series – the 600 series. This is a range of mixers that all feature 8 sub-group outputs, and which are more or less aimed at Fostex B16 users. Even the 32:8:16:2 is quite small and Soundcraft may have made the mistake of getting the design *too* compact. The market for this machine is largely dominated by the small-studio owner who wants a reliable, flexible console which also impresses the clients. The 600 series is a snatch short of being 'impressive'.

PROFILES AND REVIEWS

The mixers are modular in design, with four-band EQ (2 sweepable mid bands); subgroup metering is via multi-segment two-colour (green and red) LEDs and the master outputs (left and right) are VUs.

Soundcraft have also produced a PA version of this console, which I think is to be termed the 500.

All Soundcraft desks offer operational broadcast-quality performance. Sadly, most of them also offer more than is necessary. The prices of these desks have always been reasonable, although the series 200 desks are perhaps (in the light of recent competition) somewhat overpriced.

Allen & Heath Brenell Desk 16:16 System 8 MkII: Review
Price: TBA

When a product is successful, the order of the day has until very recently been for the company to advertise and publicize the popular unit(s) and then concentrate its R&D in other areas, thus slowly infiltrating the market in all areas and gaining a good reputation. However, since Japanese products have invaded the electrical side of the market, these old tactics have seen the death of many companies. Price and format wars have forced companies to be on their toes every single minute of the day; in short – to be standing still is to be going backwards.

Thus, in the light of the format revolution (8 tracks on 1/4″, 16 tracks on 1/2″ and so on), Allen & Heath Brenell have decided to update their popular System 8 range of mixing consoles. Improvements include new, 100mm 'ultra smooth' faders, which have improved attenuation characteristics and are now much harder wearing. Each of the channel input sections now has a push-button EQ cut facility, for signals needing no extra bass, mid or treble lift/cut. Connection of the multitrack recorder output is now required only at the tape input jack sockets (on the back panel); internal connections automatically route the signal off tape into the corresponding channel line inputs. This means that you can process signals from tape using all the features on the normal line inputs, which are usually used for mikes and instruments. These internal connections are, however, defeated when plugs are inserted into those channels that are already being fed from the multitrack machine. The tape input gain is now increased to boost the loudness of off-tape signals in the stereo mix. Another new addition is the facility of phantom power (+48 volts standard), for microphones that require it.

The construction is of very high quality. The mixers have steel main panels and covers, with a hard stove-enamel paint finish and an epoxy-ink screen-printed legend. The series is semi-modular, which means that the internal pcb assemblies are easily accessible – but you do have to take the main panel away first of

PROFILES AND REVIEWS

all. There's no doubt about it: this form of construction can be an awful nuisance (especially when you have a breakdown in the middle of a session), but, in all fairness to AHB, not many mixers under $3,000 are fully modular.

The control layout is very clear, with the input channels on the left, the group outputs on the right and the main control stereo pair of channels in the centre. One of the features on the System 8 that I particularly like is the set of illuminated VU meters along the back of the control panel, which do their job perfectly and, in addition, look really classy!

On each of the input channels there's a mike/line push-button selector, 20dB pad and a gain pot; the EQ section includes high frequency shelving +/− 16dB at 12kHz or 8kHz and low frequency shelving +/− 12dB at 120Hz or 80Hz and MID peak/dip +/− 12dB, 400Hz to 6kHz. There are three auxiliary pots with independent pre- and post-fade permutations for effects such as reverb; then there are routing buttons and the pan pot which is used for stereo imaging and routing alike, and finally, above the fader, there is a mute button that switches the output of the channel off, the PFL selector (pre-fader listen) which is used for soloing the input source of that particular channel, and also a peak-level LED which is pre-fader and responds to EQ adjustments.

I found the 16:16 I had for review extremely easy to use, thanks to the logical control layout and the nice 'feel' of the mixer in general. It was uncommonly quiet for a mixer in this price range and the routing system was particularly simple and straightforward to use. Throughout the week or so during which I had it rigged up at my studio, it performed all its functions admirably and without a single hitch. The new faders are excellent.

For anybody who is looking for a mixer, and doesn't want to spend an absolute fortune, the System 8 offers fantastic quality and features for this sort of price. Now that AHB have developed a 24:16 and a 24:8 in the System 8 range, it's going to be very difficult for potential studio-owners at either end of the market to ignore the AHB challenge.

Allen & Heath Brenell CMC range of mixers: Profile
Price: 24:16:2 $4,500

With the optional CMS64 interface, the CMC range of in-line desks can be linked to the Commodore 64 or 128 machine so that all

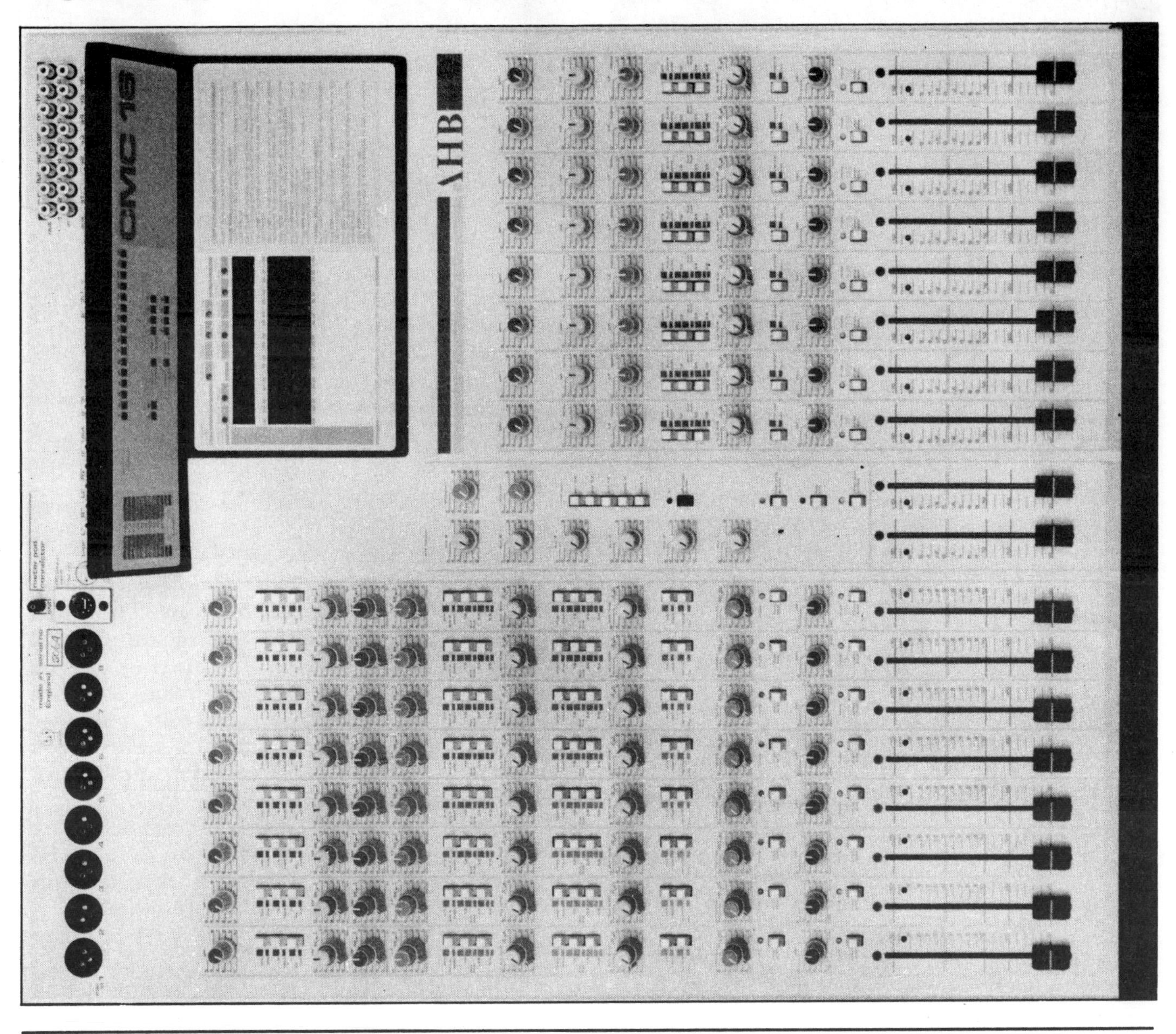

PROFILES AND REVIEWS

manner of clever little tricks can be played as far as routing destinations and muting are concerned. The CMC series from AHB is extremely compact and quite light, with the design policy aiming at somewhere between full-function and (extended!) budget facilities. The CMC24 has a full complement of 24 inputs, 16 of which offer three-band sweepable EQ, no less than six auxiliary sends and balanced mike inputs. The remaining 8 channels offer a slightly less comprehensive range of facilities, with only two-band EQ, but still retain full routing capability. These inputs are routed to any one (or all!) of the sixteen sub-group outputs via a built-in non-volatile microprocessor. A number of patches can be stored inside the memory and recalled at will. These patches can contain not only information about individual routing arrangements for each channel, but a whole desk configuration!

The real fun with the CMC begins when you add either the Commodore 64, or (as will soon be possible) the new 128K machine. The CMC will allow you to dump extended numbers of patches into the system, and muting can be sequenced either off tape or from a drum machine sync pulse. This is an excellent feature for a desk at this price. Synchronized muting can open a whole new world of 'tight' music energy!

Furthermore, the graphics facilities on the Commodore computer enable you (via AHB software) to put your routing and/or muting information up on a TV screen in colour.

The beauty of the CMC lies in what the machine is *potentially* capable of, rather than in what it can actually do the moment the power is switched on. Being software-driven, the CMC consoles should be able to give you synchronized, automated mixdown, with control not only over routing and muting, but over channel levels and – hopefully – auxiliaries too.

Even without computer link-up, the consoles in the CMC range from AHB offer unparalleled flexibility and features for the money. At the moment, you can buy CBM64s for *under* $100, while the CMC24:16:2 retails for *under* five thousand dollars. You should be able to get together a computer, a TV and the latest software – thereby creating a full computer-assisted mixing set-up – for around $7,500!

True, there are a great many other 16-buss contenders at this price and considerably below, but none of them offers computer compatability, and, as I say, you buy a CMC as much for its potential as you do for what it is *actually* capable of. For serious, articulate mixing flexibility, the AHB CMC range offers everything one could ever reasonably ask for.

The MTR 642 In-Line Mixer: Review
Price: TBA

The MTR 642 is a 6-input, 4-out and 2 (stereo)-output, 'in-line' mixer, with four of its input channels acting as outputs to a tape machine. It is basically designed for use with 4-track set-ups, either on cassette or reel-to-reel. But, of course, it'll also work as an excellent, straight 6-into-4-into-2 for submixing keyboards, drums, vocals – anything!

The 642 is an extremely good-looking, well-

built mixer, and boasts a surprising number of features – considering its size and price. The overall construction is excellent and the back panel utilizes jacks (the most common sort of connector used for 4-track recording and stage/studio-submixing). Throughout this mixer, a lot of care and attention has been applied with regard to the arrangement of controls and the sort of components used. The care taken in designing this unit means that it is extremely fast to use, as there is no need to re-patch your connections every time you want to switch tracks on your machine, or, for that matter, if you want to remix or listen to a 2-track machine in the middle of a session.

It has mono jack inputs that will accept high- and low-feed mikes, and also line-level inputs for outputs from a multitrack tape deck. Also, there is FX insert send-and-return on all six of the channels. This means that you can have Channel 1 going through a limiter or compressor, a flanger, chorus, or indeed anything you care to think of! This is a feature you'd be lucky to find on mixers for $1,500! This really puts the MTR in a class of its own. It also has two auxiliary channels; either these can be used for FX, or else the return socket for aux.2 can be used as a seventh line-level input! Also on the back panel, there is a stereo monitor out to the driver amp for the monitors, as well as stereo outputs and inputs to the mastering machine, which enable you to monitor what's going (and gone) on to tape in the final mix.

This mixer has so many unique features that I could happily continue this review for another page or two. I shall confine myself to saying that I used it successfully in my studio for a week or so, in all sorts of configurations – once as an FX mixer, the next day for submixing keyboards – the lot! The three-band EQ really does its job well, without turning the sound harsh or making acoustic sounds unrealistic or excessively thick. It seems to have (more than) everything you could expect from a mixer of this size (it fits under your arm comfortably!). It has PPI LEDs on each channel and is remarkably noise-free. I'm looking forward to the day when I can use one of these little wonders on stage: the sub-grouping/routing system is fully professional, and I should think it would be invaluable for multi-keyboard/digital drum performers (like me).

This unit gets my vote for being the best product to have appeared so far in 1984 – and it is definitely the best product from all the 'spring collections' launched at Frankfurt. And now for the real shock (and the key to this machine's assured success in the future) – the price: under $400!!! What's more . . . it's British! Well done MTR.

Microphones

AKG Microphones.
Offering a surprising number of high-quality microphones for around the $150 mark, AKG are particularly renowned for a couple of models, namely the D202 and subsequent permutations and the equally excellent C414B and related special-application capsules.

About a year or two ago, AKG stunned the recording business with the release of a microphone that offered all their usual sonic qualities, but retailed for *under* $50. This was the now world-famous D80, which has found its way into small and huge studios alike.

The BBC picked up on the D202 for broadcast applications and as far as dynamic mikes go, I've found no other all-rounder of such good quality as this. Employing a double-capsule system, and user-definable multi-position detented bass roll-off, the D202 gives a massive, rich, warm sound on acoustic instruments

PROFILES AND REVIEWS

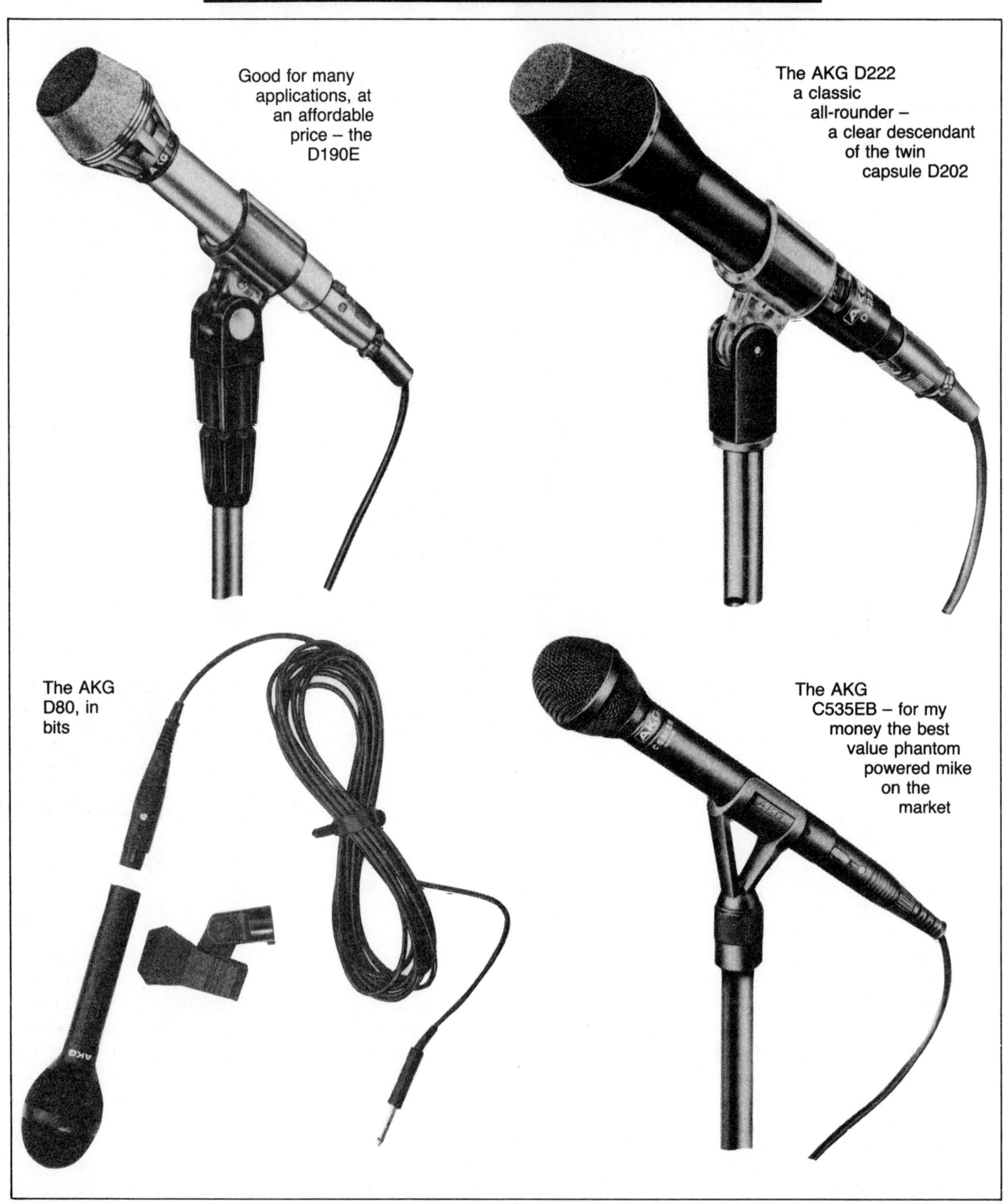

Good for many applications, at an affordable price – the D190E

The AKG D222 a classic all-rounder – a clear descendant of the twin capsule D202

The AKG D80, in bits

The AKG C535EB – for my money the best value phantom powered mike on the market

PROFILES AND REVIEWS

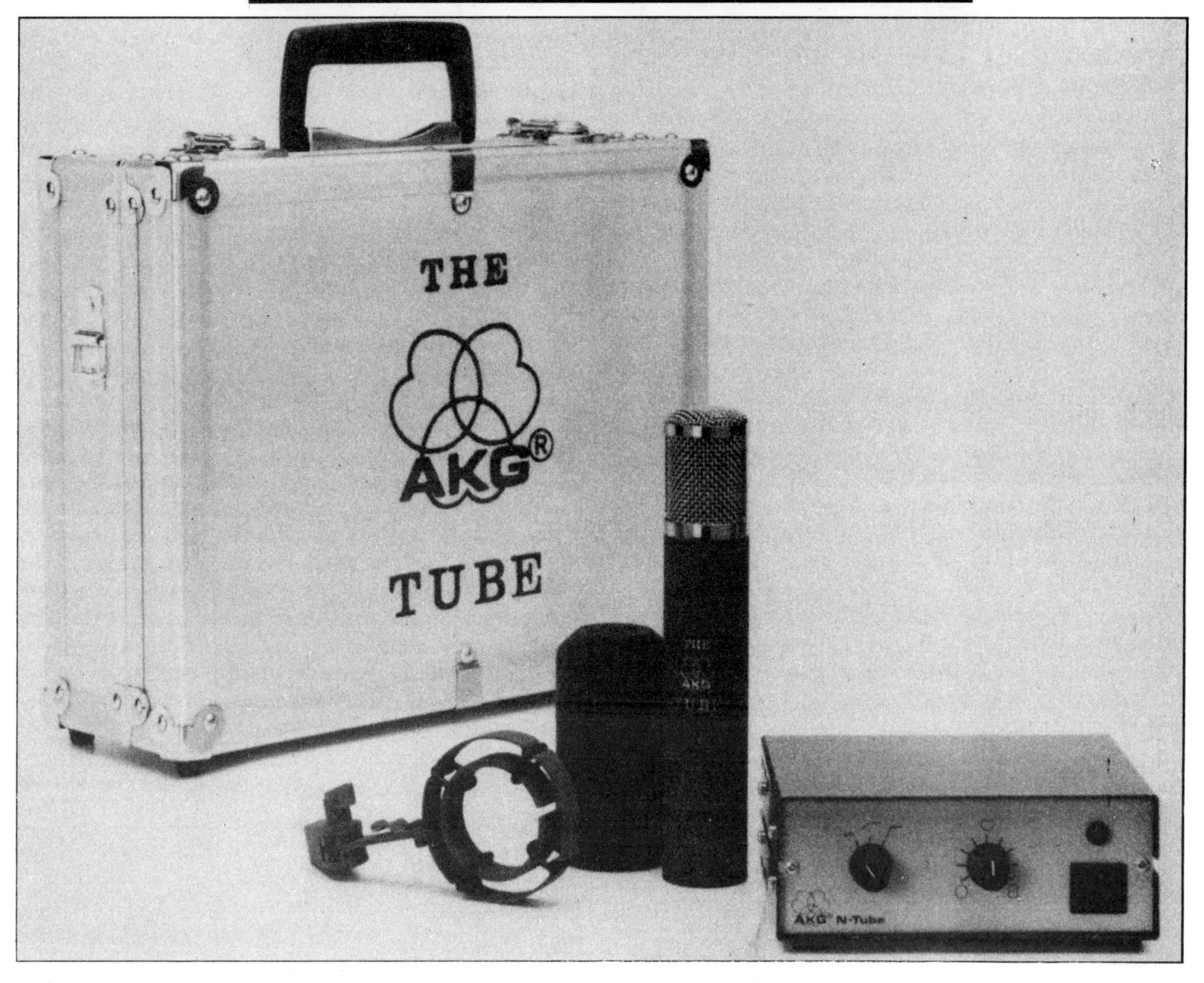

(especially guitar) and for the money is practically unsurpassable. You have to go a long way up AKG's product line to find something better (in my opinion) than the D202.

With a non-reflective matt black coating, the C535EB has become known to some PA engineers as *the* live mike – for vocals in particular. However, for a modest $250 or so, I bought one on the strength of its sonic capabilities rather than for what AKG originally intended it to be used for. Rugged and able to stand up even to *extremely* rough treatment, the C535EB offers the optimum balance between sturdiness and sound quality. It is also superb for drums.

I cannot close this section on AKG without mentioning their most recent legend – the AKG Tube. A beautiful and expensive microphone, it offers all the sonic qualities of the famed Neumann U87 in a slimmer package. Incorporating a smooth valve pre-amplifier and (unlike the U87) working on a stereo pick-up pattern, the Tube has gone down in microphone history as one of *the* all-time musts for any professional mike library. The price is high, but so will you be after recording drums with a Tube!

Cutec Microphones.
The mikes in the CDM series from Cutec offer

what is probably the most for the least, with even the most expensive (the CDM6) still hovering a generous distance below the £50 mark. A recent change-around has resulted in a new model called the CDM3. The top-of-the-range CDM6 has an excellent specification, and personal experience suggests that this is probably the most serious threat to mike manufacturers since the AKG D80 hit the market. These are high-impedance mikes, which means they are subject to the restrictions I outlined in the 'Art of Noise', but basically, considering the amount being asked for what they are, very little real criticism can be made.

Model	Pick-up Pattern	Type	Imped-ance	Frequency Response	Price
CDM2	Cardioid	Dynamic	600	80-12K	$30
CDM4	Cardioid	Dynamic	500	60-15K	$50
CDM6	Cardioid	Dynamic	600	50-19K	$70

Beyer Dynamic Microphones and Headphones.

The Beyer DT100 headphones have been adopted by more professional broadcast and recording organizations around the world than any other. Though the technology behind them has been superseded – even by models Beyer are now producing at half the price – the DT100s will go down in modern recording history as the cans most used on some of the world's more historic classical and rock sessions.

The DT100s have never been a personal favourite of mine, the newer DT220s seem to offer more for less money in my book (pun!).

As far as microphones are concerned, Beyer Dynamic are responsible for some classics, but unfortunately, these have been priced in the $300+ bracket. The M69 and M400 mikes at around $160 offer what I consider to be the best value in the range.

As far as I know, you could count on one hand the number of professional studios on this planet which *don't* own one of the CK series mikes. These are judged by many to be Beyer's best turn-out and I tend to agree. Quality doesn't start too expensive, with the transparent sounding CK701 (HF boost) at around $210 kicking the range off.

Beyer Dynamic: highly recommended microphones and headphones.

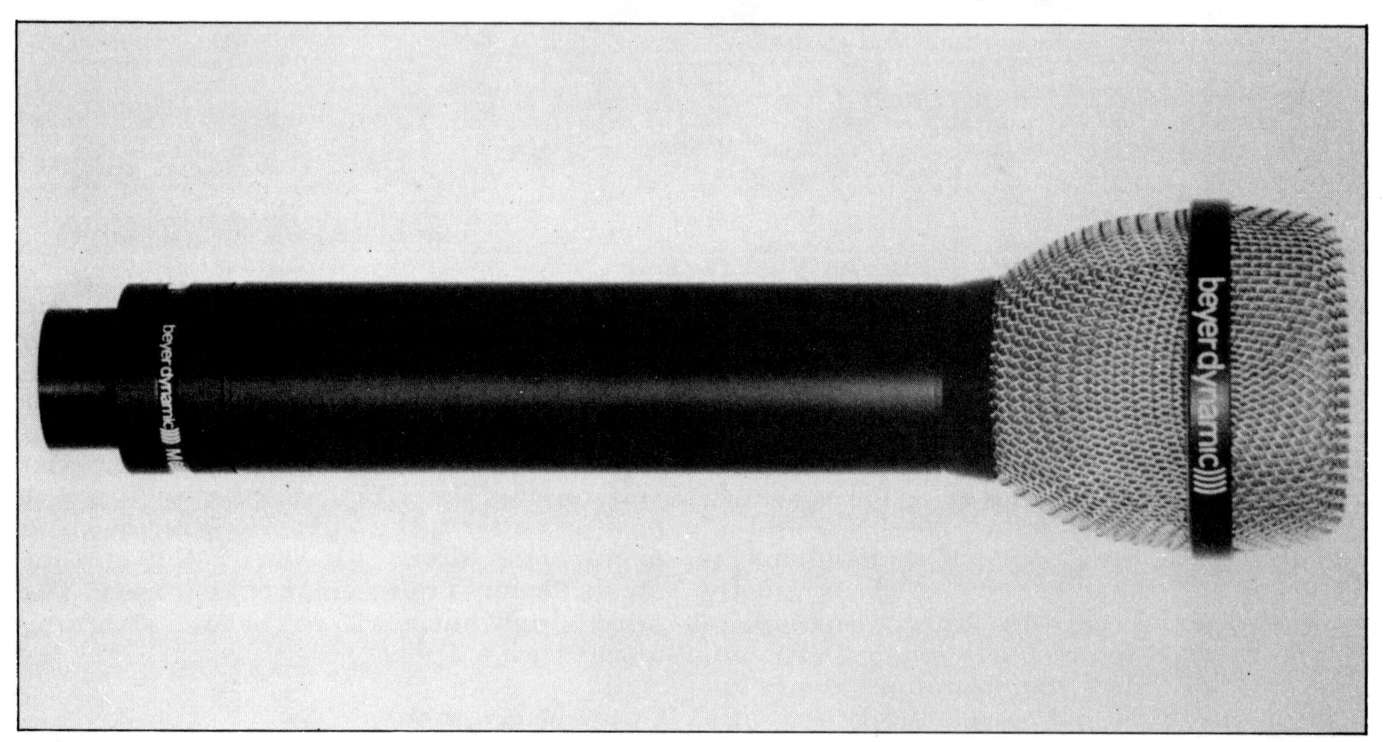

M69

PROFILES AND REVIEWS

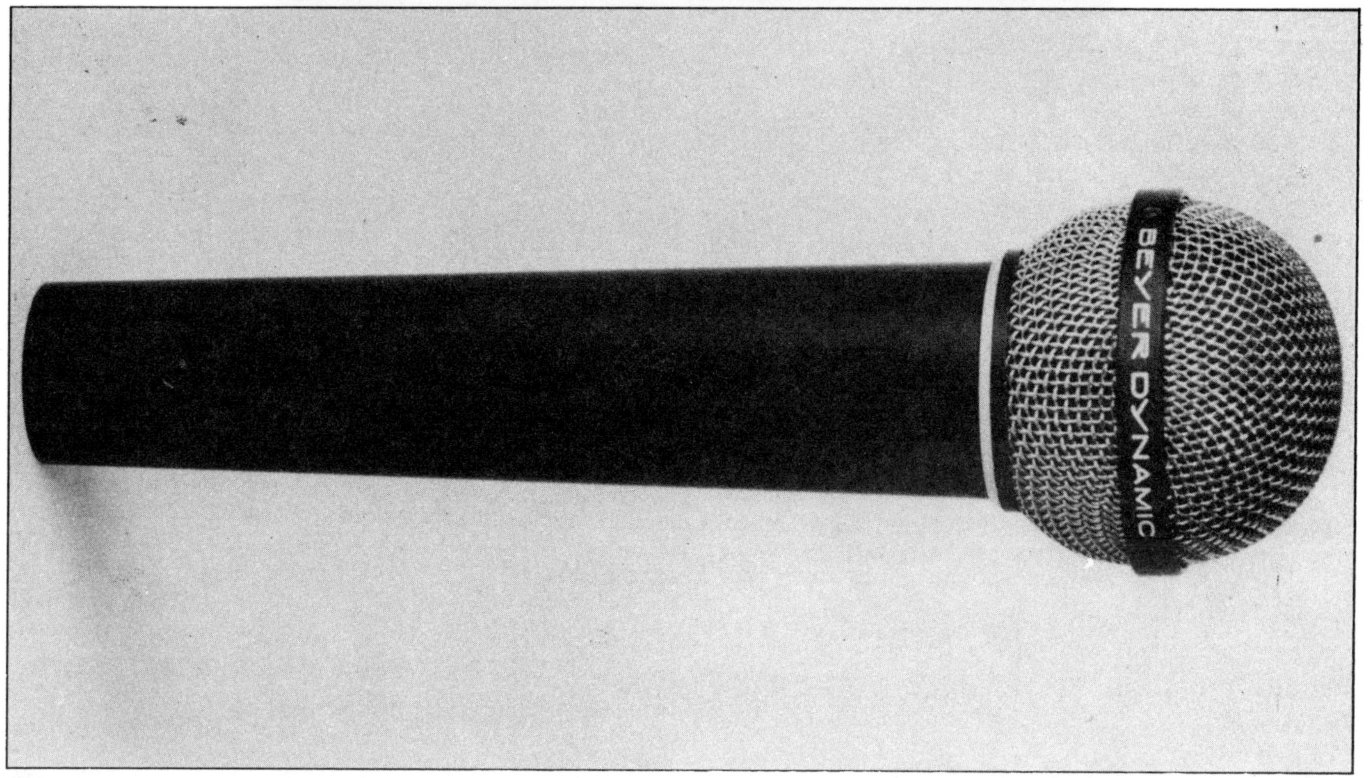

M300

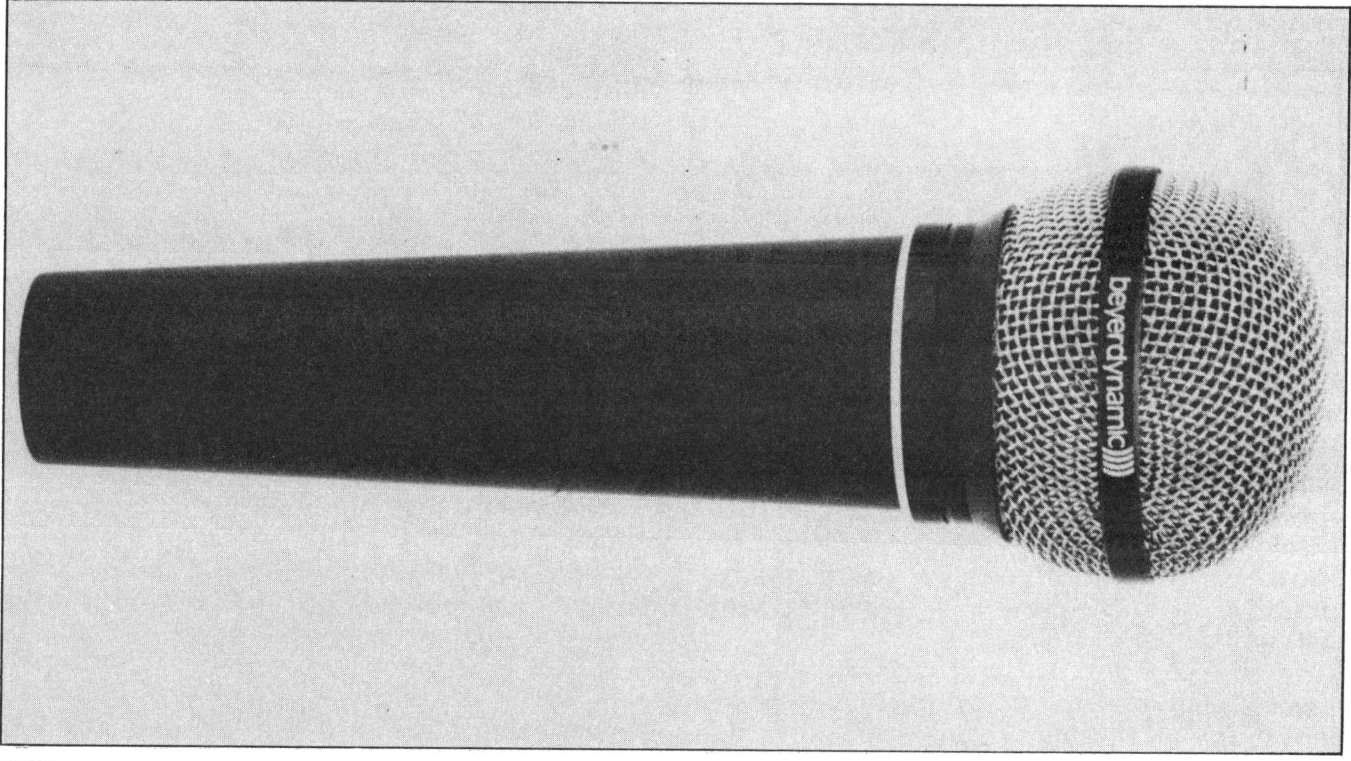

M400

PROFILES AND REVIEWS

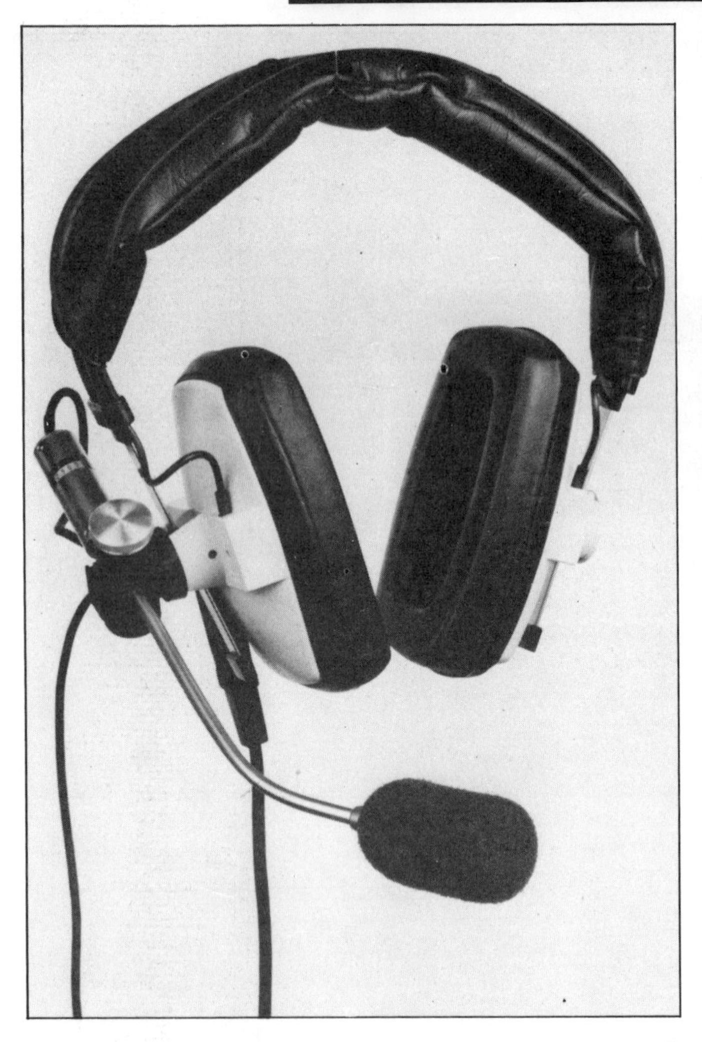

A permutation of the DT100 headphones.

Three of the excellent Prologue mikes by Shure.

Shure Microphones.
Earning their reputation in the tough world of PA set-ups, Shure microphones, from the USA, can be counted amongst the absolute best in the world. The legendary SM58 has been used to record more contemporary snare drums than any other mike. At a smidgen under the $200 barrier, you'd expect high quality and the SM58 never fails to please. The famed SM63 omni-directional mike is another personal favourite. At $110 or so, it offers truly astounding vocal finesse.

In their home country, Shure microphones enjoy a reputation which any manufacturer would envy. The company also produce special lecture/conference application microphones which have found their way onto some of our most legendary modern drum recordings!

The prices are, of course, completely governed by the dollar/pound relationship, but even at today's high prices there are a number of gems in the Shure range which are undoubtedly excellent value for money.

Perhaps performing best in the vocal area, nearly every Shure mike possesses an uncanny aptness for a huge range of applications, and on no account should you ever buy a mike without getting to know at least the SM58, 63 or 77 a lot better.

Sennheiser Microphones & Headphones.
I own more Sennhciser microphones than any

PROFILES AND REVIEWS

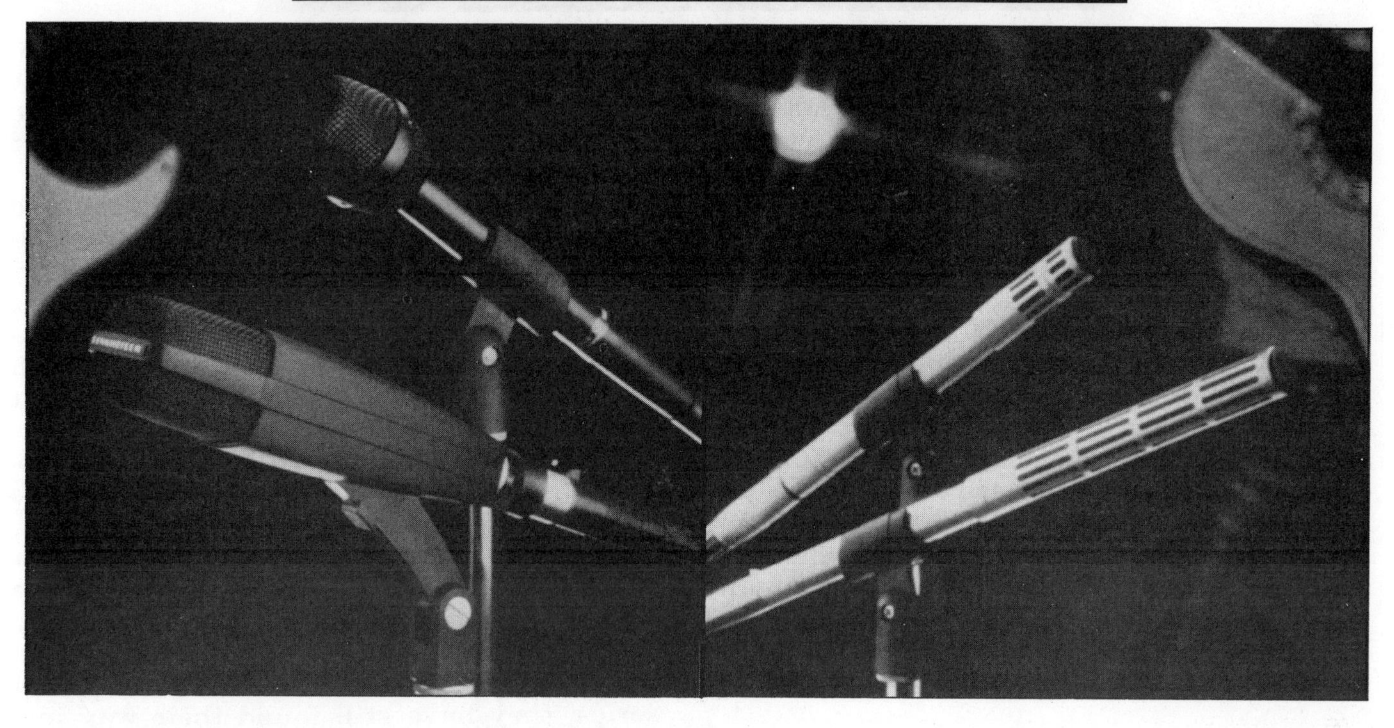

Some of the exceptionally well-crafted Sennheiser range of mikes.

Audio-Technica mikes – good quality at sensible prices.

PROFILES AND REVIEWS

other brand. Offering a comprehensive range of exceptionally well-crafted products at below the $250 mark, no potential microphone purchaser should miss the opportunity to try out the mikes in either the ME or MD series.

The MD421 is a personal favourite, offering broadcast quality at just $332 or so.

Undoubtedly, Sennheiser have carved out a name for themselves which will stand the test of time. Offering value for money and excellent quality, the aforementioned ranges represent one of the best price to performance ratios on the market.

All Sennheiser headphones are highly recommended too, with their comprehensive choice of low priced, high quality products, ruggedly built, not to mention some very fetching ear-pad colours! The BBC and many ILR and ITV stations now use Sennheiser headphones in preference to any other make.

Audio-Technica Microphones.
Recently, the BBC bought some of AT's ATM41 microphones. I wasn't too surprised, knowing that this company have consistently come up with excellent quality units for a good number of years, but I was truly shocked to find that the ATM41 costs *under* $250! So, at last the BBC have decided to start using the licence fees sensibly: the ATM41 offers them broadcast quality at an unreal price of around $210.

Designed for vocal use, I have it on good authority that the ATM41 also gives an excellent performance with instruments too. Offering a cardioid pick up pattern, and a 50-16kHz bandwidth, the printed specification is not as impressive as some mikes half the price, which means that the AT ATM41 is ideal proof that you can't believe everything you read. At some point or another, you have to allow the feelings your ears are conveying to your brain to take over from the coldness of spec sheets.

Audio-Technica are also well known for their stage-orientated Performer and Pro series microphones, which offer extremely good value for money. Although, on the whole, their spec isn't up to the excellence of the ATM series, they have still found their way into many recording set-ups.

Clearly, whether you choose Pro, Performer or ATM, AT offer good quality mikes at extremely sensible prices. You should never buy microphones without looking at the above ranges.

Outboard

Outboard: A General Introduction.

Most commercial studios nowadays rely on their outboard equipment (or 'toys') to bring in the customers – that's *after* they've discovered what type of desk the studio has. Outboard equipment can offset almost any studio's shortcomings: a room simulator (or a digital reverb with room size parameters) can substitute for a variety of studio acoustics and studio space; in-line graphic or parametric EQ systems can make the best of dodgy control room acoustics and there are a couple of other notable instances where a comprehensive array of outboard can 'save the day'.

Starting up as a home recordist, your outboard shopping list should read as follows:

Reverb
Digital Delay (w. modulation)
Compressor
Graphic EQ (if you're happy with the desk EQ section, you can skip having aux. EQ)
Flanger
Phaser

The first three items on the above list should be of reliable quality and be bought in the order listed. *All* FX you hear today (barring those utilising harmonizers or pitch changers) are either reverb, time-based digital delay FX, or compression. In fact, they are more than likely to be a combination of two or even all three.

Your reverb and DDL should be of a reasonably high quality, with a s/n ratio of not less than 65dB. Having a direct output is not essential, but is handy should you need to split feed the signal to another piece of equipment. Nor is a stereo reverb strictly necessary, but as GBS, Accessit and Vesta (amongst others) all offer inexpensive stereo spring units, it is a luxury one can afford without feeling guilty!

Many of the cheap stereo reverb units utilise cross phase pseudo-stereo. This entails the unit operating in a pre-defined internal arrangement, where wet signals from the original 'mono' input source are leaked out through the 'left' and 'right' outputs after going through a slightly different set of springs. Phase control cancellation is also employed to give an extra feeling of 'detachedness' to the sound.

However, there is a major drawback: if you play your finished master through an amp and depress the 'mono' button, you stand a good chance of your signals going 'dry' owing to the phase circuits being reversed or twined and proper cancellation will occur. The original input source may also be deadened and weakened. If possible, go for units with independent channels.

A digital delay can only offer minimal advantages over a comprehensive reverb if it has no modulation section. This takes the form of a low frequency oscillator with control over rate of sweep and depth of effect which is applied to the delayed or processed signal. With such a facility, you can obtain flanging and chorusing – two essential effects. However, digital delays (unless blessed with a strong enough depth and rate maximum) can't get real, powerful flanging or chorus effects and thus you will need dedicated units. This is something I'll go into in a while – and don't worry, it isn't *too* expensive.

Compression is a must. A dual channel unit, with (switchable) stereo link is the optimum arrangement, though a single channel unit (such as an FX pedal permutation) is better than no compression at all. I'll explain compression in full later on (when I suggest some good units). Suffice to say for now that compressors are the least understood of all popular FX units and many manufacturers claim that compression can give you different sounds: accurately speaking, this is utter bullshit.

A reverb. A digital delay. A compressor. How much should you spend on each item? Well, I would say that spending up to a maximum of $400 on your reverb, the same on your DDL and $250 on a dual compressor would be taking a middle way. Conversely, you could end up spending as little as $500 for all three. You are the one who has to decide how much to spend. . . This brings me onto another important point: people get scared of pedal FX. In the early Seventies, pedal FX were crude, noisy and nasty. However, for the last six or so years, pedal FX quality has gone up in leaps and bounds, while the prices have stayed relatively stable (thus in real terms actually going down in price).

There is no such thing as a pedal reverb unit, so in this instance you *have* to buy a rack mount unit. But, you can buy pedal compressors whose specifications are only slightly worse than their racked cousins. Boss (Roland) have also managed to stick the guts of a DE200 rhythm-sync rack DDL into a standard pedal! Because fewer materials are used in a pedal housing, these units are on average 30% cheaper than the corresponding rack effects. Do *not* think pedals are useless. *Always* try them out. If the noise figures are acceptable and the facilities are there, why not buy them? In fact, on mixdown, having foot control over compression and flanging etc. is extremely beneficial and lets your hands do that little bit more knob-twiddling! This is where I come back to my earlier point about dedicated flanger and phaser units not costing too much: for this sort of back-up outboard (if you already have a digital delay), pedals are more than acceptable.

The only thing against pedals is the fact that they are frowned upon by potential clients. You have to do more of a *sell* on your outboard, to convince people that the quality loss (if any) doesn't make any difference to the final product.

This is why, on the fact of it, this outboard section may seem too short, and indeed flippant, to include or even mention pedal FX devices. 50% of getting your studio 'right' is working out and sticking to your priorities. As this will hopefully be the first edition of an annual series, I've opted to concentrate on reverb (in particular), DDLs and compression in this book. Mastering the techniques of the above FX devices will enable you to trim, sweeten and manipulate *any* sound to your own (and your client's) taste.

Reverb: A General Introduction

Reverb is the most important effect you will ever have to buy. I've said much about the applications of reverb and quite a bit about the different types available. To recap, there are three sources of non-natural reverberation.

1. Spring lines. These are the cheapest of all reverb units on the market. Utilising one or more (usually four) stretched helical springs sitting in a suspended tray, the unit receives the signal and transmits this along the springs. This signal is picked up by a receiver at the other end. Some spring units have a mixer pot to balance the output between 'dry' and 'wet'. The sound you get from spring lines is very much dependent on the mechanical structure of the springs used. If more than one is used, they must be sufficiently different from each other to simulate reverb patterns found between two parallel walls and in large rooms.

Spring units tend to suffer from 'boing-boing' effects where low frequencies (which take longer to travel through the springs) overexcite the springs and the vibration becomes less than subtle.

Spring lines which produce usable, realistic reverb are quite difficult to manufacture and so are relatively expensive. The Vesta Kozo RV range of units is counted amongst the best of the budget spring lines, mainly because they utilise internal limiter circuits which cut out the aforementioned 'overexcitement', even at powerful input levels.

AKG have developed spring-based reverb units, but these are difficult to buy second hand and are astronomically expensive.

Spring reverb is an effect which relies more on the engineer than on a system's capabilities. Even with digital and plate at hand, I always keep a spring line in the control room for those extra special sounds created by opening up the casing, accessing the spring tray and placing metallic objects next to the springs. I recommend you buy yourself a spring line whether or not you can afford the two other more expensive systems.

2. Plate Reverb. The cost of plate reverb units even second hand is grossly inhibitive for the domestic recordist. Usually, they require suspension from the ceiling to isolate them from traffic rumble and footsteps. The system works on the same principle as a spring line,

PROFILES AND REVIEWS

The Lexicon 224X Digital Reverb and remote – a popular unit in professional studios.

though sheets of metal (or plates) are used instead of springs.

A 'plate' sound is an effect much sought after by many MOR producers, and EMT are the world leaders in plate reverb technology.

NSF do offer some exceptionally cheap ready-made and kit-form plate reverbs. However, since the introduction of the Yamaha R1000 digital reverb at under $800 and the subsequent flood of rival units, even building your own plate from scratch works out dearer than walking into your local shop and buying a digital reverb at list price!

3. Digital Reverb. This is by far and away the most popular form of reverberation in the contemporary music field. The top line units, such as the Klark Teknik DN780, Lexicon 224XL, and AMS RMX16 cost staggering amounts of money, but a few digital units have been appearing with acceptable price tags.

The aforementioned Yamaha R1000 is a preset unit, giving you four options and no added dimensions to the sound. For instance, with a pre-delay circuit which, used in conjunction with a reverb preset, you can create a whole host of different ambiences, including 'Intruder' type 'rooms'. The new Lexicon PCM60 costs about $1,000 and for my money is not as good value as the new Alesis XT, mainly because 'room' parameters are so important. The Alesis is a smidgen under $800, which I feel is reasonable (but only just) for such an important effect.

Yamaha R1000 Digital Reverb: Profile
Price: $795

The pre-reverb, side chain access is the saving grace of this machine and the principle factor

PROFILES AND REVIEWS

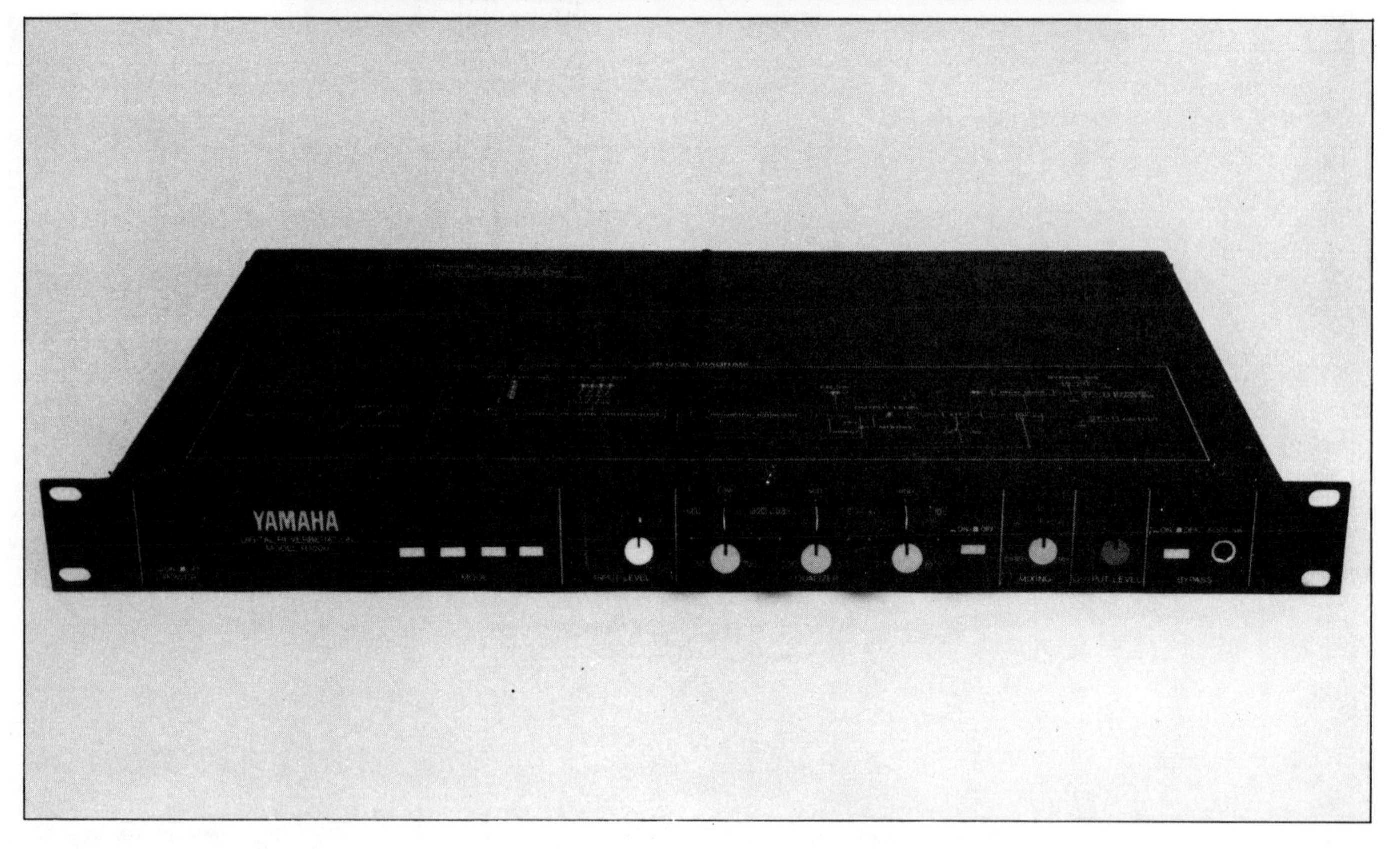

in my decision to buy one.

Despite its limitations, having four presets on a digital reverb is better than having no digital reverb at all. This is the conclusion of the majority of R1000 purchasers when they discover the dynamic performance and decay that can be achieved by digitising sound, and knowing full well that the next machine up is going to cost over $1,000 and therefore be completely out of the question.

The presets are not that different, offering more permutations on reverb intensity and EQ balance than on decay. Two of the four presets have decay times less than 3ms apart.

The unit is quiet and well built. The EQ section is a simple three-band affair which, together with the balance/mix output pot, can offer something like ten or twelve quite distinct permutations from the four presets. The s/n ratio is very good considering the price and the reverb signal bandwidth extends to 10K; reverb bandwidths are not to be taken too seriously – anything above 6K and you know the reverb is still going to be realistic. The much-revered (though its reputation has decreased with the recent appearance of rivals on the market) Quantec room simulator originally had a bandwidth of around 8K.

For about $795, the Yamaha R1000 offers excellent value for money. It is quick and simple to operate, producing quite powerful reverbs at 10% of the cost of some of the big professional machines.

I strongly recommend it.

Fostex 3180 Spring Reverb: Profile
Price: $400

Cleverly, Fostex have incorporated an analogue pre-delay circuit in this spring line unit to simulate the first reflection characteristics of rooms. And yet they haven't had the sense to put even one pre-delay parameter (nope, not even a straightforward level control) into the hands of those people who are paying for lots of

PROFILES AND REVIEWS

Japanese businessmen to play golf every Sunday in paper pagodas – you and me!

The 3180 follows the same basic lines as the Vesta RV2 and RV3: dual channels to create either stereo or completely isolated images.

The sound is not bad, although it has the wrong sort of mid range to suit many digital reverb fanatics. I like it, I think it is usable, but only just. The proof of the pudding is in the decay time, which is of medium length.

$400 or whatever price you manage to pin your local dealer down to, is a lot of money for such a one-track effect unit (note that I didn't use the plural). Fostex is OK, but I'd go for the Vesta units because of the limiting function. However, the Fostex is better built and I have a feeling the components used are of a higher quality, though *audibly* I don't think there's any difference. Strangely, a rack mounting unit, but with front fascia-mounted ins and outs. Very odd. Quite a good reverb though.

Specifications
Input: Unbal. Phone jack (Front panel), Unbal. Pin jack (Rear panel)
Input Impedance: 50k ohms
Input Level: Minimum -30dB (30mV), Maximum +30dB (30V)
Output, Normal: Unbal. Phone jack (Front panel)
Normal: Unbal. Pin jack (Rear panel)
Stero: Unbal. Pin jack (Rear panel)
Output Load Impedance: 5k ohms or higher
Output Level: 0dB (1V), adjustable
Maximum Output Level: +17dB (7V)
Reverberation Decay Time: Approx. 3 sec. (ref. to 1kHz)

Pre-Delay Time: Approx. 24 msec.
Frequency Range:
Dry 20Hz–20kHz
Reverb 200Hz–7kHz
T.H.D. Dry: Less than 0.02%
Signal-to-Noise Ratio:
Dry 80dB unwt'd, 82dB wtd.
Reverb 58dB unwt'd, 60dB wtd.
Power Requirements: 120V, 60Hz, 9W (USA/Canadian Models), 220V AC, 50Hz, 9W (European Models), 240V AC, 50Hz, 9W (UK/Australian Models)
Dimensions: 3½(H) × 17″(W) × 8¼″(D) (88mm × 430mm × 210mm)
Weight: Net 8¼lbs. (3.7kg) Shipping 9lbs (4.1kg)

PROFILES AND REVIEWS

The Great British Spring Reverb: Profile
Price: $300

Nip outside, smash up the neighbours' drains, drag a lump of drainpipe upstairs, get a pair of garden shears, cut up your parents' bed, extract some of the springs, stretch them, stuff them inside the drain pipe and solder the negative and positive wires from a mains plug to the whole lot . . .

Apart from probably getting arrested for the first action in the above step-by-step guide, you will also run the risk of electrocuting yourself. You will, however, have grasped the basic principle of the Great British Spring. The idea was first hit on by the Turnkey-associated company, Bandive, only they executed the project somewhat less dramatically. Consequently, you can now purchase the standard unit from your local dealer without risking life and limb.

The GBSR is constructed from a long piece of pipe and twelve springs of different mass and thickness. The unit is about two or three feet long and can be screwed to the wall. Two versions are available, one with balanced input and output circuits, and the other with a normal permutation, sporting unbalanced jack input and output. There is also an input level control (screwdriver adjusted) and, cleverly, Bandive have seen fit to make the hissing and humming bit (commonly known as the mass production power supply) separate. The only real control you have is the level pot. Failing that, you can while away hours of expensive studio time throwing things at it, hanging from it, scraping your nails along the casing, shouting very loudly close to the casing (making the springs inside vibrate), tapping it and generally finding ways to abuse it.

Without all the above paraphernalia, using the unit as a straightforward spring unit, you can achieve quite long, solid effects, with little or no systems hiss at all.

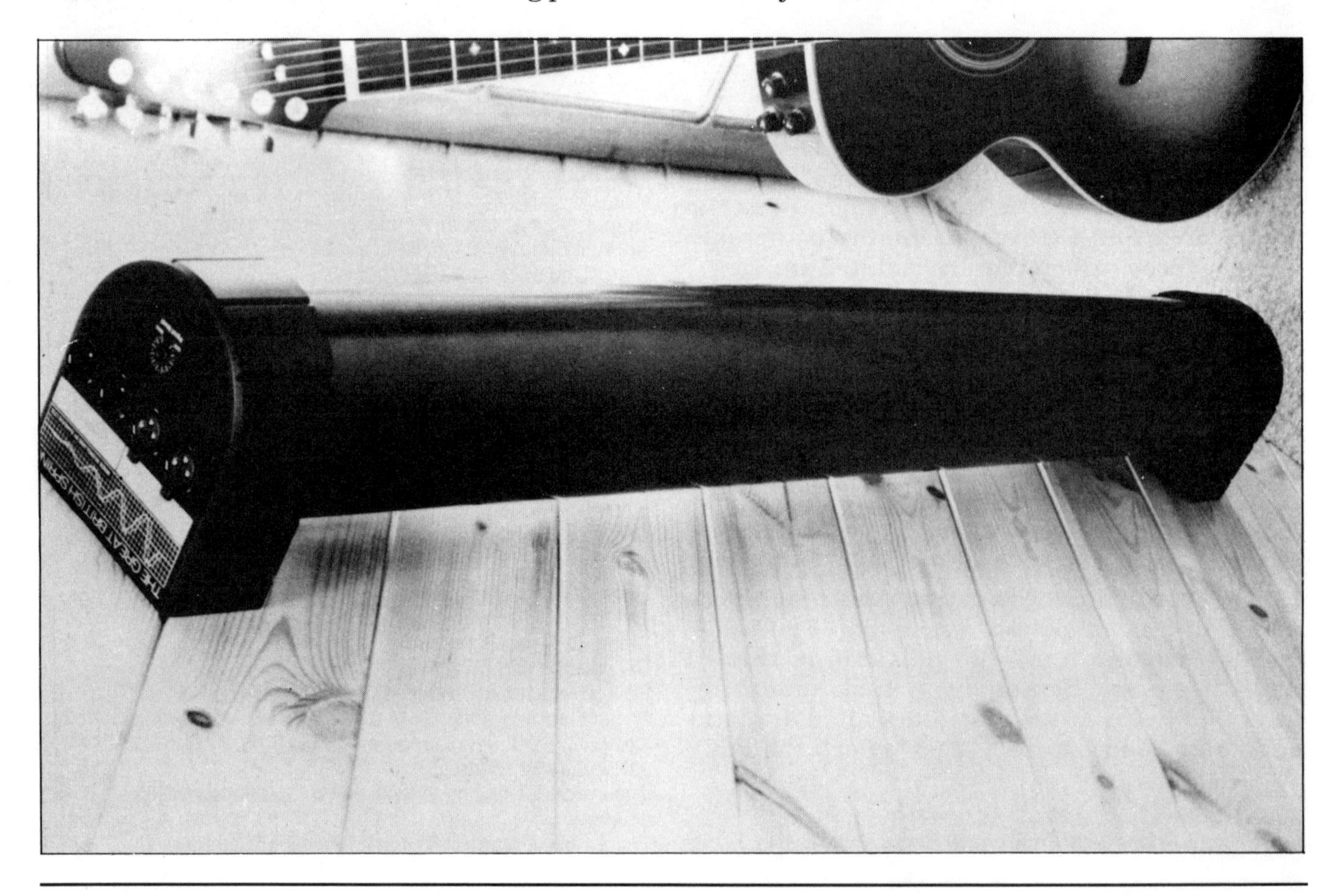

PROFILES AND REVIEWS

The GBSR is cheap and good – what more can you ask of a piece of drainpipe with twelve springs stuck inside it?

MXR 01a Digital Reverb: Profile
Price: $1,995

Originally released as the MXR 01, until the reverse reverb software was developed and fitted as standard (when it became the 01a), this machine is the cheapest programmable digital reverb on the market. Using a keypad on the front panel, it allows you to call up sets of parameters stored at an earlier date.

The audio quality is not great and my studio experiences with the MXR 01 and the new 01a have led me to the conclusion that you cannot take too many risks with the unit levels – that's if you want the noise to stay less than audible. Reverb bandwidth is somewhere in the region of 14K.

One of its best features is the fact that you can plug a normal foot pedal into the hold/freeze socket on the back panel and grab 'snapshots' of time, freezing the signal going through the delay at the time of depressing the pedal for as long as you want.

The front panel is surprisingly simple, with red LED displays showing you program and parameter information at a glance.

After some concentrated and serious tinkering with the machine, I've come to the conclusion that this machine is more of a straight plate reverb machine than a room simulator. With no internal control over frequency cut

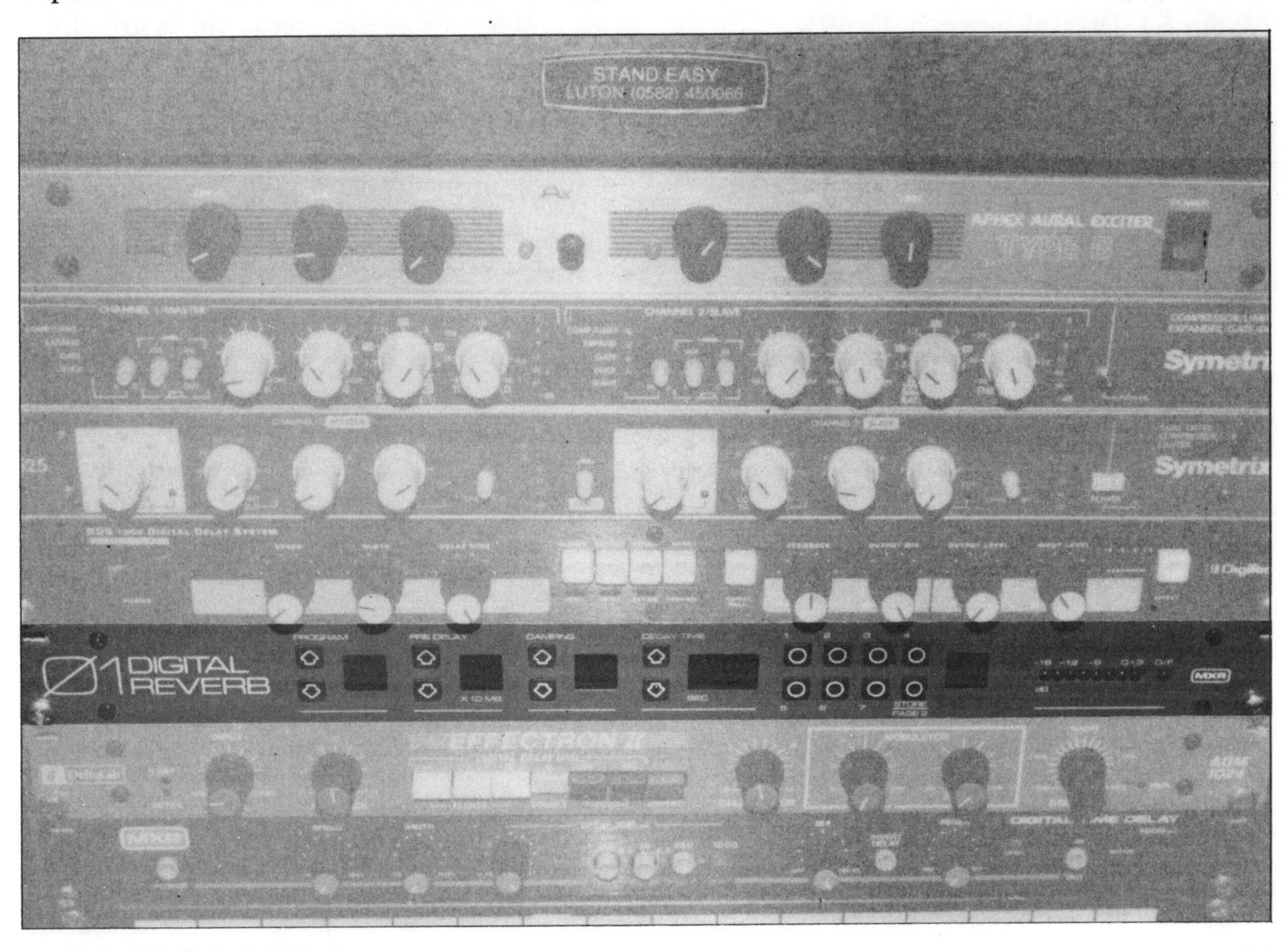

(just an overall damping mode), every straight reverb you get out is up-front and tight.

The pre-delay circuit is very powerful, giving you enough torque to introduce all sorts of weird and wonderful 'big rooms'.

I hope there will be some more software updates soon. The last was excellent and cost around fifty dollars, which is great value for money. Undoubtedly, the MXR offers the most for the least: its reverb control is unparalleled for less than three grand, and the footpedal and remote control options mean working with the 01a on long, tiring sessions is that little bit easier.

Well done MXR.

Alesis XT Digital Reverb: Profile
Price: $1,495

The Alesis XT digital reverb is reasonably priced and has become very popular with many small studio owners.

Parameter control is the all important key to creating really different reverb textures. The Yamaha R1000 is preset and any variation in sound has to come from the 'outside'. Similarly, the new Lexicon PCM60 has what I call 'limited' parameter control and you are very much tied down to the forty or fifty possible permutations – no more. What makes the Alesis XT a real breakthrough is the number of definable parameters placed at the user's control. Decay time (a parameter which largely defines the size of a reverb 'room') is a simple rotary, giving you at minimum 1/5 of a second decay, and at maximum a whole 10 seconds, which is superb.

If you refer back to my advice on reverb usage in 'The Art of Noise', you'll know that high and low frequency decay times are different on 'wet' signals. The XT has three buttons which control the frequency content of the

PROFILES AND REVIEWS

reverb signal: 'HF damp', giving you a very 'distant' reverb; 'LF cut' which creates a strong closeness to the reverb signal; and 'HF cut', which produces a much more highly defined version of the first EQ parameter.

The pre-delay circuit is coupled to the decay pot and the intensity and length of pre-delay increases as the room size gets bigger. Pre-delay is selectable – in or out.

Room simulation seems to be the dominant design policy behind the XT and they've included a selector which when depressed sets internal parameters to a small room formula and, when released, creates a large room. Though, as I've already said, the decay pot has a lot to do with creating an impression of size and, in all cases, it is the 'integration' of parameters rather than single controls which enable you to produce defined effects.

Special DDL type effects can be simulated via the slapback control which offers a sort of signal cascading effect, but without the clinical accuracy of a good DDL, the sound being warm, loose and distant on the majority of settings.

A diffusion selector cuts in and out a circuit which is designed to simulate the expansive, silky wash of reverb attainable from plate units. With this button depressed, reverb signals are less coherent and seem to consist of several 'detached' elements. Beautiful to listen to, but damned hard to put into words.

Updates: like all good pieces of equipment, the XT is software updatable, and some new FIR (Finite Impulse Response) filter chips, capable of simulating backwards reverb, are awaited. No prices have been fixed yet, but an update for an XT will probably not cost more than $100 or so.

The Alesis XT is one of the most affordable and versatile FX units in the history of modern recording. A snip under a grand, with stunning software updates in the pipeline, I seriously recommend you to try one – even if you can only afford to hire one on a daily basis, rather than shelling out the greenies.

I'm buying one!

Specifications
Frequency Response: 30Hz to 14KHz
Dynamic Range: Rev: 75dB typ.
Dry: 100dB typ.
Distortion: Rev: 0.1% typ.
Dry: .025% typ.
Levels: In: +20dB max
Out: +12dB max
Impedances: In: 500K ohms
Out: 600 ohms
Dimensions: 1¾" EIA RACK, 9¼" deep
Warranty: One Year

Lexicon PCM60 Digital Reverb: Profile
Price: $1,040

"Hello, I'm from England . . ."
"Sorry . . . where?"
"England . . . I have a studio in London . . ."
"Oh right, yeah, England . . . uh huh . . ."
"Would you like to tell me a bit about the new Lexicon digital reverb?"
"Oh, hey, yeah . . . yeah, I mean . . . this is a new digital reverb from . . . well, firstly, I should tell you that it sells for *under* two thousand dollars, which is really good for a unit of this kind . . ."
"Perhaps you'd like to let me hear it?"
"Oh, sure . . ." (plugs in headphones to home made amplifier running off a PP3 battery), "Here ya go . . ."
(Wearing headphones – sound quality surprisingly clean, but not loud) "Do you mind turning it up a bit?"
"Oh, well, it's only got four room sizes . . . you'll have to push the end one . . ."
"What?"
"*I said,* it only has a few room presets, you'll have to try the end one . . ."
"But it's not loud enough . . ."
"Sorry, that's the factory presets for you . . . it's really a very good machine, would you like to buy one?"
"Sorry, no, not at the moment, I'm going to go and get someone who can demonstrate this new Lexicon reverb for me . . ."
"Oh, for God's sake!"
"What now?"
"Have they gone and brought out another one? How can they do that?"

PROFILES AND REVIEWS

This dialogue records my first meeting with the new(ish) Lexicon PCM60 in New York a few months ago. Happily I found time to sit with one for the best part of a morning (on a good demo system) and came to the conclusion that what it offered was very good, but was not as good value for money as the MXR 01a digital reverb.

The subsequent release of the Alesis XT has put the PCM60 in *third* place, mainly due to the lack of rotary definable parameters. Lexicon have decided to put the two major parameters – room size and decay time – into four way selector banks, giving you a maximum of (yes, you've guessed it) just four permutations for each function.

I do not feel that this is good design sense at all. True, it is possible to create a multitude of permutations, but without pinpoint control over important parameters only a couple of really distinct sounds can be created, as opposed to the hundred or so options on offer with the XT or the MXR 01a.

Sound quality: there is some hissing (as in the case of the two aforementioned rivals), but this is minimal and can be easily lost. The plate and room selectors give 'classic' reverb sounds with none of the quality loss which is sometimes experienced with old (valve) plates and microphone/monitor set-ups in rooms.

It's well built, and the front panel is well designed. The sounds available are all good. They are typical of the smooth, silky sound and dynamic range which most people want when they turn to digital reverberation. It is a *Lexicon* sound. Whatever your reverb preferences, the PCM60 can undoubtedly offer some settings which will make your toes wiggle, but with a maximum decay of 4.5 seconds (longest plate) and no pre-delay control, the PCM60 does not deserve the price being asked for it.

If it hadn't been for the recent introduction of the Alesis XT, I would have given the PCM60 a more enthusiastic review. Some people may buy it for that certain 'Lexicon' quality, some because they want to put Lexicon on their studio rate cards. Do not buy *any* digital reverb without listening carefully to a PCM60 first. It is already becoming popular, but not to the same degree as the XT, I suspect.

Specifications
Frequency Response

PROFILES AND REVIEWS

Reverberant Signal: 20Hz to 10kHz, +1dB.
Direct Signal: 20Hz to 20kHz, +0.25dB.
Dynamic Range
Reverberant Range: 80dB, 20-Hz to 20-kHz noise bandwidth
Total Harmonic Distortion (THD) and Noise
Total Harmonic Distortion (THD) and Noise
Reverberant Signal:
0.05% @ 1kHz and full level.
Direct Signal:
0.025% @ 1kHz @ 3 V out
Reverberation Time
Room Program: 0.3 to 0.8 seconds
Plate Program: 0.2 to 4.5 seconds
Frequency Contouring
Bass and Treble pushbuttons for increasing or decreasing low- or high-frequency reverb time; actual contouring functions are program dependent.
Audio Input One input
Levels
+4dB: −8 to 18 dBV balanced.
−20dB: −23 to +3 dBV unbalanced.
Impedance
+4dB: 40 kilohms parallel with 150 pF balanced.
−20 dB: ‹500 kilohms parallel with 150 pF unbalanced.
Connector
2-in. tip/ring/sleeve phone jack.
Audio Output Two outputs
Levels
+4dB: +10dBV into 600 ohms; +16 dBV into 10 kilohms or greater.
−20dB: −8dBV into 10 kilohms or greater.
Impedance
600 ohms; unbalanced.
Connector
2-in. tip/sleeve phone jack.
Effects Send
Level
0dBV at machine operating level.
Impedance
600 ohms unbalanced.
Connector
2-in. tip/sleeve phone jack.
Effects Return
Level
0dBV for full machine level.
Impedance
‹50 kilohms parallel with 150pF unbalanced.
Connector
2-in. tip/sleeve phone jack.
Bypass Remote
2-in. tip/sleeve phone plug for connection to momentary footswitch; for use with optional Lexicon footswitch: 750-02834.
Power
Nominal: 100, 120, 220, 240 Vac (−10%, +5%) switch-selectable; 50 to 60 Hz; 20W.
RFI Shielding
Meets all requirements for FCC Class A computer equipment.
Protection
Mains fused; voltage crowbar and/or current limiting for internal supplies.
Dimensions
Standard 19-in. rack mount: 19″w × 1¾″h × 11″d (483 × 44 × 280mm).
Weight
9.2lb (4.2kg); shipping: 11lb(5kg).

Accessit Spring Reverb: Profile
Price: $200

Irresistibly small. It sounds very nice. Easy to control. The reverb springs enclosure can be vibration-free mounted, the control box racked away (with two other Accessit units) within arm's reach. Such are the unique features of the Accessit spring reverb unit. At a silly price of just over a hundred smackers, the most astute of you will realize that buying two (or even three) of these units may turn out to give you more flexibility than lashing out on a Vesta or Aces spring line at roughly the same price.

For abusing, especially with car keys, cigarette lighters, twist-and-spurt $10 specials (I'm not joking – one studio I visited recently were using one to create 'echoing vibrations' for a video soundtrack!), steel rulers, coathangers, etc. etc., this is the boy!

The separate control box has an input level pot with peak LED, mix pot (dry to wet), and a boost/cut filter (sweepable, of course) for the reverb signal. I don't think it has any limiting circuits, but in use I did not experience any low frequency 'boing boings'. Having an LED peak indicator is a *must*.

The spring housing is quite well made (for the money) and is attached via a reasonable length of cable, though if you wanted to put this less than handsome part of the reverb out of sight, I'm sure it wouldn't be impossible to lengthen the cable.

I haven't got round to opening one of these lads up yet, but I'm going to buy one in the next couple of weeks and have it fitted with some extra springs. Spring trays in kit form can be purchased from companies like Phonosonics in Orpington, Kent for about $25. For a throw-away FX device to customise yourself, the

PROFILES AND REVIEWS

Accessit is ideal. The sound is not too expansive, but the noise created is a useful one.

NOTE: sticking objects into *any* home recording equipment will invalidate the guarantee!

Digital Delays: A General Introduction

It is quite common for established 24-T and 48-T studios to spend upwards of $12,000 just on digital delays: AMS dominate the top end of the market and the above sum would only get you *two* of their excellent 80S machines with an average amount of memory – probably no more than 3.5 sec each. Steve Levine, Culture Club's producer, has an 80S with over twenty seconds of memory in it – at roughly a thousand pounds a second, we are obviously talking about *essential* equipment.

But why is the amount of *memory* a DDL has so important? Well, firstly, a DDL is an analogue-to-digital processor which stop-frames incoming information and converts sound energy into a binary code which can then be manipulated via additional electronics and converted back into an analogue sound signal for release through the 'delay' or effects output(s).

In simpler terms, the DDL is constantly (a good few thousand times a second) catching the sound being fed into it, storing it in RAM chips, and letting it out again, with the consequent delay being decided by you via the front panel controls.

Your average DDL usually has about 1024ms of memory (1.25 sec approx.). Some have a hold function which allows you to freeze the signal caught in the RAM chips and re-trigger it via a front panel switch, or, more excitingly, from a drum machine pulse. This is

PROFILES AND REVIEWS

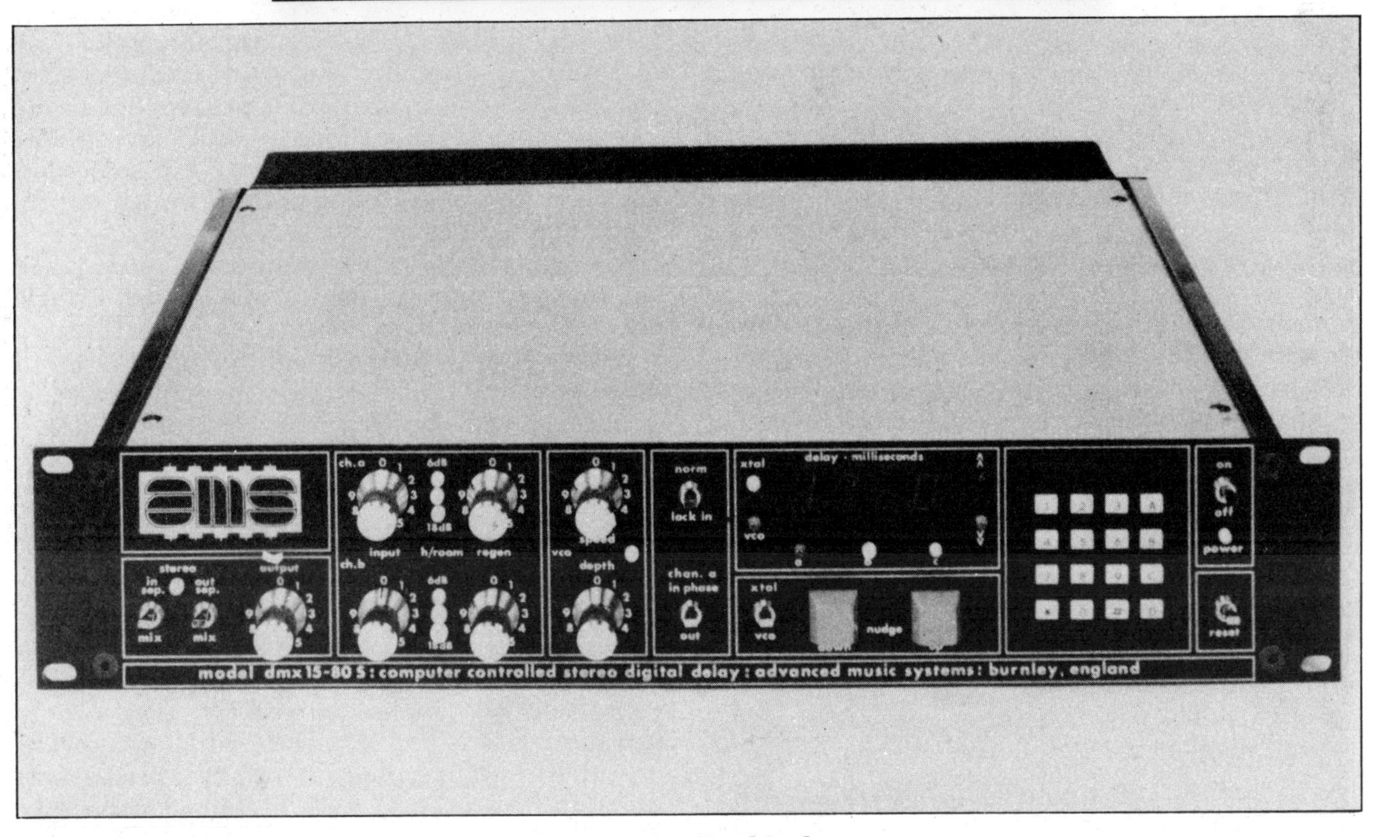

The AMS 80S DDL, undoubtedly the finest unit of its kind.

the same basic principle of sound-sampling keyboards: the designers of the Fairlight, Emulators and Ensoniq Mirage just went one step further and added interface electronics for a chromatic keyboard to control the pitch or speed at which the information is regurgitated, thus making any sound playable on a musical scale.

A hold function is extremely useful, though without manual or drum-sync re-triggering electronics, the effect (on short, sharp sounds which have been caught in the memory from a drum kit, for example) can be limited to recreating 'n-n-n-n-nineteen' machine gun type patterns.

Fortunately, a couple of small companies (in association with some retailers) are offering mods which allow you to make any DDL re-triggerable from a drum or tape pulse.

By regulating the time-delay knobs (up or down) it is possible to change the pitch of a sample held inside a DDL. If you seriously want to use your DDL as a sampler, then make sure the above function has an extra 'fine tune' knob, so that accurate chromatic tuning can take place. If all you have is one control in this section, make sure the knob isn't detented or internally calibrated so that it doesn't 'jump' between one playback pitch (or delay time) and another.

In short, a DDL can completely open up your creative horizons. Prices start (for full function units with mod. rate and depth) at around $400.

Some would argue that a DDL is *more* important than a reverb, as reverb-type effects can be created with a DDL which has regeneration or feedback (intermittent hold function governed by the amount of information being processed via RAM inside), control and invert function. This latter reverses the envelope of the processed signal and, in conjunction with feedback or regeneration, can result in a series of wishy-washy fading repeats. However, only DDLs with extremely high sampling or processing resolutions are capable of a truly convincing reverb, since on the less expensive units, which are much slower at processing and regurgitating information, the separate segments of new and old processed information can be heard individually, giving the effect of a medium length reverb decay with someone turning the volume up and down, fifty times a second.

Unfortunately, DDL units started life as top-line luxury recording processors and lower priced models only started appearing two years ago. Consequently, there aren't *that* many easily affordable units around, with the vast majority (over 80%) costing $750 upwards. This section is not very long, as my thinking on the subject tends to be: if you *do* have the odd $750 to spend on digital delay technology, buy *two* units rather than one. *Two* point source FX units are always better than one . . .

Boss DE-200 Rhythm Sync DDL: Profile
Price: $395

For well over a year now, this has simply been the best value DDL on the market – no question. It has the ability to receive trig-pulses into the back panel jack socket (wide range of acceptance) for the 'hold' or, in this case, 'sample' function. It's a 12 bit processor, which is the accepted standard on all equipment of this nature costing under a grand. You get a bandwidth trade-in above 640ms, with the figure dropping from 10kHz to just 4.5kHz on the maximum time-delay setting of 1280ms. But I wouldn't feel hard done by, if I were you – the DE-200 offers roughly 260ms more memory than its competitors and I can honestly say that the compansion circuits included are of the highest quality. So the minimum bandwidth stated above is quite acceptable for 90% of all DDL functions. Remember, treble starts at around 3kHz, and 4.5kHz is by no means the end of the world.

The fact that you can stick this machine on external sync sets it well above its competitors. And not only does it offer this almost unique facility, but at a price which currently makes it the third cheapest DDL on the British market (the other two also being Boss products!).

Extremely well-built, with the usual powerful Roland modulation section, the DE-200 is

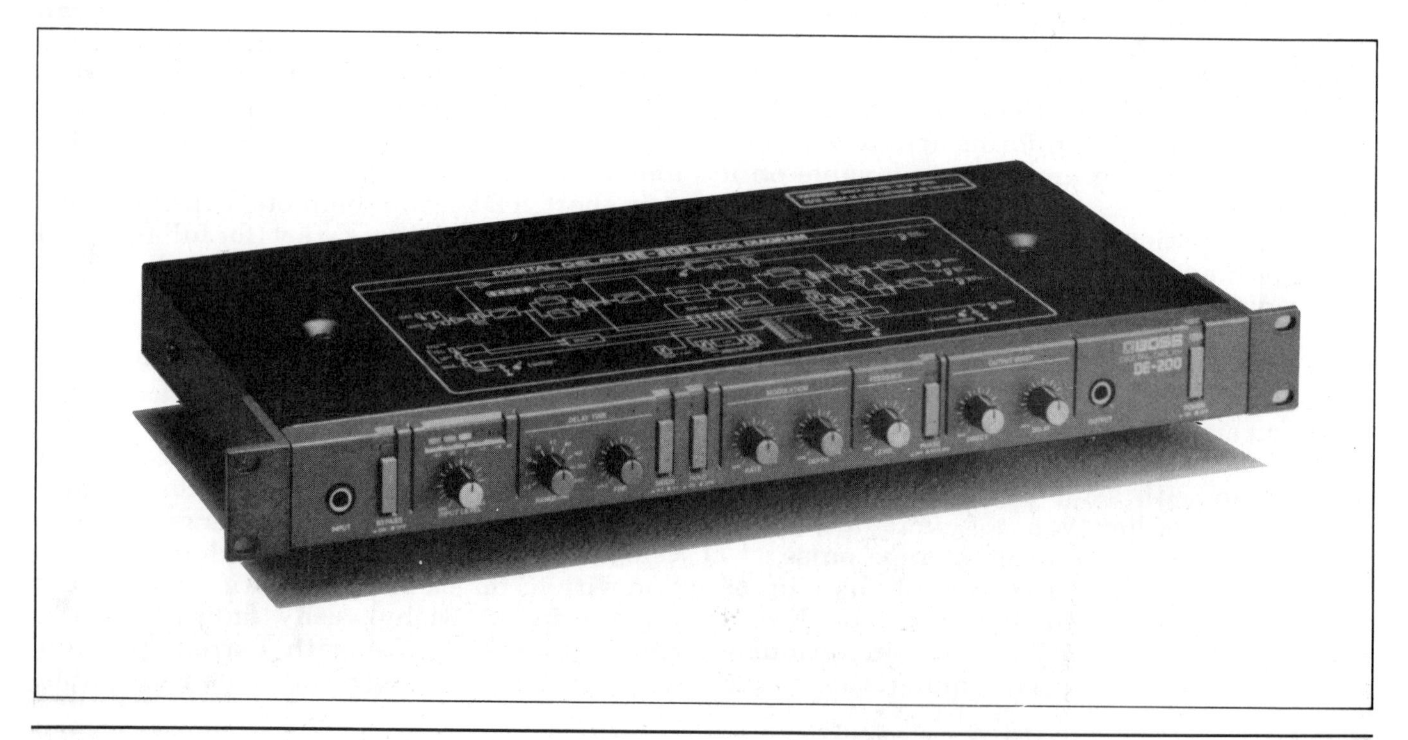

PROFILES AND REVIEWS

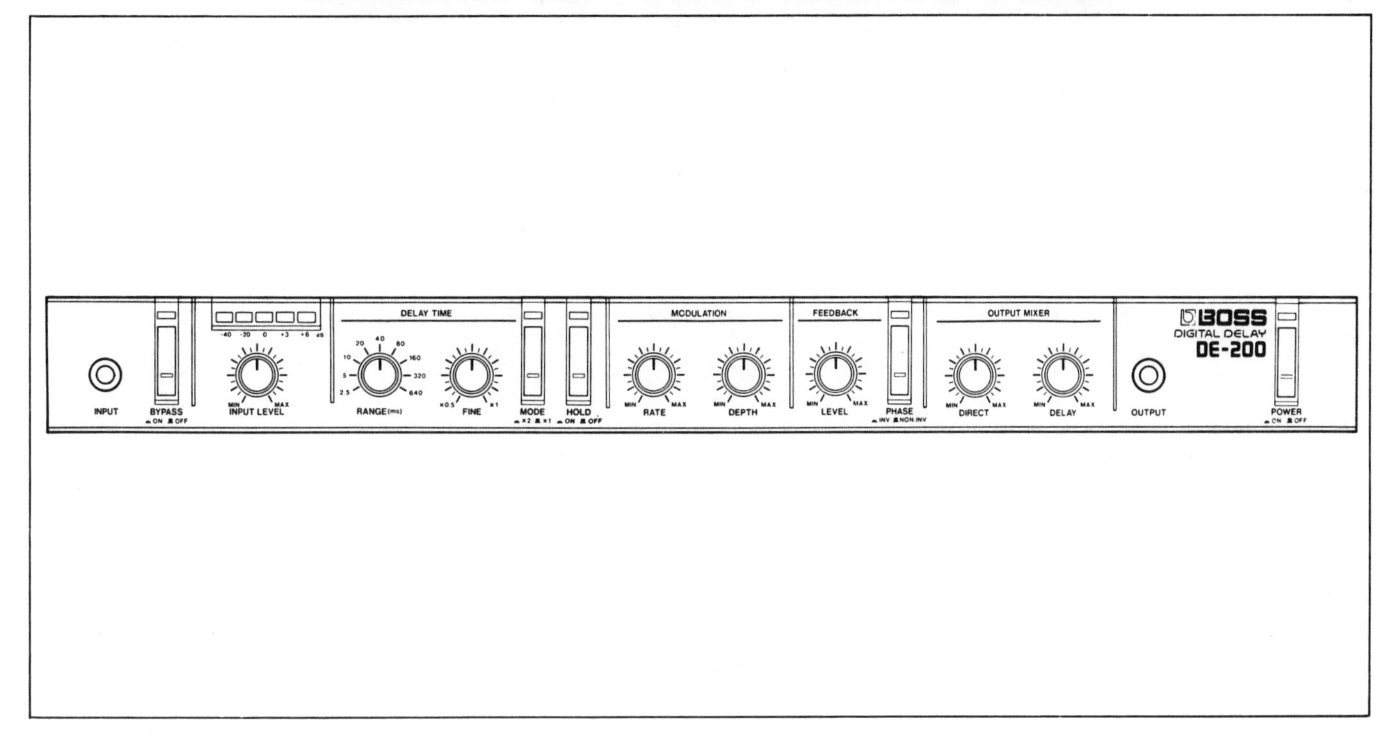

exceptional value for money. Only the new DIG-411 from Vesta seriously challenges the DE-200's price/feature equation. The DE-200 and DIG-411 are set to do battle this coming year as never before . . .

Korg SDD-1000/2000 DDLs: Profile
Price: $495+/– (SDD-1000)

With a very similar model number to the programmable Roland SDE-1000, but sporting expanded facilities compared to the Boss DE-200, the Korg SDD-1000 gets my vote for being as good value for money as the Boss unit.

Offering the same sample facility, retriggerable from an external source (jack socket), this Korg unit looks good on the surface, but lo and behold, things get even juicier as a quick perusal of the literature reveals that it has *double* the memory of the DE-200! Samples of up to 2040ms can be stored at what is quite a modest bandwidth, but excellent frequency response figures *are* attainable on shorter samples. At 1024ms, the Korg offers above-average DDL bandwidth.

You can also trigger the repeat function externally and have your on-line delayed signals repeating (and fading) in time with a drum machine or tape pulse of suitable amplitude and voltage content.

An updated version, called the SDD-2000, was released recently, which retails for around $795. I believe this offers somewhere in the region of five seconds' sampling time and can be controlled from an external keyboard via MIDI. There are cheaper monophonic sampling machines on the market, but having a MIDI buss *should* offer extra scope for control.

The SDD-1000 is a machine I suggest you seriously consider buying.

Fostex 3050 DDL: Profile
Price: $400

Offering two extremely useful electronic circuits – an input limiter with associated LED to combat overload, and a phase inverse button on the output, the 3050 from Fostex does look

PROFILES AND REVIEWS

like incredible value for money. However, it's not all plain sailing and after my initial enthusiasm I looked at the spec. sheet to discover it contains less than 300ms maximum memory.

The internal processor is only 8 bit and quite a powerful companion circuit has been used to get the best possible dynamic range and s/n ratio on the delay signal, which is quite acceptable.

For ADT, flanging and chorus, the 3050 is very good, with the clean delay settings giving you a sort of cut-short slapback effect at maximum.

You may be lucky and find a dealer offering one of these in conjunction with another piece of equipment in a cut-price package, but if not, the current competition (especially the new RDD-10 from Boss) does seem to have the 3050 on the run. However, knowing the excellent design team Fostex have in Japan, their current standing in the DDL market is almost certain to improve.

Roland SDE-1000 Programmable Digital Delay: Profile
Price: $550

A *programmable* digital delay has more to offer a PA sound engineer than a recording engineer, as delay FX are developed in the studio through a period of careful parameter selections and adjustments. Once you get to know your machinery really well, you won't need to use memory banks so much as you will be able to create whatever sound you want as and when the need arises. However, having said this, having a DDL with memory locations in the studio is a superlative luxury – especially when working on scratch-type material (or any other fast moving 'tunes') where the switching between patches on-beat can create impressive and unworldly juxtapositions.

The SDE-1000 is extremely good quality with a delay dynamic range of about 100dB and a maximum bandwidth of 17kHz at short delay times, the bandwidth dropping a few K at full tilt. The amount of memory available is not dissimilar from that offered by the Boss DE-200 (1125ms), it is simply the four user-programmable locations which push the price up (and of course the aforementioned electronics/processing performance).

With its powerful mod section – excellent value for money – the SDE-1000 offers quite staggering delay potential for well under my self-imposed $750 limit. But, we must ask, are two DE-200s better value than one SDE-1000? It is your choice.

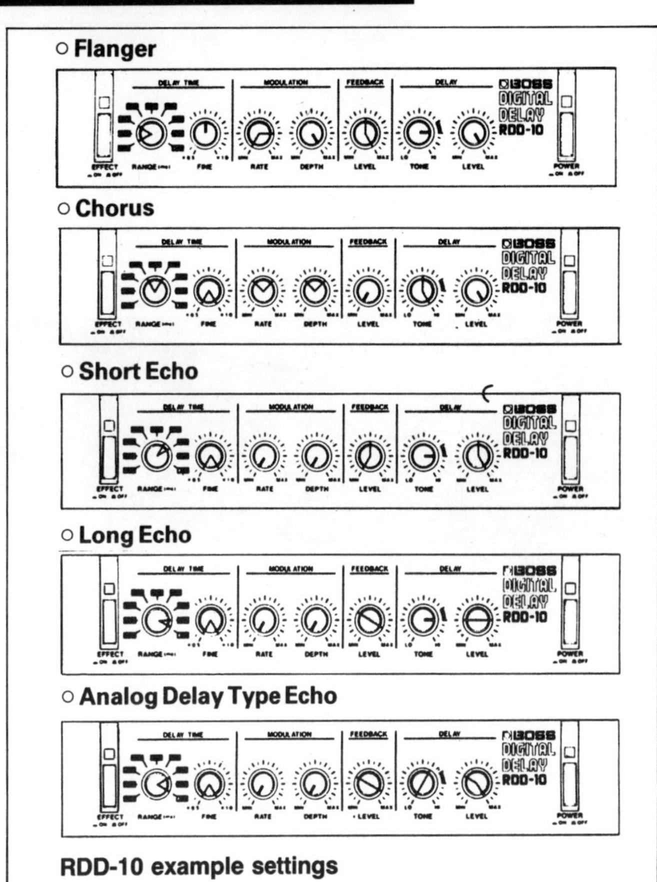

RDD-10 example settings

Boss Micro Rack Series Digital Delay, RDD-10: Profile
Price: $250

This is the newest of all the DDLs featured in this section. It is also the most expensive Boss Micro Rack Series product. It sports a truly devastating feature: the ability to link two RDD-10 modulation sections together (back

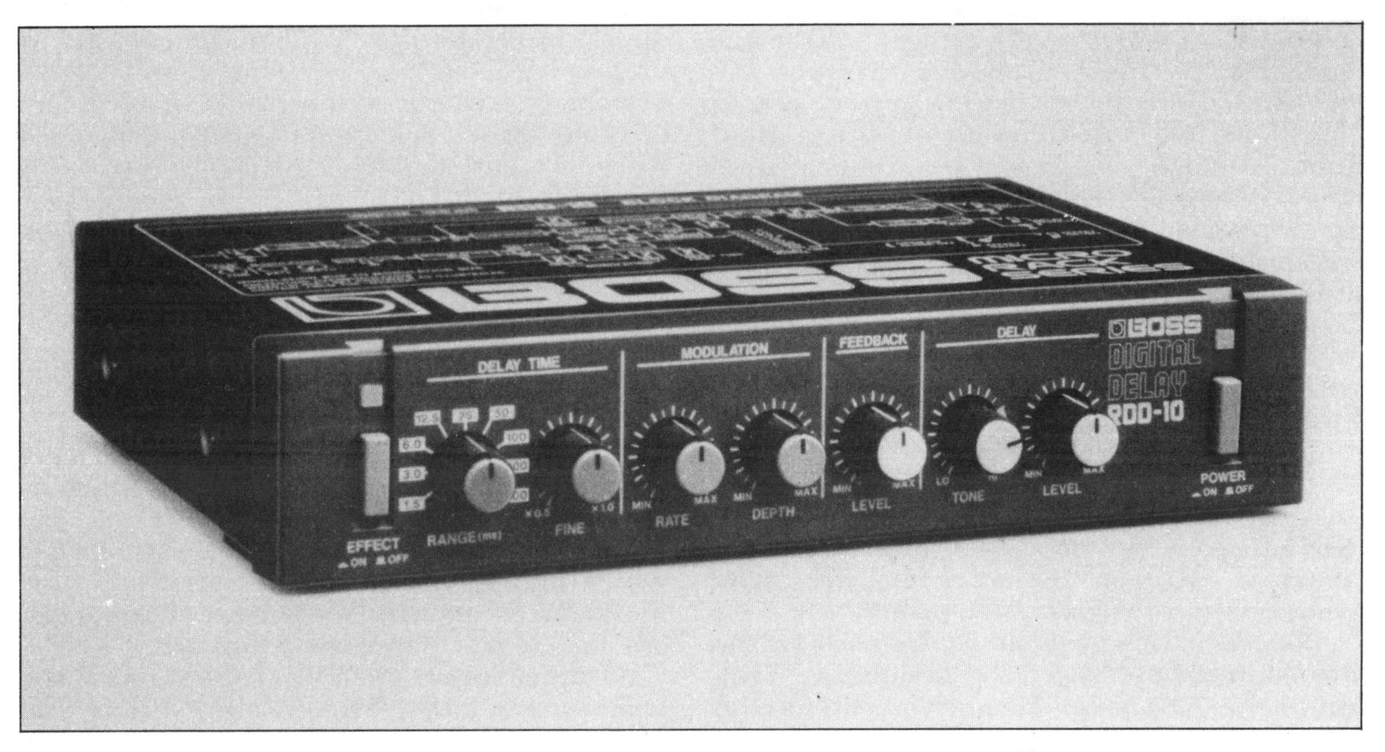

PROFILES AND REVIEWS

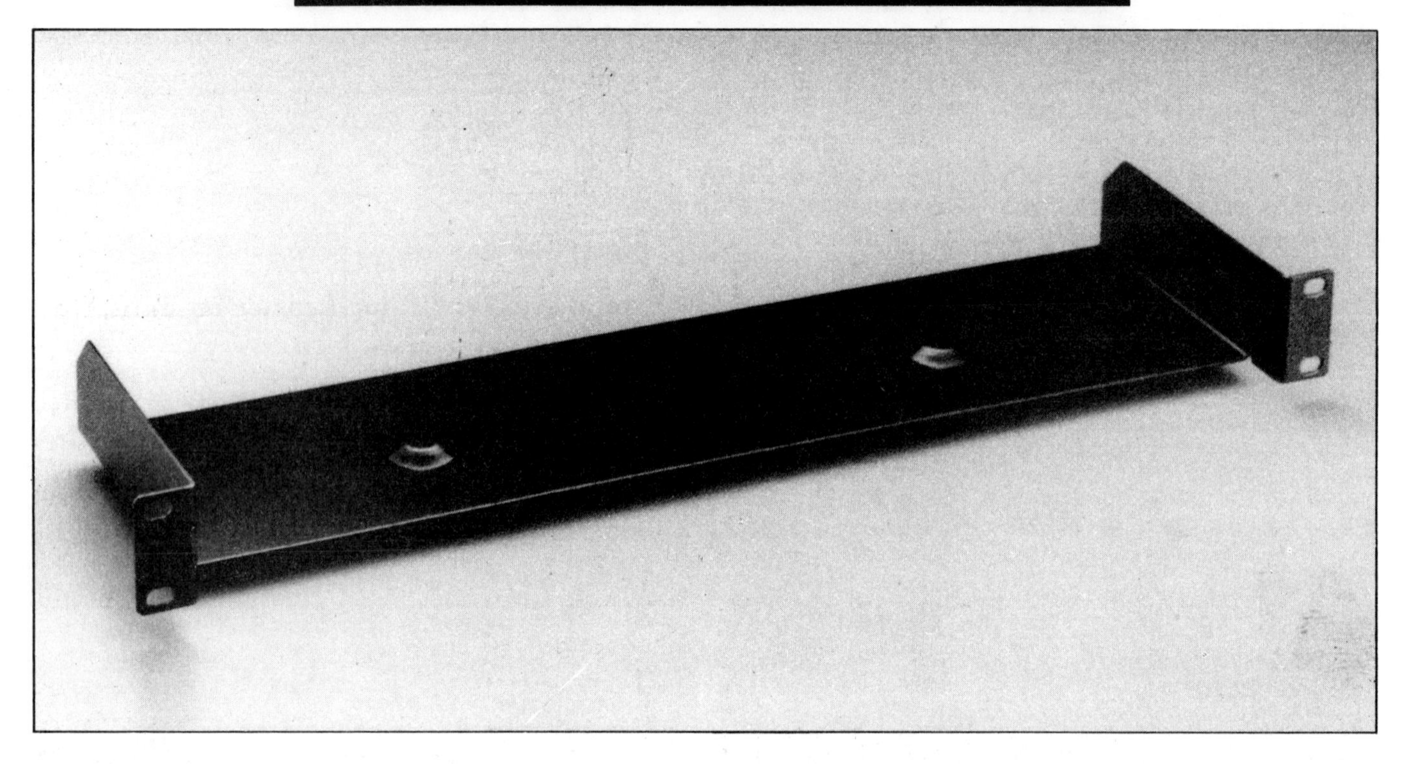

panel connection) so that double cross modulation and two independent effects can be produced simultaneously.

Quality is very good indeed, with a delay bandwidth of 16kHz. Most budget DDLs have a bandwidth which rarely exceeds 16kHz, and as long as the figure is above 10kHz, you will be able to create convincing repeat echoes which are not *that* different from the original input. Judicial EQing can get the best from any DDL output, and a bandwidth of 16kHz, as in this case, means the delay signal is of exceptionally high quality.

My only real grudge against the RDD-10 is the lack of memory, a maximum of 400ms is more than a little limiting, and the time delay on offer is capable of stretched slapback echo effects and nothing more complex than that. This is obviously a high quality digital ADT/chorus/flanging DDL, the VCO modulation section and its capacity to link up to another RDD-10 save the day. Let's face it, it's the cheapest DDL on the market – yes, even cheaper than the Boss DDL pedal!

Boss deserve a good pat on the back for the development of the Micro Rack Series. Each unit is half the usual size and two of them can sit happily on Boss's standard 19″ dedicated rack housing.

I'm planning on buying at least one of these DDLs. They are undoubtedly *the* ideal stablemate for side chain access FX, especially digital reverb units. Well designed, with a unique link feature, very good quality, at an extremely realistic and sensible price (hopefully the selling price will be nearer $200 or so within a month or two), the RDD-10 is truly an excellent little DDL, with more modulation potential than some units costing fifty times the price!

Compression and Limiting: A General Introduction

Of all the misleading information which is bandied about in the British music press, none has done more damage than the fairytales which manufacturers and subservient 'journalists' have spun on the subject of compressors and (to a lesser extent) limiters.

So many times, when I've been at one of the trade shows, either here or in the States, and also when producing and/or engineering for new bands, I get the same misguided questions about compressors. The people posing the questions have been completely led up the garden path and the most notable of all these quizzes is: 'What is the best sounding compressor on the market?'

Are you sitting comfortably? Then I'll begin ...

Compression is simply a method employed to control the dynamic range of signals before going to tape. Drum kits are the most 'compressed' of all instruments, because the signals change rapidly from the lightest sixteenths tapped on the high hat, to thundering, nerve-racking, bone-crushing tom runs. When setting the optimum level for the drum track, the loudest sound dictates where the fader on the sub group output is set so that you don't saturate the tape and produce nasty distortion. This level is always fairly low and consequently the quieter passages get lost in the quagmire of tape hiss, the s/n ratio becoming appalling.

So, an automatic method of smoothing everything out is needed ... and that is what a compressor does. Compressing your signals via desk insert points or auxiliaries allows you to squash the dynamic range down, and the control of this is spoken of in terms of ratios and 'gain reduction'. A compression ratio of 2:1 means that for every 2dB of volume going into the input of the compressor, only 1dB (or 50% normal amplitude transients) will come through the output.

Consequently, everything is much easier to handle, with the difference between quiet and loud passages reduced to a user-definable level which will all fit neatly onto the tape emulsion – above the noise floor, but below saturation level. There are some side effects as a result of all of this trickery, the worst of which, aesthetically speaking, is the loss of natural 'light and shade' one experiences when standing next to a drum kit. Massive compression ratios (over 4:1) tend to make quite flighty, transient signals sound flat and very much 'on the surface', with the natural perspective created by differing sound pressure levels being mixed together practically lost altogether.

The hard, no-nonsense, 'compress-it-out-of-existence' approach can create quite astounding results, especially on drum kits, though on vocals compression at even mild ratios can make the sound seem disjointed and jerky. For this reason, advanced compressors have 'threshold', 'attack' and 'release' controls which make the art (and it *is* an art) of compression that much easier on light, fluffy sounds.

Threshold: This parameter defines at which point the compressor electronics kick in. A very high threshold and the signal will remain quite natural (full of transients) with only the very loudest parts of the input signal being compressed. A low compression threshold will result in even quiet passages kicking the electronics into action and reducing the gain according to the defined ratio.

Attack: This defines how quickly or slowly the compression of a signal starts after the threshold has been passed. This is extremely useful for vocals, where the signal may only contain differing transients on the chorus and a medium slow attack on the compression means that gain reduction will be brought in very smoothly, without a nasty squeeze being audible (granted, to experienced ears) once the signal trips the defined threshold.

Release: This, as in the case of attack, is user-definable from a millisecond to a couple of seconds or so. The release time you set dictates how long the compression electronics will take to fade out once the signal has dropped below the threshold.

Dual Channel Stereo Compressors

Sometimes it is necessary to compress a stereo signal and a dual channel system will have to be employed – either a dedicated 2 in/2 out unit or two independent compressors. The biggest drawback to stereo compression is that there has to be some sort of link, otherwise if a loud signal appears on one side and trips the threshold and not on the other, the listener (especially on headphones) will experience a nasty, unnatural imbalance. A link must be employed so that if one side is tripped, the other reacts accordingly and the stereo volume balance is maintained.

PROFILES AND REVIEWS

Cheap compressors do not usually have a link socket, but remember that it is rare to compress a two channel signal. However, I compress reverb quite a bit and having a stereo reverb set-up means that I *have* to employ a dual channel system for that alone. Remember, there aren't any *real* rules, stereo unbalancing can be used to great creative (if somewhat strange) effect.

Limiters

A limiter is usually included in the electronics of many compressors because the principles and control parameters are almost identical. Whereas compression works on a ratio theory, limiting works on a no-nonsense barrier system which means that the threshold you set is absolute and *no* transients pass that point. Horrific limiting can be heard on Radio 4; the BBC have never been too hot on all this new fangled stuff! Generally, limiting is quite a tough and totalitarian effect, useful mainly on wickedly hot vocals and drums. On the whole, compression and limiting techniques are applied mostly to percussion, vocals and brass.

A compressor is a must.

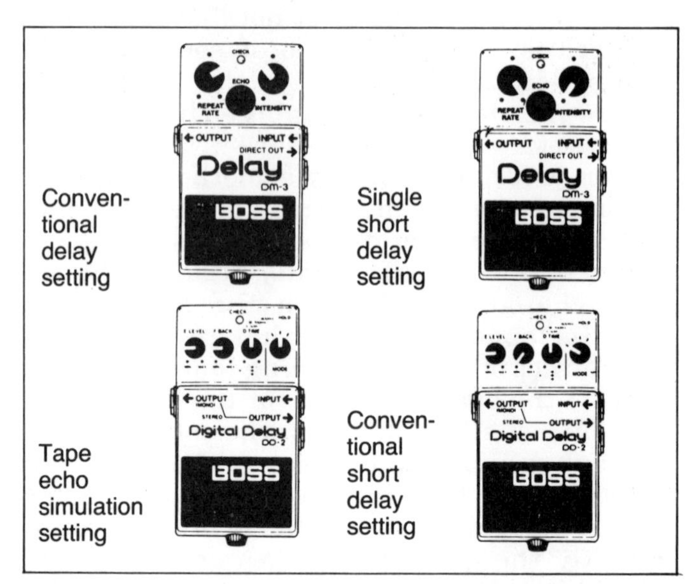

The new range of cost effective FX pedals from Vesta – strangely named, but I highly recommend them.

PROFILES AND REVIEWS

Slow vibrato | Fast vibrato | Conventional chorusing | Vibrato chorus | jet-style flanging | Metallic flanging

Accessit Compressor: Profile
Price: $100

The smallest and one of the cheapest compressors on the market, offering single channel operation with just two control parameters: input level and release time. It has an illuminated rounded meter which works horizontally and is highly reminiscent of the clapometer on *Opportunity Knocks* – easily the worse prime time entertainment in the history of television (Chris Everard 1985).

This minor objection apart, the compression ratio is a hefty 6:1, with a range of 30dB. The meter works backwards. It is able to accommodate both mike and line level inputs with the added advantage of being able to enter the electronics via the mike input and out the line output, thus giving you something of a microphone pre-amp/DI interface.

The 'Sound Vice', as the manufacturers prefer to call it, is very good quality and sports the usual Accessit din-socketed 24V DC power input.

It usually sells for around $75, which, taking into account this unit's cleanliness and no-fuss operation, really does make it remarkably good value with only the Vesta rack unit (which runs off a PP3 and sports many more features) able to compete with it at roughly another $50 more.

Yamaha GC2020 Compressor/Limiter: Profile
Price: $310

A recent addition to the Yamaha outboard family, the GC2020 may have broken the $300 barrier, but is excellent value for money all the

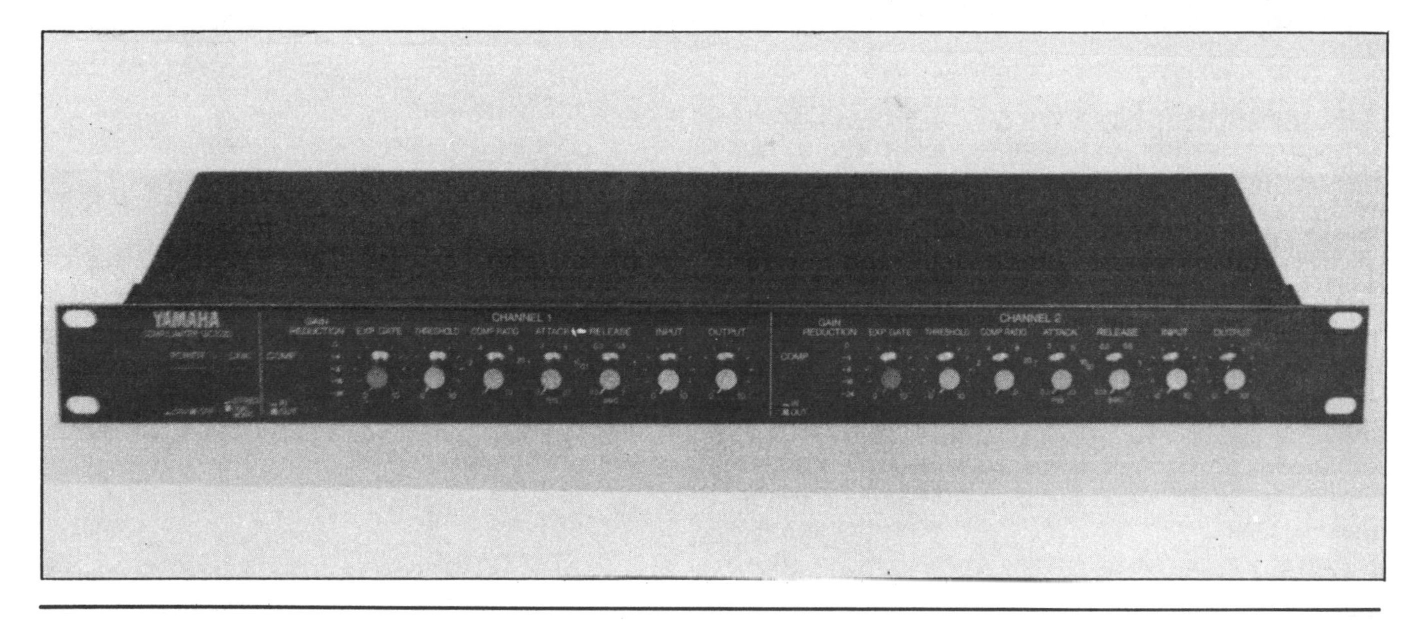

PROFILES AND REVIEWS

same. A dual channel device which can operate independently or with the two sides linked for stereo applications, it is all housed in a neat, professional, well-made 19″ rack-mounting package.

The performance of this machine is unquestionably good, offering a full complement of features, with the compression ratio covering everything from 1:1 to 00:1, which means that the compression available at that setting lets nothing through at all without the gain reduction affecting every contour of the input signal relative to the original amplitude.

Naughty manufacturers have been lengthening their spec. sheets and the initial appeal of their units by referring to the in-line noise gates found on these sophisticated compressors as 'expanders' or 'expander gates'. A noise gate is a useful feature to have built in as on powerful compression settings, background noise (of any description) increases in relative volume. To achieve tight, uncluttered results a noise gate can be introduced to cut out completely the various nasty gremlins which can creep into a processed signal.

All in all, the Yamaha GC2020 is a fine unit with fairly professional specifications for what is really quite an unprofessional price tag.

Boss Micro Rack Series RCL-10 Compressor/Limiter: Profile
Price: $150

The Boss Micro Rack Series compressor/limiter seems to offer very good value for money (as do all the units in the series) and is built to Boss's usual exacting standards.

Sporting the lengthy title of Compressor/Limiter/Expander/Noise Gate, the RCL-10 offers comprehensive compression parameters, including attack and release, together with adjustable ratio which provides more than enough torque. The gate section (as on many more sophisticated models) can be used in its own right, but lacks the finesse of control one attains by purchasing a separate noise gate system.

Once again Boss have cracked the price/performance permutation, to come up with a flexible, well-designed, high quality little box for a modest price. With the additional plus of

an external key-in trigger facility for the gate side of operations (the ability to open and close the gate using a separate signal from the one latent at the input and output), the RCL-10 should be investigated by anyone wishing to buy a compressor/limiter – regardless of their budget. As in the case of DDLs, two compressors are better than one and you could purchase three of these units for the price of some of the more widely used studio-standard compressor/limiters.

Dbx Compressor/Limiter 160 Series Units: Profile

For many recording engineers working in the

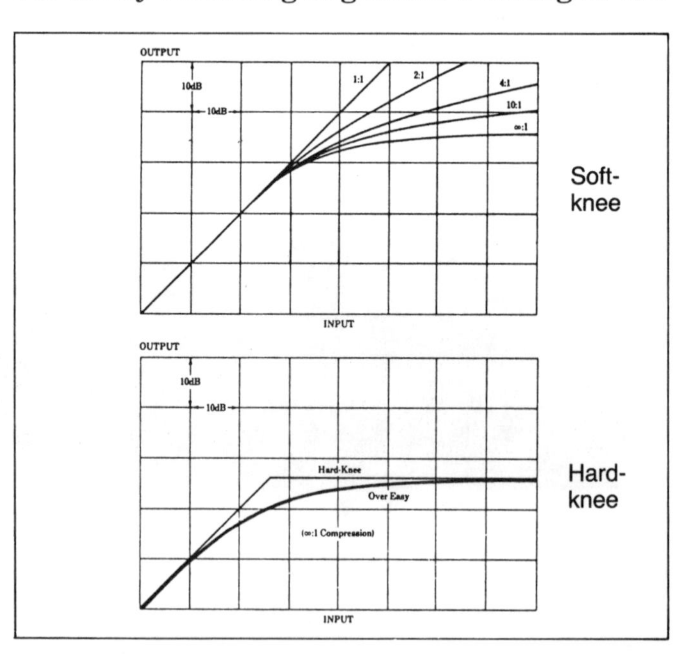

professional field, dbx compressors are considered to be the business for the money asked, which is quite high, but only relative to the amount of control offered by any one of these units.

'Soft Knee' or 'Over Easy' compression is dbx's package entailing a 'feed forward' detector system which looks at the signal in advance of its entering the compression circuits and adjusts attack and release in accordance with the envelope of the incoming signal. This is unlike normal compression circuits which (on the whole) work on the principle of having a detector loop fitted to their output(s) which adjusts the amount of processing applied (in accordance with the ratio setting) to the input. 'Over Easy' compressors offer a smoother and generally less obtrusive control system and thus, on infinite:1 ratios where the input source is reduced in level as soon as the threshold is tripped (limiting), no nastiness is encountered and the contour of the output signal is always smooth and relative to the input.

Dbx 160X Compressor
Price: $429

This is the most popular of all the dbx units and can be found in many, many pro studios around the world. Clean and unobtrusive and offering 'over easy' compression or normal characteristics, the price is set for the higher budget studio owner, but you can find these second hand for about a hundred quid if you're lucky.

The 160X has two expanded-scale LED meters, one to show the amount of gain reduction (or compression, if you like) and the other to indicate either the input or output level. Working on balanced (professional level) line input, the 160X offers a single channel of classic compression which can be twinned with another unit for stereo operation. Having no user-definable control over attack and release, the 160X offers limited flexibility but extended performance over competitors priced much higher than this.

163 Over Easy Compressor
Price: $149

Not very impressive to look at and the subject of some controversy on its release, the dbx 163 has just one slider on the front panel, which determines the threshold, the rest is regulated internally – including output gain. An expanded LED meter shows you exactly what's happening, but for some engineers the lack of control (especially over attack and release) rules it out for really ultra-serious sessions.

There is a dual channel version of the 163,

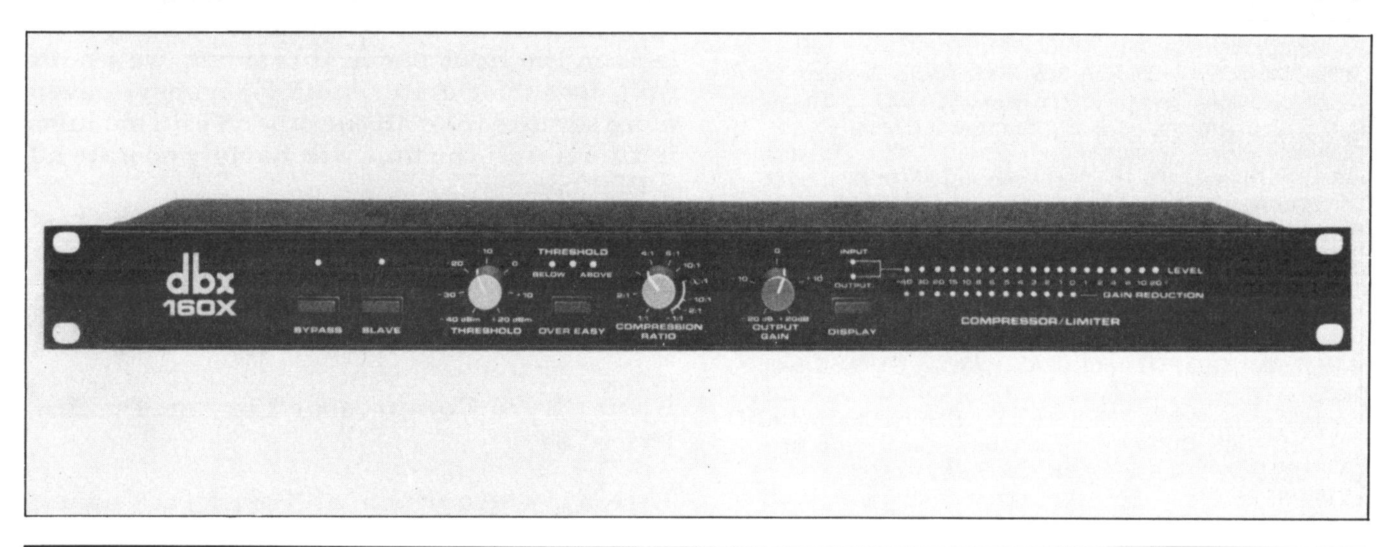

which is just as straightforward, called the RM-163 and a further permutation, called the 164, which is stereo-linked.

Specifications
Input impedance: Signal input: 50kn, unbalanced; ‹100kn balanced. Detector input: 230kn, unbalanced; ‹460kn, balanced, 25kn, unbalanced
Input level: +24dBm maximum, +17dBm nomina maximum, +24dBm clipping point
Output impedance: 22n, designed to drive 600n or greater, 47n (active low impedance output)
Output level: +24dBn into 60n or greater, +18dBm into 2kn
Threshold range: Variable from −40 to +20dBm (7.8mV to 7.8V RMS), Variable −36dBm to +4dBm (12.0mV to 1.2V RMS)
Compression ratio: Over Easy: Program dependent, affected by THRESHOLD, COMPRESSION RATIO settings (COMPRESSION RATIO control determines maximum compression ratio), continuously variable from 1:1 to oo:1 to −1:1, Hard-knee: COMPRESSION RATIO setting defines exact compression ratio, continuously variable from 1:1 to oo:1 to −1:1. Automatically varies from 1:1 below threshold to oo:1 above threshold in accordance with Over Easy threshold curve
Maximum compression: ‹60dB, ‹50dB
Threshold characteristic: Over Easy or hard-knee (switch selectable). Over Easy
Attack time[1]: Program dependent: 15ms for 10dB increase in input level (above threshold), 5ms for 20dB, 3ms for 30dB. Program dependent: 15ms for 10dB increase in input level (above threshold), 5ms for 20dB, 3ms for 30dB
Release time: Program dependent: varies automatically from 0-500ms, affected by settings of front panel controls. Program dependent: varies automatically from 0-420ms affected by settings of front panel control
Output gain: Variable from -20 to 20dB. Variable from 0 to +40dB depending upon settings of front and rear panel controls
Slew rate: ‹10V/us. ‹10V/us
Dynamic range[2]: ‹113dB. ‹106dB
Equivalent input noise (unweighted):
-89dBm, 20Hz-20kHz.
-89dBm, 30Hz-20kHz
Frequency response: +0, −1dB, 20Hz-20kHz. +0, −1dB, 30Hz-20kHz, 5kn load, +0, −3dB, 30Hz-20kHz, 2kn load
Distortion below[3] threshold: 2nd harmonic 0.07%, 3rd harmonic 0.07%. 2nd harmonic 0.1%, 3rd harmonic 0.1%
Distortion above[4] threshold: 2nd harmonic 0.07%, 3rd harmonic 0.2%. 2nd harmonic 0.1%, 3rd harmonic 0.2% (measured at −10dBm nominal level setting)
Metering: 19 LED INPUT or OUTPUT display from −40 to +20dB, 12 LED GAIN REDUCTION display from −1 to −40dB. 12 LED COMPRESSION display from −2 to −30dB
Meter zero set: −15dBm to +10dBm. Fixed
Indicators: BELOW/threshold/ABOVE (green, yellow, red) INPUT (red), OUTPUT (red), SLAVE (yellow), BYPASS (red). None
Controls and switches: THRESHOLD, COMPRESSION, RATIO, OUTPUT GAIN, DISPLAY function switch, meter zero adjust, BYPASS switch, SLAVE switch, OVER EASY switch. COMPRESSION (front panel) nominal operating level switch, adjust (rear panel)
Connectors: Input/output: TRS phone jacks and barrier terminal, Detector: barrier terminal, Strapping: TRS phone jack. Input/output: phono jacks
Dimensions: 1¾″H × 19″W × 9¼″D (4.4cm × 48.3cm × 18.4cm), 1⅞″H × 9″W × 6 7/16″D (4.8cm × 22.9cm × 16.3cm)
Weight: 6.5lbs (3.0kg), 2.5lbs (1.1kg)
Power requirements: 115/220 VAC +10%, 50-60Hz, 8W, 117 VAC +10%, 50-60Hz, 6W
Accessories: AB-1 active balanced output card, RM-18-1 rack mount kit for a single 163, RM-18-2 rack mount kit for two 163s

Vesta Fire MLM-1 Limiter: Profile
Price: $125

Designed to fit into their 4U high 19″ rack mounting powered frame, the MLM-1 from Vesta Fire is somewhat of a strange beast. Like the 'Sound Vice' from Accessit, the MLM-1 gives you a set compression ratio of similar proportions. Unlike the Sound Vice, though, it does offer you adjustable threshold, attack and release. Attack time is adjustable from 1ms (the standard minimum) to 50ms (a sensible maximum) and the release time minimum is 300ms, with a maximum of 5sec.

Because of the preset compression ratio, not *all* the control one would expect from a compression unit is available, but, as in the case of the Sound Vice, this does not make the MLM-1 unusable – far from it. To call it a limiter is more accurate. With a single LED to show when the threshold has been violated for the system to go into full operation and a stereo tie jack on the front panel, this smart, well-built unit does offer great value for money – even more so since (like all the other Vesta modules in this series) the unit will happily operate off a PP3 battery.

Full marks to Vesta for producing the best value limiter on the market.

Fostex 3070 Compressor/Limiter: Profile
Price: $400

This is my favourite of all Fostex rack mount

PROFILES AND REVIEWS

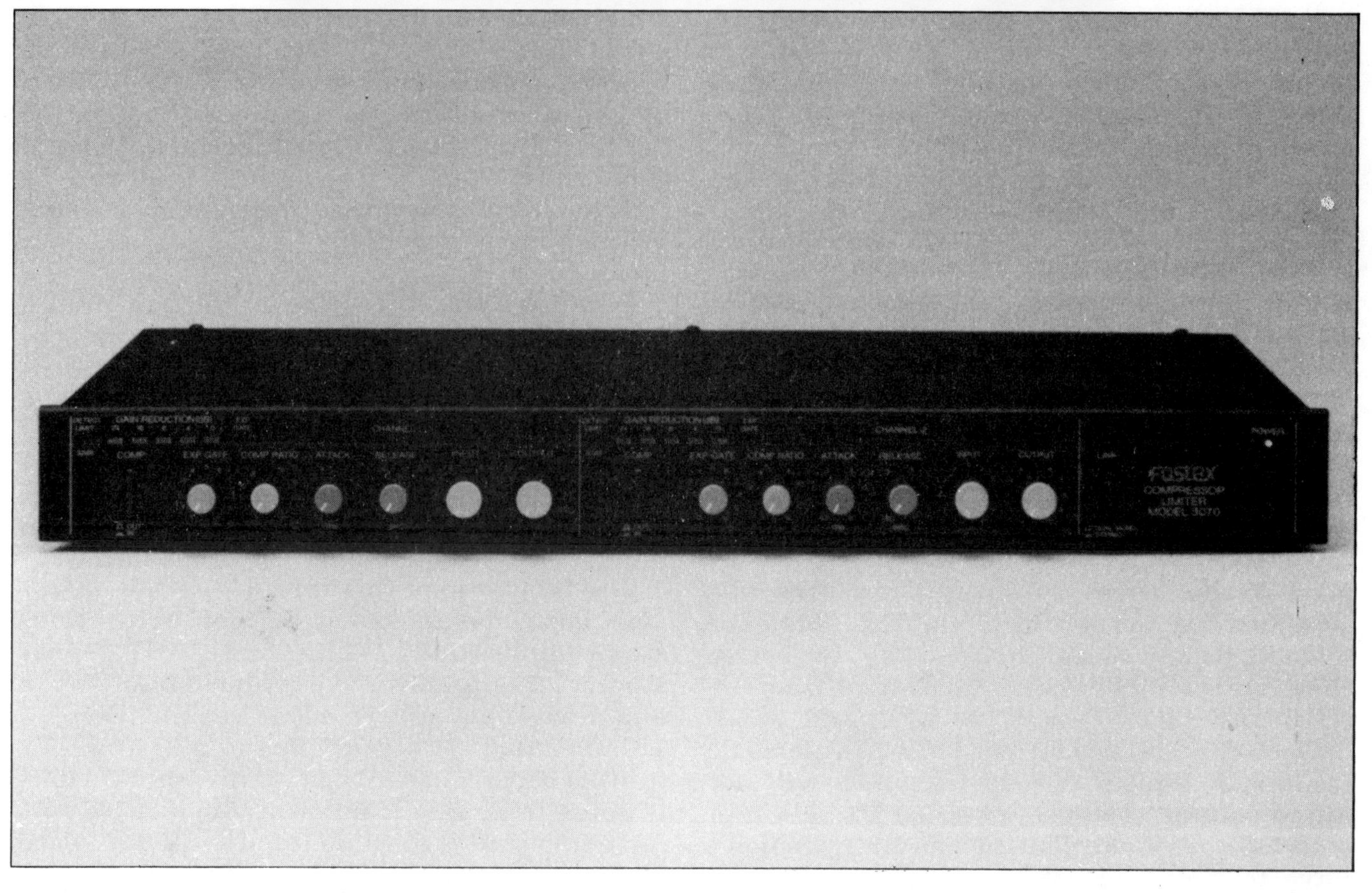

(minus ears) units. Extremely similar in design and operation to the Yamaha GC2020, it is a dual channel system which has a front panel stereo link selector. Each side has a five segment LED gain reduction meter and the 'expander' noise gate can be used independently, with or without compression being introduced, which is a feature I loudly applaud.

Attack is adjustable from 0.2ms (excellent) to 20ms, and release is adjustable from a minimum of 0.5ms (extremely fast unity gain recovery) to 2sec.

Very well built, with a professional s/n ratio, it has only one real rival in the form of the Vesta SL020 and SL200 units. The Yamaha GC2020 doesn't quite make the running here, as the Fostex and Vesta gear sport detector-loops (similar to auxiliaries) for in-line equalisation of the compressed signal – ideal for getting rid of sibilance (the effect which isssss ssssso annoying, espesscially when you're watching Crosssssroadssss!)

The 3070 offers everything a comp/lim should at a fairly reasonable price. I hope they come up with a single channel unit soon, giving people the extra option of buying one compressor and then another at a later date.

Ten out of ten.

Vesta Fire Dual Spring Reverb RV2
Price: $450

The RV2 is a dual reverberation device incorporating four springs per channel. It's in a standard 19″ rack-mounting format and is ideal for all types of recording. The RV2 has the same clean sound as its predecessor, the RV1. Like all of the Vesta units on the market, construction is very good. All the controls are colour-coded, in a logical layout. The unit uses normal jack sockets for every in and output. On the front panel, each of the two channels has its own low-cut toggle switch, input level control, output control and a very good three-colour overload/limiter indicator. On the back, there's a slider pot to control whether the outputs are made up of a mix of the original input signal(s), or just the reverb. Coming back to the front panel, there's a jack control footswitch input for each of the two reverb channels, which makes life easier when doing complicated mixes and both hands are tied up.

The low-cut toggles switch in a circuit which filters out frequencies below 100Hz and cuts them down by 6dB. This prevents the springs from rumbling and wobbling when a bass guitar or drum is put through the reverb. I must point out, though, that I still got very good results when the low-cut circuitry was switched out, the spring assembly could handle deep, boomy sounds quite easily, far better than any spring I've ever heard (apart from the AKG and Klark Teknik spring units).

Each channel has its own built-in automatic limiter. A limiter is a device which will not allow volume increase (or gain) above a pre-selected threshold. This means that you don't have to keep a constant eye on the volume level being fed to this unit, when you're busy doing something else. I found that the indicators could glow red quite a lot before any form of distortion to the output signal was audible. The three-coloured plasma meters indicate that the limiters are in operation when the lights flash red.

As mentioned, each channel is made up of four springs which have different lengths and, therefore, different tonal characteristics. The overall reverb decay of this unit is quoted at 2.5 seconds, though in practice the decay changes in accordance with the strength and intensities of the input source. The sound of this unit is in keeping with today's tastes – in other words, it is a distinctly metallic reverb, high in overall tone, but still a very realistic 'big room' sound. It's certainly comparable with a low-priced plate reverb. The main drawback of many reverbs on the market is that there's too much mid-frequency 'ring' to the decay and it's more or less impossible to get a truly high-toned reverb that will cut through a mix. The RV2 has plenty of top, which some people may choose to cut down a little with a bit of EQ for certain types of music. Personally, I have found that it's much better to have a good sharp 'top' to the reverb that can be tailored to suit the music, rather than a spring unit which is incapable of ever reaching such tones.

Because Vesta have gone for the dual design approach, you can have, in effect, two independent reverb effects simultaneously. However, there's a facility on the RV2 for crossing the paths of the output so that the reverb of channel one appears at the output of channel two and vice versa. This is useful for getting usually thin sounds to spread over the stereo image – very effective for drum machines.

The S/N ratio of this unit is 80dB, which is very good and makes it suitable for serious studio applications. While I had the RV2 at my studio, I manipulated the sound in many ways and always got superb, clean results. Being a 19″ unit and not a drainpipe or a 4′ × 2′ box (unlike certain other types of reverb) this unit is going to appeal to home studio owners who have to consider the amount of available space when purchasing equipment. I used the RV2 in conjunction with a graphic and an aural exciter and the reverb effects I got were mind blowing! At well under $500, this unit demands attention from prospective purchasers. A good'un!

Powertran MCS-1 Sampling DDL: Review
Price: $995 (Kit)

Providing a much-needed boost to Powertran's elderly range of kit-built electronic gear, the MCS-1 is a notable first. It's the first DDL to allow you to control sampled sounds via MIDI *and* CV – the AMS and Bel are CV only unless you use an external ADC and that's cheating. It's also the first self-contained sampler to break that all-important $1,500 barrier. However, since its launch towards the end of

'84, we've had the Korg SDD2000 and Akai S612, so how does it compare now?

Housed in a 2U 19" box but minus the usual hi-tech silk-screened block diagram, the MCS-1 offers the usual plethora of digital SFX – chorus, flanging, ADT, echo and phasing, in addition to its sampling capability. Flanging apart, which is weak, these are adequate – like most DDL's (with the exception of Deltaphon's wonderful 2FX), the MCS-1 can do the lot but none particularly well. A good, general purpose DDL, though.

Sampling is this baby's big selling point, so what are you getting? Important proviso no.1: the MCS-1 is monophonic. No.2: you cannot edit a sample internally – shock, horror! Neither is there any tape dump to store samples. To do that you have to fork out for a BBC B micro, Powertran's BBC interface, two disc drives, monitor, etc, etc – anyway, you get the picture. The upshot of all this is that you're still gonna need your Revox and razor blade, with all the aggro that implies. On the plus side, there's infinite sustain (looping to you) and LFO if you want to add vibrato to your sampled headless chicken.

With a maximum sampling rate of 32KHz, you can store about two seconds of sound at 12Khz, which is fine. You can also sample at just 300Hz which, if you were stupid enough to try it, would give you 32 seconds of sound. This would not be fine. 'Flat' and 'unmusical' are the words that spring to mind. Basically then, that's it – the MCS-1 excels at bass and other sounds with low frequencies, which is a roundabout way of saying its top end ain't much good.

I only had one MIDI keyboard to hand, a Juno 106. The MCS-1 responded perfectly until it came to a bit of 'I wanna play gee-tar' pitch-bending. The Juno transmits and the Powertran should respond, but . . . well, somewhere along the line it wasn't happening.

Those of you who still admit to owning CV gear – forgive me, Father, for I have a Moog – will be pleased to know that the MCS-1 can also be controlled by this. You will be less pleased to discover that the usable range is only 1-1½ octaves. After that, the tuning goes up the spout.

So there you have it. About six months ago, this would have been a Best Buy but such is progress . . . The Korg SDD2000 has 64 MIDI accessable memories and a price tag of only $750 or thereabouts, nearly $250 cheaper than the MCS-1. Yer pays yer money and yer takes yer choice . . . Whichever you choose, one thing is clear. You've left it too damn late to sell that Mellotron . . .

Cutec GS-2200 Stereo Graphic & P.N. Generator & Spectrum Analyzer: Profile

The GS-2200 from Cutec is a 10-band stereo graphic equaliser with a spectrum analyser and built-in pink noise generator. It looks good enough to go into a HiFi rack, but its quality is far superior to the usual 'swank' graphics that you see in your local retailers. It has an S/N ratio of 75dB which makes it suitable for home recording and slightly more serious studio work alike.

The inclusion of a pink noise generator is chiefly to measure acoustic levels, and, used in conjunction with the spectrum analyser, to line up tape machines. (Pink noise is sound containing all frequencies at equal levels.)

The frequencies on each side of the graphic are 31.5Hz, 63Hz, 125Hz, 250Hz, 500Hz, 1K, 2K, 4K, 8K, 16K. These are all adjustable by + and – 12dB from the centre detent. Each of the frequency bands is displayed on a 20-segment blue LED scale, which also has a display showing the master volume of the input source. The display can be switched between the left and right channels at any time.

On the back, you have three sets of stereo inputs and two sets as outputs. On my review model, all the ins and outs were jack, though I have seen phono versions in advertising literature. The pink noise generator had a mono jack.

This is going to be invaluable to anybody doing cassette duplications or trying to get the best from their control room monitors. All in all, a very handy piece of well-designed equipment.

PROFILES AND REVIEWS

Other FX units

I don't wish to keep blurting out this same old line, but the next volume will deal with all the other FX units available in greater detail – there is only so much you can fit into three hundred odd pages; it is better to have a review section based on quality rather than the *quantity* of editorial.

The outboard market is an exciting one, with manufacturers world-wide competing at trade shows for potential customers more than in any other sector within the industry. But after you've acquired yourself a decent reverberation system, delay facility and compression unit(s), the next thing is to get a graphic. Graphics enable you (as I've explained before) to 'fine tune' a signal, with the mono 31 band models offering the maximum flexibility. Using non-programmable reverb units, such as the Alesis XT, Yamaha R1000 and Lexicon PCM60, a dedicated graphic latched to the output prior to the processed signal entering the desk will give an added dimension of control. But 31 band graphics are, on the whole, too extravagant for this sort of application; a system I favour and employ myself is to have a dual 10 or 15 band stereo graphic, and to use one side to process the signal *pre*-reverb and the other half to sweeten and modify the *post*-reverb signal.

The cheaper FX units on the whole tend to have no input filtering whatsoever; many manufacturers will swear blue-in-the-face that there is no such thing as input 'sweetening' circuits on their units, but they *do* exist. Cymbals can often be the subject of a bit of high frequency cut pre-reverb, often quite contrary to what the direct signal is being EQd like on the desk. Setting up different EQ relationships between direct and reverberated signals can create some eerie and quite disarmingly sensational effects.

Indeed, you may find that purchasing a split reverberation system, comprising a basic reverb unit with side chain access, a delay, noise gate and graphic would be preferable to getting a self-contained dedicated unit such as the Alesis XT.

What did he say? . . . a noise *gate?*

The 'Glossary' (as in almost every subject covered in this tome) will concisely inform you what, in this case, a noise gate does; it has been briefly covered already. It is certainly the next most important thing (probably shoulder to shoulder with the graphic) to buy for your outboard rack. It is important to point out that only the much more expensive digital reverbs (namely the Klark Teknik DN780 and AMS RMX16) sport software which offers gated reverb parameters. Gated reverb is a partially subliminal effect, much loved by Phil Collins and Hugh Padgham, who are the world leaders in gated reverb techniques, especially on

The world's first budget-priced, rack-mounting Harmonizer from the well respected Japanese company, Ibanez.

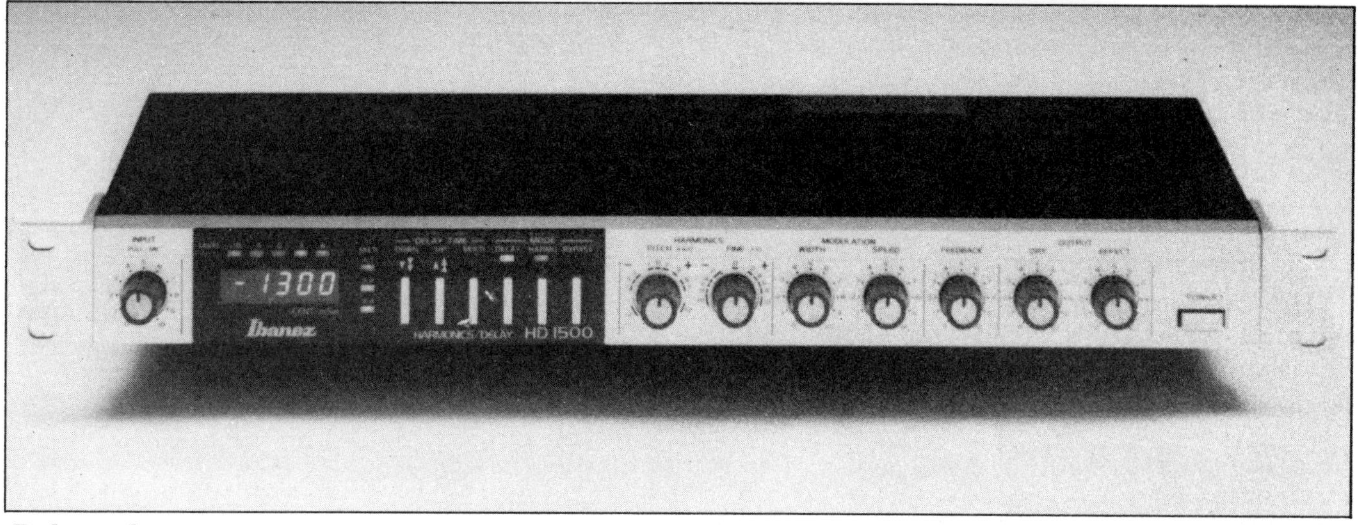

Released as we were going to press, the new HD 1500 Harmonizer. Both these units offer DDL facilities too. At around $500 second-hand, the HD1000 offers incredible value for money.

drums. On-beat severe 'shut-downs' on reverb signals can add immeasurable amounts of punch and hardness to a mix.

In their own right, noise gates can be 'fine-tuned' to cut out unwanted background noise and systems hiss. I would recommend a minimum of two, though having four is the optimum arrangement – any more than that and you are obviously a percussion compression junkie!!

SECTION SEVEN

Glossary
Appendix

Glossary

Attack: The beginning of any sound. A fast attack is one which takes very little time to develop. A slow attack usually refers to a sound which takes quite a time to reach maturity. A bass drum sound has (usually) a fast attack, while cellos, violins and double basses have slow attacks. When novices refer to a 'lack of punch' to a sound, they are usually referring to the presence of a slow attack.

Attenuator: A pot which is used to reduce the gain of an incoming signal. Commonly found on interface units which have to span the gulf between two industry code standards. 'Attenuation' is referred to mostly when dealing with the control or 'trimming' of input signals at the initial stage of processing.

Audio Sensitivity: This is a term used to describe the ability of either the human ear or any piece of electronic equipment to pick up soft or loud signals. Commonly referred to in parallel with 'audio range', audio sensitivity can also be used to refer to the range of frequencies capable of being picked up and faithfully reproduced by either the human ear or (for example) an amplifier.

People have a dreadfully inconsistent audio sensitivity; most of us are equipped with ears which can reproduce frequencies from roughly 20Hz to 20kHz, but as we grow older and our ears get subjected to the odd rock concert, a top frequency of about 18kHz is more usual.

Backbeat or Backing Track: To many, this will be self-explanatory. A backbeat in its most traditional sense is a reference to the second and fourth beats in a 4/4 bar; most commonly though, a 'backbeat' is a reference to the entire backing picture to a recording, as is the 'backing track'.

The violation of the above term is largely down to the NYC-based electro-pop/funk guys, who are famous for recording and treating drum and bass lines as a whole, rather than separate entities.

Backline: A much-loved phrase, referring to the amplifiers available from either a studio or hire company.

Baffles: Also referred to in the Soundproofing section as isolation panels and box screens. Baffles are just convenient boards or boxes, designed to soak up sound.

Band Pass Filter: Commonly found on synthesizers from a few years back, band pass filters limit the frequencies by a predetermined amount either side of a desired frequency range.

Bins (as in 'bass'): A bin is a term used to describe the massive enclosures used on PA rigs to handle the lowest of frequencies.

Bottom End: Sometimes referred to as just 'bottom', it has little or nothing to do with Pia Zadora's best asset. It's just a lazy term used to describe the bass content of a signal.

Bouncing: A term referring to the trusty system employed by many compact multitracker owners to get more information onto any one cassette or reel of tape. Simply, it means transferring the information of one track onto another in addition to any new signals. Commonly, it is possible to record ten different lines of music or information on a compact multitracker which has full 4-T capability. Less scrupulous members of the profession call the technique 'ping ponging'. Bouncing will result, in the majority of cases, in a loss in quality on initial tracks, as the information will be subject more than once to the dreaded noise performance of a multitrack recording system.

Break: A favourite term amongst many punters to describe a change or reversal in a piece of music or recording. A 'break' doesn't necessarily refer to a gap of nothingness, a 'guitar' or 'drum' break can be a reference to a solo section featuring (to the exclusion of all else) the stated instrument.

Bus or Buss: Familiar to modular synthesizer and home recording equipment owners alike, a buss is just a routing circuit which allows a single or group of signal inputs to be sent to one or more outputs. Example: A 'CV' buss is one designed to facilitate the routing of control voltages.

Calibration: The process of aligning recording equipment to frequency, level and EQ standards. A fully calibrated multitrack is one which has had all of its electronics lined up to accept a certain brand of tape. A lot of myths surround the subject of calibration; increasingly nowadays, tape recorders and all other pieces of equipment that include user-definable calibration pots come ready-aligned for accepted industry standards and brands.

Moving from one studio to another with multitrack masters will warrant a certain amount of re-calibration, but with modern equipment design going the way it is, the need to bring in an experienced engineer to calibrate any of your equipment is fast disappearing.

Chords: Known to some 'natural' musos as 'shapes' on key or fret boards, chords are the accepted way of playing groups of notes. The most basic of all standard chords usually comprise three and no more notes. A chord structure is a term used to describe the sequence and placing of separate chords within a complete piece of music.

Chorus: Commonly referred to as a 'hook' to a song, the chorus is the bit we all remember and hum to ourselves on the bus; classical buffs sometimes call it the 'refrain'. Chorus is also a word used to describe the effect of two or more similar signals meeting our ears at slightly different times. A chorus unit is a time delay based effect developed by the clever Roland people in Japan. What it does is split the input signal into two and delay it for a short while, usually 5-45ms, then let it out in a mix with the original signal. Introducing a low frequency oscillator to modulate and change the pitch of the delayed signal gives a swooshy, stringy sort of effect on less energetic sounds. Flanging is an extremely similar (though more boisterous) effect.

Click Track: Sometimes referred to as a sync track, this is an increasingly common way of recording backing tracks. A click track takes the form of a series of on-beat pulses recorded onto the multitrack which are there as either a strict guide for drummers to stay in tempo, or are pulses which contain the right amplitude to drive a drum machine or sequencer, or both.

Compressor: This is an extremely popular effect. A compressor will automatically control the output dynamics of the input signal by a user-definable ratio. Compressors are used to bring signals which contain a lot of high transients under some sort of control. A vocal signal will usually contain a lot of high transients, though the average signal will be of quite a low level. Putting a signal such as this through a compressor at a compression ratio of (for example) 2:1 will result in an output level of 1dB for every 2dB going into the input. Compressors are an indispensable tool for creating 'meaty' drum tracks in modern day recording.

Console: Term used to describe a mixing desk.

Crossover Unit: This is a device used to split a full frequency signal into component frequency bands. This is a technique most favoured by separate amplification system designers. A crossover unit is usually used to split a signal into three parts; highs, mids and lows, each section being sent to the relevant amplifier or loudspeaker.

Cue: This is also known as talkback or foldback. A cue system is either included in the spec of a desk to facilitate communication between engineer and artist, or to send previously recorded material to the headphones of performers so that overdubs can be executed, or simply a word used to give a starting prompt to anyone about to be recorded.

Cut: This is an American term used to describe the master or shop shelf recording of a master tape.

D/A Converter: Exactly the opposite to an A/D converter. This is a device which converts digital code back into analogue waveforms.

dbx: A system of noise reduction, which utilizes exactly corresponding compression and expansion circuits. Sometimes referred to as 'compansion', the system is usually much less expensive than the longer established Dolby laboratories' technique. Most half-inch 8-T machines currently in use have associated dbx noise reduction units as add-ons. dbx is also the trading name of the company who are responsible for the system's development and initial manufacture.

Decay: The retardation in amplitude of either a whole piece of music, a single note or a reverberated sound. It is also a parameter included in the spec of an envelope generator on your average synthesizer. Many digital reverbs have the decay time as a programmable option, usually displayed in milliseconds and/or seconds.

Decibel (or dB): This is the universal unit of sound measurement. 0dB is usually meant to mean the threshold of hearing, while a Jumbo flying overhead commonly exceeds a level of 125dB. Around the 130dB mark, the human ear begins to hurt. The average speaking voice fluctuates between 60 and 75dB. For long periods, listening to levels above 100dB will result in serious ear damage which (up until the present day) is irreversible even via laser surgery. If you are to monitor things louder than 100dB, you should not exceed a total listening time of about two minutes in any twelve hour period.

Delay: This is in reference to an electronic means of slowing down the arrival of a signal via either analogue or digital technology. Pre-delay is a parameter included on many digital reverbs, it introduces a space between the direct original signal hitting the reverb electronics.

Demo: What this book is about really! A demo is a live performance with usually one instrument, played to give others in the room a rough idea of what you wish a piece of music to be delivered like. A demo recording is the commitment of the above performance to tape.

Desk: Common term used to describe the small to medium sized mixers in studios or on the road. SSL, Harrison, Neve monsters et al are usually termed as 'consoles', which is a term used in studios exclusively.

Direct Injection or D.I.: This refers to the bypassing of microphones with signals going straight into a mixing desk. If an instrument is being D.I.'d, it is usually always referring to an electronic instrument, though with more and more dedicated electronic pick ups being developed for cellos, violins, violas, pianos etc. etc., it is not uncommon for the term to be transposed to these too.

Dolby Noise Reduction: Invented by Mr. Ray Dolby, it was the first noise reduction system commercially available. Split into two sections (as all present NR systems are), Encode and Decode, the system splits the input signal into several frequency bands and boosts the high frequencies (which is where the hiss is) well above normal levels. On playback, in Decode mode, the process is reversed, with the high frequencies being reduced to original strength, resulting in the hiss being brought down to inaudible levels. Some engineers swear by Dolby, others curse it. I personally feel that the dbx noise reduction system (if well lined up) offers a slightly better end result; this conclusion is based on my theory that you shouldn't mess about with a signal more than you have to and the Dolby system of splitting the sound into preselected frequency bands, going through a process of level emphasis and then sticking them all back together again, is a bit long winded. Dbx takes the signal as a whole, compresses it as a whole and then expands it as a whole. However, my remarks should under no circumstances be taken as law without you yourself experiencing and using the effects of the more professional multitrack and mastering machine Dolby units.

Most HiFi cassette decks now have two Dolby systems to choose from; Dolby B and the better Dolby C. The Type A units are the most widely used in the professional recording field.

Double-Tracking: Many foot pedal and digital delay lines offer 'Automatic Double-Tracking'. It is a technique which entails a vocal or instrument to be recorded twice on two tracks. Some of the most effective vocal double-tracking can be heard on Phil Collins' *Face Value* album. The Beatles also used it extensively on some of their tracks under the masterful hands and ears of George Martin. It is an effect which produces what many would describe as a 'thicker' sound.

Electronic double-tracking units work by splitting the signal and very slightly delaying one side of it. An introduction of a low frequency oscillator to modulate the delayed side of the signal in pitch will, in effect, let you enter the world of chorus and flanging. In fact, most chorus units with their rate and depth controls set to minimum will result in quite an acceptable, clean double-tracked signal.

Downbeat: 1: The first beat of a bar. Most electronic metronomes signify the downbeat by giving it an accent over the other clicks. 2: A term which is sometimes used instead of 'laid-back', in reference to injecting a bit of lightness and space into a piece of music, either via the arrangement or outboard equipment (such as digital and plate reverberation). 3: Term used to describe something or somebody who is dowdy or unsavoury. For example: 'Hey man, this Colombian is a bit downbeat . . . know wha' I mean?'

Drop in: When a track contains a small mistake or wrongly placed passage, it will be necessary to enter record (drop in) and exit record (drop out) with the tape in motion to allow a performer to just re-do the passage which contains the mistake. It is also referred to as 'punch in' and 'punch out'.

Drop out: 1: See above. 2: Loss of signal off tape due to a flaw in the emulsion. 3: Unsavoury character who has opted out of the normal rigours of life.

Dry: 1: This is the opposite to 'wet'; it refers to a signal which has no added reverb or delay. 2: A dry room is the same as a dead one, which means the room's acoustics offer no natural reverb or flutter echoes at all. 3: A dry session is one which is conducted with no members of the crew under the influence of alcohol – probably the rarest of all recording phenomena!

Dub: 1: This is a style of delivery which Reggae singers have developed; it employs over-the-top use of echo and/or delay effects. 2: Commonly used abbreviation for the word overdub. 3: To make amendments and additions to an existing soundtrack.

Echo: A commonly used substitute when people are referring to repeat FX from DDLs (see **Delay**). It refers to the distinct or indistinct repetition in part or whole of the original sound. Echo should not be used as an alternative word for reverb.

Echo Chamber/Room: Many of the older, larger studios still have echo chambers. This is (in its most simple arrangement) a room containing a microphone and speaker(s). The desired signals are fed to the chamber speaker(s) and the reverberated, echoing sound picked up at the other end of the room by the microphone(s). A similar system can be recreated at home in the bathroom. However, because of the sophisticated DDL and digital reverbs now on the market, new studios are opening without the need for an echo chamber.

Editing: See **Splicing.**

Envelope Generator: Commonly called an ADSR, it is something which crops up on many synthesizers and sampling keyboards. It allows you to shape a sound via four parameters: attack, decay, sustain and release.

Equalization: This refers to the 'trimming' or 'sweetening' we sometimes carry out, adjusting the frequency response of an input signal to achieve a better (or different) sound.

Equalizer: Taking the form of either parametric or graphic equalization, this is a unit which enables you to select almost any frequency in the audio spectrum and boost or cut it by a definable amount, usually up to +/− 15dB.

Expander: This is the opposite to a compressor. It is a unit used to increase the range of dynamics in audio signals.

Fade Out: A common occurrence at the end of recorded music, a fade out is when the master outputs or certain faders on the desk have been closed down to eliminate sounds slowly from a mix. When implemented *during* a track (rather than at the end), the odd fade out can be quite a subtle, subliminal effect; as indeed can fade ins which are the exact opposite.

Feedback: Rarely encountered in the studio, the ear-piercing howl and squeal of feedback is usually the result of a mike picking up its own signal from a nearby speaker. Feedback circuits are often added to DDLs (see **Delay**) nowadays; these return part of the affected signal back to the input stage to simulate recurring, almost continuous echo FX, or indeed to make up for system deficiencies.

Filter: Commonly part of a parametric EQ section, a filter is the part which can boost or cut selected frequencies.

Flange: Outer rim of tape spool.

Flanging: Originally discovered (so I've been told) by John Lennon and George Martin on one of the Beatles' sessions at Abbey Road. They created the effect, which so many of us now induce via commercially built electronic devices, by putting pressure on the tape spool flange as it went round. Electronically though, flanging works on extremely similar principles to phasing.

Flat: A term used to describe a signal or group of signals which have had no external equalization. A 'flat' pair of speakers are ones which do not colour the input signal at all.

Flutter: A small variation in the constant speed of a tape recorder. These lightning variations effect the pitch of the recorded signals. Flutter is commonly ganged with another measurement parameter (wow) and their combined test results shown in a percentage relative to the tape speed itself.

Foldback: The same as Cue, this is the term used to describe live and off-tape signals being sent to the cue or foldback amp which feeds the performer's headphones in the studio itself.

Front End: Engineer's slang for any apparatus appearing at the beginning of a signal chain. Front end equipment is usually used in reference to microphones and the inputs/gain section at the top of mixer channels.

Frequency Response: This figure is usually quoted in its extremities. The frequency response of a good microphone may be from 40Hz–20kHz. This means that the microphone is able to pick up all frequencies between 40Hz and 20kHz and reproduce them faithfully. Bad microphones usually have a frequency response which is much less; a common budget microphone FR is 100Hz–10kHz. Consequently the latter mike is unable to reproduce any signal which contains HF content in excess of 10kHz. Most of us can only hear up to 17.5kHz or thereabouts, so any equipment which has an FR above this should be able to reproduce signals without any audible difference. Most audio equipment tries to have a faithful response from 20Hz to 20kHz. However, many manufacturers quote a self-styled sort of frequency response and often make their equipment look a lot better by quoting an FR with a relative plus or minus dB number before or after. Make sure that you are not being conned. An untampered FR should be in reference to 0dB (normal flat response). An FR which is 100Hz to

10kHz +/− 8dB means that the sound deviates by up to 8dB in some frequencies. This means that the sound is going to be far from flat! A good FR trace should take the form of a straight line from 20Hz through to 20kHz – rising and falling *outside* these limits.

Gain: This refers to the amount of amplification (if any) added to an incoming signal at the input stage of a channel on a mixing desk.

Graphic Equalizer: A unit designed so each frequency in the audio spectrum is represented by a cut/boost fader, giving the user usually about +/− 6dB of attenuation.

Harmonizer: Eventide, in America, make the most famous of all harmonizers. They are also known as pitch changers. Effectively, they enable you to change the pitch of an incoming signal without effecting the speed at which the sound is reproduced.

Headroom: The safety margin all amplifiers and recording systems refer to when expressing their top end capability before distortion is audible.

Headstock: Lately this has become the part of the guitar that has been shaved right down or done away with altogether. Traditionally, the headstock is where the strings terminate at the top of the neck and where the machineheads are situated.

Hertz (Hz): A simple unit of measurement used for expressing frequencies.

Hum: The dreaded hum of a home recording system is the most common of all flaws to be heard in works recorded on a domestic set-up. Hum can be introduced into a system by (for example) a bad mains earth.

Image: A term used to describe the ability of a pair of speakers to reproduce a faithful stereo image of the original sound(s).

Impedance: This refers to the amount of current which will flow in a circuit when a certain number of volts is applied. Impedance matching is important should you require the best from your system. However, in the domestic situation, the question of impedance matching will only arise when connecting amplifiers and speakers together. Check that the wattage rating of your amplifier corresponds to the impedance of your speakers. Most amplifiers will only give optimum performance through 8 or 4ohm speakers. A 60wpc amplifier into 8ohms will in fact give you 90wpc into 4ohm speakers. Alternatively, if you run a PA stack (rated at say 32ohms) off a 100wpc amplifier, you are not going to get music power of more than a handful of watts.

Inboard: The opposite of outboard equipment. Solid State Logic, which make the world's most popular professional mixing consoles, include inboard compressors and limiters.

Input: The exact opposite of output; an input is the point at which a signal enters a piece of audio equipment.

ips: Inches per second.

Jack Plug: The male part of the world's most common audio connection, it connects to the Jack Socket. Available in two types, mono and stereo, the jack system can either be a dual or triple termination connector.

Joystick: Commonly found on EMS synthesizers, it is usually a control for modulation and/or pitchbending. In some ambisonic and quadrophonic systems, the pan pots (which have 360 degree control) have been replaced by joysticks. Nasty.

KiloHertz: One thousand Hertz.

Layering: Another term for overdubbing or, even more inaccurately, bouncing.

Leader Tape: This is the coloured bit you find at the beginning and end of spool and cassette tapes. The broadcast industries have intricate colour coding standards with leader tape. Its primary function is to allow you to lace up a transport without handling the tape itself *and* to tell at a glance whether you are at the beginning of a tape or have mounted it on the spool 'end-out'.

Leakage: The nastiest side-effect of bad

soundproofing. This term is used to describe sound 'spilling' into unwanted areas; either structurally or in a recording situation when two or more mikes are being used.

LED: Light Emiting Diode. A popular indicator used by many manufacturers.

Level: The amplitude, or volume, of any given signal. A signal of 'varying' amplitude is one which contains transients.

Limiter: A signal-processor which reduces all gain of an incoming signal once the electronics have been tripped in via a self-defined threshold. Basically, unlike a compressor, a limiter will not allow *any* volume or gain increase at all. Horrendous limiting can be heard on Radio 4. The BBC have still not learned how to use their inboard limiters!

Lipsync: An attribute the dubbing engineers on the PG Tips chimp commercials don't worry about too much. When you hear a producer shouting at a performer for being 'out on lipsync' in a performance for television, all he's actually saying is that the performer can't mime!

mSec: Millisecond; one thousandth of a whole second.

Manual: 1. The opposite of automatic. 2. A keyboard on an instrument.

Master Tape: This is the complete stereo recording from any performance or multitrack session. It is the tape that acetates are cut from to form the 'mother' and 'father' plates from which the presses make the records.

Mixer: The central part of most studios, the mixer is used to gang together different signals, and gives you control over balance, tone and volume in recording and mixdown.

Mixdown: Once you have completed all the performances necessary for a piece of music on the multitrack machine, you then hook up the 2-T and mix all the tape return signals into stereo; this is called a mixdown.

Modulation: Usually used in reference to a shifting waveform. Soundwise, modulation results in a cyclic movement of tone and/or pitch. Having a modulation section on a digital delay is essential should one wish to create flanging or chorusing.

Monitor: Loudspeaker of sufficient quality and audio performance to be used in a control room.

Multicore: A bundle of cables or wires, packaged in an overall sheath.

Multitracking: The art of recording several things onto more than just one track of tape. Ninety-five per cent of all contemporary recording projects now entail the use of multitrack technology at one stage or another.

Multitrack Tape: Coming in various widths and emulsion types, this is the material you use to store all the separate tracks of magnetic information on from a multitrack machine. The smallest multitrack format (strictly speaking) is your common-or-garden compact cassette; in compact multitrackers, all four of the available tracks (side A stereo left and right, side B stereo left and right) are used for recording on, and the tape is only an ⅛ of an inch wide. The widest multitrack tape currently in use is for sixteen and twenty-four track recorders; it measures exactly two inches across.

Mute: Occasionally found under the title 'dim' on recording consoles, this is a control which, when depressed, reduces the monitor level in the control room by a predetermined amount. Handy for taking phone calls!

Noise Gate: This is a handy device which closes down all the audio signals being fed to it should they drop below a selectable threshold. Extremely useful for creating ambient and yet claustrophobic drum sounds. Some gates have a 'key in' socket which allows you to control the action of the gate according to an outside signal – regardless of what signal is actually being gated. One of the most common applications of the above feature is to key-in the signal from a bass drum which has the bass guitar signal 'on-line'. This will result in the bass drum envelope (fast and punchy) controlling what you hear from the bass guitar. On the whole, this technique results in a sharp, tight sound.

Noise Reduction: Found in a few different forms, the two most popular noise reduction units are built by Dolby and dbx. It is a method by which the annoying tape hiss, encountered on even professional analogue systems, can be reduced and, in perfectly lined-up encode/decode cards, result in the complete elimination of it.

Notch filter: Since the introduction of the Fairlight, notch filters have been entering contemporary studios more and more. A notch filter is a device which enables you to emphasize or eliminate frequencies which can accurately be pinpointed. They are ideal tonal adjustment devices for eliminating the awful, constant 'digital shit' hum that all the early Aussie samplers suffered from.

Octave Divider: A pruned down harmonizer, usually found in a foot pedal configuration which can produce higher and/or lower octaves by tracking any given input signal. Costing often under £90, an octave divider provides a cost effective way of producing thicker, deeper or higher textures from simple signal sources such as brass. Superb on acoustic guitars, an octave divider is a *must*.

Outboard: Otherwise referred to as 'toys' or 'FX', these are the bits of equipment which 'sell' a modern-day recording studio to clients. Certain pieces of outboard are more important than others such as reverbs, delays, comp/lims and gates. However, the more outboard you have, the more chances you have of creating unique textures.

Out of Phase: When two signals are 'out of phase', certain frequencies contained in them are cancelling each other out, due to the reversal of polarity from one to the (relative) other.

Output: The exact opposite of input.

Overdubbing: The art of building up tracks of information on different channels of a multitrack machine.

Op-amp: These could be looked upon as the analogue equivalents to microprocessors. Op-amp is an abbreviation of operational amplifier. Op-amps are found most commonly inside recording consoles used in filter and amplification circuits.

Pad: Found at the top of input channels, a pad cuts down the incoming signal by a predetermined amount – usually 10 or 20dB.

Panning: This is a term used to describe the positioning of a sound or group of sounds across the left to right sound stage.

Pan Pot: Abbreviation of panoramic potentiometer, this is just a cross-wired stereo volume control, so that the left and right outputs fade in opposite directions which produces a defined 'movement' or shift between the loud speakers. A panning control may also take the form of a joystick.

Parametric EQ: This is different from a graphic equalizer, as the frequency bands selected can be continuously selectable and emphasized or de-emphasized, instead of the choice being restricted to six, ten, fifteen, twenty-seven or thirty-one factory defined steps.

Parameter: A word recently revived from obscurity by the flood of Digital Access Control System synthesizers, such as the Yamaha DX7, Korg DW6000 and Roland JX8P. Parameter is another word for a single or group of increments which are adjustable. A parameter is a dimension of control or attenuation.

Passive Circuits: Anything termed as being passive is a device which works without the need for electricity. The vast majority of electric guitars and basses are passive – the opposite being 'active'. Overwater and Status are just two companies now producing 'active' electric bass and guitar designs. These incorporate a battery compartment, usually for a 9V power cell which is turned on and off when the jacklead is plugged in and out.

PA System: The good ol' Public Address system. Since Woodstock, the PA has become more and more complicated, splitting the component frequency ranges (bass, mid and treble) into specialized cabinets and enclosures. It is now common for 'small' gigs to hire a PA system which can kick out a kilowatt and use it at three-quarters volume!

Patching: The art of connection via patchcords on a patchbay. In a well thought out system, any number of audio signals can be manipulated and ganged together and sent to dual or single destinations by just a handful of patchcords.

Phase Shift and Phasing: A vastly overestimated flaw sometimes encountered in audio systems. I can't stress strongly enough that the human ear is *extremely* sensitive towards pitch and amplitude, but *not* phasing or odd phase shifts. Most 'technical' writers seem to have a personal aversion to phasing in its unwanted, natural, almost accidental form. This has a lot to do with the fact that, on this point at least, they let their brains rule their ears rather than the other way around, leaving them in a state of panic and disgust should unwanted phase shifting be picked up on a meter or scope – even though the phasing present is inaudible to the human ear. It is one of my saddest observations that any institutionalized or 'educated' 'engineers' all seem to have hearing that is perfect up to 20kHz and are extraordinarily sensitive to phase. I often believe that two requirements for gaining a place on the Tonnmeister course are to have a pocket dictionary full of condemnatory adjectives for you to spill out should you detect any phase abnormalities, and to be able to listen to the compact disc version of Phil Collins' 'Sussudio' through a pair of Celestion SL6s or UREI 815s without tapping your feet!

Potentiometer: Posh talk for a variable level control – whether it be for tone, amplitude or whatever. This can be a rotary or linear control. A fader is a linear potentiometer.

PPM: See **VU Meter.**

Preamplifier: Initial amplification stage for signals before they go to the main amplifier circuits.

Punch-in: Exactly the same as drop-in. It is the method of slipping into record while the tape is in motion to re-do a passage where a mistake may have arisen. To slip out of record while the tape is still in motion is called a punch-out or drop-out. This control is often via a footswitch.

Quadrophonic Sound: A much-explored but never commercially acceptable form of listening which enabled the music or whatever programme material you like to be listened to from all directions via four loudspeakers. I believe that Quadrophonic sound is better than ambisonics. Ambisonics are only around today because quadrophonic failed. Quadrophonic sound *could* be brought back to life by the marketing of four-channel amplifiers and by putting all popular material on *cassette*. Surely all these years of developing a one-direction, four-track transport for compact multitrackers can be made to pay off in the domestic consumer market? Anyone who went to see any of the Pink Floyd or Mike Oldfield quadrophonic concerts *must* know that it offers ten times more than stereo.

Release: The final parameter in a four-stage envelope generator. This determines how long a note takes to die away after the key has been released on the keyboard.

Reverb: Strictly speaking, this refers to the sound characteristics of an open space or, more commonly, a large room. Reverb is an ambient quality, produced from soundwaves being reflected off hard surfaces, such as brick walls or mountain tops.

Riding: Boosting a certain dimension of the sound by a roughly calculated quantity to make up for system deficiencies. In a studio where you know the speakers are bass 'light', engineers sometimes 'ride the bass'.

Roll off: Technical term for a de-emphasis in either high or low frequencies, ie bass roll off and HF roll off.

Rough Mix: Self-explanatory, universal term for any mixdowns that are done as tests prior to the final mixdown session.

Routing: The system all consoles employ to move single or groups of signals from the input stage through EQ and/or aux electronics to single or ganged outputs.

RF: Abbreviation of radio frequency.

Sel-sync: A term which in recent years has been shortened to 'sync', sel-sync is short for 'selective synchronization' and refers to all tape recorders which allow you to monitor off-tape signals via the record head. As I've explained, the modern recorder headblock is made up of three heads in a line. The first of these is the erase head, the second the record head, and lastly the playback or monitor head. If you record a performance and replay it via the monitor head while recording an overdub, your performance off-tape will be out of time with itself owing to the short time lag between the tape passing the record head and playback head. Information will be heard from the monitor head and the timing for the subsequent overdub will be based on that signal (naturally). But because information stored on the tape has *already* passed the record head, the whole signal being recorded will be committed to tape *after* the required points have passed the record head. Therefore, all multitrackers and advanced 2-Ts have a record head which can playback too. This is termed the sync head by many manufacturers and engineers.

Separation: The art of acoustic separation is one which can take many years to learn and perfect. A multi-instrument, multitrack master which contains pieces recorded in just single takes that offers you 'clean' tracks of instruments to mix and sweeten, with little or no 'leakage' between groups of instruments, is known as a track or take with good 'separation'.

Sequencer: A data recording device which remembers and playbacks sequences of notes from synthesizers and/or samplers. Advanced units offer programming in step time (chronological, beat-by-beat exhaustion of the Random Access Memory) *and* real time (the inputting of data from an instrument in time to a metronome produced by the sequencer which is directly related to the amount of memory selected for recording).

Splicing: The same as editing, it is the art of joining two pieces of magnetic tape or film together, end to end, to produce an undetectable join in the programme material.

Stage Box: A handy connection centre linked to a long piece of multicore cable which links the microphone and line inputs from the stage to those on the PA desk in the auditorium. Lots of studios parallel link inputs and/or patchpoints around their studio walls to save the need for massively long connection cables. These connection boxes in studios are also sometimes called Stage Boxes.

Synthesizer: In its simplest form, a monophonic keyboard instrument which can simulate real sounds via an oscillator (VCO), filter (VCF) and four-stage envelope generator (VCA section). The first polyphonic synthesizers appeared in the early to mid-seventies from companies like Moog, Roland and Sequential Circuits. Since then, many more tone generation and control parameters have been added to the basic analogue synthesizer, such as complicated dual and triple low frequency (inaudible) oscillators for the modulation of audio waveforms, glissando and portamento, sixteen-note polyphony and digital and analogue chorus circuits, to enhance the sounds created by the operator.

Recently, three other forms of synthesis have emerged, utilizing different technology but more importantly offering voice generation capabilities which can result in the synthesized sounds rivalling those of real instruments. PPG from Germany are famous for their Wave series synthesizers which do away with voltage controlled oscillators (VCO) and rely on factory-embedded libraries of waveforms. The beauty of this system is that all normal 'synth sounds' can be created because the standard analogue synthesizer waveforms, such as square wave, triangle, ramp wave and white noise, are included in the PPG's library. Sounds are created by combining numbers of these waveforms and introducing modulation and filtering. These new waveform combinations can be stored in 'combi programs' and recalled at will. There are also extensive envelope generators which can manipulate the final shape of the programmed sound.

Yamaha have developed a hugely popular form of additive synthesis based on frequency modulation technology – a full explanation of this can be found in the Yamaha DX1 keyboard review in the MIDI Synth section.

Finally, the fourth type of synthesis currently available comes from the Japanese microchip kings, Casio. Released while this book was being written, Casio has perfected phase distortion synthesis which has some surprisingly similar sonic qualities to those offered (at much greater cost) by digital waveform and frequency modulation synthesis.

Synthesizers are the most used of all instruments and their influence on modern-day recording *techniques* must never be underestimated.

S/N ratio: Short for signal to noise ratio, this is the measurement we refer to when describing how hissy or noisy a piece of equipment is. More accurately, the figure quoted shows how much louder the actual signal (music, for instance) is than the hiss and/or hum inherent in a system. An acceptable S/N figure is about 65dB, which is the typical performance you'd get from a non chrome cassette with Dolby B. The higher the figure, the better the performance in relation to the absence of hiss or noise. Most digital tape recorders have a S/N ratio of about 90–95dB!

Talkback: The same as foldback in the sense that this is a common facility on more advanced desks, which offers a direct mike line input into the cue circuit(s) to assist communication between control room personnel and the performer(s) in the studio.

Tape Echo: The art of using a three-headed tape recorder to produce delayed signal FX, such as ADT, slapback echo and flanging/chorusing (for which your chosen machine will need a varispeed). You simply feed signals to the sync head and replay them from the monitor head. The aforementioned time lag between the two heads is your source of delay. Running the tape at fast speeds and fluttering the varispeed at the same time will result in chorusing and flanging, while having the tape run at very slow speeds of perhaps 1⅞ips will enable you to create very deep and long delays.

Tape echo has its drawbacks – mainly the hiss you get from running even ¼-inch tape at less than 7.5ips, but also the inconvenience of having to change the tape every once in a while. However, it is still one of the FX that I use most, and however sophisticated AMS digital delay systems get, there is a certain uniqueness of control one can achieve by using tape echo.

Transport: A general term used to describe all the motorized and non-motorized components in a tape recorder which ferry the tape from the supply spool, across the heads to the take-up spool.

Transients: Sharp bursts of sound energy usually associated with percussion instruments. Transients are the most common reason for tape saturation (distortion) and are therefore nearly always the things pinpointed for compression, which reduces the transients to within a manageable dynamic range.

Transpose: To move up or down a note or passage of notes into another key either by electronic means or sheer brainwork!

Voltage Control: Used in reference to first generation analogue synthesis, where each note on the keyboard is linked to a different voltage output which controls the pitch of the oscillator(s). The pitch is therefore 'voltage controlled'.

VU Meter: This is short for volume unit meter – a scale and needle device used to represent volume. This system is sometimes coupled with PPM (peak program meters) which are much more instantaneous in showing transients in any given programme material.

White Noise: A signal containing all frequencies which rise in level by 6dB every octave. Many synths have white or pink noise generators which can produce breath and wind sounds when filtered properly.

Appendix

You, Your Demos ... and Stardom ...

If you wish to become a professional musician – and home recording is just a means to an end, then it would be stupid of me to neglect this fact and not give you any pointers as to how you go about presenting your recorded masterpieces.

Presenting and 'marketing' yourself and your music via your demos is a fine art and a subject which merits considerable care and attention; but for the time being, here is a basic guide.

Record companies often employ 'spotters', more traditionally referred to as 'talent scouts'. They report and are usually part of the Artist & Repertoire department (or A&R). This is the department which is constantly in direct contact with the artists on its books. It is the department responsible for strongly recommending, and increasingly taking, the ultimate decision as to whether a new act should be given a deal – either for publishing, recording or both.

The A&R department is the first rung on the ladder, should you wish to pursue the accepted way of making a living in the contemporary music field.

Guidelines

1. NEVER 'Doorstep' record company A&R executives; they are extraordinarily busy people.
2. ALWAYS try to discover the name of someone in the A&R department to receive your demos, but don't bother them directly, always enquire to an assistant or the telephonist.
3. ALWAYS clearly label your demos, with the case listing(s) correctly corresponding to the material contained on the tape.
4. ALWAYS use fresh cassettes of high quality, which contain no unwanted material or garbage.
5. ALWAYS include a contact phone number and address.
6. ALWAYS state which NR system (if any) has been used.
7. ALWAYS include an informative *concise* biography, details of where the songs were recorded and (if applicable) where your next gig is, with a definite confirmation that at least two places have been reserved under your target record company's name on the guest list.

Setting up an interview between yourself and an A&R man is also an accepted way of going about self-promotion, though the average day in the life of an A&R man necessitates them always on the whole to hear the music before getting involved with direct contact.

Both musically and technically, the demos presented to your target companies must be a faithful representation of your abilities.